ONLY A
BREATH
APART

ALSO BY KATIE McGARRY

THE PUSHING THE LIMITS SERIES

Pushing the Limits

Crossing the Line

Dare You To

Take Me On

Breaking the Rules

Chasing Impossible

THE THUNDER ROAD SERIES

Nowhere But Here

Walk the Edge

Long Way Home

OTHERS

Say You'll Remember Me

Red at Night

ONLY A BREATH APART

Katie McGarry

TOR TEEN

A Tom Doherty Associates Book

New York

ONLY A BREATH APART

A Tor Teen Book
Published by Tom Doherty Associates
175 Fifth Avenue
New York, NY 10010

www.torteen.com

Tor® is a registered trademark of Macmillan Publishing Group, LLC.

Library of Congress Cataloging-in-Publication Data

Names: McGarry, Katie, author.
Title: Only a breath apart / Katie McGarry.
Description: First edition. | New York : Tor Teen, 2019. | "A Tom
    Doherty Associates Book."
Identifiers: LCCN 2018044554 | ISBN 9781250193858 (hardcover) |
    ISBN 9781250193872 (ebook)
Subjects: | CYAC: Love—Fiction. | Family problems—Fiction. |
    Farms—Fiction. | Best friends—Fiction. | Friendship—Fiction.
Classification: LCC PZ7.M167156 Onl 2019 | DDC [Fic]—dc23
LC record available at https://lccn.loc.gov/2018044554

Our books may be purchased in bulk for promotional, educational,
or business use. Please contact your local bookseller or the
Macmillan Corporate and Premium Sales Department at
1-800-221-7945, extension 5442, or by email at
MacmillanSpecialMarkets@macmillan.com.

First Edition: January 2019

Printed in the United States of America

0 9 8 7 6 5 4 3 2 1

For Ann, Peter, Phyllis, and Leon—
because you gave me my love of land.

A friend loves at all times. They are there to help when trouble comes.

Proverbs 17:17 (NIRV)

ONLY A
BREATH
APART

JESSE

Six Years Old

You need to pack your bag." Jesse's mom crouched in front of him and grabbed hold of his shoulders. From the glow of the nightlight, he could see a red mark on her face. Sort of like how his skin would look when he had fallen from a tree and landed hard on the ground.

His mom smelled weird, a strange combination of salt and sweat, and the foul stench made him want to vomit. If fear had a smell, this was it, and it rolled off of her in waves.

Before she had shaken him awake, he had been sleeping in Mom's big bed. The one she shared with the guy she kissed. This guy wasn't the same one from last year. She said this man was different, but Jesse didn't think so. Like the last man, he never smiled.

Jesse hugged the blanket his gran had crocheted for him to his chest. The bedroom had a strange, dreamlike quality to it, too many shadows, and it made him think of his older cousin Glory. She was in her twenties and talked too much about ghosts. "Why am I leaving?"

Mom had promised him he could visit longer than his normal few days, and his head hurt as he tried to understand what he did wrong to be sent away so soon.

She smiled even though her eyes were filled with tears. "Don't you miss Gran?"

Jesse swayed on his feet from exhaustion. He'd only been here a few days, but he did miss Gran and home. He missed how there was breakfast in the morning, dinner at night and how she would laugh with him as they made oatmeal cookies together. He missed his swing in the backyard, walking the land with Glory and catching fireflies with his best friend, Scarlett. He missed a full stomach, sheets that didn't smell and people who didn't yell.

Mom hugged him, and he felt her tremble. She pulled away, grabbed a duffle bag and threw clothes into it from the open drawer. "Hurry, Jesse. Gran wants to see you."

In his Spiderman PJs and no socks, he stumbled across the room. His feet were cold against the wooden floor of the second-floor apartment. It was an old house, and it had too many people in it. Most of them angry, staggering as if their feet didn't work, or they were passed out on the stairway.

Jesse knelt on the floor and felt for his shoes under the bed. As his hand came in contact with a shoelace, there was a shout and a door slammed. "Ophelia!"

"Let's go." Mom snatched Jesse's hand, yanked him to his feet, and he ran to keep up.

The man who his mother said was going to take care of her, maybe both of them someday, came roaring toward them from the kitchen. "Where are you going?"

"Home."

"No, you're not." The man grew louder as he got closer. Jesse's heart convulsed, and he clung tighter to his blanket and his mother's hand. Then pain shot down Jesse's arm, his blanket fell from his grasp and he yelped as the man attempted to tear him away from his mom.

His mother released him, and fear ripped through Jesse. She was going to leave him. Nausea clawed at his stomach, but his mother didn't bolt for the door. She turned, and the sound of her slapping the man reverberated across the room. "Don't touch my son. No one ever touches my son!"

The man drew back and threw his fist into her face, blood squirted from her nose, and Jesse screamed. His mom stumbled forward, into the man, and then the man fell, his hands covering his privates. In seconds, Jesse was in the air, his mom tossing him onto her hip.

Jesse looped his arms around her neck and squeezed. Tears streamed along his cheeks and onto her skin. She sprinted down the stairs, and once outside, yanked her car door open. She shoved him across the seat to the passenger side, but he didn't let go. She pried his fingers from her neck, secured him with the seatbelt, then started the car.

His fingers closed into a fist, and he felt nothing. Jesse's sob cut past the roaring engine. "My blanket! We forgot my blanket!"

The house grew farther away, and Jesse cried louder, yet they went faster until his mom slammed on the brakes. Tires squealing, the car lurched.

"Stop it!" Mom shouted. "We aren't going back. We're never going back. Never!"

Jesse's chest split open, and his entire body writhed as he cried harder. That was his blanket. The one Gran had made for him. The one she said he could take anywhere and would mean he was never alone. Now, he would be alone, and he hated alone more than anything.

His mom slammed her hands against the steering wheel, and the slapping sound made him jump. "Stupid! I'm so stupid!"

Her voice broke, and her lower lip quivered. One tear fell, then another. An emotional cold slap in the face, and he shook. He'd made his mom cry, and she already cried too much.

Slipping through the seatbelt, he wrapped his arms around her. "It's okay, Mommy. I don't need my blanket. I don't. I'm sorry. Don't cry."

She sobbed harder, spit coming from her mouth as it opened. She leaned her head against the steering wheel, and Jesse held her, shushed her, then she stopped holding the steering wheel and held on to him. His mom smelled of flowers, sweat and smoke. This time, the smell didn't bother him nearly as much.

He closed his eyes and wished they were at Gran's. Gran could make it better. She always did.

With a shuddering breath, Mom encouraged him to sit on her lap. The darkness of the parking lot didn't seem so bad then, and the rain pattering against the roof didn't seem so loud.

Jesse placed his head against her chest, listened to her heartbeat and focused on her inhales and exhales. Why couldn't he be enough to make her happy?

"Can I tell you something?" she asked, and he nodded. His heart hurt with how much he loved his mom, and he wondered why love had to be so painful. "Our family is cursed."

Late at night, after Gran had tucked him in, he had overheard Mom talk about this with Glory and Gran.

"A long time ago, our family was rich. The richest family in the county, but we hurt people to make that money. We stole land by force, beat them. We even killed. Your grandpa said the money was cursed so we became cursed. A real-life southern gothic tragedy."

She gave a hollow laugh, but Jesse didn't think it was funny. He snuggled closer to her as the shadows thrown by the street-light moved, drawing nearer, as if they were ready to reach out and grab him.

"We're cursed, baby. There's no way to deny it, but I think I figured out how to break it." Mom gently eased him back so she could look him in the eye. She combed her fingers through his hair, and he wished for the millionth time she would stop trying to make them a "family" with some weird guy, and instead let their family be her, him, Glory and Gran.

"People say our curse is that when we fall in love with some-one, something horrible will happen to them, and we're left to grieve forever."

He nodded again, because that's what the people in town said.

"But we aren't cursed because we love or because of something somebody did a long time ago, we're cursed if we leave the farm. The land is what protects us, gives us our strength. As long as we stay on it, as long as we let it nourish us, as long as we respect that the land is alive and is a part of us, we'll be safe. Do you under-stand?"

He did, and he didn't.

"As long as you never leave the land, you'll be safe, and you'll be happy. If we leave, the land will reject us and we lose the pro-tection. That's when our life falls apart. That's when we hurt the people we love. Once we leave, the curse sets in and there's no cure. Returning doesn't help. To stay protected, you can never leave. You have to live there, forever."

Jesse shook. This had to be wrong. He loved the rolling hills, the rows of corn, the cattle in the fields and the trees he and Scarlett climbed. His land could never hurt him or his mom. "You're wrong."

"I'm not. My life fell apart after I left, and now the people I love are in pain over me." His mother winced as if saying the words hurt her. "You're in pain over me, and every time I return home, I hurt you more and more. You're better off on the farm with your gran and without me."

"I'm okay." He just needed her to be okay. Jesse patted her arm, but she didn't seem to notice his touch. "I'm better with you."

"Don't be me, Jesse. Don't go chasing after shiny paths. Stay on the land." She tilted her head and tried for a smile that quickly failed. "After me and Gran, you're the last living Lachlin and the land will be yours."

"I don't want it." *Not if it hurts people.* "Glory can have it."

"She's a third cousin. She can't own the land. But the land isn't cursed, *we* are. The land will keep you safe. That's what I need you to understand."

He frowned, and she cupped his face. "When you get old enough, the land will belong to you so promise me that when you're older you'll never leave the farm. Do you understand? Never, ever leave. Promise me, Jesse. Promise to never leave the land."

Jesse looked into his mother's sad, green eyes and gave her his most solemn promise he'd ever given anyone. Even to Scarlett. Even to his gran. "I promise I'll never leave the land."

SCARLETT

Seven Years Old

Daddy left late last night, and Grandma arrived this morning. Those two things never happened, and while Jesse had promised to show her the new calf born on his land, Scarlett was hesitant to leave. Daddy yelled last night, and Mom had cried. Scarlett had done what she was told and stayed tucked in bed, not daring to dip a toe from beneath the covers. Not even when Jesse had thrown rocks at her window at midnight in an attempt to lure her to come out and play.

Mom sat at the kitchen table while Grandma poured hot water into two teacups. One for her, one for Mom. In the dining room, Scarlett was crouched into a ball in the corner. In a spot where they couldn't see her, but she could see them.

"I don't know what to do," Mom said. "It's not getting easier. It's getting harder."

"Men are complicated." Grandma sat in the chair beside Mom and placed her hand over hers. "But you have to think of all the things that Bryant provides for you and Scarlett. As long as you stay with him, you and Scarlett will never want for anything."

"I don't know—"

"Do you want Scarlett to grow up like you? Always struggling to make ends meet? Wondering where your next meal will come from? Do you want to end up alone like me? Do you want Scarlett to end up alone?"

Scarlett shivered at the idea of being alone. She didn't want to end up that way—she didn't like the idea of no one loving her.

"Figure out what upsets Bryant and avoid those things. He works extremely hard, and it's your job to make sure he returns to a happy, stress-free home."

Scarlett's nose tickled and though she tried squishing it to stop the sneeze, it happened anyway. Mom's and Grandma's heads snapped in her direction, and Mom started toward her. "Scarlett, I told you to stay in your playroom."

Yes, she had, but she had wanted to make sure Mom was okay.

"Go play outside. I'll even let you play with Jesse, but remember the rules."

Rule number one: Don't upset Daddy.

Rule number two: Be home by four, plenty of time before her father returned home from work. Daddy worried and needed to know where they were, at all times.

Rule number three: Don't tell Daddy she played with Jesse. Since she started school, whenever he heard that she had been playing with Jesse, there was a pinched disappointment in his face that made Scarlett apologize to him immediately. She hated letting her daddy down.

Yet, she couldn't stay away from Jesse, not even for her dad, so instead of playing together as much during the day, they snuck out to be together at night. She couldn't explain this pull she had toward Jesse. It was a lot like needing to breathe.

"And don't tell anyone that Daddy was angry. He'd be sad if we did." With a gentle pat, her mom sent Scarlett out the door. Scarlett flew across the street and onto Jesse's land. She bypassed his trailer and sprinted toward the barn in the west field. If a calf was born, that was where Jesse would be.

Over the first hill, a gust of wind blew through the trees. Scarlett heard a whisper; a voice in the breeze. It was a comforting voice, a lot like that of Jesse's grandmother when she'd give Scarlett a hug. She slowed and glanced around. Besides the sun, the grass and the birds, she saw nothing. Not even when she spun to be sure.

Scarlett, the breeze whispered again, and she squinted as she tried to listen. No, the voice wasn't on the breeze, it was coming from below her—from the land.

"Scarlett," said a solid voice. From the tree line, Jesse's older cousin Glory emerged from the shadows. "You need to go home."

As always happened when Scarlett tried to talk, there was a great pause. She did her best to remember what her speech therapist had told her. How to take a deep breath before speaking and focus on forcing her tongue to form the words correctly. "Mom . . . Mom said I could play with Jesse."

Not all the words came out right, but she was proud she didn't fully stutter. She said the first word in a sentence twice, but her therapist told her it was okay. They would work on that next . . . right after she had a good handle on the "th" sound.

Lots of kids made fun of her for how she talked, but Jesse didn't and that was all that mattered.

Glory walked toward her in her long shimmering skirt. "I know Jesse would love to see you, but you know how I've told you that I have angels who talk to me?"

"Yes." Glory's stories equal parts terrified and fascinated her.

"My angels have a message for you and then you need to head home."

"W . . . Why?"

Glory lowered herself to Scarlett's level and tucked her black hair behind her ear. She had a gentle smile that made Scarlett feel safe. "I don't know why, but they came to me and told me that this is very important."

Scarlett squished her mouth in disappointment, but she wasn't going to disobey an adult.

"The angels told me that the land likes you, and if you let it, it'll keep you safe when you're scared. I'm curious, though—can you tell me what it is that scares you?"

Scarlett fiddled with the ends of her shirt because Mommy said she wasn't allowed to talk about Daddy being mad. Glory reached to the ground and when she brought her palm back up, she held a fat multicolored caterpillar that crawled along her skin. "Do you know what caterpillars become?"

"But . . . butter-fies." *L*'s were still difficult for her.

Glory offered Scarlett the caterpillar, and she happily took it in her hand. Girls at school squealed at bugs. She and Jesse actively searched them out.

"When you see this caterpillar again, it means that the land is waking up for you. It will be a dangerous time for you, but a time of much-needed change. When you see this caterpillar again, you need to find me if I haven't found you already. There will be things I need to teach you. Do you understand?"

Before Scarlett could answer, Glory's eyes widened. "Run home, Scarlett. Now."

Scarlett turned and sprinted, her lungs burning as she didn't slow, not even for the hills. Fear pumped into her veins at the sight of her father's car in the driveway where her Grandma's car had once been. He was home early. He never came home early.

She ran up the driveway, swung around back just as her father opened the back door and yelled out her name. She did her best to control her breathing as she said, "I'm . . . I'm here."

The surprise on his face was better than anger. Was he surprised to see her or surprised her sentence was close to clear? Her mother came up behind him, placed a hand on her father's shoulder and mumbled to him that she had told him that Scarlett had been playing around the house. Her father turned to her mother then, gathered her close and they hugged as her father whispered to her mother over and over again that he was sorry.

Her mom held him tight, and the look of pure relief on her mom's face settled the uneasiness in Scarlett's stomach. Everything was okay. Now they would never be alone.

SCARLETT

I'm defying my parents by attending a funeral. Reckless and adventurous teenage behavior, I know. Most seventeen-year-olds lie to their parents so they can go on a date with a forbidden boy or attend a party where there will be questionable behavior. Me? I'm outright lying to my dad, and it's because Jesse Lachlin's grandmother died.

The entire way here I've questioned my sanity, but I don't know how I'd live with myself if I stayed home. Jesse Lachlin used to be my childhood best friend. We were inseparable. We had the type of friendship people strive to have, and then, a few years ago, he cut me so deeply that I still bleed. But ten-year-old me would have never abandoned a hurting Jesse. So today I'm not only honoring the memory of Jesse's grandmother, but also the memory of our dead friendship.

On my way to the funeral, the high grass of the field swats at my legs, but I don't mind the sting. I love walking barefoot in grass, I love the smell of the earth and I love that brief feeling of freedom open spaces can provide.

It's the dog days of August. The type of hot that starts when the sun rises and makes you sweat through your clothes within minutes. While my skin and palms are on fire, the pads of my feet are cool against the dirt. The heat is unwelcome, but the sky is deep blue and the sun is bright, and for that, I can be grateful.

Walking out of the field, I stop short of crossing the one-lane road to slip on the flats that dangle from my fingertips. My mother would be mortified if she knew I was entering a church in a cotton daisy-print sundress. It's not one of the dresses with stiff fabric and impossible back zippers she would have picked for me at an overpriced department store. It's the type that's machine-washable and breathable. The type of dress Jesse's grandmother would have given her stamp of approval.

I can practically hear my mother heavily sigh and mumble my name, Scarlett, as if it were her personal, private curse word. Mom believes there's a certain way to dress and behave, and I'm breaking all sorts of her rules today. Watch out, world. I'm officially rebellious.

I smile to myself because I'm the opposite of rebellious. For the last few years, I've followed every rule. I'm the teacher's pet and the girl with straight *A*'s. I'm the poster child of perfection, and have earned every snarky ice princess comment Jesse's friends whisper about me in the school hallways because he and I no longer speak.

There are only six cars in the parking lot of the white church, and that makes me frown. I thought more people would have wanted to attend. Jesse's mud-covered pickup is there, and so is an unnaturally clean black Mercedes that belongs to his uncle. This ought to be interesting. Jesse and his uncle have a mutual hate for each other that runs deeper than any root of any tree.

Movement to my right and I slowly turn my head. Shivers run down my spine at the sight of Glory Gardner. Even though I'm seventeen and too old for ghost stories, I still can't shake the ones regarding this woman. Girls would whisper over lunch boxes that Glory was a witch. As I grew older, I understood that witch meant con artist. She claims she can read palms, tarot cards and "sees" spirits from beyond the dead. All for a glorious fee.

She's a beautiful woman—long dirty blond hair that's untamed, even in a bun, and she has an eclectic taste in clothing. Today she wears a white peasant shirt and a flowing skirt made of material that shimmers in the sun.

Glory watches me like I watch her, with morbid curiosity. I knew her as a child, back when Jesse and I ran wild in the fields near her home, but we haven't talked in years.

She stands under the shade of a towering weeping willow. There are lots of those trees around here. Mom says it's because there is too much water in the ground. I say it's because the people in this town have cried too many tears. Mom doesn't like my answer.

I tilt my head toward the church, an unspoken question if Glory will be joining me. She shakes her head no. I'm not shocked. According to rumors, Glory will go up in flames if she enters the house of God. But who knows? Maybe I will, too.

The church is one of those picturesque, historical, one-room school buildings squeezed between a cornfield on one side and a hay field on the other. A huge steeple with a bell attempts to reach the heavens, but like anything created by a human, it falls tragically short.

The foreboding wooden door makes no noise as I open it, and I'm able to slip in without a huge, squeaking announcement. Orange light filters in through the dark stained glass windows, and its struggling beams reveal millions of dancing particles of dust.

On the altar, there's no casket, but there is an urn. My heart dips—Suzanne is dead. I used to wish she were my grandmother, and many times, she treated me as if I belonged to her. Suzanne was the epitome of love, and the world feels colder now that she's gone.

Choosing a spot in the back, I drop into a pew, and as I scan the church my stomach churns. How is it possible that this place is so barren?

Besides the Funeral Brigade, or the FB, as I like to refer to them, there aren't many people here. The FB are the older group of women who attend every funeral in our small town even if they didn't know the person. Attending funerals isn't my idea of fun, but who am I to judge?

The FB sit directly behind the one person the town believes to be the lone sane member of the Lachlin family, probably because he isn't blood related—Jesse's uncle.

On the left side of the church is Jesse. Only Jesse. And that causes a painful pang in my chest. Where are his stinking friends? The anarchists in training who follow Jesse wherever he goes? Where is the rest of the town? Yes, Suzanne was polarizing, but still, where is any respect?

Quietly, so I don't draw attention to myself, I slip from the right set of pews to the left. Someone should be on Jesse's side, and it's sad it has to be me.

A door at the front of the church opens, and the pastor walks out from the addition the church built on as a small office ten years ago. I would have thought any pastor assigned to this place would be as ancient as this church. Sort of like an Indiana Jones Knights Templar scenario where he lives forever as long as he stays inside. But no, he's the youngest pastor from the main, newer church in town. His name is Pastor Hughes, and he's a thirty-something black man with a fit build who is just cute enough that he should be starring in a movie.

The pastor looks up, and he flinches as if startled. I peek over my shoulder then sigh. Clearly, he's surprised to see me. Flipping fantastic.

His reaction, and the fact he won't stop staring, causes every person to turn their heads. Lovely. I've had dreams like this where I enter a room and become the center of attention. Only in my dreams it's at school, it's my classmates and I'm naked, but still, this is disconcerting.

Eventually, the FB and Jesse's uncle return their attention to the front, but Jesse doesn't. He rests his arm on the back of the pew, and it's hard to ignore that he's made me his sole focus, but I do my best to act as if I don't notice.

To help, I concentrate on what my mom taught me as a child—to make sure the skirt of my dress is tucked appropriately so that my thighs don't show. I then fold my hands in my lap and straighten to a book-on-head posture. I can be the ice princess people claim me to be.

Five pews separate me and Jesse, and it's not nearly enough. My cheeks burn under his continued inspection. Jesse has done this a handful of times since our freshman year. Glance at me as if I'm someone worth looking at, someone worth laughing with a little too loud and smiling with a little too much. Then he remembers who I am and snaps his gaze to someone else.

But he's not looking away now. I inhale deeply to act like I don't care, but I do. Jesse may not be the same person he was before high school, but he has the same beautiful green eyes, and the same mess of red hair that curls out from under his baseball cap— because only Jesse would wear a baseball cap to a funeral.

I can't help but notice the scar on his chin from when the branch of a tree we climbed broke and we smacked the ground hard. He took the brunt of the fall, catching me so that I would land on him. I cried when he bled. Being Jesse, he laughed at the adventure.

While so much has changed since we were friends, there is so much that hasn't. Jesse is still rebellious, unconventional and lost.

The preacher welcomes us, starts into some scripture that must mean something to someone other than me, and Jesse returns his attention to the front.

As the pastor gives the eulogy, my chest aches. It's not the pastor's words that suck the air out of my body, but Jesse. Strong Jesse. Carefree Jesse. Peter Pan in the flesh. But with each excruciating minute that passes, his shoulders buckle and his posture slouches until he's bent over. Arms on his legs, head down and fingers clasped together as if he's in prayer.

Jesse doesn't pray. At least I've never known him to, and if he is now, it must mean he's dying.

". . . and if Suzanne was known for anything, it was love. She might have been unorthodox, but her love was intense." The pastor had mainly been preaching on the side with the most people, but he edges his way to stand in front of Jesse. To the person Suzanne had taken care of for most of his life. "And she loved you the most."

Jesse's head drops into his hands, and I wince as if I've been punched. He loved his grandmother, and she loved him in return. That was one of the problems with Jesse—there weren't that many people who ever truly loved him.

I loved him once—the way a six-year-old loves with abandon. I loved him how I once loved myself. Jesse was freedom when so much of my life meant confinement. He was laughter during dark nights, he was the warrior who scared the monsters under my bed away . . . he was my friend.

I stand. Abruptly. In such a rush that all eyes are on me again, but I don't care. I walk up the aisle and refuse to acknowledge a single soul. The pastor pauses, and when I sit next to Jesse, it's still with some space between us, but I'm closer than anyone else.

The pastor continues again, for another fifteen minutes, and when he stops there's silence . . . as silent as a church can be . . . awkward and eerie. The Funeral Brigade leaves first, and they're the type who don't start chatting until the door to the church is open, but once sunlight drifts in, their voices sound like the buzz of bees.

Jesse's uncle rises to his feet, approaches the pastor and whispers in his ear. The pastor nods then says, "Jesse, if you want to talk, I'll be in my office."

Jesse doesn't respond, doesn't gesture, doesn't do a thing. He keeps his head down, his arms on his knees, his hands clasped. I raise an eyebrow at the pastor, an unspoken plea that he do his magical pastoral stuff that makes people better. Maybe *Hallelujah* him a few times and slap him on the back of the head to declare him saved.

Instead, the pastor leaves with Jesse's uncle. Both of them are jerks.

When the door to the secret back room closes, I wish the pastor and Jesse's uncle to be "blessed" with a short burst of food poisoning. Of course, wishing doesn't do anything and wishing won't help Jesse.

I lace and unlace my fingers. What do I do? What do I say? I look over at Jesse and try to find the right words, but there are no words. I have absolutely nothing to offer him. Maybe I'm as bad as the others.

Perching on the edge of the pew, I raise my hand to perform a pat on the back, and I open my mouth for the standby of, "I'm sorry for your loss," but before I can carry either out, Jesse says, "Stay, Tink."

Stay, Tink. It's like he ripped out my heart, and I'm watching

it pump in his hands. Tink was his nickname for me. It's a reminder of how simpler life was over three years ago.

The part of me that still hurts from when he ended our friendship wants to tell him where to shove the idea of me staying, but
the part that used to look forward to capturing glowing fireflies
in a jar slides back into the pew and stays.

JESSE

Today feels like the worst day of my life, but the scar on my back is proof it's not.

My uncle follows me into the trailer and shakes his head in disgust. It's what he does. Sticks his nose up when he walks in as if the place stinks like a garbage dump. But like it has for as long as I can remember, the trailer smells of oatmeal cookies.

This place is home. The furniture filling the trailer is antiques from the farmhouse Gran was born in—the aging and condemned building next to the trailer. On the blue walls of the living room are paintings of moss-covered trees bending over long, straight paths. Being a neat freak, Gran had everything in place, everything right, everything but me.

Thinking the curse was ridiculous town folklore, poor Uncle Marshall married into the family. He lost his wife, my aunt Julia, two years after they married. Even still, he doesn't believe. His fancy law degree and shiny practice make him too practical for the reality that there's something soiled in the blood of my family.

Gotta admit, I feel sorry for the man. He loved Aunt Julia. She loved him. Just because I pity him doesn't mean I like him, and it doesn't mean he likes me. The sole reason the two of us have stayed civil died two days ago.

"How are you?" Marshall asks, and from his tone, he's sincere, but the question is stupid. I lost my grandmother. He knows how I'm doing.

"Okay." I rest Gran's urn on the mantel of the heater that was built to look like a fireplace then place a hand on the side of the urn as if I'm touching her.

God, I miss her already. Holes in hearts hurt, and I have too many holes for me to be breathing. Gran poured her love into me, so much, I should have been fixed, but maybe that's the problem with having too many holes. All the love that's poured in falls out.

A year ago, Gran dragged my ass out of bed to help her pull weeds. She wore that old floppy sunhat with a foot-long brim, wearing overalls like she was the one who would be getting dirty. She didn't get dirty, though. She sat in her lawn chair as I dug in the earth and bossed me around. *That's not a weed, Jesse, that's an onion. I raised you to know the difference.*

Are you sure? It looks like a weed.

I had held up the onion and fought the smile on my face. I knew what I was pulling, and I knew it would piss her off. Seeing the onion in my hand, Gran had gone into an eloquent swearing rant that could make a sailor blush and me smile even in my darkest moments. At the end of her rant, at the end of most every rant, she laughed. Good and long.

From her lawn chair throne, she readjusted the hat on her head and ordered me back to work. She was the queen of our sad sod of land.

"You were wise to not scatter her ashes in the cemetery." My uncle tries again for cordial. This is why Gran liked him, why she kept him tied to the Lachlins even though he moved on, remarried and started a family with someone new. "She would have wanted to be spread on her land."

Scattering her ashes . . . my eyes burn, and I turn my back to Marshall to open the living room curtains. Scarlett's massive home comes into view. It's towering, made of stone, and when I was a kid, I used to think it was a castle.

The Copelands' mini-mansion and my trailer are the only homes on our long gravel road. We're a mile from a paved road, and even farther from a decent subdivision. We're literally the edge of nowhere with no other signs of life besides birds and the occasional lost deer.

Across the road, Scarlett walks barefoot to the mailbox. She holds her shoes in her hand and her sundress swishes with her stride, occasionally showing more leg than she typically allows. Her hair is tied in a knot at the base of her neck. When we were kids, she was all knees and elbows with a tomboy attitude, but now she's grown-up and gorgeous.

Long black hair, blue eyes, Scarlett. . . . my Tink.

The service. Shoes in hand. She walked. I lower my head and silently curse. I should have noticed she didn't have a ride, should have offered her a way back instead of leaving her alone. I should have done a lot of things differently, but I didn't. Story of my life.

Oblivious to me watching, Scarlett flips through the letters. Too many times, in the dark moments of night, I think of her and lazy, hot days under the willow tree. I think of the endless summer nights chasing fireflies in the long blades of grass. I think of her tinkling laughter, her obsession with bright stars in the black sky, and of her daring smile.

Cobwebs of the past have overtaken my brain, and if I continue to linger, I'll suffocate in the web. The past isn't a place I like to play, as most of my memories are too brutal to visit.

Here and now. Stay in the present and stay focused on the goal—my land.

I take off my baseball cap and run a hand through my hair as I cross over the invisible line of the living room to the kitchen. I open the fridge and there's not much there. Sliced ham, two individual prepackaged slices of cheese, leftover pizza and beer.

"The church property was one of the first pieces of Lachlin land sold off," Marshall says as he sits on the love seat. It's not a comfortable piece of furniture, but it's probably worth more than my life. That is if I could find someone stupid enough to drive to the middle of nowhere to appraise it as an antique. "Did you know that?"

Yeah, I did. Gran told me every bit of information on the Lachlins. My own personal bedtime stories in the vein of the Brothers Grimm. My family lineage is so messed up there are days I would have preferred being told I was three-quarters troll.

Over half this county used to belong to the Lachlins, but slowly the land has been sold off. Generation after generation, year by year, parcel by parcel, in order to keep the Lachlins from going under in debt. Now, the six hundred acres and me are all that's left. I'm land rich but cash poor. Not a good combination.

I keep staring at the fridge because my mind is running slow. In the sink is Gran's empty china teacup. I can't bring myself to wash it. It's as if I do, I'm admitting she's gone. A tightness in my chest and I suck in a shaky breath. God, I'm dying.

The refrigerator motor kicks on and draws me back to the near-empty shelves. I shouldn't do it. Won't help Marshall's opinion of me, but I lost the only person in my life I allowed myself to love. A beer buzz sounds good.

I pull out a beer, and because Gran loved southern hospitality, I tilt the bottle in his direction. "Want one?"

"You're not old enough to drink."

I'm not, but Gran never cared. Marshall's answer wasn't a firm no so I grab another and slide it to him across the coffee table Gran said was imported from England by her great-great grandfather. I sit on the only piece of comfortable furniture in the room—Gran's recliner.

I pop open my cap and drink. Marshall stares at the bottle in front of him. He's considering it, and that makes me slightly like him.

"Your grandmother made me the executor of her will."

I know this. He's a lawyer. I'm not. I'm seventeen. He's boring and forty.

"I'm your legal guardian," Marshall says, "but let me be clear, I will not clean up your messes. As we discussed in June, you think you're old enough to live on your own, and I'm going to respect that decision. The state will only care if you dig yourself a hole. It's up to you if you're going to dig it."

His eyes flicker to the beer in my hand, and I place it on the coffee table.

"If there are problems, I'm moving you into my house, and you'll live by my rules. The only way I'll allow you to live here is if you stay out of trouble, do you understand?"

"Yes." He's not pushing me into his house because he doesn't want me around his wife and children.

"Until you turn eighteen, I'll be handling the accounting for anything associated with the land." This isn't a shock. Gran listed Marshall on the farm account six months ago. She said when the land officially becomes mine so would the account. "That doesn't mean I'm personally helping with anything associated with the farm."

That's his stuck-up, suit-wearing way of saying he's not the type of guy who can stand dirt under his fingernails. It must suck to be him. "I can handle taking care of the land." I've been doing it most of my life.

"If you need money, send me an email detailing exactly what you need, why you need it and a detailed cost analysis as well as bids/costs from three places. Do not spend a dime on this farm without clearing the purchase with me, do you understand?"

"This isn't your stuffy office where I need a purchase order number to buy a hammer. It's a farm."

"A farm is a business. That's a lesson you need to learn."

"Do you know a thing about farming?" I counter.

He ignores me. "Your gran told me you've been saving money in a separate account so you could handle the bills associated with living in the trailer after her death. Is this true?"

I nod. It's not much. Most of the money I made went into the land account to keep the property afloat. If I'm careful with what I tucked away in the personal account, I won't starve—yet.

Saving wasn't easy, but like damn squirrels Gran and I socked away as much as we could. Beyond the six hundred acres, we're broke. Gran was living off of social security, and she made money by leasing our land to other farmers. Not able to take care of the land herself, she allowed other farmers to use our land to plant crops for themselves or to graze their cattle, and they pay us rent. They also pay me to work their fields or tend to their animals.

Last year, I convinced Gran to let me keep some of the property for hay. Problem was, I had to rent equipment to cut and bail the hay, and I didn't make any money. In fact, I barely broke even. Farming's an investment, and it's not cheap.

Marshall leans forward and rubs his hands together like he's nervous. He and I don't get along, but I'm playing nice and so is he. The nervousness is out of place. He reaches into his man-bag overstuffed with papers, pulls out a crisp folder and slides it to me.

A few paragraphs in, I sway as if I've been hit in the head. "What the hell is this?"

Another rub of his hands. "A test."

I toss the folder back in his direction and wait for a better answer. He stares back because he knows I can read, process information and, according to some tests, I'm smart.

"This land is mine," I say, "so this joke isn't funny."

"The acre that contains the trailer will remain yours regardless of what happens."

"This land is mine," I repeat slowly in case he hadn't caught on the first time.

"I told your grandmother to give you this acre alone, let me sell the rest and put the money into a trust for you, but she disagreed. I don't believe you can handle the responsibility of this land. She did, but she understood my reservations. So we split our differences and agreed to set up a tribunal."

"A tribunal?"

"Three of us are going to watch you and make the decision if you're responsible enough to own the land. We'll vote when you turn eighteen in May. If the vote goes against you, the farm will be sold. The payments will be spread out over ten years to guarantee you'll make good financial decisions. This test, the tribunal, is a good plan. A fair plan. It gives you a fighting chance to own the land."

My uncle is a bastard. "How did you talk Gran into this? Did you lie to her? Did you make her sign papers she didn't even know she was signing?"

"I didn't have to do anything. Your grandmother was worried about leaving you such a big responsibility at a young age. I have to admit, I'm worried, too."

I bitterly chuckle. "You're worried? Last I checked, you hate me."

"I don't hate you, Jesse. I think you make bad choices."

"I make plenty of good choices." Choices that kept my grandmother happy over the last years of her life. Choices that were hard on me, but helped the people I loved.

"You believe that?" Marshall challenges.

My eyes widen in affirmation.

"Drug possession."

"It was pot, and that's legal in some states." And I bought it for a friend.

"Suspension from school for fighting."

"The guy was an ass. You would have hit him, too."

"You buck authority, have no grounding, ignore rules, and you have no idea what it means to take on a farm of this size and not run it into the ground."

My head jerks back as if his words were a physical blow. "No sense of responsibility? Who do you think had been taking care of Gran?"

Marshall looks me square in the eye. "Me."

My muscles tighten, and it's hard as hell not to punch him in the face. Yeah, Marshall took care of Gran's finances, but it was me who took care of this place, me who made sure she was eating and me who watched over her day after day.

"Farming isn't owning a shovel and throwing down some seeds. To make this a working farm, you'll have to take out a loan to buy equipment. The only equity you have is the property—this acre and trailer included. If you default on the loan, you'll be left with nothing. That idea terrified your grandmother."

I stand because I don't know what else to do. What the hell was Gran thinking? Searching for support, I go to the window and lean my hands against the frame. "I won't lose it."

"I also wouldn't be doing a good job as the executor of your grandmother's estate and your guardian if I didn't consider the possibility that you'd sell the land yourself the day of your eighteenth birthday and blow the profits within the first year."

I round to glare at him. "You honestly think I could sell?"

"Before her death you had asked me about selling."

A small portion, just a few acres. Because I wanted to help Gran. I thought maybe if I had more money we could find a new specialist, a better specialist, someone who could help her live longer, but he didn't believe me. He never believes me. "So you're the decision maker now?"

He waits too many beats before speaking or maybe not enough. "I took on this role because, believe it or not, I care. I won't pretend to understand the pain you've gone through, and I won't pretend to understand your connection to this land. I've watched you grow up. I know, for you, this farm is like a Band-Aid on cuts that won't stop bleeding."

If that was meant to make me feel better, it didn't. "You'll never vote for me. You're biased."

"I'm not biased."

For days I've been a stick under pressure, being bent too far. Finally, I snap. "I know you told Gran not to take me in after Mom died and to put me in foster care. You told her I was too broken and couldn't be fixed. I know because I heard you. Tell me now you're not biased."

Guilt flashes over his face, and he tries to hide it as he flips through the folder in his hands. "If it helps, that's why your grandmother set up the tribunal and chose two other people to help make the decision. Majority vote will win, and she believed you'll rise to the challenge."

I'm not sure if I respect him or hate him for not denying what we both know is true regarding the foster care. I'm also not sure how I feel that he doesn't apologize either.

"She chose people who will give you a fair shake," he continues. "This isn't a death sentence. It's a wake-up call. It's August, and you have until May to prove you're responsible. You have time. Take it. Prove me wrong."

A growing sense of purpose takes root within me, and I do my best to funnel my anger and grief into it. "Who, besides you, is on the tribunal?"

"If I tell you then I run the risk of you putting on a show for those people. This is your chance to change for the better. Take advantage of it." Marshall leaves the paperwork on the antique table, shoves his folder back in his leather bag and stands. "If it's any consolation, I want you to succeed, but I want you to truly succeed. I won't vote for you to keep the land unless you show me you understand what it means to run a farm of this magnitude."

It's no consolation. That's him attempting to ease his guilt for when he votes against me.

"I'm sorry for your loss, Jesse. If you need to talk or if you'd like to stop by for a meal, you're welcome at my house. And if you get tired of being here alone, you can live with us. We have plenty of room."

I don't believe any of that, but I nod because doing so will get him out of my home faster. Marshall stares at me for a few more seconds, as if contemplating saying more, but he doesn't. Instead he walks out, shutting the door behind him.

His engine purrs to life and rocks crack under his moving tires. Then there's silence. Maddening silence. I drop into Gran's recliner, lower my head into my hands and close my eyes. I've lost Gran, and now I could lose my land. The only thing left that I love. The only thing in my life that brings me peace. "Why, Gran?"

I strain to listen in the silence, and my gut twists that there's no response. "I miss you."

Still no response and my head begins to throb. My cell in my back pocket vibrates. I dig it out, expecting to see a text from one of my friends, but I pop my neck to the right at the sight of Glory's name. *You need to stop by tomorrow night.*

Me: *No*

Glory: *I know of your grandmother's plan.*

Me: *So do I*

Glory: *But I know who the people are who will be deciding your future.*

Me—stone cold frozen.

Glory: *Stop by tomorrow at nine. I should be wrapping up my last session then.*

Me: *I won't be there.*

Glory: *Yes, you will.*

SCARLETT

The two signs attached to the purple canopy that covers the craft table full of crystals for sale makes life seem incredibly simple: *Let the spirits help guide your way.* The other: *Have questions? The cards have answers.* Life, though, as I'm well versed, is never that simple.

The Watermelon Festival is bustling with people, young and old, and Main Street is lined for as far as the eye can see with fair vendors. A gaggle of children are gathered on their tiptoes at the we-bring-the-birthday-party-to-you business that's set up next to Glory's booth. The whish of air being pumped into a balloon and then the associated screech of it being twisted into the shape of an animal is like music coming from the Pied Piper.

My friend Camila Sanchez is in the center of the mob. With her sleek, recently dyed platinum-blond shoulder-length hair and ambitious personality, Camila is surrounded by a plethora of children. She manhandles balloons while simultaneously explaining the pricing of the parties for her parents' business. Due to the smile stretching across her lips, no one would know she hates children, balloons and balloon animals.

When a little girl complains that her dog's legs are uneven and not long enough, Camila's smile widens, but it's not sweet. "It's a short dog."

I snort, and she glances around. Camila spots me then gives a conspiratorial wink. It's 5:45, and her parents are letting her off at six. Mr. and Mrs. Sanchez are awesome parents, and if they said six, they mean six. They're the parental unit of my dreams.

"I thought you said you were meeting Camila."

I jump at the sound of Dad's voice and spin in his direction. "I am."

Dad studies me, and I hide my hands behind my back to conceal the slight quiver that could announce my guilt. When I left him, he was in good spirits, but his moods can quickly shift. There are two patched-up holes in my bedroom that can testify to this. Dad replaced the drywall, covered it with fresh paint, but the perfection can't take away the memory of the way my heart pounded through my chest as he drove his fist through the wall.

He inclines his head toward the booth of balloon animals. "Camila appears to be working."

"She's getting off soon," I say too fast as I bite back the need to ask why he didn't go home like he said he was.

"Why did you leave us if she's still working? You said Camila would be done by five-thirty."

My mouth dries out, and the tremble in my hands travels to the rest of my body, but I force out a cleansing breath. *Show no fear. Don't give him any reason to doubt a thing I say.* "She was supposed to be off by now, but her parents asked her to work a few more minutes."

"If Camila isn't getting off until later, you should have told me." There's a subtle sharpness to his tone that causes hurricane warnings in my brain. "I was showing you a great deal of trust by letting you find Camila on your own."

"She's only running a few minutes late. Her parents are watching me so I'm okay."

Out of the corner of my eye, I glance over and my heart lifts when I notice Camila's mom watching us. Her stare gives credibility to every falsehood rolling off my tongue. She's not watching because she thinks I need a babysitter, but probably because she's mentioned to Camila that she's perplexed by my father's strict rules.

I touch the crystals on the table as if I'm interested in them. It's difficult to act normal as Dad looks at Camila's mom then studies me. *Please believe me, please believe me. Please.*

I'm so stupid. I should have never left Dad early. I should have never lied. But I did. Dad was having fun at the fair, Mom was having fun and my sister, Isabelle, was having fun. They were all laughing and smiling. They've forgiven him, and I haven't. I can't, not again, and this is one of the many ways life is no longer simple.

I want to peek at him in an attempt to understand my fate, but I don't. Eye contact doesn't help when he's angry. It only makes it worse.

Being in public won't soothe his temper. He'll just be more discreet. Like last year when Dad had arrived early to pick me up at a football game and saw me heading to the bathroom by myself. After I had returned to my friends, he called me away with a smile on his face. He had placed a seemingly loving arm around my shoulder, but his fingers dug into my arm as he severely whispered in my ear how I was irresponsible and that it was time to go home.

Dad didn't cause a scene at the game. The yelling started the moment we were alone in his car and continued until he left me in my room. I stayed on my bed for hours, curled up in a ball and sobbing.

My throat swells as I think of how this will play out. Will it be like Christmas? Will he throw a lamp and force Mom to clean it up as I watch? Or will it be like this past spring and he'll flip the kitchen table, breaking all the dishes that had been placed there for dinner?

Dad steps closer to me, and I'm filled with dread. "Next time, in a situation like this, you return to me and have Camila text you when she's done working. I don't like the idea of you being alone."

All I want is to be alone, for my thoughts and actions to belong only to me. But he's not angry, he's believing me, and I release the breath I had unknowingly held and take the small win. "Okay."

"I worry about you," he says with such sincerity that I feel guilty for causing him anxiety.

"I know." I keep my eyes locked on the crystals on the table, terrified if I meet his gaze, he'll change his mind and flip out.

"I only worry because I care."

"I know," I say again.

"I miss you talking to me. I miss us being close."

Me, too, but I stay silent because I don't trust either of us to continue this conversation—for his mood not to change and for me not to cry.

There's a beat of awkward silence, and I wish he would leave. I take a risk and peek at him. Dad's staring past the tent and into the hole his mind goes to when he thinks of his sister.

Dad and I are opposites. In mood, demeanor and appearance. Where he has light brown hair and brown eyes, I resemble Mom with my black hair, blue eyes and some long-lost generation of Mediterranean olive complexion. There are many times when I'm thankful I favor Mom. When I look in the mirror, I'm glad I don't have to be reminded of my father.

"Your mom and Isabelle are feeding ducks at the pond." Dad blinks as he returns to the real world then grins at me as if the gesture can wash away the past few minutes. "Do you remember when you were Isabelle's age and you fell in the pond feeding the ducks and I jumped in to save you? Do you remember, to make you laugh, I put duck feathers in my hair?"

I do remember. I had ruined my favorite outfit, I was cold, I was wet and I was crying because I had gone under the murky water and couldn't swim. But my father had rescued me, had hugged me, had given me his jacket to make me warm and then made me laugh.

Standing beside me now, Dad has this expression like he's considering good-naturedly bumping his shoulder into mine, just like he did when life was easier. I step away from him, not a ton, just a fraction. Enough to let him know I'm not ready.

Necklaces dangle from an iron holder, and I run my fingers along the different-colored stones tied to the leather cords. The black stone beckons me. It's cool to the touch, smooth, and makes me feel safe.

"Would you like one?" Dad asks. "I'll buy the necklace for you."

I've gone out of my way to avoid situations like this—where Dad has the ability to buy or do something for me. After what's happened between us, accepting anything from him makes me feel like he's purchasing tiny portions of my soul that I wasn't even aware were for sale.

"It's obsidian." Glory Gardner approaches us from the other side of the table. Locks of her curly, long dirty-blond hair fall from the jeweled barrette near the base of her neck. Her gray eyes meet mine. No, not meet—lock with mine and her stare causes an itch near my bones. "Obsidian shields us from psychic, physical and emotional attacks. It's a very powerful stone."

I swallow because the way she said it is like she *knows* what I'm hiding, and Dad must feel the same way. He shifts beside me and rubs the back of his neck. Dad doesn't ask if I want the necklace again. He's probably scared I'll say yes.

A customer asks Glory a question, and she wanders to the other side of the booth. Dad stares at the ground before meeting my eyes again. "Scarlett, I know you're upset with me."

My eyes to snap to his, and my heart stalls.

"I know you're disappointed, but I don't feel comfortable with you applying to the University of Kentucky and being so far from home."

Yesterday, Dad informed me he's sending me to the private college in town. Dad and Mom agreed it was perfect. I could live at home and continue my education. My choice of study was up to me, but my choices there are limited.

I want to become a speech therapist—to help children like how my speech therapist helped me. I haven't stuttered at school in years, my articulation is fantastic, and I can't remember the last time anyone teased me over how I spoke. My experience with speech therapy was life altering. I want to save someone like my therapist saved me.

The closest this college has to my chosen field of study is one class in public speaking.

"Do you see those girls over there?" Dad motions toward the group in a tight-knit circle. "Each of them are going to graduate from college with huge student loan debt. They would give their right arm to have what I'm offering you. I'm paying for all of your college education. We don't even have to fill out a single scholarship application form or fill out the FAFSA. In return, all your mom and I ask for is that you stick close to home. Just for four more years."

My dad is controlling, and I hate it. But I also understand. His older sister disappeared when she was a freshman in college. He loved her, very much, and one day she went to a party and then no one ever saw her again. My father says that not knowing what happened to her is like having a terrible slashing pain in his muscles he can never reach, even if he digs into his skin with his own fingers.

I know that must be awful, but what he's doing to me—it's smothering. What happened to his sister gnaws away at him like a flesh-eating parasite. But living with my father, with how his emotions can spiral in a blink of an eye . . . I place a hand on my abdomen as my stomach churns.

Behind Dad, several booths away, Mom has Isabelle by the hand. With her eyes, Mom begs me to not create problems for her, Isabelle or me. I can almost hear her in my head. *Please play along and allow us the good day. It's been so long, and we deserve it.*

There's fear in Mom's eyes, a fear that plays a constant game of hide-and-seek in my psyche. So rooted in me that it's now part of my DNA.

"Please tell me you understand our decision," Dad pushes. "I don't like you upset."

Mom tilts her head in an additional plea, and I hate that somehow my entire family's happiness depends on me. "I understand." I don't, and I'm not sure I ever will.

Dad's smile is good-natured, and I should feel like I was just rewarded, but I don't. I don't want to live like this for another five years. I don't want to live like this for another day, but I don't know how to escape. "Mom's waiting for you."

"Promise you'll stay near Mrs. Sanchez until Camila is off and then text me when you get to her house," Dad says, which means he'll be watching me from a distance until Camila is by my side. "I want to know you reached her house safely."

"I will."

"Don't stay out late. There are too many people on the road late at night who drink. I want you at her house by eight, and you should be home by ten."

"Okay," I say, and I'm willing him to end this lingering goodbye.

"I might call her parents to check on you."

I'm aware.

Dad acts like he has something else he wants to say, but instead shoves his hands in his front pockets. Maybe he's thinking of how I used to voluntarily hug him when we'd say goodbye. Maybe he's thinking how I used to laugh and joke with him before I would hit him up for money. Maybe he's thinking of the few times I used to ask him to explore the festival with me. Maybe he's not, but I am, and that makes the ache in my chest turn into a piercing sting.

"Be safe," Dad says.

"I will."

"I love you." His declaration sends a shock wave of hurt through my body because loving him back is torture. I inhale deeply, as the only way to survive is to never feel.

He finally leaves, and the breath I release is so audible that Glory raises an eyebrow from down the table. I ignore her because I can't deal with anyone else.

"Would you like me to read your palm?" Glory asks as she walks toward me.

Unlike most of the girls in my senior class, I've never had my palm read by Glory Gardner. There's a part of me that's curious if the "spirits" and "cards" in question can possibly have more insight into my life than I do. If this, in theory, other realm can wade through the meddled mess of emotions that causes me to be unclear on very clear questions: Is it possible to love someone who hurts you? Is it possible for the person who hurts you to love you? When the person in question asks for forgiveness, is forgiveness possible?

Then there's the most important question: Does he mean it this time?

Each time I think it's impossible for my heart to hurt any more than it already does, it finds another painfully imaginative way to twist.

Glory's forehead furrows, and her eyes slide around my body as if she sees something I don't. "Yes, you need your cards read."

"Sorry," I say. "No money."

I have money, but that's to grab a bite to eat later, and even if I did have extra, I wouldn't waste it on something as frivolous as someone who thinks they can hear dead people.

She does another sweep of me with her gaze and purses her lips. "You definitely need your cards read. I'm assuming you remember where I live?"

Um . . . "Yes." Jesse used to take me to her house when we were kids, and it's awkward she remembers.

"Come to my place tonight at nine. I'll read your cards for free. Your aura is indicating you're ready for a change."

That wasn't intuitive. We live in a small town. Desiring change is a way of life. But I have never heard of Glory doing anything for free and this suddenly seems dangerous. Dangerous as in a person in an unmarked white van asking if you want to pet the puppy.

"Hey." Camila bounces up beside me. "What are we talking about?"

Mental whiplash. "I thought you were working."

"I was, but now I'm not."

"We were discussing how Miss Copeland is going to stop by my home at nine this evening to receive a free reading," Glory says.

"I'm sorry." Camila raises her hand to cup her ear. "Did you say *free*?"

"And for you as well as long as you bring Miss Copeland with you."

"Oh, we are so there," Camila says, and before I can intervene to explain that I don't think this is an amazing idea, Glory is called away by two women in mom jeans.

"How did you convince her to do a free reading?" Camila asks, but I don't bother answering because she has started talking about their family trip to visit her mother's family in Mexico over fall break, and she's terrified she'll be tragically injured by a shark bite.

I raise an eyebrow at her in a *boo-hoo*. I'll take shark bites, exotic beaches and her grandmother's mouthwatering cooking any day over my family. In fact, I'd willingly give a kidney if her family adopted me.

"Have you heard from Evangeline?" Camila asks, and the hint of sadness in her voice is unlike her. Camila and Evangeline have been best friends since kindergarten, but they argue constantly. Unfortunately, this summer, they're fighting over a boy.

I've been part of group texts where Evangeline described her trip with her family to China, and I can tell by the way Camila holds herself she hasn't heard a thing.

"She's asked about you." It's not a lie. Evangeline misses Camila, too.

Camila takes my hand, and we start toward the food trucks. She tells me how we're meeting some guys from school, and if she notices me cringing, she ignores it. Dating isn't on my radar and neither is her two thousandth attempt to fix me up. She specifically mentions Stewart Mitchell and Bryan Langston, and I wonder which one she wants to date.

As we walk away, I look to the right and find my father staring at me from a distance. Goose pimples rise over my flesh and I quickly glance away, over my shoulder, and find Glory watching me as well. A good portion of me wonders if accepting Glory's offer is a good idea, but telling Camila no would cause greater issues. Though, I do have to admit, when it comes to Glory, I am curious.

JESSE

The sky bleeds red as the last light of the roasting day fades into night. I walk out of the tree line made up mostly of towering maples and willows and into the circle of cut grass that surrounds Glory's home.

The cottage is the original homestead built hundreds of years ago when a Lachlin made it over the Appalachians. Gran let Glory live here rent free because she said Glory was family. Family in the eighteenth-cousin-twice-removed type of way, but still family. Blood meant everything to Gran; so did this land. That's the reason why I have my grandmother's maiden name.

The place isn't much—a living room, bedroom, kitchen and bathroom. There's a staircase that leads to an attic that's fit for boxes and spiders. The original stone fireplace works, but I wouldn't light a match in it without fear of the place going up in flames.

Only way here is by foot or to take U.S. Highway 25 to the narrow, broken road that leads to the winding dirt path that ends at Glory's. Moral to the story—you have to want to find the place. For someone who runs a con business that requires people locating her, her choice of residence is irrational. But that's Glory to the core—strange.

I didn't drive, I walked. Since the funeral, I haven't been able to take a lungful of air, but by walking on my land the strangling sensation has been downgraded to a minor choke. When I can't breathe, the land breathes for me. And Marshall wonders why I don't want to give it up.

Two cars are parked off to the side. One is Glory's blue Beetle. The other a shiny black Escalade with out-of-county license plates. People come from all over the state, some across the country, to meet with Glory. They'll pay good money, too. What a waste.

The door that needs to be stripped of the peeling, blue paint is closed, and the porch light is on. All nonverbals Glory is knee-deep in a session and knocking would disturb the "spirits."

I climb the wooden stairs and cross the porch for the swing. Faint light pushes through the layers of white sheer curtains of the window, and beyond that I can barely make out two silhouettes settled at the round wooden table Glory claims was made out of some tree that helps with psychic energy. Odds are she picked it up from the Salvation Army when she was twenty.

I adjust the cap on my head, stretch out my booted feet and lay an arm along the swing. The shadows behind the curtains move then the front door opens with an ominous squeak.

Out walks a thin woman in her sixties who wears a pantsuit and oversize sunglasses. She and Glory say goodbyes in hushed tones. The older woman dabs the corner of her eye behind her glasses with a handkerchief and then lightly runs it along her nose. Glory offers her a comforting hug and then the lady ambles down the steps.

The two of us stay silent as we watch the woman start her car and pull away with the slowness of one who has no idea which way to go—even when there's only one way out.

"She lose someone?" I say.

Glory leans her shoulder against the beam of the porch. "Her son died several years ago."

"Do you ever feel guilty about what you do?"

"Are you referring to the serenity I gave her by letting her know that her son is at peace?"

"How much did peace cost? One hundred dollars for an hour? Two hundred for two?"

Glory examines me—head to toe. Hat, Guns N' Roses T-shirt,

jeans, work boots. She gets that faraway look in her eye—the I-tout-lies stare—and I raise a hand in the air. "Mention you're sensing Gran's spirit, and I'll convince Marshall to evict you by the end of next week."

"It's too early to see Suzanne. Souls need time to build up energy before I can sense them."

I click my tongue in admonishment. "There's a flaw in your perfect gift after all."

"We all have flaws. Some of us don't mind admitting them. Your gran asked me to read your palm after her death so I could help guide you. Would you mind giving me your hand?"

My gran believed in Glory, but I don't. "I have no interest in knowing my future."

"That sounds like you believe I have the gift, and you're scared of what I'll tell you."

"I believe you're a hustler who makes a buck off people who are easy reads."

"Nothing about you is easy. In fact, everything about you is very difficult."

"Let me guess, I'm a tortured soul, and next week I'm going to see a bluebird and that bluebird's going to represent a dead family member of mine who is there to tell me to be at peace with my soul."

The ends of Glory's mouth edge up—sarcastic and dry. "It'll be a blackbird, actually, and the bird will not bring peace to your soul. The sight of it will trouble you."

Another keen observation based on things every person in town already knows—my soul is always troubled.

"You believe you are cursed. Is it so hard to stretch your belief in the Lachlin curse to thinking there are those of us who possess a supernatural gift?"

"I'm cursed because I have to listen to you spew lies about spirits beyond the grave."

Glory has the balls to smirk at me. "I know what you really believe, and I know how you think you can break the curse."

She doesn't know anything, and I'm ready for this conversation to be done. "Gran told you about the tribunal."

"Yes, and I also know you can't evict me so your threats are hollow."

True story. I read the entire file Marshall left behind, and Glory can stay on the land for now. "But I can evict you when I inherit the land."

"*If* you inherit the land," she corrects. "Come inside, and I'll warm up some leftovers."

The mention of food causes my stomach to grumble, but pride keeps me full. "I'm good. Tell me who's on the tribunal."

"We used to be close. It seems like yesterday when you and Scarlett Copeland were playing in my garden and smuggling cookies out of my pantry. You're grieving, I'm grieving. Let's eat and remember Suzanne together."

Anger tightens my muscles. I don't want to remember Scarlett or Gran. "The tribunal."

Glory sighs heavily. "Your grandmother didn't want you to know who the two other members of the tribunal are."

"Then why am I here?"

"Because I spent last night searching your future."

I roll my neck as my shoulders cramp. "Gran may have believed in your fake gifts, but you don't have to play with me. I know you're a con."

"There are too many variables to predict your future," she continues as if I hadn't spoken, "but the odds of you keeping the land improve if you know who is in the tribunal. If Suzanne knew this before she passed, she would have told you the truth."

Those words—the truth—are a hook to the head and a front kick to the gut.

"I'll tell you who the two other members of the tribunal are, but I have two conditions."

I'm sure she does. Glory's all about payment. "What do you want?" Because if it's money, she'll be a sad, sad psychic.

"First, if you inherit the land—"

"*When* I inherit the land."

"*If*," she emphasizes. "Because your future is still very unclear . . ."

"You're a nutcase."

"If you keep the land, then you'll let me remain in the cottage, rent free, and you will leave the surrounding acreage alone. I need the privacy and the energy the woods provide."

For the first time since Gran passed, I find clarity. Negotiating, manipulating situations to my favor—this is my world. "Fine. Number two."

"Before I get to my last request, you should know that one of the members has no idea the tribunal exists. They're to be told a few days before the vote. Your grandmother and uncle felt it would be unfair to this person to have such a decision weighing on them for so long."

Whatever. "What's your last condition?"

"That for the next hour you do absolutely everything I ask of you. Even in the moments you'd rather set yourself on fire, you are to stay and do everything I tell you to do."

She wants to have dinner, we'll have dinner. "Fine, but you tell me the names first and which one knows and which one doesn't."

A breeze drifts over the trees, and wind chimes of varying sizes hanging from the roof clink together and create a tinkling symphony. The scent of lavender fills the air and the smell reminds me of the times Gran dragged me to Glory's to plant, weed and help harvest her garden.

"I'm assuming you already know Marshall is one of the members," Glory continues.

"Yeah."

"The second person is the man who performed Suzanne's funeral, Pastor Hughes. He's aware he's a member of the tribunal."

I yank hard on the bill of my baseball cap. From his increased visits with Gran over the past six months, I should have seen that one coming.

"You have your work cut out with him," she says. "But he'll be easier than your uncle."

"No kidding. Who's the third?" Because I need this one to be a slam dunk.

"It's the passenger of the car coming up the road, and when this person comes into my house, you will follow and that is when your hour will begin."

I glance down the driveway that's now fallen into darkness. There's no car, no sound of an engine, or tires crackling over rocks on the road. There's crickets singing, frogs croaking and the high-pitched chirp of a bat flying out into the night.

"I'll warm up the leftovers and leave them in the microwave. Eat as soon as you come in as things will move quickly. I'll see you inside in a few."

The screen door closes behind Glory with a clap. On cue, there's the purr of an engine and then headlights poke through the trunks of the trees. Got to give Glory credit: she's a con, but she's a good con. Timing on that was perfect.

The car parks awkwardly a few spots down from Glory's car, and I hitch my thumbs in my pockets as I wait to see who the third person is deciding my fate. The mailman? The receptionist at Gran's doctor's office? The guy down at the hardware store?

The driver's side door opens first, but it's the passenger side door I watch. Scarlett Copeland emerges, and the moment her eyes meet mine, my gut twists and the smile that had been on her lips fades.

I am screwed.

SCARLETT

It's hard to ignore Jesse Lachlin when he's built like a brick wall, and he's one of four of us who are squished in a room that's the size of a kitchen pantry. But ignore him, I do. I was nice to him at church, and then he discarded me as if I were a Sunday school volunteer application. There's only so many times in a day I can allow myself to be walked all over and hurt, and I reserve that time for my father. There's no room for anyone else to hurt me, Jesse included.

Glory, Camila and I sit at a chestnut wooden table that's the right size for us to extend our palms to Glory. Glory is currently studying Camila's hand, and my palm sweats because, when it's my turn, I'm not sure I want to hear what Glory has to say.

On the table is a large raw crystal. It's not pretty or very shiny. It has too many sharp edges, and something about it makes me uncomfortable. To be honest, this entire place makes me uneasy. I rub a hand along my arm as if I'm cold. I do have a chill, but it's mental as there's no air-conditioning. Even with multiple soft lamps and candles lighting the room, the entire place feels dark, as if I'm being smothered by a storm cloud.

"Everything's fine," Camila says in a low tone. It's clear that she meant it as a private conversation between me and her, but I'm sure Glory heard. I glance at Glory to see if she reacts, but she's too busy studying Camila's hand.

"If he calls again," Camila whispers, "Mom will handle it."

I nod like I'm not worried about Dad, and that the thought of him discovering we left Camila's house never entered my mind, but worry gnaws at me. The constant fear of making Dad angry is a sludge in my veins that leaves a path of underlying panic.

We couldn't leave Camila's house until my father called Camila's mom to confirm I was there. When Dad calls to check on me, he'll also ask her mom to hand her cell to me so my father can hear my voice. Camila's mom is awesome. After Dad's initial call, she'll shoo me and Camila off with encouraging words for us to be teenagers.

It's a miracle that his behavior hasn't scared off Camila or her parents.

A beep of a microwave and the scent of something Italian fills the air. Seconds later, Jesse walks in to the room, plops down onto a red velvet love seat in the corner and places a plate of spaghetti on his lap.

I stare at him, and for the first time since I exited the car, he looks at me. His red hair feathers out from his cap and there's a hint of a five-o'clock shadow along his jawline. He's handsome as always, but the heaviness in his eyes shows his grief and exhaustion. Jesse shouldn't be here. He should be home, but then again, maybe home is too painful.

"I hope the two of you don't mind Jesse being here," Glory says in this mystical, singsong voice as she releases Camila's hand. "I forgot I had promised him dinner when I had invited the two of you over."

Camila drops a grin on Jesse that's a combination of flirtatious and deadly. Exactly like how I'd imagine a black widow spider must appear seconds after mating. Camila has two modes: friendly and dangerously blunt.

"I don't mind him staying," Camila says. "That is, if he can figure out how to be a decent human being."

And then there are the times that her honesty wanders into mean. But I remind myself that Camila is standing up for me. I didn't pick Camila, she picked me. When Jesse dropped me as a friend and then said terrible things about me to other people on the first day of our freshman year, she was the one who found me crying in the bathroom and told me it would be okay. For that, I will forever be grateful.

Jesse leans back in the chair as relaxed as a lion in the sun. "Once I figure that out, I'll pass along my tips to you." He really is Peter Pan. Frozen in his immaturity.

Camila loves a good sparring match, and while sometimes it's entertaining to watch when her opponent is worthy, I don't feel like watching today. Jesse is free game to her any other time, just not this week. "Can we move this along? I would like to know my future before the future happens."

Rolling with the change in the game, Camila shrugs one shoulder. "You're right. He's not worth it."

"Scarlett, are you okay with Jesse being here?" Glory asks as she gestures for me to offer my palm.

"I can go," Jesse pipes in and edges to the end of his seat. "I'm sure you have plenty of secrets you don't want an audience for."

Camila jerks her head toward me, an unspoken question of what Jesse could possibly know that she doesn't. Besides fireflies in jars and memories of uninhibited, pure joyous laughter when he and I were children, Jesse, like Camila, doesn't know my secrets.

Trust and friendships are hard for me. Because of that, Camila is the closest I have to a friend. I'm that friend Camila calls when she's ticked everyone else off, like when she and Evangeline aren't talking. I'm there when she needs someone, then I don't complain when she's made up with other people and she chooses to hang with them over me.

It hurts at times, but I'd never tell her that. I'm the one who has the weird father, and it's not her fault I'm friendship impaired.

"I don't have anything to hide," I lie, then speak the absolute truth to Jesse as I give Glory both of my hands, palms up. "You know nothing about me."

I steel myself for his retort, but there isn't one. Each second of silence that passes doesn't make me relax, but instead causes nausea to frolic in my stomach. Jesse used to know me better than anyone else, and I wonder if my words hurt him as much as they hurt to admit.

A fork scrapes against a plate, and I assume he's eating. Like always, life goes forward for Jesse.

Glory brushes her finger along a line of my left hand then my right. She frowns as she studies my hand as if she's learning how to defuse a bomb. Lightly, so much so that I hardly feel it, she traces circles on my right hand. She lifts her head, and it's disconcerting how quickly she switches to a smile. I can spot forced happiness better than most. "We'll start with Camila."

Camila's eyes twinkle as she winks at me, and I genuinely smile back. This is why we're friends. Camila lives life while I, on the other hand, focus on getting through the day.

Glory hands Camila a deck of tarot cards and asks her to shuffle them. She does, hands them back and then Glory lays the cards out in the design of a Celtic cross.

She looks over the arrangement of cards as if it's an interesting piece of art then digs in. There are things about Camila Glory nails: like how Camila is vivacious, tenacious and driven. My friend eats it up, and I sit back in relief. I needed fluff and fun.

I soak in the perky energy that flows out of Camila. When I didn't think my friend could soar much higher, Glory tells Camila that she'll soon need a passport, will be on a beach and that the boy in Mexico who has been on her mind has been thinking about her and that they'll go on a date that will include snow cones. She even tells Camila that she and a close friend will soon reconcile. Camila nearly bursts from her skin.

Besides Mexico and snow cones, the "psychic" reading is vague, it's harmless, and worth the cost of admission: free. There are worse ways to spend an evening.

Glory gathers her cards, organizes them into a full deck and Camila performs a little clap as she angles herself toward me. "This is so much fun! I can't wait for her to read you."

I expect Glory to hand the deck to me, but instead she tilts her head and stares straight through me as if she sees a ghost. A chill runs along my spine and goose bumps raise on my arms. I'm afraid to glance behind me, scared there will be a specter hovering in the air, yet I do look because curiosity is stronger than fear.

There's no ghost, only Jesse and he's watching me. A tingling of electricity in the air, and I wonder if anyone else can feel it.

"What's happening?" Camila asks.

"We're waiting." Glory's expression is eerily set in stone.

"For?" Camila pushes.

I strain to listen to the silence, as if that will provide a clue. It's weird how still the house is. No ticking of a clock, no radio being played for background noise, not even the sound of our breaths. It's like the world has been frozen.

A phone rings, and I jump as adrenaline courses through me. Camila laughs so loudly that it hurts my ears. She places her right hand on her chest, and her left hand on my wrist. "Oh my God, this is so much fun! You were scared, too. Don't lie. I saw you jump."

Camila continues to laugh as she reaches into her purse and accepts the call. "Hi, Papá."

The way she says "Papá" is as if the name were a hug. Camila's relationship with her father is so open, so harmonious, that she still refers to him with the joy that belongs to a child.

Camila's laughter fades, and she glowers. "No, I put the contracts in the binder. They should be there. I counted them and double-checked before I left the binder in your office."

A few seconds of silence, and Camila closes her eyes. "Can it wait until I get home? I'm out with Scarlett."

She mashes her lips together. "Okay. I'm on my way." Camila ends the call, and I'll admit to being disappointed. Even though I had my reservations, it's been fun and I'm not ready to leave.

"Papá can't find the contracts we signed for the parties today. I'm sure I'll find them as soon as I walk in." Because her father's office is a perpetual mess. "The timing stinks."

It does, but I can't argue with her responsibility to her parents' business. I reach for my purse and offer Glory my practiced smile. "Thank you. We had fun."

"But I didn't do your reading," Glory protests.

"It's okay."

Camila stands, balances her purse on her wrist, then grabs the table. "Oh my God."

"Are you okay?" I ask.

"I may have left the binder at the fair. I remember putting it on the table, but I don't remember putting it in the box of stuff to go home. This is not good."

But fixable. "We'll swing by the fair, see if it's there, and if it's not, I bet it's in your dad's office. Didn't your mom and dad hire someone to work the booth tonight?"

"Yes."

"Then I bet it's safe and sound at the booth."

While I congratulate myself for avoiding that mini-crisis, Camila blows up my fix. "If I go back to the fair, I can't get you home in time for curfew. I have to find the contracts, Scarlett. I can't lose those."

My stomach drops, and I stare pleadingly at my friend as she gives me the same imploring stare in return. I've never broken curfew, and after the close call at the fair, I don't plan on breaking that rule tonight.

"I can drive you home," Glory suggests.

"What?" Camila and I say at the same time, and Jesse coughs.

"I know where you live," Glory's eyes sparkle as if she's given me the best solution, "and it sounds like Camila needs to get into town and then home swiftly. Your home is in the opposite direction. Plus if you stay, then I'll be able to do your reading."

She's right, on all accounts, yet I'm unsure. I was comfortable with Glory at six years old, but that was back when I had absolutely no sense of self-preservation. Camila sucks in her lower lip, and I can tell she's already made her decision. She needs me to accept Glory's offer.

Fabulous.

"Thank you." I drift back into the chair. "That would be amazing."

Camila throws her arms around my neck, kisses my cheek, then she's out the door. She will owe me for life, and by the fleeting smile she sends me before she walks out, she's aware.

Glory focuses on the tarot cards as she shuffles them, and I ready myself for nonsense. Maybe she'll tell me that I'll meet the love of my life at the next high school football game. Maybe she'll tell me that he's cute, loaded and is ready to sweep me off to his private island where all I'll have to do for the rest of my life is read books.

"Scarlett," Glory says slowly, and my eyes narrow, as nothing good ever comes from anyone saying my name in that tone. "There's a reason why I asked you here—and I'm hoping you'll be accommodating."

And here's the ulterior motive I've been waiting to rear its ugly little head. "What?"

"I do want to read your cards, but Jesse's cards need to be read as well, and I know with everything that is inside me that I need to read your cards together."

JESSE

Ichoke and slam a hand to my chest to dislodge the knot of spaghetti. "What did you say?"

"I need to read your cards together." Her merciless eyes land on me.

I always knew Glory was a con. Knew she had to have a dead heart to exploit people the way she does. But to mix things up between me and Scarlett with the knowledge of how we used to be tight and then how we aren't—that's subzero.

Pieces of Scarlett's long black hair fall over her shoulder as she risks a peek at me. She's not happy either, and that only increases my rage at Glory. Why can't she leave the two of us alone?

The fork clanks loudly against the china when I drop the plate onto the wooden floor. Scarlett sags in her chair as I sink into the seat left empty by her demonic friend.

I go to stretch out my legs, but my boots hit the table, so instead I bend my knees. My jeans come in contact with Scarlett's warm thigh and electricity shoots through me. I jump, and Scarlett straightens as if I shocked her with a Taser.

She tries to scoot her chair to the side, but it hits the base of one of the towering bookcases. Because this room is the size of a refrigerator box, there's nowhere for either of us to go, nowhere for either of us to put ourselves without touching the other.

I resettle so my leg is a fraction of an inch from hers. Even though we aren't touching, I can still feel her heat. Scarlett is the most gorgeous girl at our school. I know that. Every male who has been in a one-mile radius knows that. I've had to work hard to keep from staring at her like the other idiots at school and that just pisses me off more. Scarlett and I aren't friends anymore, and I shouldn't find her attractive.

Glory watches us with an amused glint in her eyes, and too angry for a decent comeback, I cross my arms and glare.

Scarlett angles her feet in the direction of the door and tucks her hair behind her ear. "While I greatly appreciate you offering to do a free reading, I think I'll skip it, but I would highly appreciate it if you could give me the ride home. Now."

Straight to the point with some salt at the end. Nice to see some things about Scarlett haven't changed. When we were friends, she would have never hung out with the likes of Camila: social climber, soul sucker, eternal self-appointed judge to the entire school. Now the two of them are as thick as thieves.

Being Glory, she ignores the direct request and places the stacked deck in between me and Scarlett. "Whoever feels led should cut the deck. The other should shuffle. And, Scarlett, this reading was a direct request from Suzanne before she died. She knew it had been on my mind, but I never felt pushed to act on it until today."

If looks could kill, Glory would be withering on the floor taking her last breaths. But because Glory doesn't die, Scarlett cuts the deck, slapping her half of it next to me with enough anger the table shakes.

"Guess I'm shuffling the cards," I say.

"Guess you are," Scarlett shoots back without looking at me.

This should be fun, like having my fingernails ripped off. I gather both piles, do a sloppy slip of a few cards from one position to another, then slide the cards back to Glory so they topple over in a waterfall. If that pissed her off, she doesn't show it as she gathers them in her hands and starts placing them in complicated patterns.

As Glory flips one of the cards onto the table, Scarlett jerks.

"Are you okay?" Glory asks.

Scarlett slightly quakes, like a light aftershock. "Just a chill."

Glory looks pleased—the type of pleased a hyena has when a gazelle takes a nap in front of him. She points at the card she laid down. "Does the Chariot mean anything to you?"

The Chariot is this kingly-warrior-looking guy being pulled around in—surprisingly enough—a chariot. Unlike most of the other cards, it's faced away from Glory.

"It's a card," Scarlett says.

"And it's in reverse," Glory says, like that proves some sort of point.

"I'd really like to go home now," Scarlett says, and if we were friends, I'd offer her a fist bump, but we aren't so I go back to ignoring her like she's ignoring me.

"Soon." Glory finishes laying out the cards then studies them before speaking again. "You both have very clear and specific goals, and you are both determined to succeed."

On cue I slump in my seat. Wow—another earth-shattering statement.

"You feel as if you've lost control of your lives. You feel stuck, like there is no forward momentum. You also both understand pain, more than someone your age should. Scarlett, your pain and secrets are such that I highly advise you to carry obsidian at all times."

Scarlett flinches. I glance at her, trying to figure out if that was real or a glitch in my brain. I can't tell. She sits there, all perfect, as if nothing could or would faze her. This girl is nothing like the Tink I remember.

Our freshman year, Scarlett became a replica of her mother: perfect posture, manicured nails, and hands folded in her lap like a princess. She even inherited the uncanny ability, with a subtle flick of her eyes, to look down upon me and my friends.

Glory starts into some nonsense about how this will be a trying year, but a defining year—a year that we will both look back upon and have fond emotions for—and I can't help the sense of pride that washes through me as Scarlett arches a brow in disbelief. That's the girl I remember. The one who had no problem calling me or anyone else out on their crap.

"You both have secrets," Glory says. "Secrets that unless you figure out how to bring them to the surface and confront, you'll never find happiness."

"Can you be any more vague?" I ask, and Scarlett smirks. The edges of my own mouth move up. It's been a long time since the two of us were on the same side of anything.

"Would you like me to be more specific?" Glory asks with a taunt. My smile falls. Anything Glory knows about me isn't because of magical cards. It's because my grandmother trusted her when she shouldn't have.

"Why don't we wrap this up," Scarlett says.

"Tell me what you want to know," Glory says to Scarlett, and I find myself curious for her answer. Scarlett has everything. Her father owns the lone manufacturing plant in the county, their family is loaded and whatever she or her mother wants appears out of the air with a snap of their fingers. Scarlett has never had to struggle.

"Will I do it?" she asks. "Will I reach my goal?"

Glory scoops up the cards, shuffles them again and says aloud, "Will Scarlett and Jesse reach their goals?"

Once again, she lays out the cards in an elaborate pattern and her eyes flicker from one card to the next. "There are many obstacles in your paths, and you both will be tested."

My fingers tap against my still-crossed arms. Glory is like one of Gran's records that's been scratched and plays the same section of music over and over again.

"I can't one hundred percent say if either of you will succeed."

"Of course you can't," I mumble.

"I can see that if the two of you work together, there will be a clearer path of success."

"If we work together?" Scarlett balks. "Please."

Glory looks straight at me, and I see more than I want. See a truth that twists my gut. I had been hoping that Glory was wrong. That after Scarlett left, Glory would tell me she had made a mistake, Scarlett wasn't one of the tribunal and Glory would be offering me excuses as to why her psychic powers had been out of whack.

But this. . . . I take my cap off and run a hand over my head in an attempt to recover. Screw me, Scarlett really is the third vote in the tribunal.

"Are you kidding me?" I say, and the contempt in my tone tastes bitter.

"No," Glory says. "The two of you must definitely work together."

SCARLETT

I'm out of my seat, purse in hand and I'm ready to go. Camila's reading was fun. This one was a joke, at my expense, and I'm not laughing. "Take me home."

A cell rings, and I glance at Jesse, waiting for him to answer, but instead it's Glory who crosses the room and grabs her cell. She accepts the video call and gives a brilliant smile. "Hi! Do you mind giving me a few? I need to wrap up with a client, and I'll call you right back."

My entire body seizes. "You're supposed to give me a ride home."

Glory ends the call and offers me an apologetic expression. "I forgot I had a phone meeting. I'll take you home, after the call, but this will be a lengthy session."

Meaning I won't be home by curfew. "Reschedule."

Glory has a thoughtful look as she approaches me. One that makes me feel like I should run. She leans forward and says in my ear, "You felt something when you saw the Chariot."

The moment she placed that card on the table I felt as if I had sprinted headfirst into a wall. It was a stunned feeling, as if I were lost in a fog, but I won't admit that. Not to her, not to anybody.

"You've been asleep for a very long time," she whispers. "It's time to wake up, Scarlett. There's a whole world of possibility waiting for you."

I step back from her because this lady is insane. "I need you to take me home."

"I can't, but I'm sure Jesse can lead the way."

Um . . . no. I spin on my toes, and I'm out the door, down the stairs, and I head east for home. Seconds later, the screen door slams shut again, and there are heavy footfalls on the wooden steps.

"Wait up!" Jesse calls out.

Nope. Not going to happen. I enter the tree line and curse the sky above that there's no moon. This is the country, which means that besides the fading light from Glory's house, I'm in complete darkness.

"Scarlett!" Jesse tries again. "Wait!"

But I don't. I walked this land hundreds of times with Jesse, sometimes by myself so I could find him when I needed a friend. I can do this on my own.

"Let me find you so I can walk you home," Jesse says.

He's to my right, and I hurry because I don't want to be found. My pulse pounds in my ears, and my blood tingles with this need to stay hidden, to stay alone.

Once upon a time, Jesse was my best friend, and then one day he froze me out. He stopped answering the door when I knocked, he ran away when he saw me coming across the field and then when we were forced into the same space on the first day of our freshman year, he humiliated me in front of the entire school.

Jesse Lachlin crushed me, and while I feel sorry for him because his grandmother died, I don't forgive him for leaving a scar on my soul.

"Dammit, Scarlett, stop being so stubborn."

My jaw clenches, and it takes an immeasurable amount of self-control to not explain to Jesse in a very loud tone that he's the biggest jerk I've ever met. Doing so will inform him where I'm located, and I need him to leave me alone.

I push forward, faster this time, but then my foot snags on a root. My balance is thrown and my arms swing wildly in the air. I attempt to reach for something to break my fall, but my fingers catch air. The sensation is like the first massive hill of a roller coaster as my stomach lifts, and I brace myself for impact with the ground.

I close my eyes, tense my muscles and I'm caught. Strong, warm arms weave around me from behind and then my back is pressed flush against a solid chest. My heart leaps, and my lungs are robbed of air.

"You okay?" Jesse's mouth is incredibly close to my ear, and his hot breath tickles my skin. I tremble, because of the adrenaline or because of this achingly beautiful intimacy, I don't know.

"Are you okay?" he asks again, and this time his arms tenderly squeeze me as if he's offering comfort, as if he honestly cares. It's been so long since anyone has hugged me that a part of me melts into the embrace as if I'm dry ground welcoming a warm rain.

"Scarlett?" Jesse gently urges me to answer. "Are you okay?"

No, I'm not. I haven't been okay in years, and he's partly to blame. A rush of anger fills me, and I shove Jesse away. "I'm fine."

He straightens as if I had slapped him. Something I should have done our freshman year when he embarrassed me at lunch, making me the laughingstock of the freshman class. People still whisper about it. "Yeah, you seem fine."

We've wandered far enough into the woods that the lights from Glory's cottage are no longer visible. Above us, through the thick foliage, thousands of stars twinkle in the night sky. I blink, and my sight finally adjusts to the darkness. I'm still surrounded by blackness, but I can make out some of the trees and most of Jesse.

"Are you ready to accept my help?"

"I know my way home."

"You were walking toward the state highway."

I cross my arms because I had no idea I had been heading in the exact wrong direction of home. "I was trying to lose you."

"Then lose me. But lose me when you cross the street to your home. I don't need police officers and FBI agents roaming my land for weeks because you can't figure out east from west."

"Scared they'll find your drug stash?"

Jesse yanks on the bill of his baseball cap. I have no idea if Jesse does drugs or not. Rumor at school is that he was arrested for possession, but his uncle had the charges dropped.

"Get your phone and use the flashlight app," he says. "Last thing I need is your dad suing me because you can't walk without tripping."

Jesse isn't reaching for his cell, and I know why. Unlike me, Jesse knows this entire land so well that he could walk it blindfolded and with his arms tied behind his back.

"The light will blind us," I say, "and I remember how to get home."

He releases a long breath like he doesn't believe me then starts to walk in the opposite direction of where I had been heading. "Then at least stick close."

As much as I hate it, I do. Even when I roamed this land daily, I still didn't know it as well as Jesse. No one could. Jesse and the land aren't just connected. They are one.

JESSE

Through the woods, Scarlett followed me, walking where I walked, but as soon as we step into the hayfield, she catches up to be by my side. She has a slight limp, and I shake my head. She's wearing sandals. Not even sturdy sandals. Ones that were made for show and not for comfort. And she thought walking was a good idea, and I thought she was smart.

"Let's take a break." I expect her to argue, but instead she plops down on a log.

Good thing the hayfield was cut last week or we'd be thigh deep in grass. I prop my back against the trunk of an oak and watch as she takes off her sandals then circles her ankles.

"You used to be able to run from Gran's to Glory's without stopping," I say.

"But I never did it in sandals."

True story. Though, during the summer, she used to run this land barefoot.

"Know where you're at now?" I ask.

She scans the area then nods. This time, I believe her.

"The creek's to the south." Scarlett turns her head in the right direction then her gaze wanders to the north—to the location of the huge sugar maple my great-great-great grandfather planted when he was a boy. She doesn't mention the maple. I don't bring it up either. I guess some things are better left in the past.

I lean my head against the tree and can feel the lingering

warmth of the day radiating from the bark. Breathing in deep enough, I can still smell the sun. Scarlett used to tell me I was wrong—she said the scent was that of life. She thought the aroma was created when the leaves absorbed beams of light for food. With all the seriousness that a ten-year-old could have, Scarlett pinned me down with a glare and declared the smell green.

That was back when she would admit she could smell colors. Now I'd bet she would tell me she smells nothing.

The leaves surrounding us clap with the breeze and a new scent fills my nose. It's sweet honeysuckle on the vine with a hint of wild grass, and I frown. There's no honeysuckle near here, it's the wind having fun at my expense. That scent belongs to Scarlett. I glance over at her and she's watching me.

"I was always envious of you for that," she says.

"Of what?"

"Of how you could touch any part of this land at any time and look as if you truly belong. As if it's alive and you're having a conversation no one else can hear. Sometimes it made me think that the Lachlins are spiritually gifted and that Glory might really be psychic."

"Glory's a con," I say.

Scarlett studies me. "You have to admit the phone call Camila received was weird."

As was Scarlett showing up in the car exactly as Glory and I were talking about the third member of the tribunal, but that boils down to . . . "Coincidence."

"She knew a lot about Camila, and some things she said regarding me were true."

"It's a game. She throws out broad statements, and people are more than happy to latch on to her lies because they're excited at the idea of believing in something."

"So you don't believe we're meant to work together?"

I believe I need her to vote for me in May. "What do you want?"

She freezes while wrapping her hair into a bun at the base of her neck. "Excuse me?"

"Glory said you had a goal. What is it?"

"Why do you care?"

She has a point. To go from years of ignoring her to attempting to sneak into her private thoughts doesn't exactly add up. "Just making conversation."

Scarlett finishes with her hair then gives me her best princess to pauper look. It's equal parts tempting and annoying. "What do *you* want?" she turns the question around.

I could lie. Give her some lame goal, but she's watching me, testing me. I have nine months to win her over, and it's going to take all that time to undo what's happened between us. The pure truth will drive her away, and odds are she still knows me well enough to ferret out the lie so I give her half of the truth. "I want my land."

"This is your land. It's been your land since the day you were born."

Exactly. "Gran didn't give me it outright. Marshall will decide when I turn eighteen if I'm mature enough to own the farm."

"Are you?"

That was direct. "Yes."

She gathers her sandals and stands. "Then I wish you luck." With a gentle sway of her hips, she pivots on her toes, and this time heads in the right direction.

I push off the tree and join her. We're so deep into the heart of my land that there's no sound of human life, no rumble of a truck from the road, no music from speakers, no stray conversation lingering in the night. Just the occasional sound of a cricket trying to get laid.

She wishes me luck. As if she doesn't believe in me. As if she sides with Marshall on her opinion of me. "I'm responsible enough to own the land."

"Okay," she says, but doesn't sound convinced.

"I'm responsible enough to own the land," I say again. Silence on her end and that pisses me off. "What makes you think I'm not responsible enough?"

"With how you behave at school, I'd say you're going to sell the farm the moment your name is on the deed. What will you blow the money on? A field party for the ages?"

I spit out the same words she threw at me earlier, and I'm a bastard because I want them to hurt her as bad as her saying it hurt me. "You don't know me."

She doesn't respond, just keeps on walking like what I said doesn't matter.

"You don't know me," I say louder.

"I guess that makes us equal."

"What makes you think I'm irresponsible?"

She makes a soft derisive sound, and my teeth grind.

"Don't act insulted," she bites out. "You've been suspended from school, you've been arrested at least twice, and your friends are a bunch of losers who sit in the back of class and make fun of anyone who is not the four of you. That is the definition of juvenile delinquency."

"You think you have me and my friends figured out, don't you?"

"Three years of high school, and each year, you guys act like fools, so, yes, I have a good handle on the situation."

Every muscle in my body tenses. "Like you and your friends are any better?"

"Well, none of my friends have been arrested."

"Your friends are mean and talk more crap than my friends ever do. My friends would never hurt people like your so-called friends do."

She picks up her pace. "Unlike some people, my friends don't ridicule people in public."

"Guess I should tell my friends that the great Scarlett Copeland told me it's only proper to throw shade if we do it behind people's backs."

"Do whatever you need to ease your conscience. You're the jerk here, Jesse. Not me."

"You and your friends believe you're better because your clothes cost more, but you aren't better. Your life is a show. You guys complain how hard life is because the hotel you want for prom is booked. Not a single one of you know what it's like to struggle."

"Wow." Her chin lifts and her nose is definitely in the air. "And to think, I spent years wondering why you didn't want to be my friend anymore. I had no idea you had done me a favor. Thank you for helping me figure out that I like it better when we don't talk."

I become rooted on the spot. Idiot. I'm. An. Idiot. I'm supposed to be repairing my friendship with Scarlett, not rehashing years of pain.

Scarlett keeps going, and when I catch up, it's clear she's going to ignore that I exist. The walk goes by too quickly or not fast enough. Depends upon one's feelings on heavy, angry silences. The beaming porch lights of Scarlett's massive house come into view, and I can see the outline of my trailer. Home sweet home.

We reach the old, rusting metal swing set my grandmother bought for me when I was five. Back then, I thought she gave me heaven. I pause by the seesaw that looks like it would crack in two if touched. Scarlett and I had spent hours on this thing. Going up and then down. A fantastic metaphor for our lives. Scarlett, though, must not feel sentimental. She keeps walking. I guess she's not saying goodbye.

"Scarlett," I call out, and I'm shocked when she stops. Her back's still toward me, but at least she's not running. "I told you what I want. I'm curious what you want."

She glances over her shoulder at me. "Why?"

"Maybe Glory's right. Maybe we can find a way to help each other."

Scarlett scans the yard, and I wonder what she sees. With her here, I see our ghosts as children—hear our laughter, taste the honeysuckle we ate as we talked for hours and the way she'd place her hand in mine when we'd walk across this field.

"Even though you obviously did me a favor, why did you stop talking to me?" she asks. "After all those years of seeing each other day in and day out, why did you stop being my friend?" She pauses, and I lower my head because each and every word is a paper cut on my heart. "What did I do wrong?"

I shake my head because I got nothing. Nothing that will make sense to her. What's worse, I don't have anything that makes sense to me. At least not anymore.

When it's clear I'm not going to give her the Disney ending she was hoping for, she digs into her purse and pulls out a key. She's going to leave, and I'm losing my shot. I should have listened better in health during the sex education talk. Maybe Coach had some great pearls of wisdom on how to talk to girls, and I missed it in order to take a nap.

"Can you get me a job?" she asks.

"What do you need a job for?" Her father is loaded.

"I want to go to UK."

My eyes narrow as I try to figure out where this is headed. "The University of Kentucky?"

"Yes. I want to become a speech therapist, and they have a great program. So I need a job. Can you make that happen for me?"

She's met with more stone cold silence from me.

"I didn't think so." Scarlett walks across the road and back to her pristine life.

SCARLETT

I close the front door and place my house key on the hook. My mother calls from the kitchen, "Scarlett? Is that you?"

"No, Mom, it's a burglar."

Like always, she laughs. It's a good laugh, a soft laugh, and it makes me smile. I walk down the long, wide hallway made of dark hardwood and enter our bright kitchen. At the table is Mom and my sister.

In her typical seat and in footed pajamas like it's December instead of August, my sister's legs swing. Her toes barely skim the floor. Isabelle's long black hair, complete with bed-head knots, falls wildly over her shoulders. I'm betting this means nightmares. Again.

I force a smile and choose the seat next to my sister. "Why are you awake, squirt?"

With her fingers curled around a cup of tea, my sister gives me a beaming smile. There's a new empty slot in her mouth, which means she must have lost another tooth. I have never appreciated how many teeth are in a human's mouth until my sister began losing hers at a horrifying rate. She's six, and I'm concerned she's going to be nothing but gums by seven.

"Sometimes we need a cup of tea," Mom answers for her, then squishes her nose in a cute way at my sister. "Don't we, Isabelle?"

Isabelle overenthusiastically nods and takes a sip of her tea for effect. On the seat next to her is the American Girl doll my father

bought her during their Chicago trip. The doll is dressed in matching footed pajamas, and I understand the heat-inducing nightwear.
I lift Isabelle's doll, and my stomach twists. Band-Aids cover her
doll's right eye and forehead, and a sock is tied like a tourniquet
on her doll's right wrist.

I shoot Mom a ticked-off look, and Mom lowers her gaze to
her own cup of tea. "Would you like some tea, Scarlett? It's cham-
omile, and I'm sure the water's still hot."

No, I want my sister to not be a textbook psychology case. I
turn the doll so Mom can read my thoughts. Mom merely slips
out of her seat and heads to the stove.

I tip Isabelle's doll in her direction and move it as if it's the
one talking. "Why don't you go upstairs, dig out some books and
I'll come up and read to you?"

My sister's eyes twinkle in agreement, and she snatches the
doll from me as she runs out of the kitchen. Her feet make a
cute *click-clap* padding sound as she makes her way up the stairs
while Mom busies herself with putting away dishes from the
drying rack.

After being in Glory's cramped house with three other people,
my house feels ostentatious. Especially with the two stoves, hardwood flooring and marble countertops.

At Glory's, when sitting next to me, Jesse couldn't fit his long
legs anywhere without touching me. A tingling in my chest at the
memory of Jesse's knee gliding against my thigh and how he caught
me in the woods.

Heat creeps up my neck, and I touch my warm cheeks. I've
never dated anyone. Dad told me I'm not allowed, but I also haven't
felt comfortable enough to even consider accepting an invitation.
The thought of permitting someone to touch me makes me sick, but
then Jesse touched me and, oddly enough, it sparked something
new within me. Something foreign, something that feels alive.

"Who's Stewart Mitchell?" Mom asks.

"Some guy at school." I glance at her over my shoulder. "Why
do you ask?"

"Your father noticed he's been liking your posts on social
media and that he posted a picture of you this evening. You know

how your father feels about dating, and he's not happy you didn't tell him of all your plans. "

For some people, social media is fun. For me, it's my father's way to track my every movement. "I'm not dating Stewart, and Camila and I ran into him at the food trucks. I'm not psychic and can't tell Dad about things I don't know about until they happen."

"Still," Mom says, as if that's a real response and that I *should* be psychic. "You're home early."

"Camila forgot some paperwork at the fair. If I went with her, I'd be late for curfew."

Mom carefully pours steaming water from the pot into a teacup, sets the pot back on the stove then brings the cup over to me. Out of habit, I swirl the bag of tea in the water one way and then another. Mom reclaims her seat across from me, and I love and hate how she is my best friend. *Was* my best friend. I scowl. I don't know anything anymore.

"We were at Glory's," I say, because if she's still my best friend, I should do what I used to do: tell her everything. "When I was at the fair, Glory offered to give us a free reading if we came to her house, and I accepted. When Camila had to leave, I walked home."

"You shouldn't have done that," Mom whispers, and her gaze swings toward Dad's study, as if she can see through the walls and possibly spot my father's reaction to my words. "If your father finds out, he'll be unhappy."

Dad's always unhappy, but before I can respond, Mom says, "How were you able to navigate the Lachlin property at night?"

"Jesse walked with me."

Mom circles her new gold bracelet. She's thinking. In theory, she's done a lot of that lately, but she's proof that thinking things through doesn't always yield good results. "We should keep this to ourselves, but please try to make better choices next time."

I wonder if I'll be lying every day for the rest of my life. I hope not. That sounds exhausting.

"Your father likes knowing you're safe, and if you do something outside of the expected plan, then that stresses him out," Mom says. "He worries."

Yes, we all worry, but somehow Dad can't figure how to suck

up worry like the rest of us. "Did you talk to Dad about letting me get my driver's permit?"

"I'm waiting for a good time to discuss it with him."

She'll be waiting forever, and I'm tired of being in purgatory. "When you do talk to him, can you tell him I don't want to go to a business college? I want to become a speech therapist."

Her blue eyes meet mine. There are so many emotions swirling in them, I can't tell which one she feels the most. Fear? Regret? Sadness? "Can we please not talk about this?"

"We need to talk about this. These decisions affect the rest of my life."

"Yes, they do, and think of the opportunities your father is giving you. You'll receive a fantastic education, and you should hear how excited he is about you interning with his company while you're in college."

Am I speaking English? "I don't want to work for him, and I don't want to go to a business college."

"I thought you wanted a job. You've been begging us to allow you to work."

"I do want a job, but a job I pick." My father isn't a fan of me working while in high school. His excuse is that he makes enough money and that I should focus on my studies.

But here's the thing: he has never allowed my mother to have her own bank account or a job. Not even to sell makeup or Tupperware or cooking utensils like half the moms I know at school. Not even when I know my mom has been interested in doing something a little more with her life. Dad always told her that he wanted her attention solely on raising me and Isabelle. I never thought much about Mom's desires and Dad's excuses until I *did* start to think about them, and now I want a job. "I want to be a speech therapist."

"Don't you understand? Your father is grooming you to be a part of his business. He's giving you the entire world. All you have to do is accept."

"But this isn't what I want."

"Give yourself some time to wrap your head around what your

father is offering. You'll come to see how amazing this opportunity is. You are so blessed to have him as your father."

Blessed? I whip my head up so fast that the kitchen spins. "Dad hit you."

I freeze and so does Mom.

Crap.

I didn't mean to say the words out loud. It was a terrible slip. If he heard me, he'll be mad, but as I strain to listen for his footsteps, for his loud angry breathing, I hear nothing. Hope sparks in my chest. Maybe, just maybe, I can talk to my mom. Really talk to her . . . about how we both need change.

Mom's pale and rigid, and the sight reminds me of what happened last month. Of how Dad yelled at her—no, not yelled. It was beyond shouting. It was something dark, something evil, something barbaric, like a possession. He was out of control, and she wore the same expression then that she does now—a woman knowing that she is about to be destroyed.

A quick sweep of the room, as if searching for the boogeyman, because talking to Mom—talking to Mom about Dad—it's forbidden and it's dangerous.

"He hit you again," I whisper.

"I know. Last month. We've had this conversation and—"

"Mom . . ." She doesn't understand what I'm trying to say. "I know he slapped you last night."

Mom's eyes widen. She thought it was her secret. As if the walls in this house are impenetrable. "That didn't happen."

It did. I know it, she knows it, yet she's lying . . . to me. Since her mom died, the only person she has been close to honest with is me and now she's not.

Last month, Dad did more than slap her. He devastated her. My gut twists with the memory of me screaming, of Isabelle crying and of my mother begging him to stop. A cut on her forehead bleeding into her eye, one side of her face swollen, the bruises across her back.

My mother was shattered, and I shattered. I've never cried so much in my life. Even for days after. My mother was so concerned about me, even though she was the one who wore the bruises. She laid with me in bed begging me to stop, but I couldn't stop.

I was broken.

From across the table, Mom says nothing and my brain wavers toward crazy. "You promised me if he hit you again that you'd make him leave."

To get me to stop crying, *Dad* swore if he ever hit her again that he'd leave.

"He hit you again," I say, "and everyone is acting like nothing happened."

"I told you he didn't slap me."

I blink repeatedly because she can't be for real. "I heard it. A hand across the face is a pretty distinctive sound."

"I don't know what you think you heard, but that isn't what happened."

"He did. But let's say he didn't; what happened to you last month was bad enough, and I don't understand why he's still living here."

"Because he's changing, and I promise, this time, the change is real."

"He always changes!" I snap then lower my voice. Dad gets angry. I don't. That's his job. Not mine. "Yet we end up in the same place. Sitting at this table with the same cup of tea having the same tired and pathetic conversation."

Mom's face twists with concern—for me—as if my emotions and reactions are off base. "I don't understand why you're upset. He didn't hurt you. He's never hurt you. He doesn't even mean it when he hurts me."

Has she lost her mind? "Dad hurts me every time he lays a hand on you."

"He gets stressed, and the stress makes him angry. It was a mistake, and it's a mistake I've forgiven." Mom wrings her hands then circles the bracelet again. "To be blunt, this was never your problem to forgive so you need to get past this."

My head moves as if *she* had slapped *me*. Mom combs her fingers through her hair then stretches her hand out to me as if she wants me to touch her. "I have been married to your father for twenty-five years, and he has only hit me five times. When he hurts me, he doesn't mean it. He loves me, he loves you and he's so sorry for what he's done. More sorry than you know. He's cried over this, and your father never cries."

Yet it's okay for me to cry.

"You act as if your father is some belligerent drunk who beats me all the time. Your father adores me and worships you and your sister. I understand you're sad, and what happened is a shame, but if you pause for reflection, this is merely a bump in a long life. Look me in the eye and tell me you honestly think your father doesn't love you. That he doesn't love me. Think of the times in between those bad moments. Think of the way he has loved you."

I close my eyes, because I don't want to remember those times. I don't want to remember how, as a child, he read to me every night before I went to sleep, how he would smile with pride when I brought home a report card full of *A*'s or of how, in an attempt to make me laugh, he tossed a whipped-cream pie in his face after Jesse broke my heart.

"He's sorry," Mom says in a soft voice, a sincere voice. "It's killing him that you won't forgive him. I'm begging you to please give him a chance. You've never held a grudge this long before and you've been so cold. You've always been able to find a way to forgive him. Why is it different this time?"

"You promised—" My voice breaks as my throat becomes thick. "You promised if he hit you again you would throw him out and not allow him back. He promised he'd never hit you again."

"He didn't slap me last night, Scarlett. We argued, but he didn't touch me. Believe me."

But that's the problem—I can't. Not anymore.

Mom lays her hands flat on the table, and I notice the new diamond on her right hand. Guilt gifts. It's the new Christmas. "Your father and I are going to counseling, and it's been very good for us. He's trying, and I'm trying. We're learning how to communicate and how to stop being in a toxic cycle. We're making great progress, and our counselor thinks it would be good if we brought you to some of our sessions. He also thought it would be good if you and your father had some sessions on your own."

I shake my head because I don't want to go to therapy, and I definitely don't want to talk to Dad. I need space. Mom needs space. We all need space, and I don't understand why this is tough to comprehend.

Mom's frown deepens. "I thought you wanted me to go to counseling. I thought you would be happy your father is getting the help he needs. The help we all need. I don't understand why you're so focused on the negative instead of the positives."

"How should I feel?"

"Not upset. I don't want you upset."

"I keep making this stupid mistake that this is somehow my life, so why don't you walk me through how to behave as a puppet."

"Don't be like that," Mom says in reprimand. "There's no need to make this dramatic."

Dramatic? Dad slapping her across the face then punching her in the stomach was the dramatic portion of this past month's events. "I'm upset because he's going to hurt you again."

"I said he didn't slap me last night."

"But he will. If he doesn't hit you, he yells. If he doesn't yell, he breaks things. If he doesn't break things, he hits you. He spins out of control and it's terrifying. He will hit you again, and I don't understand how you don't see this!"

"Again, he didn't touch me last night, and as for last month . . . he didn't hurt me nearly as bad as you think."

"Yes, he did!" I wipe at my eyes, ticked off with myself that I'm getting upset while she sits there so calm and she's the one Dad hit. I'm not crazy. Dad did hurt her and he hurt her bad. This isn't in my head, not at all.

I can't watch him hit her again, and I can't watch her bleed. I can't keep living in a house where every second of every day I'm wondering if this is the moment he's going to snap. I can't think straight, I can't sleep and I don't want to eat. I need to feel okay, and I don't.

I plead with her on the most basic level. I give her my fear.

"Dad needs to leave, and you need to make him leave because I need space. If Dad leaves then maybe I'll feel safe again because I don't feel safe with him around."

"The counselor said you might not understand," Mom says calmly, so calmly that I want to throw something at her. "And that you would be upset for a while. But he also said that we can't let your negativity hurt the progress your father and I are making."

The world sways. I'm dizzy with rage, and that terrifies me. How can I be filled with rage? Does that mean I'm my father? "You told your counselor he hits you?" Mom and Dad aren't known for public honesty. In fact, they've sworn me to secrecy.

"He hit me, not *hits*. Only five times in twenty-five years. And, yes, our counselor knows."

"What crackpot of a therapist thinks you staying with *him* is a good idea?"

"Forgiveness is freeing," Mom says. "It's so much better than how you've been behaving. You need to let this all go and be happy again."

Happy? I'm drowning, and I've told her what she needs to do to help me survive, but instead of reaching into the water, grabbing me and pulling me to the surface, she's wringing her hands and watching me flounder from the dry dock.

I can't do this anymore. I stand and the china cup rattles with the movement. "I'm going to bed."

"Scarlett," Mom calls as I walk away, but I ignore her. "Please don't leave things like this between us."

She won't sleep tonight. She doesn't like it when anyone is mad at her, and she'll twist and bend herself in order to appease. I should care and should make her feel better, but I can't. Not tonight.

My entire life, my mom and I saw eye to eye. A united front standing in the middle of a hurricane, but we aren't the duo I thought we were.

As I round the corner for the staircase, I catch my father sitting in his favorite chair in the living room. The TV isn't on, his computer isn't in his lap, and his phone is on the end table.

He's sitting there, perched on the edge, his hands clasped

between his legs as he leans forward as if he's the one who has the right to be upset. He lifts his head and looks at me.

Terror flashes through me and my hand drops to my stomach as it roils. He wasn't in his study. He was here, in the living room. Did he hear me tell Mom how I went to Glory's? That I broke his precious rules and neglected to tell him where I was at every second of the day? That I want him to leave?

Run.

It's a small voice inside me. A demanding voice. The voice that has kept me safe all these years, but there's a crazy feeling within me that stops me from sprinting up the stairs. If he's going to be angry with me, then I want him to be angry with me for a good reason. I want him to know how much I despise him. I raise my chin and glare. "I will *never* forgive you."

He shuts his eyes as if he's crushed, and I should leave, but I don't. There's a part of me that wants to see him bleed like Mom did several weeks ago. I want him to beg for my forgiveness. I want to see him on his knees, but instead he merely lowers his head into his hands.

"Do you know what it's like for me to love?" Dad says through his fingers in this wrenching tone, the sound of a wounded animal on the verge of death. I grab the bannister, because while that voice inside me screams to run, his brokenness is so abnormal that I'm drawn to stay.

"After losing my sister, I didn't think I could love again." Dad raises his head and there are tears in his eyes. Tears, and that causes my mouth to turn down. Mom had said that Dad has cried, but I've never seen it. Never in all my years.

"I see so much of your aunt Megan in you. She was also beautiful and smart and had this smile, just like yours, that could light up any room." Dad pauses, then looks straight at me and the pure agony on his face makes it hard to glance away. "I was made fun of a lot when I was in school, did you know that?"

I shake my head. I've never heard any of this before. He doesn't talk a lot about Megan, he's never told me that I was like her, and he's never let on that his life as a teen before her disappearance was anything short of perfection.

He shrugs his shoulders as if what he said wasn't a big deal, but it is—to me. "I was an awkward child and teen. I bloomed late in life. My feet grew faster than the rest of me, and I had no coordination. It didn't help that I thought quoting lines from *Star Trek* would impress girls."

It's as if he's talking about somebody else. Not him—not the man this community loves.

"I didn't have many friends," he continues, "but it never mattered because I had Megan. She stuck up for me, was my best friend and gave me confidence when I didn't have any."

A tear rolls down Dad's cheek and my throat constricts as I try to fight off a wave of sadness.

"After Megan went missing, I felt like I died. I didn't just lose my sister—I lost my best and only friend. For weeks, for months, I went out looking for her. I saw her on every street corner and behind every tree, and every time I got close and realized it wasn't her, it was like losing her all over again. I would lay in bed and wonder what happened to her—if she was alive, if she was scared, if she was hurt or if she had died and if she died in pain—"

Dad chokes, and I can't find the ability to breathe.

"I didn't think I could love again," he says between broken breaths. "I didn't want to love anyone because losing Megan hurt too much, but I did learn to love again. I love you, I love your mom and I love Isabelle. I messed up, and I'm sorry. So sorry. You don't understand how much I love you, Scarlett. You don't understand how I'm terrified I'm going to lose you like I lost my sister." His head falls into his hands again. "I can't do that. I can't lose anyone again."

My chest is heavy, an ache that is so strong that I'm nearly doubled over. My pain, my father's pain, all of our pain surging through me and it's too much to control.

"Please forgive me, Scarlett." Dad's word are muffled through his tears. "Please forgive me. I can't take this anymore. Knowing you're upset with me and that you hate me, it kills me. I can't lose anyone else. I can't."

I rake a hand through my hair, pulling at the strands until pain pricks my scalp as a war wages inside me. My eyes burn with tears I don't want to shed. "You can't hit her anymore."

"I won't," he cries. "I promise I won't."

Dad sobs, his face in his hands, and his shoulders shudder. He's hurting, and I understand hurt. Against my will, my feet shuffle forward, and I end up on the floor in front of him. I place a hand on his shoulder. An offer of comfort, comfort I wish someone would offer me, as if I'm loved. There's a screaming inside my soul yet I say, "Don't cry, Dad. Please don't cry. I'm sorry. Just please don't cry."

JESSE

By being on the land, I'd been able to keep my mind off losing Gran. I cut the hay in the back field, helped Mr. Bergen move his cattle from one pasture to another, then helped harvest corn in the east fields. Unable to enter the trailer, I slept three nights in the hammock.

I spent a lot of that time absorbed in memories of Scarlett. I don't know why. Maybe it's because thinking of her was easier than thinking of Gran. But I try not to think of Scarlett anymore, at least not as my Tink. She's changed and so have I. Life sucks that way.

The first day of school is tomorrow, and I need a shower and a decent meal. As I approach the front of the trailer I raise my eyebrows at the sight of Veronica sitting on my steps.

V is all of four foot nine, ninety pounds, has striking blue eyes, a head full of tight blond curls and takes adorable to another level. Yet the girl used to smoke Marlboros like a southern boy hooked on NASCAR, and when she's pissed she cusses with the eloquence of a retired combat marine. When she's happy, she rivals unicorns puking rainbows, and that's when the scary really begins.

Finding her on my front steps with an expression that reminds me of the Reaper doesn't sit well. In fact, the shifting in my gut informs me my aorta is about to be slashed.

"Jesse Lachlin returns." V takes a drag on her cigarette, blows out the smoke and then smashes out the tip on a rock by her foot. She only smokes when she's having a bad day.

If I ask her what's wrong, she'd get pissed and deny she's having problems. That irritates me, and I'm not into fruitless conversations, so I keep my mouth shut.

"My butt got numb an hour ago waiting on you to show. Here's a piece of advice: answer your texts so I don't have to hitchhike to confirm you're still alive."

I stop at the bottom of the steps and look at V, but I don't see her. Instead I imagine the inside of the trailer. It's dark. The air possibly stale from no one being in or out for days. A genuine tomb.

My stomach sinks because the last thing I want is to cross the threshold and spot Gran's ashes on the mantel. There will be no smile at me walking in covered in dirt from working hard. No glare for not coming home for the last three nights. No comfortableness as we watch TV in silence. A heaviness in my chest, and I briefly close my eyes at the pain.

"Why didn't you tell us your grandmother passed?" V asks, and my insides flip at the sympathy in her tone. I hang with V because she's not sentimental. She's steel; so are the other two guys we hang with. None of us have room for emotions.

I hitch a thumb over my shoulder. "Want to get off my steps so I can shower?"

She nods as if she's agreeing to how I need this to play out. V stands to the side, allowing me access to the door, and after the lock clicks open, I swallow. This is it. This is how life is going to be now and forever—alone.

I push the door open, flick on the light and breathe out when I walk in without ripping in half. At least not physically. The emotional might take a few decades.

"Are you going to invite me in?" V asks from the door.

Like a vampire afraid she'll burst into flames, the girl won't go into any house without permission. Does it make sense? No. Will V tell any of us why she's like this? Never. Maybe she is a vampire. Those monsters are supposed to be super-teddy-bear cute on the outside and deadly on the inside, right? "Come in."

She does and follows me into the kitchen. A red light flashes from Gran's old-school landline phone, and I push *play* on the answering machine.

"Hi, Jesse. This is Mrs. Haig." My guidance counselor from school. "I'd like to pass on my condolences, and I'd like you to drop by the office on Monday so we can discuss the plans you had for your senior year. I know that you worked hard to gather enough credits to graduate by December, but now that things have changed, I'd like to discuss other options."

Options meaning she would like me to stay in school and graduate in May. She was never a big fan of me graduating early. I was doing it so I could take care of Gran full-time. Now, thanks to Marshall, my future is blurry.

Mrs. Haig says a few more things then the message ends. I go to the sink, wash my hands, and V props herself on the counter. She wears a black shirt that falls off the shoulder, a short skirt, and neon-pink and black striped socks that reach her knees. She's a funked-out Wicked Witch of the West.

"Are you going to tell me what that message was about?" V asks.

No. "Who brought you here?"

"Leo and Nazareth. They sat with me for a bit, but then they had to go to work. They'll be here later to take me home."

I turn off the water. "You've been here all day?"

"And yesterday." She shrugs one shoulder. "I had two days off at the grocery store and was bored. Here's better than home anyhow."

True story. V's alone a lot and her house is bizarre. I don't scare easily, but that place makes the hair on my arms stand on end.

"Look," she says. "None of us are warm and fuzzy and not a single one of us knows what to say about your gran dying, and if we did attempt words, we'd probably tell you something stupid like 'suck it up and get laid.' So instead of saying something that'll make you kick our asses, how about we agree to ignore it and yet you know that we aren't complete jerks because our silence doesn't mean we don't care."

I slowly finish drying my hands, and she rakes nervous fingers through her shoulder-length curls, a rare moment of insecurity.

"Unless you want to talk," she continues. "I mean, I guess we can do that. I'm a girl. I can do feelings."

The right side of my mouth tips up with how she shivered with the word *feelings*. She might be more jacked in the head than me. I doubt it, but it's possible. "Hungry?"

"Starved."

The shower will wait. I open the fridge and find nothing besides mustard, ketchup and barbecue sauce. "Want to get a taco?"

She's already on her cell, and I don't have to ask to know she's telling Leo and Nazareth to meet us at Cosmic's, the only Mexican place in town.

I go down the hallway, and I'm grateful I closed the door to Gran's room because I'm barely holding it together now. Seeing her room without her in it might make me drop to my knees and bawl like a baby. At least with the door closed, I can pretend she's still alive.

"Mind if we go shopping afterwards?" I call out as I switch jeans and peel my shirt off. She gets a 15 percent discount at the grocery store and that discount is going to help me survive until the land is mine. Possibly for a while after, until I can get the farm up and running right again.

"As long as it's not the five-finger discount, I'm in." V leans her shoulder against my doorframe and stares at the maps on my wall. One is of the world. The other of the U.S. Along the other walls are smaller maps of other states and regions. V raises an eyebrow as if today will be the day I offer her an explanation for my map obsession. I don't offer one. Instead, I dig my keys and wallet out of my old jeans and slide past her for the front door.

We walk out and I see the light is on from Scarlett's second-floor bedroom. She said her goal is to attend the University of Kentucky. Her CEO daddy could empty his pants pocket and have enough to buy her an entire wing at the school. But I saw the expression on her face, understood what she didn't say—Daddy must have said no.

I don't need to understand the why for the scenario, I just need the girl to like me well enough to vote for me to keep the land.

"I need a favor," I say.

V pauses at the front of my rusting truck and studies my face. Asking to use her discount, that's something we all do. Other than that? I don't ask for favors.

"What do you need?"

"I need you to help someone get a job at the grocery store with no questions asked." A job is what Scarlett asked for, but I don't think she fully understands her request.

If Daddy has dug in his feet, and the University of Kentucky is something Scarlett really wants, she'll have to become a big girl and do it on her own like the rest of us peasants. That means money and money means a job. That responsibility will probably scare the hell out of her.

V's been employed at the Save Mart since she was fourteen and has worked herself up to assistant manager. It sounds big, but it means she has to fight with people over returns. V's sweetly mean enough to say no with enough force that people listen.

"Will you buy me dinner tonight?" All negotiations for me and her come down to food and money. It's gritty and simple. "And tomorrow night, then once a week after that."

"I'll buy dinner tonight, tomorrow night and then I have the option after that to either buy you dinner once a week or make you dinner once a week." Dinner out can get costly. Even at ninety-nine cents per taco.

She bobs her head as if she's weighing the pros and cons. "Fine, but if you make dinner then it's hot and it isn't something frozen that you put in the microwave to warm up. Real food, Lachlin."

"Deal."

"Then have whoever it is show after school on Tuesday. I'll find something for them." She walks backward then spins for the passenger side door of my truck. As soon as we're in, gravel flies from the back tires and screeching guitars blare from the broken speakers. I peek over at Scarlett's window, and I swear the curtain moves.

SCARLETT

It's the first day of my senior year, and near the library's auto-biography section, Camila and Evangeline have repaired their friendship for the thousandth time. This makes me, once again, the odd man out, but I'm fine being on the periphery.

Friendships are built on secret-sharing and trust. I'll listen to what anyone has to say, at any time, and I'll never repeat another word to anyone else. I'm good at keeping secrets. But there's this impenetrable wall surrounding my heart that keeps me from opening up, and it grows by the day. I should be ashamed to admit I like the wall, but I'm not. I embrace the inner ice princess. Emotions are overrated.

Except for a few required classes—math, English and science—I have more than enough credit hours to graduate in the spring, so the period before lunch, along with Camila and Evangeline, I'm an aide in the library.

I'm at the circulation desk, the librarian's in her office at the computer and the rest of the place is dead. Staying awake isn't easy. Last night I participated in my persistent, not-so-favorite hobby: worrying. Thoughts circled my brain like vultures, then those vultures dipped down and picked me apart, leaving me feeling bloody and bruised.

Dad and Mom argued last night. Not really argue as much as Mom pleading about something and Dad telling her no. Their voices carried down the hallway from their room to mine, a constant barrage of the buzzing of angry bees. Sometimes the buzzing would intensify, but it never got loud or angry, nor could I make out the reason for the fight.

With the covers pulled tight to my chin, I kept waiting for the ax to fall. For Dad's loud bellowing voice to echo along the hallway, for doors to slam so hard that the picture frames on the wall rattled, for Mom to cry, and then I waited for the sickening sound of flesh hitting flesh.

Five times in twenty-five years. But the last time was so heinous, so bad, and it was only a few weeks ago. Over the years, Dad has become more controlling . . . or has he? Is this how it's always been and I'm the one seeing the world differently?

Last night, my worst fears didn't become reality, but the waiting for the worst caused me to end up on my bathroom floor, vomiting into the toilet. No sleep for me.

I fight exhaustion by scrolling through the internet as Camila catches Evangeline up on everything she missed when she went with her parents to China to adopt her newest sister. Evangeline was born in Africa and lived in an orphanage until her parents adopted her at two. Now Evangeline is the oldest of five Henderson children, all of whom have been adopted from around the world.

"Then Glory knew about my upcoming trip to Mexico, and she knew that the two of us were fighting and that we would make up," Camila says. "Everything she said is true. It was as if she was inside my mind. You have to get a real reading from her. Not the cheap ones she does at the street fairs."

"I want to go," Evangeline says, then calls out to me, "Scarlett, can you get me a free session?"

My response is an are-you-for-real glower. Evangeline and Camila giggle because for some reason they find me amusing.

The Glory conversation comes close to zealous, and Camila and Evangeline enter a near frenzy. *Maybe we should all make an appointment with Glory and have a group reading. Maybe we should see if she would do house calls. Wouldn't it be fun to hear what Glory has to say about everyone?*

No, actually, it wouldn't. But it's a free country, and therefore they can willingly throw away their money on useless things like Glory's "predictions." My prediction was worthless. As if working with Jesse Lachlin could help me attend the University of Kentucky. That is insanity.

"We should do it at Glory's place," Camila says.

"But you said her house is small." Evangeline twines her finger around one of her long braids. "There will be at least six of us who will want to go."

"Yes," Camila draws out. "But one of the fun parts of being at Glory's was Jesse Lachlin."

My eyes snap up at this, and I'm not a fan of how Camila glances at me with this sugary smile as if she's privy to what happened between me and Jesse after she left. As if she knows how he chased after me, how I fell, how he caught me and how my skin still tingles with the memory of his touch.

"What about Jesse Lachlin?" Evangeline asks.

"He was there." Camila waggles her eyebrows. "Every inch of his towering tallness and hard muscle. He sat in the chair behind us all brooding, sarcastic and handsome. I'm game for being in the same breathing space as him again, as long as he stays mute. His looks more than make up for his awful personality."

Evangeline fans herself. "That boy is hot."

Hot isn't exactly the word I would use for him. *Hot* somehow feels . . . lacking. *Hot* is for some boy in our gym class who has recently grown facial hair. Jesse Lachlin is no boy. He has fire-red hair, a sun-kissed tan from all the hours working on his land, deep green eyes and a body made to handle rough, rugged days.

I might have been ignoring Jesse for years, but I've seen him. Every girl in this school has gone out of her way to drive or walk along one of the country roads to watch Jesse as he works his land. Living across the street, I've had a front-row view. His shirt off, drenched in sweat, muscles rippling as he moves, the way he sometimes pauses in his front yard and looks across the road as if he knows I'm watching. A fluttering in my chest and then—

"Would you date him?" Evangeline asks.

"No." Camila's answer is swift. "And it's not like he dates anyone. Except for his friends, the boy is a recluse."

"Why wouldn't you?" The knee-jerk question surprises even me when it pops out of my mouth. Camila and Evangeline look at me as if I those were the first words I'd ever spoken. If I could hide under the circulation desk without making this moment worse, I would.

"Besides the fact he's cursed and anyone a Lachlin falls in love with drops dead?" Camila walks toward me and Evangeline follows. Camila watches me with more curiosity than I care for, but it's nice that she's moving the conversation in my direction. "Jesse's a train wreck, and he taints anyone in his vicinity. Dating him would be a social, emotional and literal death sentence."

I'm familiar with the curse, and it's no truer than Glory and her prophesies. "That sounds melodramatic."

"It's not." Camila has a swear-to-God seriousness to her. "Mom and Dad had Bible study at our house last night, and Pastor Hughes came. Everyone thought I was in the basement, but I went to the kitchen for something to drink, and I heard Pastor Hughes ask everyone what they knew about Jesse."

Eavesdropping. How Camila.

"Did you know that before Veronica started hanging with Jesse that she was on track to be a concert pianist?" Camila says.

"Seriously?" Evangeline tilts her head in disbelief, and I'll admit to putting down my cell.

"Seriously. And Leo Wheeling was a star soccer player, predicted to be the first freshman to play varsity for our high school, and then he started hanging out with Jesse."

Faint middle school memories of hearing Leo's name over the announcements regarding soccer emerge in my mind.

"Then someone said that before Nazareth Kravitz moved here, he had taken the ACT in the seventh grade and received a perfect score. He moved here, met Jesse and the rest is history."

Nazareth sleeps through most of our classes, that is, when he bothers showing up for school.

I nibble on my bottom lip as I'm not sure how much I like the Jesse-is-the-devil enthusiasm. I may share the opinion, but that doesn't mean anyone else should.

"Of course, then there's Jesse himself. Drinking, drugs."

"The fights," Evangeline pipes in.

"Don't forget the suspensions—"

"And he's been arrested!" Evangeline finishes Camila's statement like the two share a brain. Her eyes sparkle like that precious piece of scandalous gossip was just too good not to spread.

"The boy is a walking disaster," Camila continues. "Anyone who hangs out with him *wants* to become a loser. It doesn't matter he's going to be a millionaire once he sells his grandmother's land. Anyone who spends time with Jesse is asking for hurt."

"*And* death."

The bell rings, and it startles me enough that I jump. We gather our things and enter the packed hallway. A millionaire. I knew Jesse would inherit a lot of money once the land was sold, but I never contemplated how much.

"We have maybe a two-minute lead." Camila glances over her shoulder as if she's being stalked. "I made the mistake of telling Corbin Johnson about the lunch table we want."

I give Camila a swift side-eye because she and Corbin Johnson have had an annoying flirting relationship since sophomore year, which means he's going to gun for the table Camila and I have called ours since freshman year.

"I know, I messed up." She scowls. "But you brought your lunch, right?"

I hold up the paper bag I packed with a ham sandwich before leaving the house.

"Excellent," she says.

Her loose lips mean I'm heading straight to the cafeteria. She goes left to her locker, then she'll head for the long line for food while I go straight to the table by the window because to the seniors go the spoils.

I drop my lunch bag and books on the table, sit, then count seats. There was a lot of shuffling during freshman year as personalities worked themselves in and out of our lunch group, but we've been lunch-buddy solid since the beginning of sophomore year.

Throughout the years, I've considered going solo. Maybe hiding out in the library during lunch and drifting through school as if I were invisible. I tried it once. I lasted a whole two days. Who knew lonely could be so . . . lonely.

Being in a group isn't bad, but sometimes I notice how everyone else partners out. They share a connection and sometimes my jealousy causes me to hurt. But loneliness hurts more.

I shove away the bad thoughts, prop my head on my hand and enjoy the warm sun. Our high school is on top of a hill. The view is of rolling green hills filled with full green trees. It's picturesque, it's calming and it's the reason our group has coveted this table.

A scraping of a chair, a tray full of food and I glance over with my practiced smile in welcome. It's not Camila, Evangeline, or anyone else from the group. It's green eyes, red hair, a familiar mischievous smile that used to be reserved only for me, and my blood pounds with excitement as if someone lit a sparkler in my chest. Then I frown because I'm not supposed to feel this way. Not with him. Not with anyone.

Jesse Lachlin winks at me as he sits across from me like no time has passed from when we climbed trees together. "What's up, Tink?"

Another thrill runs through me but then my muscles tighten. Stupid, antiquated reaction belonging to a dead past. "What are you doing here?"

Jesse pops a fry into his mouth, chews, then picks up another as if he has no intention of answering. I scan the cafeteria. Several people are watching us, curious as to why Jesse Lachlin is sitting with me, or is even at lunch, or even at school.

From the lunch line, Camila's and Evangeline's eyes are bugging out of their heads.

What is going on? Camila mouths.

I raise my eyebrows to inform her I have no idea. Jesse digs into his corn with his fork and that's crossing lines. "Maybe you didn't hear me, but I asked what you're doing here."

He lifts his eyes to meet mine and there's a glimmer in them that causes my lips to flatten. Fantastic. He's here to make my life a living hell.

"It seems obvious," he says.

If he remembers anything about me, he should recall I was never known for my patience and that he should be speaking, and speaking soon. "Just answer the question."

"I'm eating lunch."

I honest to God groan in frustration. "There's no room at the inn."

He surveys the table, takes in the empty seats, my books, and then gives me a good look. A slow look. As if he's trying to memorize every inch he's drinking in. My cheeks redden because that somehow feels a little too intimate for lunch. Feels a little too intimate for someone I'm no longer friends with. It feels too intimate if we *were* friends.

I glance away, but I sense him still staring at me. God help me, I want to stare back.

"Hey," he whispers. Because I have rarely been able to deny him when he talks to me in that conspiratorial tone, I meet his gaze.

His green eyes glitter as he glances left, right, then lowers his head as if what he's about to say is a massive secret to be shared only between us. "There's nobody else here."

"I'm aware."

Jesse relaxes back in his seat. "Good to hear. I was scared for a second. Thought maybe Glory was contagious and you were going to claim you hang with dead people."

"What do you want?"

"Wow, great table. I've never considered staying in school for lunch, but this table makes remaining in this prison doable." A short blonde collapses into the seat next to Jesse, and my blood begins to boil. I stare at her, and she meets my eyes with absolutely no fear.

"You guys need to leave," I say as politely as one can while fighting the urge to scream. "I sat at this table first so it's mine."

"Still have your temper, don't you?" Jesse winks at me again, but this time my fingers twitch with the need to throttle him. "Do any of your stuck-up friends know that?"

The blonde's face scrunches. Her name is Veronica and she's part of Jesse's little group of insurgent friends who think rules don't apply to them. "The Ice Princess has a temper? Please. I don't believe it. That would mean she has emotions."

Jesse's green eyes soften at the "Ice Princess" reference, as if he's sorry for Veronica being bold enough to call me that to my face. But that "sympathy" he's showing, I don't buy it. "You need to go."

"It's a table." Jesse offers me a crooked smile, and it's reminiscent of long summer days and a plan to steal fresh cookies off his gran's counter. Seeing that smile makes me ache more than being called an ice princess. "Not a kid in a divorce."

"I promised my friends these seats so therefore these seats are taken."

"All of them?" he asks, but doesn't wait for an answer. "I guess I could be persuaded to set up a custody arrangement. You get the table Monday and Wednesday. V and I get it Tuesday and Thursday. We take turns every other Friday. If you need it in writing, I bet I could get Marshall to draw up an agreement."

"When I speak, do you understand the words coming out of my mouth?" I say. "Is it because I'm using too many words in a sentence for you to keep up? Will shorter sentences help? This is my table. It belongs to me. You leave now."

Veronica twirls her hair with her fingers. "Well, the table actually belongs to the school, and when I came in both of you were here so I could argue that Jesse was here first and therefore first dibs belong to him. Oh, listen to me. I could be a lawyer if I grow up."

I slow-blink because the world is turning red, and Jesse's watching me as if I'm the best reality show he's ever seen. As I'm about to not so nicely tell her to move her butt from this table, Jesse slides his full tray of food in her direction. "I'll meet you outside by my truck." Even though we aren't allowed to leave the building.

She shrugs then swipes up the tray without another word. I do a quick scan of the cafeteria, and I'm not liking how the two of us have become the center of attention. I've worked hard over the years to not overly stand out, and I am not happy. "Why are you here?"

Jesse leans forward, arms on the table. My response to whatever smartass remark he'll spew is on the tip of my tongue so I angle forward, too, ready to spar.

"I got you a job, Tink."

My brain officially stops working. "You got me a what?"

"A job. At the Save Mart. You start tomorrow after school."

"Why did you get me a job?"

"Because you said you wanted a job so you can go to the University of Kentucky. I'm pretty good at math, and I did some addition. Your daddy must not want you going there, which means if you want to go to UK, then you need to pay for it yourself. That means you need to become like the rest of us lowlifes and work."

My mouth gapes as I've lost the ability to speak. There were too many things in that little speech that were so wrong, so hurtful, so . . . "I . . . I nev . . . never said my father wouldn't let me go to UK."

His forehead furrows with my stutter, and I don't like how he scans my face as if searching for an answer to a personal question. "Then you're saying you don't need a job?"

A job. I want it, I need it, but Dad will lose his mind if he finds out.

"I guess your silence is the answer."

Jesse stands to leave, and I shake myself back to life. "Why are you doing this?"

He shoves his hands into his pockets, causing his jeans that were already precariously perched on his hips to sag a bit lower. "I'm going to need your help."

"With what?"

"Keeping my land."

One eyebrow rises. "I can't help you keep your land."

"Yes, you can. Gran left it up to three people to decide if I get to keep the land when I turn eighteen. You're one of them, and I need your vote. Otherwise, the land will be sold and the money will be put into trust for me."

Jesse has to be high. "None of that is true."

"Yes, it is."

"Considering that sounds like something that involves me and I know nothing about it, I'm going to call this one wrong."

"It's true."

It's wrong, but my brain goes another direction. "Why would you want to keep the land? If you sell it, you'll be set for life."

Annoyance flickers over his face. "You have a job. Are you going to take it or not?"

I have a job. Anxiety creeps into my system. I want a job. I need a job. A job can help me with application fees and tuition, but what Jesse doesn't understand is what I really need is permission. My hands start to tremble, and I hide them under the table.

If I do this and my father finds out, he'll scream, he'll break things, he'll . . . But if I do this, if I start saving now, maybe I can go to UK. Then maybe I can become a speech therapist and then—

"Are you going to take it or not?" he pushes.

Yes and thank you. It's what I should say, but those aren't the words that tumble out. No, they are much, much worse, and they are too honest. "I don't just need a job. I also need a ride. At least home. I can probably get Camila to drop me off."

Because I don't want her to know I'm working, I'll ask her to drop me off at the library as it is right next to the store. If she asks why I have a job when my father has told her father multiple times that he doesn't believe I should work while I'm in high school, I'll have to lie, and lying means more lying and that makes keeping stories straight complicated, and silence is better.

Jesse stares at me for longer than I like, and I hate that he hasn't responded. He looks at me as if he can see through me or into me, and I shift as uneasiness swirls in my stomach. A hush falls over the cafeteria as if everyone else is also waiting on an answer to my question they didn't hear.

"I'll take care of that, too," he says, and his words echo and bounce along the walls of the cafeteria.

Then Jesse Lachlin walks away, leaving me in a room full of people who are now wondering what exactly it is he's going to take care of for me.

Flipping fantastic.

JESSE

First thing I see when I walk into the trailer is V's head hanging off the rock-hard couch with her bare feet propped up against the wall. The light from the TV bounces off her face. Leo and Nazareth are also lounging in my living room. Leo on the couch with V. Nazareth in a straight-back chair. The volume's off, but they watch it as if they hear every word.

"How did V get in if I wasn't here to give her permission?" I ask.

"I walked in first," Leo says. "And then I told her to come in."

Works for me.

"You should consider locking your door," V says. "You never know who could bust in."

Noted.

"I'm starting to wonder if we should have your head examined," V continues.

"Because I don't lock doors?"

"Because you're making questionable choices." The glare she sends informs me she's not thrilled with her newest employee at the Save Mart.

I purposely didn't tell her it was Scarlett. V's not a fan. It's nothing personal. She's not fond of people in general, but people from school rub her the wrong way more. But Scarlett will continue to have a job there because V keeps her promises.

I understand V. People are overrated, and in this moment, the three other people I allow somewhat in my life are overrated, too.

The problem with having friends is that they have opinions. Wouldn't be so bad if they could keep their opinions to themselves, but my friends aren't that way. They're loud, they're blunt, and God help me, they're honest. At least what they consider honest.

From behind thick-rimmed black-frame glasses, Nazareth darts his eyes to V and then back to me. He's warning me about her mood. I flick my chin to thank him for the heads-up. The kid's a nerd with muscles and is one of those rare few who only talks when he has something worth saying. His paranoid-weirdo parents don't have a proper appreciation of him, but I do.

Nazareth has long brown hair that's pulled back in a rubber band, and the string of tattoos on his right arm is the handiwork of his mother. She gave him his first one when he was ten. I'm sure that wasn't legal, but his parents aren't about rules, normal parenting, or normal in general. Oddly enough, he and Leo are in a neck-in-neck race for the most stable household among the four of us, which isn't saying much.

Nazareth's parents are nurturing in the free-love, screw-the-government type of way. Leo's parents are the strict-rules, be-who-I-tell-you-to-be type. Their parents couldn't get much different, but they at least have dinner on the table every night.

I fist bump with Leo, and he offers me a sly white grin against his dark skin. He's one of four black families in our small farming town. That's not always an easy road for him to walk.

Leo's smile widens. It's not so much a warning that my ass is about to fried by V, but his amusement of the show to come.

V stretches, reminding me of a cat awakening from a deep sleep. "How are we supposed to stage a decent intervention if you come in late and we have school tomorrow?"

It's 11:59 on Tuesday night. Earlier today, I picked up Scarlett from her first day of work, and V saw her climbing into my truck. I knew then that my night was going to suck.

With aching muscles, I'm slow as I sit in the recliner. "Text me, and I'll schedule you in."

V mocks me with a smirk. "That would require you answering your texts. Where've you been?"

"Moving hay." I baled it a few days ago, and I've been moving it to the western barn. Mr. Bergen offered a nice price for it, but I held off accepting. I'm hoping to start a bidding war between him and Mr. Vaughn.

Leo runs a hand through his shoulder-length black curls then starts poking V's feet to agitate her. It works and she uses her toe to push the side of his head.

Leo grew out his hair when his retired-from-the-army dad made the mistake of telling Leo that he'd never allow a son of his to wear long hair. His dad was a long-deployment guy. Gone more than home. I'm assuming that's why his dad isn't aware of how Leo makes his decisions involving authority figures: find what people want from him and then does his best to piss them off. "We would have helped you with the hay."

I shrug because I'm not good at explanations. "Not ready."

For people, conversations or help.

That's the problem with help. Sometimes you only need it when you need it. The other times it's a burden. "Can we get this intervention going? I need a shower and then I'm going to bed. Speaking of, how long is this going to take? Five minutes? Ten? Maybe cut me some slack and do it in the time it takes to microwave a Hot Pocket."

Leo chuckles. "He's fine, V. But we won't be if he takes off his work boots. That stench will kill us all."

I finish untying my boot, slip it off and throw it at him. He deflects it then flashes me the middle finger.

"I'm not sure what that is about." V wiggles her fingers in the direction of Scarlett's mini-mansion. "But whatever it is, be careful. People say she's an ice princess for a reason."

"People say that or you?"

"In this specific instance, it's one and the same. Be careful, okay?"

"Is that my intervention?" I pull off my other boot, and V squishes her nose in disgust.

"Why do boys stink?"

My mouth tips up as I hold out my arms. "Some girls are attracted to all this."

"Some girls need therapy." She kicks off the wall, stands and goes into the kitchen. "I need your help, Leo."

I hear the fridge open, close and then one of the drawers open and close. I don't bother checking what they're up to, but instead look out the front window to Scarlett's. She didn't say much on the way home, and her silence created a strange pit in my stomach. I can't admit to saying much to her either, as talking to Scarlett is like handling dynamite.

"What's going on with you and the Ice Princess?" Nazareth asks. Figures they would leave the "intervention" to the one whose parents try to make him and his siblings participate in a weekly "emotions bonfire." He hangs with one of us instead.

I give the short explanation. "Scarlett and I were friends once, and Gran made me promise to be nice to her after she died."

Nazareth's gaze strays to the kitchen, and he gestures his hand at whoever he's looking at in a "see, he's fine" gesture, but V sighs so loudly that my head falls back onto the chair.

"Your turn, Leo," V says. "Nazareth, that was pathetic."

Nazareth shrugs at her then at me in apology. Yeah, I agree. People who want to talk feelings suck.

"Okay, dumbass," Leo says from the kitchen, "let's try it this way. You have hated that girl since freshman year. You don't hate people. You avoid them, but you don't hate. Now you got her a job and are giving the Ice Princess a ride. Your puzzle pieces don't fit."

Ice Princess. Since Scarlett and I stopped being friends, she's built a rep for being aloof. At school, in public, Scarlett is perfect and rarely engages, but no one would mistake her as quiet or shy. Some call her proper, but I say she smiles on cue, because, like my mom, Scarlett's smile never touches her eyes. Unlike my mom, who cried all the time, Scarlett's blue orbs stay ice cold.

But I learned the other night she still has fire and that raging temper. To be honest, that gave me hope that my Tink still exists. It also makes me wonder how much of her life is a show, and if it is, I can't help but wonder why.

"You're grieving." V places a plate full of cupcakes on the coffee table. "Grieving can make us do stupid things with the wrong people."

Is that what she's scared of? "I'm not rebounding with Scarlett."

V extracts a lighter from her back pocket, squats next to the table and looks directly at me. "Just be careful."

I've permitted V, Leo and Nazareth to see pieces no one else has, but they don't know everything. I've allowed them this close, but not close enough. Life for them and me is easier that way.

"You're not the kind of guy to hook up," V says quietly. "I know hurt, and I know searching for comfort. You're the type who would regret it. I guess I'm saying, don't be stupid. You've been hurt enough. Don't bring on more pain than you need."

After seeing Mom chase after guys for years, I don't want to kiss someone to feel. I'd rather kiss someone because I'm feeling.

Seeking comfort with Scarlett, though . . . that beautiful long black hair and those gorgeous curves. She's the type of girl guys nearly break their necks to sneak a peek at. I've been looking for years. There's not a day since sophomore year that she hasn't taken my breath away. If I was going to seek comfort, it would be with a girl like her, but there's only one Scarlett in the world, and I can't go near her, for both of our sakes.

"I'm helping Scarlett with a job," I say, "and she's going to help convince my uncle that I should inherit the land when I turn eighteen. That's all this is."

"Why wouldn't you get the land when you turn eighteen?" Lines form on V's forehead, and I shake my head because that's not her business. That's mine.

Knowing I won't budge, she clicks the lighter and Nazareth turns off the TV. The candle in the center of the cupcake bursts to life. "Leo and Nazareth made these so say thank you."

"Are you trying to kill me?" I ask. "A bullet to the head would be faster and more humane than food poisoning."

Leo punches me in the shoulder, I punch him in the back and he grins as he drops onto the couch. "Don't trust the frosting. V stuck her tongue in the container."

I lower my head because I hate to do this. "My birthday isn't until May."

"I know." V stands and rubs her hands against her jeans, which are more rips than material. "This is to celebrate our anniversary."

I glance at Leo and Nazareth for an explanation, but they don't give me a thing. "Anniversary of what?"

"Of when you and me became friends. Leo is next week and Nazareth is in November. It's not every day when people who are lost find a way to be lost together. Now, make a wish and blow out the candle."

My throat thickens. She's never done this before, but this obviously means something to her. I'm a jerk because I don't know how to tell her that she, Nazareth and Leo mean something to me, too. Doing what I'm told, I make a wish then blow out the candle and plunge us into darkness.

SCARLETT

Two hours a day, after school, I stock, sweep floors and clean the bathroom. Best parts about the Save Mart? Number one: it's next to the library so I'm only lying about where I'm at by ten feet. Number two: Dad doesn't check in on me because it is after school and he doesn't have time. Number three: Mom and Dad don't shop here and neither do their friends. This place sells generic labels, and my mother would have a hot flash at the idea of being seen someplace so cheap.

The manager of the store offered to let me work weekends, and while the lure of more money was appealing, I declined. Mom and Dad believe I'm studying with Camila after school at the library. Regular work on the weekends might press my luck.

Like he has for the past week, Jesse's waiting for me in his ancient red pickup truck in the last spot of the parking lot. He has a blue baseball cap over his red hair and he drums the steering wheel as if he's listening to the beat of an amazing song.

Typically, walking to Jesse's truck feels like tiptoeing along a plank of a ship in the middle of the ocean, and each step is mental preparation for the long drop. He's not exactly a conversationalist. Then again, neither am I. Our ride home is silent, and it's awkward. But today, I'm skipping to the truck because I got paid.

Metal grinds against metal as I crack open the passenger door then heave myself into the truck which is higher off the ground than should be legal. My first inhale is of Jesse—turned-over earth, cut grass and a summer breeze mixed with a rich, spicy scent that I can't quite describe. The scent is calming and each inhale makes me warm all over.

The pleather seat I'm sitting on is ripped, and I have no confidence in the aging seatbelt as I click it into place. With one hand on the wheel, Jesse glances over at me as if he's curious. "You're in a good mood."

I wave my paycheck in the air. "I got paid."

Jesse offers me a hesitant smile, the type that ghosts the Peter Pan one he gave me regularly when we were children. For some reason, I blush.

Maybe it's because of the way his green eyes glow, maybe it's because Jesse is beautiful with how he's currently looking at me. Maybe it's because Jesse is huge in this small cab. He encompasses every inch of it, and I'm scared if I move just the slightest we might touch, setting off the same sparks of electricity that happened at Glory's.

I glance away, yet Jesse still watches me. Under his attention, my skin becomes sensitive, as if his gaze were a brush of his fingers. After several beats, he looks away, turns over the engine, and we sputter and backfire our way out of the parking lot.

Because his air conditioner is busted, both windows are rolled down and my hair blows wildly in the wind until I take a ponytail holder off my wrist and tie my hair into a bun.

Jesse's dressed differently today. More like I would have thought he should have dressed for his grandmother's funeral. Instead of jeans, a T-shirt and work boots, Jesse's in a long-sleeve blue gingham button-down with the sleeves rolled to his elbows, tan slacks and black boots that appear shined. He's cleanly shaved, and I have to admit I miss the red scruff on his jaw.

I'm tempted to ask him where he's going, but decide I won't like his answer because it appears he's dressed to go on a date. Though it's stupid for me to care. What he does is not my concern. To keep myself from asking, I open my paycheck then frown. My ten dollars an hour wasn't nearly as promising on paper as it sounded in theory. Taxes, social security and who the hell is FICA?

"Want me to take you someplace to cash it?" Jesse asks.

His question stops me cold. I don't have a bank account so I'm not sure I can cash my check. My mother doesn't have a bank account either, and I'm not sure if she has ever owned one. Her name isn't even on Dad's accounts. She just has a credit card she shares with Dad.

Since I'm a minor, I'm required to have a parent sign for me to open an account, and my father continuously tells me that there's no reason for me to have one when he's more than happy to cover my expenses.

"I guess you don't cash checks," Jesse continues with a grin like we're sharing a joke, but I don't find him funny. "You probably put it in your overflowing savings account. Tell me which bank, and I'll take you there. When you enter a bank, do angels sing and do the people who work there fall to their knees like you're royalty?"

Embarrassment of my reality sweeps through me, and it's chased by a shot of anger. Every time I start to think Jesse has a shred of something redeemable in him, he speaks. I shove my check back into the envelope, cross my arms and wish for the awkward silence to return.

Jesse narrows his eyes on me. "What can you possibly be mad about?"

He is living proof that boys are incredibly dense. "You insulted me."

"I what?"

I gesture at the road because his attention is on me and not on driving straight. Dying is not on my list of things to do for the day.

He looks forward, and the tendons in his neck are strained as if he has the right to be annoyed. "I didn't say anything bad to you."

I roll my eyes, and he catches it. "Is this how you want to play this out, Tink? I get you a job, drive you home and then you find the slightest reason to get upset?"

"You make wrong assumptions about me, and I don't appreciate it. And where do you get off calling me Tink? Like you and I are somehow friends."

Red splotches appear on his face. "Do you need to go to the

bank or not? And I'm not insulting you with asking. I'm being nice. You should try it sometime."

I want to kill him, but then if I did I wouldn't have a ride.

"Home or bank, *Scarlett*?" Jesse stops at the light on Main Street and looks over at me. "Third time I've asked the question, and last I checked it's proper to answer, even for you."

My spine goes rigid. "You mean even for an ice princess?"

Jesse's lips thin out. "Home it is, then, or down the street from home since you can't stomach me dropping you off at your driveway. For the record, you are an ice princess. I get you a job, give you a ride and you can't stand to let your mommy and daddy see me with you. That's cold, even for you."

The light turns green, and his truck barrels down the road. Obviously Jesse believes the speed limit is more of a suggestion than law. It should take longer than it does to reach the road that leads to my house and Jesse's trailer, but that's what happens when you do fifty-five in a thirty-five then eighty in a sixty.

Like I asked on Tuesday, he drives halfway down the mile road then stops. The manners my mother drilled into me are begging for me to open my mouth and say, "Thank you for the ride," but my pride is demanding that I leave the truck, slam the door behind me, then stomp down the road. Because I'm torn down the middle, I don't do either. I'm paralyzed, and I stare straight out the window.

"Are you getting out or not?" Jesse sounds as exhausted as I feel.

"Why did you get me the job? In fact, why are you picking me up from work and taking me home?"

"Being neighborly," he bites out. "It's what decent people do."

"For years you've frozen me out. I take that back, you froze me out after you spent weeks saying terrible things about me at school. Things that have clung to me like mud I can't wash off, and now you're doing nice things to be 'neighborly'?"

"What do you want me to do here? Because anything I do or say is going to piss you off."

He's right. I fist my paycheck, reach to the floorboard for my purse and when my fingers grab air, I go numb. My pulse beats hard in my ears, and I quake. I forgot my purse, which means I forgot my cell, which means Dad is going to catch me in a lie. How could I be so stupid?

Sweat breaks out along my brow. I need my purse. I need my phone. If Dad finds out I have a job . . . I cover my cheek with my hand, wondering how painful the slap would be.

"I forgot my purse at the store." My voice is strained, hoarse.

"Let me guess. You expect me to take you back."

My mouth goes dry because the answer is yes, but I don't know how to ask him. I don't know why he's helping me. I don't know why he stopped being my friend. More important, I don't know how to return home without my cell. I have to plug my cell into the power cord in the kitchen every night before I go to bed, in the slot that's right next to my mother's. The slots my father checks before he goes to bed.

I don't know what Dad will do if I don't have my cell, and I don't want to find out. And what happens if someone from the store finds my purse, calls my home and Dad answers? Oh my God, what have I done?

I meet Jesse's eyes and will him to do this for me because I can't bring myself to open my mouth and ask even though I should. Even though it shouldn't be a problem for me to do so, but I can't ask for help. I . . . can't.

Behind me, a crow caws and while the sound does nothing for me, Jesse's eyes snap over my shoulder. He blinks once, twice, a third time, and then with a low curse, he slams into reverse. Dust flies from the rear wheels as he backs into the grass then lurches toward town.

I glance behind me, through the back window, and the massive crow perched on the wooden horse fence bordering our property flaps its giant wings in agitation. A chill runs along my skin, and I rub my hands down my arms for warmth. I swear to God that bird is watching me and that's not normal. Nothing feels normal.

Jesse takes the left onto the state road and something in the bed of the truck shifts. It's a shovel, and then my heart sinks as I notice more gardening tools and flowers. All of them in flimsy containers that suggest the flowers are ready to be planted.

I don't have to be a brilliant detective to figure out where Jesse was going after he dropped me off. I bet he had plans to scatter his grandmother's ashes today, and that he was going to mark the spot with her favorite flowers.

My stomach churns, and I slink down in the seat, sick to death of being me.

JESSE

If it weren't for that blackbird, I would have thrown Scarlett out of my truck and took my chances on the votes. Maybe the pastor will be called on by God to vote for me. Maybe hell will freeze over and my uncle will believe I'm responsible by May. But I did see the blackbird. I felt that *caw* all the way to my marrow. That bird was a dull knife plunged into my chest, and it made me think of Gran.

Scarlett stays silent the entire ride to the Save Mart, holding on to the seat as I take turns at breakneck speeds. It's her silent protest I'm going too fast. I am, but I don't care. Being reckless makes me numb.

I pull into the Save Mart lot and back into a spot. Scarlett doesn't bother acknowledging me as she jumps out and slams the door. I might as well go ahead and put a *For Sale* sign in the front of my trailer and have the land sold now for how well things are going between me and her. Even though I got her what she wanted, Scarlett's a brick wall.

I drum my fingers against the steering wheel in an attempt to drain some of the annoyance from my muscles. The flowers I dug up need to be in the ground and rooting soon, or I'm going to lose them and then that will really piss me off. Gran's urn is in the box on the floorboard, and the goal was to settle her ashes today near her favorite oak, next to my mom. At this rate, I'm not going to be able to start until after dark, which isn't what I wanted. Not at all.

Scarlett weaves through the parking lot toward the store. Elegance, grace, beauty. Hardheaded, stubborn and every ounce of an ice princess. My gut twists with a flash of guilt. Ice princess. That's what she called herself, and that's my fault. What the hell is wrong with me that I feel bad for hurting a girl who feels nothing for me? V's right. I do need my head examined.

Minutes pass. Cars come and go. People walk in and out. A shiny Beamer washed and waxed the way rich people pay others to do pulls in and that causes a raised eyebrow. Most wealthy people believe they're too good for discount food.

That car's familiar. Too familiar. A jolt as Mr. Copeland exits the driver's side looking as happy as someone swarmed and stung by wasps.

My mind swirls at a whirlwind pace. Scarlett asked for help with a job, needed a ride and asked to be dropped off a quarter mile from home. One plus one means Scarlett's dad doesn't know she's working here. Divide that answer by another number, and I'm betting that means Mr. Copeland might have been in the dark about her having a job at all.

I grab my cell then curse. I don't have Scarlett's number, never have, but she needs to be warned. There's a bull on steroids with sharp horns on the warpath. My hand grasps the handle of the door as Scarlett steps out of the store with her purse in hand.

Her father says her name, her head jerks up and her expression of pure fear causes my heart to stop. I've seen that look before. I saw it on my mom, too many times, and I wasn't fast or strong enough the last time.

Mr. Copeland's mouth moves, and Scarlett's eyes widen. He grabs her arm and my vision tunnels. His hand is on her arm, and it's clear she doesn't want it there. Mr. Copeland pivots on his feet, goes for his car and drags Scarlett with him.

My door screeches open, and Scarlett whips her head in my direction. My feet are on the ground, I step toward her and she shakes her head at me, violently, and mouths, *no*. I halt dead in my tracks, and I squint because there's no way she's telling me no. But she does it again. She shakes her head at me, her black hair flipping with the movement, and she mouths, *Please don't*.

I'm paralyzed. Every ounce of me needs to intervene, but our eyes meet again and her fear practically creates a direct connection between us.

If I step in will it be worse? I know she can't hear me, no way at all, yet she nods and that nod keeps me rooted on the spot.

Scarlett's father releases her at the passenger side door. She's slow to get in while he yanks his door open hard enough that if it were my truck the door would have fallen off the hinges. He starts the car, his engine too smooth to growl. He backs up without looking and slams the gas so hard that he probably hits forty before he reaches Main Street.

A glance at the bed of my truck. I have things to do, promises to keep to my gran. But I made a promise to Scarlett first, and it broke my gran's heart when I reneged on that vow, which is why I'm guessing she made Scarlett one of the people responsible for the vote.

I thought you promised her you would always be her friend, Gran had once said to me.

"I did, Gran," I mumble to the ground.

Then why'd you stop? Why did you hurt that girl? Hurting her is hurting you, and I don't want to see you hurt.

The words in my brain aren't real. Just memories of a conversation we had too many times to count. "You know why."

Keep your promise to her, Jesse. You're nothing if you aren't a man of integrity. You're nothing if you don't know how to be a real friend.

"I let her go to save her."

From who?

From me.

I want you to love.

"That's the problem, Gran. That's always been the problem."

A blackbird lands a few feet from me, inches from a dead carcass. The bird looks at me. I look at him. It's like staring into a black abyss. It's a lot like looking inside myself.

SCARLETT

Dad doesn't take me home. That would have been predictable and simple. Nope. He throws a curveball, and he takes me to church. It's not even the small quaint one where Suzanne's funeral took place. It's the huge one that was recently built in town.

This is the second time I've stepped inside a church since freshman year, and like when I had walked into Suzanne's funeral, I'm shocked when I don't go up in flames. I'm also a bit disappointed. Flames would be easier.

Mom, Dad and Isabelle attend church here. They used to go to church on the occasion that it didn't impede with sleeping in, but after Dad hit Mom last month they became the type of regular attendees who get ticked off when someone else sits in their pew. As far as I'm concerned, they're Sunday morning hypocrites.

We're in a sad office the size of a walk-in closet. There's all the religious crap one would expect for a pastor: crosses, stenciled Bible verses on the wall, apple-cinnamon wafting from a Glade plug-in because I guess that's what heaven must smell like.

On the desk are pictures of a perfect family on the beach. Each little girl is dressed in starched periwinkle dresses and wears a bow in her hair. Mom included. I suppress a gag.

I'm in the exact limb-numbing position as when Dad dragged me in here twenty minutes ago: arms folded, my ankles crossed, and I stare at the brown industrial carpet. Occasionally, I check the clock on the desk. My stomach is queasy as I don't know where

I stand with my father. He's angry, and I'm angry. He's disappointed, and I'm devastated. It's like we're a slow chemical burn bent on destruction.

"Why?" Dad shifts in the identical fabric chair as the one I'm in. Oddly enough, there's no anger in his tone, just exasperation.

"You know why," I whisper in return. While I have the courage to answer, I don't have the courage to look him in the eye.

"Is this about the University of Kentucky?" Dad asks, and there's patronizing laughter in his tone. "Do you really think you could afford to pay for school on minimum wage?"

A sharp pain strikes my chest; he makes me sound like a naive fool. The worst part? I guess I am.

"Scarlett," Dad's voice drops, "I'm not doing this to punish you, but to protect you."

Because he lost his sister. I know this, and the guilt inside me screams that I should let this all go—my hurt, my pride, this growing anger—but I can't. I've given up so much over the years, and I can't abandon this dream.

"About these . . . sessions," Dad says slowly, "think about what you say before you say it. Once words are out of your mouth, you can't take them back. I want you to use this time for you to let go of your grudge with me, but remember to think about your family."

Of course, this is all for show . . . for Mom.

The door opens, Dad goes quiet and I lift my head then lower it again. Why can't I catch a break? Wearing jeans and a white collared shirt, the pastor from Suzanne's funeral walks in. He smiles at me, but then he stretches out his hand to Dad. "Sorry to keep you waiting. I'm Pastor Saul Hughes. Pastor Morris is in a meeting. As soon as he's out, he'll come straight here."

Dad clasps his hand. "It's nice to meet you. Thank you for the last-minute meeting. I know it's after five, but I do appreciate you fitting us in."

"We're here for you and your family." All said with the same smile that's neither happy, nor condescending nor intimidating. It's there, plastered on his face, and I wonder if pastors take classes in seminary to look approachable without showing an ounce of real emotion. "In the meantime, why don't you take a seat in the reception area, Mr. Copeland, while Scarlett and I talk? Betty put on some coffee, and she would love to make you a cup."

I notice the dark disapproval that flashes over Dad's face, but I've trained myself to spot it. Like how doctors understand the subtle signs of a heart attack.

"When I spoke with Edward a few weeks ago about possibly bringing Scarlett in for sessions, I told him I was comfortable with *both* of you speaking to Scarlett. And I thought I was to be involved in these sessions."

Impressive. Dad was able to say all of that without becoming the spawn of Satan. Even more impressive, Dad's being his normal demanding and controlling self yet the smile doesn't falter as Pastor Hughes sits behind his desk. Most people back down immediately to my father.

"Edward and I believe it would be best if he continues to handle the counseling sessions for you, your wife and then for you and your wife. Now that Scarlett's agreed to meet with us, we think she'd feel more comfortable speaking to someone different. We also believe she'd be more comfortable if she meets individually with me for a few sessions before the two of you start meeting together." He meets my eyes then. "How's that sound?"

Awful.

Pastor Hughes said I agreed to meet with him. What a strange word—*agreed*. Does dragged out of the Save Mart and then driven here equal *agreed*? I don't want to be here. I want my job, I want my dreams, but once again, being here is the path of least resistance. I know I'm expected to say something to appease him and my father, but I can't.

The silence goes on for so long that it's heavy, yet I'm unable to speak.

"Fine," Dad says. "You can speak to Scarlett, and I give you permission to discuss everything with her."

Permission is what I obviously need in order to do anything in my life. I'm not sure what "permission" Dad's granting, but Pastor Hughes seems satisfied.

"We're here because we're having rebellion issues with Scarlett," Dad continues. "She's been lying to us. I just picked her up from the Save Mart, where it turns out she has been working there without our consent. And recently, she went to a funeral without our approval when we thought she was at home."

My spine straightens. He knew about the funeral? In fact, how did he know about me working at the Save Mart?

"She also went to Glory Gardner's for a tarot reading without our permission and was with a person we don't approve of when she told us she was with her friend Camila. Of which, Scarlett, your mother and I are still debating whether or not to tell Camila's parents that the two of you snuck out."

I prop my elbow on the arm of the chair, and I lean my head into my hand. At least Dad hasn't figured on that Camila's mom is in on the act, but I've been caught and I guess I should be grateful that I'm here instead of home, where he could be losing his mind. I can practically hear Mom cooing, *See, he's changing.*

There's silence, and I peek up at Pastor Hughes to find him watching me. "How did you discover all these things, Mr. Copeland?"

"Scarlett admitted that she was at Glory's, and I had a client tell me about Scarlett's job. She was working while I thought she was at the library studying."

Pastor Hughes switches his gaze to Dad. "And Suzanne's funeral?"

I raise an eyebrow. Kudos to him for using Suzanne's name. Dad readjusts in his seat yet doesn't answer.

"Only the truth is going to heal your family," Pastor Hughes pushes.

Dad rubs his neck then says, "I installed a tracking app on her cell."

"You what?" I say.

"Mr. Copeland," Pastor Hughes says, "will you please give me and Scarlett a few minutes alone?"

Dad mashes his lips together, and though I can tell it literally pains him, he stands to leave. He then places a hand on my shoulder. It's a gentle hand, a loving hand, one as a child I came to expect and looked forward to anytime he left the room.

But this hand hit my mother last month.

It's the fifth time this has happened, assuming he really didn't slap her recently. The fifth time in twenty-five years, as my mother is quick to point out. I'm vaguely aware of some of the incidents when I was younger—I don't remember the actual events as much as I remember the flashes of emotion. I'm fully aware of the one freshman year and then last month. Each of those has been seared in my brain like the crescendo of a horror movie.

"The app is on your cell so I can find you if you go missing," he says.

I'm a strange combination of hot and cold, and I close my eyes. Should I hate him? Do I hate him? Should I want to hate him?

He hit my mom, he's taking away my dreams, he tracks my every movement, but he's sad. He's broken. He loves me. He just wants to protect me.

Is this what love is?

Is love the way he decorated the living room with sparkly snowflakes when I had the stomach flu and couldn't attend the fifth grade daddy-daughter dance? He dressed up in his tux while I stayed in my pajamas. I danced on his feet, and then when I didn't feel good anymore, he watched Harry Potter movies with me.

A heaviness in my chest, and I wince because every part of me hurts.

Dad finally goes, the door clicks closed, and that leaves me and the pastor looking at each other. Besides Suzanne's funeral, I've seen him before—at this church. I used to attend with my family every week. But that was before Dad hit Mom my freshman year. After that, God and I stopped talking. Maybe I'm the one who stopped as I'm not sure He was ever talking to me.

Pastor Hughes talks. He explains that I can call him by his first name, Saul, but I'll pass on that. He explains that anything I divulge will be kept confidential, even from my parents. I pull a loose string off my shirt. He says other things that sound good, sound pretty. He asks questions I don't answer, and then I roll my neck because I want this to be over. I want this entire season of my life to be over.

Then there's silence, and somewhat embarrassed, I look up. Lost in my own thoughts I have no idea how long it's been since he last spoke. "I'm sorry, what did you say?"

"I asked how your friends would describe you."

"Can we please cut to the chase—to what you really want to know? Or can I leave?"

Pastor Hughes stares directly at me. I stare directly back. He mirrors my position, relaxed in his seat and hands folded in his lap. Who knows? Maybe I'm mirroring him, though I can't remember moving.

"I want you to know that I'm aware of some of your parents' issues," he says, "and they've given me permission to talk to you about certain things."

Sure, he is, and sure, they have.

"I'm not here as an advocate for them. I'm here as an advocate for you. What you say to me will remain confidential," he repeats.

I snort. I don't mean to, but it happens regardless.

"What?" he asks.

I shrug a response.

"Tell me?" he pushes in a kind voice.

"If Dad wants to know what I tell you then he'll find out."

"Why do you say that?"

"Because that's who he is."

"That's not going to happen. I'm not here for your father. I'm here for you."

Goody. My bad luck never runs out, does it?

"How would you describe your parents' relationship?"

Complicated. "Good."

"Good?"

"Good."

"Is the relationship your father and mother share the type you want when you're older?"

Something dangerous coils inside me. "I don't know."

"What would you list as the good qualities of their marriage?"

I scrub my hands over my face as I start to sweat. Is the thermostat set to two hundred degrees? "They love each other."

"What does that love look like?"

My face screws up. "Blue with polka dots. What type of question is that?"

"What would you list as the bad qualities of their relationship?"

All of it. Some people aren't meant to be together, and maybe they'd be better apart. "Next question."

"Is there abuse in your home?" he asks.

I flinch at how easily he says the words. Maybe he didn't receive the memo, but we don't talk about this. "I'm sorry. I think I misunderstood. Can you repeat that?"

"Is there abuse in your home? Physical? Emotional? Verbal?"

My mouth dries out, and it becomes harder to breathe. I glance around again, my eyes jumping from wall to wall, and I feel suddenly trapped.

"Anything you say in here remains between us," he reminds me. "I'm here to help."

And that is my undoing. "Why would anyone expect to come in here and be helped?"

Pastor Hughes doesn't react like I want him to. I'll admit, I wanted him to flinch but he's unmoved. "Why would you say that?"

Is he capable of not asking a question? "*If*," I emphasize the word. "*If* someone was being abused, you wouldn't help them."

"That's not true."

I laugh. It's not the cute type. It's the manic type, and I begin to wonder if I have gone insane. Like the Hatter has decided he officially has had a little too much tea. "So, *if* a woman was being abused by her husband, and the daughter happened to tell you, what would you do?"

"Talk her into calling the police."

"Why can't you?"

"I would encourage the daughter to do it first. She needs to be empowered in making decisions for her life, but if she won't do it, I would. As a mandatory reporter, I'd have to."

He makes it sound so easy. "Fine. She calls the police and the police show, what do you think would happen?"

"Why don't you tell me what you think would happen?"

This guy is a conversational moron. "The woman would tell

the police that her daughter was wrong and that the bruises on her face were due to an accident. The woman would say her daughter either misunderstood or was being overly dramatic or that she was some bitter teenager getting back at her parents. Or maybe the call wouldn't be taken seriously because the husband is golfing buddies with the chief of police."

"Did this happen to you?"

No, but it's what Mom said she would do if I called the police after Dad hit her last month. "There's no help for someone like this girl."

"What if making that call led people in authority positions to become aware that there might be a situation and that forces all the adults, even the mom and dad, to seriously search for and accept help?"

"Will calling the police fix the situation?" I demand.

"Calling will help."

"I didn't ask for help. I asked if calling will fix the situation. What's the point of calling the police or coming here if nothing will change?"

"What if it can be changed?"

"What if it can't? What if this is a waste of time?"

"It's not a waste of time. Help is available, and if there is ever abuse, the police should be called."

"Why, so they won't believe the daughter?"

"*You* call because *I* will believe the daughter."

Hope. It's there like the breaking of dawn, but that thin sliver of hope isn't strong enough to break through this incredible coldness. So cold, I shiver. He says he'd believe me, but I don't believe him.

"Does your father abuse your mother?" he asks.

I welcome the cold now, stare at the floor, and pretend I'm some place other than here.

"Has your father recently threatened you or your mother or your sister? Does he have a weapon? Has he done anything to make you think he's going to hurt you or your mother?"

My throat burns and my knee bounces.

"If your father threatens you or your family, if he hurts you or anyone else, you need to call the police. It's not okay for someone to hurt you or someone you love."

Yet it happens anyway. "What's the point of all this? Why do I have to be here? I don't hit people, and no one hits me. And I never said my father hits my mother."

Silence again as he studies me, and I feel like a sweater that's unraveling.

"How would it make you feel *if* your father hit your mother?"

"I never said he hits my mother," I say again.

"It's a hypothetical question."

I'm hypothetically considering screaming at the top of my lungs because that's the most insane question I've been asked. "I'd imagine it would feel great. How do you think it would feel?"

"How are you feeling now?"

"Fantastic. Like sprinkles on top of a sundae."

"Really?"

"No, not really. I'm angry."

"And how is that working out for you? The anger?"

I tighten my grip on the armrests because it's either that or flipping his desk. *Deep breaths. Very deep breaths. Push down the anger. Push it down and drown.* I can't be angry. I can never be angry. I can never be my father. "I changed my mind. I'm not angry."

"You're not?"

"Nope. You can go to school and ask anyone. I'm known as the Ice Princess. I don't have emotions."

"So you're not angry now?"

"I'm annoyed, not angry. You're asking me stupid questions, and I have a right to be annoyed."

"Is that the only reason you're angry?"

"No, I mean yes, I mean . . . I'm not angry." I'm so confused.

"If your father had hit your mother, do you think you'd be angry?"

"How else would I feel?"

"Is angry how you want to feel?"

"Want? There is nothing about this life I want. I don't want to be monitored every second. I don't want to go to college here in town. I don't want to be groomed to take over my father's business.

And I sure as heck don't want to—" I choke on the next words . . . *watch my father hit my mother.*

My chest is rising and falling fast, too fast. Because I didn't mean to say any of that, because I didn't mean to say anything, I stand and go for the door.

When I place my fingers on the handle, Pastor Hughes says, "Living in anger is like being a ghost in your own life. If you're willing, I'd like to help you let go of the anger. I'd like to help you be more than a ghost."

"I . . . I am . . . I am not angry!" I stutter, and a flash of nauseating heat hits me hard.

Pastor Hughes stares at me with a calmness I resent.

"I'm not," I repeat in a voice so quiet I'm not sure if he heard it.

"When you're ready to talk again, I'm here," he says.

I can't take any more, so I leave. My father shoves off his chair to his feet. "I thought you would be in there longer."

I say nothing as I walk down the hallway. There's this red-hot rage underneath my skin. Molten lava that's desperately trying to erupt.

"Scarlett, wait. I need to go to my session before we head home."

"Go to your session," I bite out. "I'm not stopping you."

His footsteps quicken as he tries to keep up with me. "Where are you going?"

"Home."

"How?"

"I'll walk."

"This is ridiculous. We live miles from town."

I spin on my toes and meet him eye to eye. He wants to do therapy, let's do therapy. Right here in the hallway for all to see. "Then it'll be a long walk, won't it? But that's my choice. Like having a job should be my choice. Like having a bank account should be my choice. Like having a counseling session with a pastor should be my choice. Like not living with a man who treats my mother the way he does should be my choice. *My. Choice.*"

Anger flashes in Dad's eyes, but I'm saved once again by Pastor Hughes. "Mr. Copeland, Pastor Morris is ready to see you."

I should become mute. I should become meek. I should lean

around Dad and say words that would make Pastor Hughes think that he somehow misheard what I said, misreading another possible act of rebellion. I should do this because the hell Dad's promising by his glare when we go home will be awful, but I'm sick and tired of being controlled.

With my arms stretched, I bow to mock my father, the king. The world belongs to him, and we're pieces to be discarded at will. I straighten, and the Ice Princess officially leaves the building.

JESSE

I've been waiting for a day to go as planned since Gran's death, and today won't be it. I try to do something nice for Gran, to honor her, and instead I end up knee-deep in mud, and not the kind I'd thought I'd be in by now. I should be planting flowers at Gran's final resting place, but instead I'm changing the tire of my truck off the side of the road. I hit a pothole and blew a tire. A poetic summary of my life.

What should have been a few minutes turned into longer. Tools broke, lug nuts were stuck, the jack ancient, my patience shot. Finally finished, I toss the tools into the bed of my truck then wipe the sweat off my brow. I glance down the road and squint. Someone's walking, a hitchhiker, maybe, and that doesn't make sense. This isn't a direct route to anywhere.

A breeze runs along the highway, and the walker's long hair blows around her head. Same form-fitting pants, same blue shirt, same strut that hypnotizes me. That's Scarlett miles from town and without her father. As she gets closer, she's watching me like I'm watching her.

Her mascara is smudged and smeared. Could be the heat. If I didn't know better, it could be tears. She has a limp and she wears dress flats on her feet. I suck in a breath to ask her what her deal is with taking long hikes in the wrong shoes, but swallow the words.

She lifts her chin, probably waiting for me to say something smartass, to shoot her down because that's what the two of us were doing the last time she was in my truck. Two five-year-olds with toy guns. Taking aim and firing.

I go to the passenger door and hold it open for her. She pauses, as if she's waiting for me to take an unfair hit. I hold my hands in the air. No more sparring. Even I'm tired. I incline my head to the cab, and Scarlett slides in. I round the front, jump in, start the engine, then pull out onto the road.

Scarlett leans against the rolled-down window, her hand fisting her hair near the base of her neck. She's known for keeping to herself, but Scarlett doesn't look like the girl who thinks she's too good to speak to me. She looks like she's been dragged out into the open by an angry mob and stoned near to death.

I have to give her credit. If I were the one on the road, I would have kept on walking, even with the offered ride. Accepting this help would have cost me my pride. Scarlett, at least the Scarlett I once knew, lives on pride.

Earlier today, her father was going caveman in a public parking lot, and she waved me off. I should leave it alone. Scarlett's not my problem, I shouldn't care, but . . . "Things between you and your dad looked intense. You okay?"

"Nope." She pops the *p* as if her answer doesn't carry weight, but she's dropped a bomb. At least to me it's a detonation. I hadn't expected her to be honest.

"Do you want to talk about it?"

"Nope."

Fair enough. "That's okay, I don't like talking about things that bother me either."

Scarlett glances at me, and for the first time since freshman year, her eyes aren't frozen. It's as if that one sentence has caused them to thaw. Now, they're a deep blue. As blue as the sky, as blue as the sea, and I'm lost in them longer than I should be.

She blinks. I do, too, and I force my focus back on the road, but I don't see pavement. I see her beautiful eyes, I see her sad eyes, and I wish I could take away her pain.

"Can I help?" she asks.

Hearing her voice jars me, and I look at her to make sure I didn't make it up in my head. "Help with what?"

Scarlett gestures to the bed of the truck. "I'm assuming this is for Suzanne. I liked her. A lot. When we were younger, I used to pretend she was my grandmother."

A stinging in my soul. "She liked you, too." More than liked. Gran loved her enough to give her power over my future. Loved her enough to mention Scarlett at least once a month—a constant reminder that Gran didn't like my decisions.

Scarlett bites her bottom lip and the motion causes another stirring, but this time in my blood.

"Or maybe that's something you want to do alone," she says, "or with your friends or—"

"No," I cut her off. "That'd be fine. She . . ." I pause because I'm close to feeling and that scares me. "Gran would have liked that."

Scarlett nods, and we continue down the road.

"The problem is," Scarlett says, as if we had been having a longer conversation or that I had overheard the one in her head, "I don't know what to say when someone loses a loved one. And I really don't know what to say to you."

If those are the rules, I should be permanently chained to the trailer. "I guess I'd say the same thing as when someone else's father acted like a jerk in a parking lot, and that person ends up walking miles for home. Sometimes, there aren't words and that's okay."

This time, her entire face softens, and Scarlett is absolutely stunning. I've never seen anyone as beautiful in my life—even with the mascara smudges, even in the ninety degree heat. I run a hand over my face because if I don't stop staring, we'll crash.

"If you want me to take you home tell me now," I say. "Otherwise, you're going with me."

She shivers as if she's cold and whispers, "I don't want to go home."

The turnoff for our road arrives, but I don't take the right this time. Instead, I keep going and eventually take the dirt road that will get me closer to the oak in the east field, toward the place where I laid my mom to rest and where I want to spread my gran. When we hit the stream, I veer off the dirt road and we go over the land I love more than my own life.

The truck rocks and jostles over the bumpy terrain, and Scarlett no longer looks hard or calculating. Just thoughtful. For the first time in weeks, I find some semblance of peace.

It's near eight and the sun is more west than it is anywhere else. Another hour and this place will be dark. I've dug, I've planted, I've sweated, I've watered, all with Scarlett by my side. She's turned over dirt, she's packed soil over new and old plants, and she's poured water onto dry ground.

We've worked for over an hour in the most comfortable silence of my life. Never once did I have to tell her what to do, never once did I have to tell her the vision I had in my head. It's like she had crawled up in the scary place and took out the blueprints for how I needed Gran's final resting place to be.

To be honest, maybe I didn't have a blueprint and Scarlett's a genius. She'd been like that when we were children, knowing what to do with my land in such a way that it had seemed like the God-given plan from the start. Like the peonies along the stream, the black-eyed Susans near the woods, and the honeysuckle near the sugar maple that we used to call ours.

I toss the shovel into the bed of the truck then scan the area to see if I missed anything in the cleanup. Scarlett's on her knees, patting the dirt around one of the rosebushes. She rubs a hand along her brow and leaves a trail of dirt on her skin.

Warmth in my chest at the familiar sight. Scarlett was like me as a kid. A day hadn't been done right unless you ended it with more soil on you than on the bottom of your shoes.

Scarlett lifts her head and smiles . . . at me. It's a gentle smile, and one that causes a spike of excitement in my blood. It's as if the sun has melted off her outer shell and has revealed the girl I once knew, and a woman I want to get to know.

My feet move, one in front of the other, even though I don't recall making the conscious choice to move. It's more a response to a gravitational call, one I can't ignore.

I crouch next to her and Scarlett busies herself dusting the soil off the leaves of the rosebush, as if the tender drops of the next rain won't be enough to wash the dirt away.

"Thanks for helping me," I say.

She continues to fuss over the plant. "Thank you for offering me a ride."

A lock of her hair falls forward and entwined in the strands is a small leaf. I reach out to remove the offending foliage then freeze when Scarlett's deep blue eyes dart to mine. I stop breathing, stop moving and my mouth dries out. My heart picks up speed because the need is to draw nearer. The urge is to touch her cheek, to cup her face, to . . . "There's a leaf."

"Okay." She slowly wets her lips, and as I draw my fingers through her hair, the leaf falls to the ground. Scarlett briefly watches it, but then returns those gorgeous eyes to me.

"Thank you," she whispers.

"You're welcome," I whisper back.

Time has halted, and the world surrounding us is nothing more than beautiful slants of light. Wind rushes through the trees; a *crack* from above and Scarlett jumps to her feet. I look up in time to catch the sight of a twig tumbling to the ground. I slowly stand, and wonder what the hell any of that was.

A leaf.

My fingers in her hair.

Possibly the most intimate moment of my life.

Scarlett's cheeks have a healthy glow. It's a blush. As if she liked me touching her, as if the moment made her shy. I shove my hands in my pockets because I'd be lying if I didn't say the moment made me shy, too. Curious, confused and shy.

"What else can I do?" she asks. "To help."

It's all been done. "I need to scatter her ashes now."

Sorrow shadows her face, and her sadness awakens mine.

"I remember climbing this tree." Scarlett glances up at the old oak, and I wonder if she sees our ghosts racing toward the top.

I reach both arms up and touch the thick low-hanging branch.

Closing my eyes, I can feel the energy of the tree barreling through my veins. The tree is old, not the oldest on the farm, but close to it. The roots run deep into the soil, into the heart of the land. Touching the tree releases a surge of power from it into me—like recharging a battery.

"How do you do that?" Scarlett asks, and I open my eyes.

"Do what?"

"The same thing you've always done since we were kids." She shrugs as if she's confused by her own words. "Touch anything on this land and look peaceful."

Twenty-three hours and forty-five minutes of my day, I have no peace, but I guess I'm lucky that my land can at least hand me fifteen minutes of no demons. "Don't give me that crap. You know what I'm doing, and you know how to do it."

Pure defiance. "No, I don't."

I smile because I like the familiar stubbornness. "Yes, you do."

Crossed arms over her chest.

"Touch the tree," I say.

"Touch the tree?"

"Touch the tree."

Scarlett grins, one reminiscent of our childhood days. The breeze plays with the ends of her hair, and I capture that moment. A snapshot of something I want to remember. Scarlett's back on my land. My friend. My foe. The person who used to push me, compete with me and made me alive. My Tink.

"Do it," I tease her. "Or are you scared of what you'll find when you do?"

"I am not touching a tree to prove a point," she says.

I chuckle because Scarlett was never one to be pushed to do anything she didn't want to do. Not even when I double-dog dared. I release the limb and head for my truck. "Your loss."

But when enough steps have happened, I glance over my shoulder to see her staring at the trunk like she's considering pressing her hand against the bark.

I open the passenger door. On the bench seat is her phone and it's surprising my truck hasn't caught on fire. Someone is blowing up her cell, and I'm betting it's her dad.

Two parts of me battle as I stare at her cell. The selfish part
wants to ignore it and continue on with my plan with her by my
side, but then the other part of me, the part my grandmother
wanted me to pay more attention to, knows what needs to be done.

I pick up her cell and stretch it toward her. "Looks like someone wants to talk."

Her posture crumbles as she accepts her cell and scrolls
through the messages. With a blink of her eyes, she hardens. A
fortress built to endure a war.

Scarlett blows out a breath then looks up at me. "I have to go."

Yeah. Saw that coming. "Hop in. I'll give you a ride."

"Thank you for the offer, but I'll walk."

"Don't be like that. I thought we weren't mad at each other
anymore," I say. Her forehead furrows, and my stomach sinks. "Are
you still mad at me?"

"N . . . no, yes . . . I . . . I," she stutters, and that keeps me from
opening my mouth and arguing with her. When we were young,
she stuttered all the time, but then she learned how to control the
stutter through breathing. After that, the only time she did it
was when she was upset and her thoughts were moving too fast
for her mouth. My eyes narrow in on her as I try to figure out the
problem.

The haunted look in her eyes—it's déjà vu. A whisper of a
memory from another lifetime. I saw that sadness in my mother's
eyes. "Are you sure you're okay?"

"I'm fine."

Her head drops with what I can imagine was her reading the
disbelief on my face.

"My father's angry at me, okay? I've pushed him, and I'll admit
to pushing him on purpose. In hindsight, that was stupid. If he
sees me with you, it'll only make him angrier."

I bristle. "Because I'm Jesse Lachlin, town menace?"

Her dad hated me when we were younger, too. He didn't think
I was good enough to be her friend then. That's why we snuck out
at night to play. I don't guess there's any reason for his opinion of
me to have changed.

"Because I'm not allowed to be alone with a boy. I'm barely

allowed to go out with my friends, but he does allow it and only because he checks my plans with their parents. He won't appreciate you giving me a ride home, and I won't appreciate any assumptions he'll make as to what I was doing alone with you."

My eyebrows raise. "Are you saying your dad would think we were having—" Her cheeks turn bright red, cutting off my words, and I chuckle. "Our conversations were different when we were kids."

"I guess they were," she says with a faint lift of her lips, but then it falls. "When it comes to my dad, I've dug myself a hole and I don't need to dig it any further."

That I can respect. I've spent the past couple of years digging holes, too. "Do you know how to get home?"

"I'm going to cut through the east field, follow the stream and hit the road a quarter mile from my house; that way he'll think I came from the main road. I promise I won't get lost this time." There's a twinkle in her eye, and it's the most adorable thing I've seen.

"That's a twenty-minute walk."

She shrugs. "I said I need to go home, not that I wanted to."

"I'll go with you. At least to the road."

"You need to stay and scatter your grandmother's ashes."

"Scarlett," I start, but she silences me with a lift of her hand. "You need to do this."

She's right, I do, and the misery in my chest nearly brings me to my knees. Scarlett rises onto her toes, kisses my cheek and I close my eyes with the tender pressure of her soft lips on my skin. She pulls back and offers me a sad smile. "Thank you for all that you've done for me. The job, the ride, for bringing me here. I needed this."

Scarlett takes her flats off her feet and starts barefoot for the stream, but I can't let her go, not yet. "Is everything going to be okay with your dad?"

That stops her cold, and she looks at me over her shoulder. There's something there in her expression that bothers me. A pulling and a nagging.

"I'll be fine," she says.

"He's the reason you took that job, isn't he? He doesn't want you to go to UK."

Scarlett stays silent but the answer is there in how her shoulders crumble.

"I'll still help you if I can," I offer.

"I don't think anyone can help me, but thank you for trying. It's more than anyone else has ever done."

"We're friends now," I say. "Friends again, I guess." I can do it again—friends with Scarlett. I'm friends with V, Leo and Nazareth, and overall, they're doing okay. As V said, we've figured out a way to be lost together.

Her entire face drains of color, and her sadness hits me deep. "I don't know what being friends means anymore. Not just with you, but with anyone. There's something wrong with me. When I look inside me, I don't see anything. I'm empty."

"Scarlett, I mean it. We're friends again."

"No offense, but you don't get to make that decision. I appreciate the job, I appreciate the ride and I appreciate you letting me have this moment with you, but you burned the friendship bridge between us years ago then danced in the ashes. After how you treated me, there's no going back, but at least we had this moment. I'm not angry with you anymore, and it feels really good to not be angry with at least one person."

I don't understand why I feel like she just reached into my chest and created a black hole, but I do. The loneliness as she leaves is close to crippling.

Partially believing she'll turn around and tell me she was wrong, I watch as she disappears on the horizon. She doesn't turn, and she doesn't forgive me. The overwhelming sense of loss creates a confusing ache.

I return to the truck and check my cell. There are messages from V, but also a message from Glory: *What she needs, ask me and I can help.*

The skin on my neck prickles, and I scan the area searching for the eyes watching me, but I'm alone. *What are you talking about?*

Glory: *You know.*

There's a crazy buzz in my head. *You're full of crap.*

Glory: *Am I?*

This is stupid. There's no way Glory knows what Scarlett needs. No way she knows anything. I throw the cell back on the bench seat, but then stare at it. What if Glory can somehow give Scarlett what she needs? Am I going to let my pride cost her?

Scarlett needs a job. One she can work from home and one she can keep secret.

Silence. Enough time that I should be smug that I called Glory's bluff, but I'm not. I want Scarlett to have a job more than I want to be right.

Glory: *You have to ask. Nicely.*

And Glory wonders why I don't like her: *Can you please give Scarlett a job?*

Glory: *Bring her to me. She and I will talk.*

I massage my neck and then hope I can pull this off. *We'll be by tonight.*

SCARLETT

The front door opens before I have the chance to place my hand on the doorknob. My stomach jumps to my throat as I expect Dad to tower over me, but it's not my father, it's my mother. Her eyes are wide, her face pale and drawn. She grabs hold of my hand and drags me into the house, closing the door behind her with great care to not make noise.

"Go to your room," she whispers. "And stay there. Don't come out until I tell you."

My heart beats at every pressure point. I'm five years old again being ushered away to a promised safety that doesn't exist. Somehow, when Mom looks this scared, I'm always five.

The back door opens and shuts with a slam. "Scarlett!"

I stop breathing and Mom gives me a look that screams *danger.* She pushes me toward the stairs. "Run."

I do. Up the stairs, but it doesn't feel fast enough. It's like I'm caught in slow motion, running through wet sand. Dad's footsteps pound against the hardwood of the foyer. "Scarlett, come here!"

"You don't want to do this," Mom says in her soothing tone. "Let her go upstairs while you have a chance to calm down."

"She walked out on me!" he shouts at Mom. "I took her to counseling and she left!"

"They told us she might act out once we brought her to counseling. That we would be drudging up emotions in her that she hasn't faced. They told us that we need to be patient. This isn't Scarlett. This is the result of her counseling session."

"She wasn't there when I left!" his voice booms. "That was her choice! Scarlett! Get down here now!"

A shiver runs through me so forcefully that I slip on the stairs. I fall, my knee slamming into the corner of the step and my head hits the railing. Pain spikes through me, but I ignore the throbbing. I have to keep going.

"Get out of my way!" he yells, and there's a crash. Glass shattering. With my hand on the railing, I drag myself to my feet and look down. In chunks and pieces throughout the foyer are the remnants of Mom's favorite vase. The one her mother gave her. The sole heirloom from her past.

With her arms outstretched, my mother stands at the bottom of the stairs, a wall between me and him. Dad looms over Mom, and while she stands strong, I cower for her.

Panic races through me. Self-preservation screams at me to lock myself in my room, but love begs me to save my mom. I do neither, instead I'm frozen, except for my lips. They move, and sound tumbles out. "Mom."

Both Mom and Dad's gazes snap up to mine. Dad's chest moves rapidly, breathing hard with his anger, and Mom somehow appears so calm that I blink because it can't be real. While keeping her eyes locked on me, Mom reaches out and slowly places a hand on Dad's chest. My heart stutters as I expect him to push her away, but he doesn't. He only closes his eyes.

"Go to your room, Scarlett," Mom says. I swallow as I feel like I should stay. Terrified if I leave, Dad will release all his anger and hit her again, but then red-hot nausea causes me to break into a sweat. What if staying makes things worse?

"Do what I ask," Mom says in a soft voice, "and take Isabelle with you."

My eyes shoot straight to the second-floor landing and there is my sister. Her entire face void of color, her little fingers squeezing her doll tight to her chest. Mom protects me. I protect Isabelle. Those are our jobs. I scurry to my feet, grab my sister, swing her up to my hip and race to my room.

Isabelle clings to me as she presses her doll and fingers into my neck. In my room, I close my door, lock it and pretend that will keep the monsters away. I climb onto my bed, and Isabelle doesn't let go. She only tries to burrow further into me, as if she could find a way to climb inside my chest and hide. I hold on to her and she holds on to me and we lay perfectly still.

Shouting.

My father irate, my mother begging for him to be calm. He blames me, he blames Mom, he blames Isabelle, he blames Pastor Hughes. Everyone but himself. And my mom, I wish she would shut up and hide. I wish she wouldn't confront him. I wish I had kept *my* mouth shut. I wish for an entirely different life.

It goes on and on. Their voices bouncing in volume as they move from room to room.

It feels like weeks pass, days pass, when in reality it's hours. A circle of loud voices that never ceases.

"Have you considered that Scarlett's rebellious behavior is because of our college decision? Maybe if we give her a little bit of freedom . . . ?" Mom's plea is clearer than any of the other things they've said. They're moving up the stairs. I pray she makes it safely.

"It's not about where she goes to college," Dad snaps. "This is about Scarlett lying to us."

"But the speech therapy degree means so much to her."

"She's trying to divide and control us. She's mad you've forgiven me. We have to stand firm together if we're going to save our family. We can't give in to her. We have to stand strong."

"But maybe if you allowed the job she'd see that as an act of faith from you—"

"Whose side are you on?" Dad roars outside my door. Isabelle and I jump and cling tighter to each other. "It should be my side! My side, not hers!"

"Please don't yell at me," Mom begs, and I choke as Mom begins to cry. "Just please stop yelling. I can't take it anymore. I just can't."

My heart rate raises. I let go of my sister and clutch the blanket. I feel as if I'm being thrown out into the vast vacuum of space, spiraling out of control. My lungs squeeze, and I gasp for breath. I caused this. If he hurts her, it's my fault.

Pain in my chest, my muscles ache, and I can't suck in enough air. Sweat beads along my skin, and as Mom continues to cry and Dad continues to shout, no air goes into my lungs. I can't breathe, and I'm going to die.

Isabelle's little body shakes into mine, her tears streaming through the material of my shirt. Mom cries louder, I see stars as I fight to breathe and then . . .

"I'm sorry." Dad sounds so tired. So contrite. Like a different man. "Please don't cry. I'm sorry. I didn't meant to yell. I never thought Scarlett would actually leave. I never thought she would outright disobey like she has. When she left, I thought she was going to wait in the car for me and then when I couldn't find her after my session . . . it scared me."

I freeze and so does my sister. It's like we're on the edge of a blade and the wrong move could cause us to be sliced.

"Don't cry—" Dad's voice breaks as if he's on the verge of tears. "Please don't cry. I love you. So much. Please forgive me. Please, just forgive me."

He continues like that as Mom continues to weep. Eventually she tells him that she forgives him and that she loves him and it goes silent, except for the eventual click of their bedroom door being closed.

Second verse same as the first.

Isabelle and I stay silent on my bed, holding one another. An hour goes by. Then another. I stop keeping count. Eventually she drifts off, and I become brave enough to bundle her up in a blanket and carry her to her room.

When I place her on her bed, she becomes barely coherent enough to lift her arms as I change her into pajamas and to whisper she loves me as I leave.

In the hallway, I pause outside my door, straining to hear anything from my parents' bedroom, but beyond my father's muffled snore, there's nothing. How can they do that? Go from one hundred to zero in minutes? From warpath to sleep, as if that's natural? I'll be lucky if I sleep the rest of the week.

I enter my bedroom, close the door, lean back against it and wonder if I should turn on the lights and read until sunrise, but a tap on my window causes my forehead to furrow.

SCARLETT

At the second tap, I turn my head toward the sound. A third tap followed by a fourth and I cross the room. It's close to midnight, it's Friday and it's August. Old habit and expectation cause my pulse to quicken. Two more taps, and on instinct, I open the window.

I search the dark ground but spot nothing. Maybe I'm hearing things that aren't real. Maybe—

My head tilts as I spot the tiny visitor on my windowsill. Inching along is a fat, multicolored caterpillar and seeing him is like reaching through the fog of memory. I've seen him before, but where?

"Hey, Tink. It's about time. I ran out of rocks."

My gaze snaps to the towering oak tree next to the house. Crouched near the trunk on the thick branch reaching out toward my window is Jesse Lachlin. He's in jeans, a white T-shirt and a blue baseball cap. A surge of panic that my father will find him floods me, but then Jesse slowly smiles—his pirate one. With that one gesture, the heaviness overwhelming my body lifts.

"What are you doing here?" I whisper.

Perched precariously on the branch, he shifts his footing and my heart slams past my chest. He shouldn't move. If he moves, he'll fall and then he'll die and that will be bad. "Don't move!"

His impish grin widens. "Why?"

"You'll fall."

"No, I won't."

"Yes, you will."

"Come on, where's the faith? We've climbed higher in weaker trees than this."

Yes, we did, but . . . "We were also seven, fifty pounds and more flexible."

He chuckles. "Speak for yourself. I'm still flexible."

I don't know why, but I smile. "You were never flexible. You had the climbing grace of a rock. If it weren't for me, you'd still be kissing the ground."

"Then come out here and show me how it's done."

My grin falters. I'm not seven. I'm seventeen. I'm longer, heavier and I haven't climbed a tree since the summer before our freshman year. My last summer being friends with Jesse. "Why are you here?"

Jesse places his hand on a neighboring branch. "As I said earlier, we're friends."

"And I told you we aren't friends."

"I need a friend right now and something tells me you need one, too."

"You have friends," I say slowly.

"Yeah, but they aren't here, and if they were I'd send them home. You're the friend I need. Come on. Climb some trees with me."

I want to, but I don't know how.

"Just give me tonight, Tink." The hopeful plea in his voice is nearly my undoing. "If you decide after this we can't be friends, then I'll accept your decision. No anger between us, just two people who were once friends."

The caterpillar crawls in Jesse's direction. A memory flashes in my mind of sunshine and my chubby fingers holding a caterpillar just like him. An elusive sixth sense consumes me; this is important, somehow, but I don't know why. "My father will hear if I go down the stairs."

"Then leave the way you did in the past—go out the window."

"I'll fall."

"No, you won't."

Causing the blood to drain to my toes, Jesse edges away from the fleeting safety of the trunk and holds out his hand. The imp-ish grin returns and in his green eyes is the spark I always adored.

The branch curves a foot from my window. It's a hardy branch, and I've shimmied myself out this window hundreds of times in my life. Each time without thought. Each time with confidence. My mouth dries out and a tremor of fear runs through me. "I'll fall."

"Not gonna happen. Give me your hand, and I'll help you reach the ground safely."

That sounds good, but . . . "I don't trust you."

"I deserve that." Sadness rolls over his face. "And you have a right to not trust me. But c'mon, Tink, somewhere deep inside you have to know I'd never let you fall."

My hands go cold and clammy, and I rub them against the dress pants I wore to work. I look down and realize that this is not a tree-climbing outfit. "Give me a sec?"

"And put on some decent shoes, Tink. I'm starting to think you don't own anything sensible."

I keep my window open but close the curtains and hurry through my room. I trip over my feet as I yank off my pants, throw off my shirt and trade them for jeans, a sports bra and a tank top. I toss my hair into a messy bun then have to rummage longer in my closet than I should for a pair of tennis shoes. Back on my bed, it's hard to tie them as my hands are unsteady.

I'm sneaking out. I'm climbing down the tree. I'm going to hang out with Jesse Lachlin. I lift my head and pause. What am I doing? This is stupid and reckless, and if Dad finds out he'll be furious, but he's always furious. Am I to be Mom and to spend my life being nothing more than a pawn to calm Dad down when he throws a fit? I rise to my feet.

No. That's not who I'm going to be. I open the curtains and accept Jesse's outstretched hand.

The moment my fingers lay in his, Jesse doesn't wrap his hand around mine like I expect. Instead, he slides his fingers along my skin and then grips my forearm. "Take my arm."

I do. His skin is hot under my touch, and his pulse beats under my fingertips. Jesse's grip on me is firm, steady, and I exhale slowly to try to calm my racing heart.

"You've done this a million times," he says. "You can do it again. Place your other hand on the windowsill for support, pull yourself up onto the frame and then put one foot on the branch followed by another. I swear, you did this with your eyes closed all through third grade to freak me out."

I did, but somehow I was braver when I was younger. I shake out my other hand to try to stop the nervous tingles.

"Don't overthink this," he says. "Just do it."

I shouldn't do this. I should let go of Jesse, shut my window and go to bed, but I need to do this. Not for Jesse, but for me. I'm in control of my life. Not my father. I can leave whenever I want, and I'm choosing to leave now.

A hand on the windowsill, one foot on the frame and I dig my nails into Jesse's skin. I let go of the window and make the massive step from my house to the tree, landing in a crouching position in front of him.

My vision narrows at the enormous distance between me and the ground. I'm going to fall. Panic sets in, nausea turns my stomach and my hand flails in a balance check. An arm snakes around my waist, and I'm tugged into solid warmth. My breath rushes out of my body, and when I glance up, serious green eyes stare into mine. "I got you."

Jesse's grip rivals steel bands. Settled on a narrow limb, I've never felt more secure. A tornado could blow through this tree, through this town, and could destroy everything in its path, but Jesse and I would still be crouched here together. His strength keeping us in place.

"You good?" he asks.

No, not really, but I keep my doubts quiet. I scan the branches, and it's like looking at a treasure map I once had memorized. A few years have passed, the tree is older, but the layout is overall the same. "I'm good."

"You sure?"

Nope. "Yeah."

"Are you sure?" he asks again.

"Don't make me put you in a choke hold and force you to tap out."

Jesse gives me a crooked grin, releases me and shifts back toward the trunk, then onto a parallel branch. Using my fingers to feel along the thinner branches above me for support, I inch toward the trunk. A quick survey of the tree finds the finger and footholds I used as a child.

I'm rusty, I'm slow, but I make it down the two stories without breaking my neck. I have to jump the last part, and the solid ground is a gift. Seconds later, Jesse lands beside me. The moment his feet hit the ground, an electrical shock runs through me. Resonating from the ground and shooting up through me from my toes.

Jesse jerks and his green eyes widen as if he felt the same thing. "You okay?"

My entire body tingles with the aftermath of the energy spike. "Yes. Are you?"

"Yeah." Jesse slips off his cap then rakes a hand through his hair as if waking himself from a dream. "Let's do this."

"Where exactly are we going?"

"Same place as always."

I'm dumbfounded as he walks toward his land. "And where is that?"

"Second star on the right then straight on till morning."

Second star on the right. I haven't been Tink to his Peter Pan for a long time. But watching Jesse head off to the land the two of us conquered in battles that belonged in our heads creates a sense of nostalgia I can't ignore. I start for the land that calls to Jesse, the land that used to call to me. It's definitely time for an adventure.

JESSE

Scarlett walks beside me. It's dark. It's silent. We have a half-moon's worth of light. Enough to cast a shadow, but we can't see too far ahead. The night's warm and the breeze that's blowing in from the west is light and welcome. The long blades of grass swat at our legs, and the farther we travel onto my land, the more the weight of the world lifts from my shoulders.

Some of the words she said to me earlier today circle in my head: *I'm empty.*

That's how I'll feel if I lose this land. I don't have much going for me, but I have the soil beneath my feet. It's my only reason to wake in the morning, and to continue to take a breath throughout a minute. I hurt for Scarlett because I've felt lost, but never empty.

"What's going on between you and your dad?" I ask. "He sounds controlling."

"I never said he was controlling."

"I didn't say the grass is green or that the sky is blue, but that doesn't make it any less green or blue."

Scarlett's glare is sharp, but then she runs her fingers along the high grass as if my words didn't penetrate her wall of ice. "I don't discuss home."

I'm aware. We were inseparable until freshman year, and other than her dad didn't like me, she never said much about her father. I can't give her too much crap because I never told her about my mom and her tour bus full of problems. I also didn't tell her about my psychotic, absentee father either, so I guess that makes us even.

"I won't tell anyone," I say, even though that won't convince her to share her secrets, and I don't blame her. Just because I call us friends doesn't wipe away the damage that's been done. "I spread Gran's ashes in the same spot where I spread Mom's. I meant to plant flowers there for years, but . . ." Never did. Not because I didn't care, but because thinking of Mom hurts.

I watch the ground and as we walk I'm swamped by the memory of the fear in Mom's eyes, the tears streaming down her face—

"I guess things have always been complicated at home," Scarlett says. "Growing up, I didn't think much of it until one day I did."

"What made you think?"

"I just did," she says quietly. "Please don't tell anyone what I've said. Dad is obsessed with his reputation, and we live in a small town. If you talk, someone else will talk and he'd know everything I said by lunch."

"You can trust me."

She purses her lips like she doesn't believe me, and I deserve her reaction. I have a lot to do to back up the words. "What's the game plan?"

Her eyebrows raise. "This is your adventure so you tell me."

"Nah, tonight's already booked. I'm talking about your plan to go to UK."

I don't like her heavy, pensive expression, and I have myself to blame. That question is a part of her home life, and she's admitted she doesn't trust me. It's time for me to back off. "Don't answer, Tink. You'll tell me when you're ready."

That grants me a surprised glance, and some of her heaviness disappears. "I was always baffled why you called me Tink. I look nothing like her."

No, she doesn't. Disney can keep their tiny, blond, green-dress-wearing fairy. I'll take the black-haired, strong-bodied beauty next to me. "Gran used to read the novel to me. The real deal—not the movie. The book was called *Peter and Wendy*. She told me once that Peter and Tink made her think of you and me."

"Really?" I like the hint of happy in her tone.

"Yeah."

"Why?"

"I'm obvious."

Scarlett laughs. A good laugh. The type that makes you want to laugh along. "Are you admitting you'll never grow up?"

Sometimes I think I grew up too fast, but instead of saying that, I wink at her. "What's the point of life if you don't have an adventure?"

"Why me for Tink?"

I weigh how she'd take the truth. If she'd be able to see Gran's heart in her thoughts. Not willing to risk alienating her, I go for part of the answer. "You're loyal."

She kicks at a stone in the grass as we near the woods. "I don't know about that."

"I do. If I hadn't stopped talking to you our freshman year you would have stuck with me until the day you died." And that was the problem.

"Why did you stop being friends with me?" It's the second time she's asked.

The first time I didn't have the balls to answer, and I was disappointed in myself. She deserves better, and now is as good a time as any to start. "I'm cursed."

Her head whips in my direction, her eyes wide, and I force a smile on my face and pray that it looks carefree. She nervously laughs and pushes her hand against my shoulder. I exaggerate my steps as if that pat could physically move me, which makes her giggle more natural.

"I thought you were being serious," she says. "You'd think people would get tired of the stupid Lachlin curse."

"I don't believe because some great-great-great-granddaddy killed someone in cold blood that I'll gain everything I want then watch it be destroyed."

"Good."

But Mom did teach me better than to tempt fate. I have a plan: stay on my land, keep that as my focus, and all will be good in my world.

"Remember when we found that stray cat that had been hurt on your land?" I ask.

"Yes."

"And remember how we were sure that cat had kittens?"

She nods, and I can tell the memory makes her sad. Back then, even though I told her I was going to try to nurse the cat back to life, she saw the truth. She knew that cat was going to die, and I remember the way her eyes welled up with tears at the thought of those babies being alone.

"I found the kittens." It took me twenty-four hours with no sleep, but I found them.

Scarlett stops walking and stares at me. "Were they alive?"

"Yeah. Barely." I shove my hands in my pockets. "There were three of them. One died, but the other two made it. They're barn cats now in the west field."

"Why didn't you tell me?"

"I tried. I saw that your window was open." Her sign to find her there. "I climbed the tree, but I didn't knock."

"Why?"

The muscles in the back of my neck tense. "You were crying, and your mom was on your bed with you. You guys were talking about Camila's birthday party."

Realization drains the color from her face. "Jesse—"

I cut her off so we can get this over with. "I overheard what you said and what your mom said. Don't worry, it's okay."

"It's not." Scarlett places a hand on her stomach. That was the night she realized that as long as she was friends with me, she wouldn't have any other friends.

"Because you're loyal you would have stuck by me even when it would have cost you your happiness. I couldn't let you destroy your future to be friends with me."

We live in a small town. Lines are drawn between groups of people before most figure out if they like peanut butter with or without jelly. I was her friend. She was mine. While her dad kept us from seeing each other except for stolen moments during the day and then at night, he couldn't keep us away from each other at school.

The whole world knew we were friends, and Scarlett didn't care until she did. Until she learned she was the only girl not invited to Camila Sanchez's birthday party. Until she learned the reason why was because she was best friends with me. She was fourteen and an outcast.

Middle school had been hard on her, and she had hoped high school would be better. That birthday party snub had informed her she was going to experience four more years of social hell.

The good folks in town decided something had to be wrong with her for willingly hanging with a Lachlin, especially a Lachlin like me with questionable parents, a questionable upbringing and a grandmother who three-quarters of the county thought was certifiably insane.

"I heard your mom telling you that your life would be easier without me. She said you would never fit in at school and that you would be an outcast as long as we were friends. So, I gave you up."

Her mouth gapes. "She meant life would be easier for *her*. She was tired of listening to people tell her she was a bad parent because they thought she approved of my relationship with you. I didn't care what anyone else thought. I wanted to be friends with you."

"Your mom wasn't wrong. Being friends with me is a death sentence."

"I didn't care!" she shouts.

"I did!"

"So you threw me away to make new friends? They're worthy, but I wasn't?"

Her anger feeds mine because walking away from her slayed me. "It hurt you to be excluded, and you were going to continue to be excluded because of me. I gave you up so you could have a better life!"

"So Veronica is strong enough to be your friend, to take the crap the world throws at her for hanging with you, but I wasn't?"

"No, that's not how it is."

"Then how is it, Jesse? Explain to me how exactly it is," she pushes. "Because this all sounds like a lot of bull! It sounds like you think you're the big, strong male stepping in to make my choices all in the name of protecting me, without any regard for what I want. Either that or you can't own up to the fact you thought I wasn't good enough to be your friend."

"You were more than good enough. If anything, you were too good for me."

"Then why did you call me an ice princess? If you did all of that to be my friend, then why did you make me the joke of the entire school?"

"Because I was fourteen and an asshole! It's a piss-poor excuse, but it's all I got. I hurt you, and I'm sorry."

"You walking away hurt me! That name hurt me! You were supposed to be my best friend and friends don't do what you did to me!"

"We can rehash this as much as you want, but it won't change what I did or why. I made a mistake. You either forgive me or you don't, but I'm telling you I'm sorry, and if I could take it back, I would."

She draws in several deep breaths, and after the longest silence of my life, she meets my eyes again. "Do you regret it?"

"Every. Damn. Day."

"Good," she says with some of the familiar attitude I'm used to my best friend having. "So you know, just because I'm still standing here doesn't mean I forgive you or that we're friends. You're on probation, Lachlin."

"Understood." Probation is better than no shot at all.

"Now, where are we going?"

She hasn't run away, and she hasn't socked me in the stomach. She's still here and that's a huge win.

"To Glory's," I say. "I convinced her to give you a job."

SCARLETT

I should be completely absorbed in Glory's every word because she's offering me an amazing opportunity, but my attention is split between Glory and Jesse. Glory is describing a job I need. Jesse and I may or may not be friends again—it all depends on me.

I pray for easy, and my life becomes more complicated. But Glory and Jesse are good complications—I think. Either that or they're tragic mistakes. I guess time will tell.

Glory pours hot water in a teacup she had placed in front of me, and like I do at home, I swirl the tea bag in the water. Her quaint yellow kitchen is too warm for tea, but it felt rude to decline, especially since this is my formal job interview. Not to mention a job interview at 12:30 A.M. From my seat at the table for two, I spot Jesse lazily leaning against the post of the front porch. His thumbs are hitched in his pockets and he stares out into the night.

The rest of our walk was silent, but the silence wasn't awkward or heavy. It was welcome and intimate. His hand occasionally brushed against mine, and each time, my heart curiously fluttered.

On the porch, Jesse rests his head along the post and closes his eyes. He possesses grace, a quietness and a sense of solid strength. It's not new. It's the same sense of peace Jesse has always had when he walks his land. It's a peace I've envied my entire life.

Glory flits around the kitchen. She's in a long blue skirt that shimmers, with a matching tank top, and her long, unruly hair flows over her shoulders and along her back. Even in the heat, she seems cool. She goes into the living room, returns and places a stack of books in the middle of the narrow table. I can't read the covers as the tops are flipped down.

She sits in the only other chair and sips from her tea. "It's hawthorn berry tea."

I lift the cup, inhale the calming scent and take a sip. The taste automatically brings on memories of me and my mother and late nights in our kitchen talking. "My mom loves tea, and this one is a favorite. She has all sorts of different types. I think she buys most of it from some specialty store in Lexington."

The pride flowing from me is evident. I miss my close relationship with my mom.

"How is your mother?" Glory asks.

I swirl the tea bag in the cup because I honestly don't know how to answer.

"My relationship with my mother was also complicated," she says. "Hawthorn berry tea helps the heart. It also helps those who have a hard time loving others and themselves."

I should probably buy this in bulk, then.

"Can I see your palm?" Glory asks, then adds, "No charge."

That causes my lips to lift, and her touch is gentle as she holds my hand. She traces the same circles she did during my reading. "These are called islands, and they aren't something I like to particularly see when doing a reading, nor do I like to see them where they are located on your palm. It means mental stress and an emotional disturbance. For you, I see that someone is standing in your way to happiness."

Nausea swirls in my stomach. "Why are you telling me this?"

She curls my fingers into a loose fist and pats my hand. "I understand why you don't answer personal questions, and I want you to know that you don't have to answer any while you work for me. But I also want to make you aware that it won't stop me from asking."

Not sure what to say to that so I take another drink.

"I'll pay you minimum wage and a half, plus bonuses for tasks done well or when I have a very profitable month. While most of the work I'll give you can be done at home, there are times I will need you at my house, but I'll do my best to work around a schedule that will suit you."

"Thank you." We talked when I first came in, and she understood up-front that I couldn't work in public as I'm taking on this job without my parents' permission. She waved off any concerns by telling me that she could hire infants to sell necklaces during craft shows, but what she needed was someone with brains.

"You will need a laptop or a computer of some sort. Do you have one?"

I squish my lips to the side because I do own a laptop, but . . . "My father monitors my computer and cell."

"Then I'll supply the laptop, but will you be able to keep that discreet?"

A secret? Hidden in my room? I hope so. "Yes."

"For jobs done on the computer, I'll be able to see how long you were on. For jobs not done on the computer, you'll need to log your hours, but I've run this business since I was sixteen. I know how long it takes to do things so don't think you can fake hours."

I set down my cup. "I thought you were psychic and would know when I was lying."

She laughs, and it's weird how carefree it is. Is it possible for anyone to be that happy? Her eyes flicker over my shoulder then settle back on me again. "I am psychic, but I'm not a human lie detector. I depend upon the universe and spirits to talk to me. They aren't always chatting nor do they tell me everything I want to know. To be honest, they are usually telling me things I wish they would keep to themselves."

I focus on my teacup to keep any sarcastic expression off my face. She's giving me a job, and while I'm still skeptical, I'm a skeptic with a job.

"You don't believe in what I can do?"

I shrug, not wanting to insult the person who is giving me a shot at freedom.

"It's okay to be honest. In fact, honesty is what I expect."

"Ghosts and angels talking to you seems . . . farfetched."

"I can respect that," she says with another quick glance over my shoulder. "People have felt that way since the dawn of time. Do you know what they used to call people like me?"

My eyebrows raise. "Witches?"

Glory's eyes twinkle as if that amused her. "Prophets. God spoke to Joseph and Daniel via dreams. In the New Testament, angels visited Mary and shepherds watching over their sheep. The number of people in the Bible who saw visions, talked with angels or had prophetic dreams are too many to count. I have a harder time understanding that people can believe in God yet think He doesn't have any more prophets."

I snort. "God's prophet charges fifty dollars for a half hour?"

"I never said I was a saint or that I was doing it right." Her smile widens, and I smile along with her. "While I'm more than likely not, as in definitely not, doing what I'm supposed to be doing with my gift, I do help people, and as you work with me, you'll understand."

I take another sip of tea as I have nothing productive to add to any of that. Glory looks over my shoulder again, but this time her gaze settles there for a few seconds and a cold chill runs along my spine. "Why do you keep doing that?"

Glory slowly returns her focus to me. "Doing what?"

My eyes widen in a *Hello?* and I wave my hand near my shoulder. "That."

She relaxes back in her seat, taking her cup of tea with her. "Don't tell Jesse because he'll be angry, but Suzanne is here. She's currently attached herself to you."

My entire body goes into a deep freeze and then I blink. Twice. "Why?"

"Don't worry. She's not present all the time. Spirits need the right amount of energy to linger in this realm, and very few have enough energy to remain long. She initially attached herself to Jesse, but since he's on the porch doing nothing, she decided to join us."

"Why?" I'm a freaking parrot.

"Because there are things she believes you should know."

"Like what?"

"This is why being a psychic is a hard job. You have to know what to say, how to say it and," she glares over my shoulder, "when not to say it."

Silence. Glory purses her lips as if she's agitated. "It's not the time, and you can disagree with me as much as you want, but it's not going to make me change my mind."

Her eyes wander toward the counter, near the window. "You can't do it. You're a new spirit." She pauses then rolls her eyes. "Very mature. Did you kiss people with that mouth?"

The temperature dips, goose bumps form along my arms and the curtain moves. Frightening electricity shoots through my blood, and my chair squeaks beneath me as I jerk. There was no wind. Not even a slight breeze. The trees didn't rustle. The other curtain didn't move, yet that one did. My heart pounds, my hands shake and there has to be an explanation.

"Good job, Suzanne, you moved a curtain. You used so much energy you won't be around when I speak to Jesse." Glory's expression softens. "Please take it slow."

Yeah. Okay. Beautiful. We've wandered well past my comfort level of crazy for the evening. Whether this is real or a great act or whatever, I'm done. I stretch my fingers because the tingle in my body is indicative of me losing my sanity. "I need to go home."

Glory stands along with me, and when she walks into the living room, I follow.

"I need you to take these two boxes with you. Put the pendants on the chains and price them for sale. I have a craft fair this week and will need those done quickly. The other box is full of receipts and purchase orders I need entered into my system. Jesse?"

The screen door opens, Jesse walks in and the way his gaze automatically seeks mine creates a warmth in my blood. A blush heats my cheeks, and I tuck a stray hair behind my ear because I suddenly have no idea what to do with my hands. He winks at me and I melt.

"Jesse," Glory says, "can you swing by tomorrow and pick up these boxes and the laptop for Ms. Copeland? How you two smuggle them into her house is not my responsibility, but Ms. Copeland, it is your responsibility to keep my property safe." She pins me with a serious look.

"I promise to take care of everything," I say. "Thank you for what you're doing for me."

"You're welcome." She glances at Jesse. "And the boxes?"

"I'll drop by in the morning," Jesse says.

"Since Ms. Copeland's father monitors her cell, if I should need to reach her, do I have permission to contact you and trust that you'll relay that information to her in a timely fashion?"

"Yeah, that's fine."

"Good. And Ms. Copeland, I highly recommend that with your first paycheck that you purchase something obsidian. Keeping in mind the islands on your palm, you'll need the protection. I'll give you a twenty percent discount on any of your purchases. Now the two of you should leave as I have a busy day tomorrow."

"You ready?" Jesse asks.

I nod because I constantly find myself at a loss for words when I'm in this cottage. Jesse walks out, but before I follow, Glory calls, "Ms. Copeland?"

She hurries for the kitchen. I stay inside while Jesse waits for me on the porch.

"You can call me Scarlett," I say.

"I know," she replies from the kitchen. "But calling you Ms. Copeland shows that I see you as an adult and you'll be making some very adult decisions soon." She returns with the books and dumps them into my hands. "You need to read these."

Three books. Two on reading palms. Another on analyzing body language. My eyebrows pinch together. "What are these for?"

"For you to learn. I've decided to take you on as my mentee."

My face contorts. Um . . . "I'm not psychic."

Glory places her cool fingertips on my wrist and gives me a squeeze. "Sweetheart, sometimes neither am I. As I said, you'll soon understand. Now go. Your father will be checking in on you earlier than normal, and Jesse will figure out he needs to talk to you."

Mental whiplash, and I stop having coherent thoughts.

"You were smart to follow the caterpillar. Continue to let him be your guide."

Unable to say anything intelligent, I offer Glory a jumbled "Thank you," then leave.

JESSE

Scarlett left Glory's with three books in her hands, and I gave them back to Glory, telling her that I'd pick them up later with the other things. It's a long trek, and I didn't want her flipping through books on the way, but talking to me. The girl walking next to me through the field is the reincarnation of my best friend from the past. She's telling me how she freaked out when Glory chatted with some "spirit." Scarlett laughs, and my soul lifts with the sound. We don't need the moon or stars to guide us. She's shining brighter than any light that could lead us home.

"I know I can keep this a secret from Dad, and I'll be able to make a ton of money and I'm going to be able to figure out how to go to the University of Kentucky." Scarlett skips ahead of me, does a circle like she did when we were kids and claps her hands. "I have a job!"

She does and seeing her happy scabs over old, open wounds.

"Jesse," there's a breathlessness in her tone that makes me feel lighter, "thank you."

My stomach drops. She needs to know why I'm helping her. I've told her before, but she didn't believe me. If I do this wrong, the wall that's currently down will go back up before I have the chance to blink. Now that Scarlett is in my life, I don't want to lose her again.

I slow when we reach my backyard. Scarlett's aglow, a brilliant smile gracing her lips, but it fades as she searches my face. "Are you okay?"

"I need your help."

"With what?"

"I need your help to keep my land." Scarlett remains quiet as I unload Marshall's lack of confidence in me, his influence over Gran, her tribunal decision and why they weren't going to inform Scarlett about her involvement until closer to the vote.

Halfway through, I have a tough time looking at Scarlett as horror overtakes her expression. I understand. I can't escape this nightmare. I finish speaking, and her continued silence is almost too heavy for me to bear.

"So you weren't kidding at lunch," she finally says in a quiet voice that creates guilt. Her doubt in me, in how I've declared us friends again, is so tangible I could reach out and touch it.

"No." I shove my hands in my pockets, and wish I could punch my fist through that wall she's throwing up. "I see your mind working, and it's not what you think."

Her eyes flash to mine, dark with anger. "Don't do that. Don't tell me what I should think or how I should feel. I get enough of that crap at home."

I scan the looming fortress of stone she calls home. Thanks to Mom's stellar choice in guys, I know how to take a hit and I know from experience a verbal hit can be just as damaging. Is that what's happening to her? Is her dad the manipulative asshole who punches with words? Better question: Does she know it?

"Fair enough," I say slowly. "You're correct, I don't have any right to tell you how to feel. Neither does anyone else." I pause, giving that time to sink in. "I want us to be friends again. Not because I need your vote, but because I miss you. This whole thing started out with me needing your help, but the rest of it has been real. I haven't lied to you. Not from the start."

"What if I don't vote for you?" she pushes. "Are you still going to be friends with me?"

It's a tough question, it's real, and I give her an honest answer. "I'll probably be mad for a while, but we'll still be friends. I'm tired of not having you in my life."

Her shoulders roll forward as if she's exhausted. "I need to go before Dad notices I'm gone."

She's heavy as we cross the street, and it almost makes me wish I hadn't mentioned the vote, but not doing so would have been unfair. We reach the tree near her room, and she pauses as she surveys the climb. Up is more daunting than down.

As I start to take a knee to give her a boost, she says, "I'll vote for you to keep the land."

My head jerks up. "What?"

"I'll vote for you to keep the land. Even if you didn't help with the job, even if you had called me an ice princess every day until the end of May, even if you had never spoken a word to me, regardless of how you treat me going forward, I will vote for you to keep your land."

"Why?"

"Because this land belongs to you. It always has. I disagree with what your gran and Marshall are trying to do. If you fail, you fail. If you succeed, you succeed. I'm sick and tired of adults acting like we're glass that will shatter if we fall. Sometimes they need to let us fall. Sometimes we need to make our own mistakes. Sometimes, adults need to butt out."

I don't think she's talking about Marshall, but that's okay. I agree with every word.

"You don't have to do this." Her tone is sad. "I promise you'll have my vote regardless."

"Do what?"

She gestures between the two of us. "Pretend we're friends."

I've seen that look before on my mother, and it's an expression I never wanted to see again. I didn't have a word for that look as a child, but Scarlett gave it a name: *empty*. Pale face, haunted eyes and a brokenness that covers her like a shroud.

Someone's hurting her—somehow. I have the urge to gather her up, hold her close and run. To take her as far from here as I can carry her, but the farthest I could take her is to the edge of my land and something tells me that wouldn't be far enough. At least not for her.

To survive, I need my land. To survive, she needs to leave. I don't know how to fix her, but I do know how to help staunch some of the bleeding. "When can you meet me again?"

"Maybe we can sneak in the boxes while my mom and dad go grocery shopping—"

"That's not what I meant. When can you sneak out your window like you did tonight?"

Her eyes widen in disbelief, as if me asking to hang with her again was never in her realm of possibilities. "I don't know. Tomorrow night I'm supposed to help Camila throw Evangeline a birthday party and then after that it's school nights so—"

"When you do have a free night, I want you to flash your light three times at midnight, and I'll meet you here, okay? There's something I want to show you. It's something that fixes me when life gets to be too much."

Scarlett eyes me with suspicion. "What if I can't get out for another month?"

She's testing me, and if I were her, I'd do the same. I'm going to have to work for her trust. The good news—I've never shied away from anything hard. "Then we hang out in a month."

"You're going to watch my window every night for the rest of your life until I'm ready?"

"Yeah, but do you want to take that long for another adventure? 'Cause that sounds like a boring life, and you're better than that, Tink."

Her lips twitch with a grin and a bit of life flares in her eyes. Me—I'm smiling everywhere. Heart, eyes and face. Yet she rolls her eyes at me. "You're impossible."

Good God, she's beautiful and I'm a lucky man because she's looking at me. I crouch then lace my hands together. "I'll give you a boost."

"How did you make it up without a boost?"

"I'm taller than you."

She frowns like she doesn't like my answer then studies the tree. Damn if she still isn't stubborn and competitive and that makes me proud. I stand because there's no way she's accepting my help now. "You'll need a running start."

"I'm aware." She motions to the lowest branch. "Did that hold your weight?"

"Barely. I had to move quickly to the one on the right before I could gain my balance."

Scarlett breathes in deeply and then she's on the run. While I jumped straight up with the sprint, she sprints up the trunk of the tree, using it as a ladder, and then grabs hold of the lowest branch. She kicks up her legs, snakes them around the branch, then uses her arms to heave herself onto the opposite side. My heart stalls as the branch dips, but it holds her weight as she scrambles to the next, sturdier branch.

Her quiet laughter eases some of the knots in my stomach. "You look sick."

I feel sick. Even though I encouraged her to climb, after that tumble we took as kids from a tree, I keep seeing her falling and breaking her neck. But I can't say anything. I take as many risks as she does, and I'm not into throwing stones at glass houses. "Go to bed, Tink. You have to be exhausted because this isn't as funny as you think."

She calls a good night, and I watch with tense and ready-to-catch arms as she weaves her way up the tree then back into her room. I watch her window, wondering if she remembers the routine we had in place for so many years. A minute later, she reappears and waves. I wave back, and she closes her curtains. I head home, happy that I found my friend again.

SCARLETT

Only in a small farming town would an AP Environmental Science teacher offer extra credit for viewing the birth of a calf. Also only in a farming community would my teacher be the one who is the owner of the mother of said calf. Mrs. Bergen works at the school while Mr. Bergen works their farm full-time. There aren't many farmers in our area who can financially survive on the farm alone. Many are like Mr. and Mrs. Bergen, and sometimes both spouses work a full-time job on top of the farm.

It's Monday, and everyone in our class received the group text as soon as the last bell rang that the calf was going to be born soon. Camila pulls up on the grass next to three other cars of people we know at school. Down the way is Jesse's truck, and there's a strange flutter in my chest at the idea of seeing him again, which is stupid because we're friends, nothing more. Actually, he's a friend on probation and there should be no fluttering.

Camila, Evangeline and I pile out of Camila's Honda Accord, and I take a picture of the barn we're heading to because Dad has demanded visual proof of where I'm at and what I'm doing: *I'm at Mrs. Bergen's house to see the calf being born. This is the extra credit I told you about.*

Dad: *How long will you be there?*

I sigh heavily. *As long as it takes for a cow to be born.*

Dad: *Did your teacher mention how long it can take?*

Is he for real? I start to type, *I'll ask the mother cow if she can rush this along so it fits into your time frame,* but decided to delete that and answer: *No. I'll text with updates.*

Dad: *Thank you.*

Camila and Evangeline are a few steps ahead, huddled in conversation, and they're speaking in code. It's their way of acting like I'm part of the conversation when I'm really not. They use only pronouns instead of names because whatever they're talking about isn't for me to know. Most days it bothers me, but today it doesn't. I'm too busy searching for Jesse.

We enter the aging wooden barn, and Mrs. Bergen smiles when she sees us. Our science teacher is short, athletically built and has long red curls pulled back in a ponytail. She's out of her normal black pants and nice shirt and in sweatpants and a T-shirt. "Your timing is perfect. The calf is about to be born."

Our feet crunch against the hay as we join our classmates along the wooden fence that separates us from the spacious stall the huge dairy cow is currently lying in. Her dark eyes stare off into the distance, and her entire body moves up then down with her respirations.

I scan the six other students and not one of them is Jesse. A pang of disappointment, and then I survey the rest of the barn to see if he's hanging in the back. I must have been wrong on the truck, as he's nowhere to be seen.

Mrs. Bergen climbs over the rail with a stack of towels in her hand. My eyes widen as she hands the towels to the person crouched near the literal tail end of the cow. It's Jesse.

"Why is Jesse in there?" Camila asks, as if she's jealous she's not the one a few inches from a cow's butt.

"This is Jesse's cow," Mrs. Bergen answers.

"Really?" I ask without meaning to, and Jesse's head pops up. His eyes meet mine, and butterflies take flight in my chest. I glance away, but then force my gaze back to his. He's still watching me and a shadow of his Peter Pan smile ghosts his lips, as if he and I are sharing our own private conversation.

The cow's body tenses up, and Jesse's attention returns to the mother-to-be. A ripple runs through the cow, and all the conversation in the barn goes silent. A white glob of something emerges from the cow and my stomach turns upside down. While my classmates and I shift away from the railing and the cow, Jesse edges closer.

More of the white blob is pushed out and my heart beats hard as inside that blob is the baby cow. Jessie reaches out, uses his gloved finger to puncture the blob, and I grab the railing as Jesse cleans away the gross stuff from the baby cow's snout. I wait for the calf's eyelids to flutter and for it to show some sign of life, but it doesn't and panic sets in.

I wildly glance around, waiting for Mr. or Mrs. Bergen to jump in, but they don't. I wait for someone to say something. For Jesse to freak, for someone to cry out that it's dead, and from the way everyone else at the railing is looking at each other, I'm not the only one in dread.

Another ripple goes through the mother cow and the entire barn is eerily quiet. Jesse is silent, the mother cow is silent, the calf is silent.

Jesse grabs hold of the calf's front legs, and with the contraction, he gently helps as the rest of the calf's body is expelled. Jesse takes the blankets, wipes the nose and the mouth again and whispers gently to the baby, "It's okay. Come on, honey. Your momma is going to be on her feet soon and she needs you to be awake."

Please be awake, please be awake. My lungs start to hurt as I hold my breath and silently beg the universe for there to be life.

The calf blinks, she blinks again, then she inhales. I breathe out, and Camila grabs hold of my arm as if she's having trouble staying on her feet.

"That was intense," she whispers to me and I nod, unable to take my eyes off of Jesse tending to the baby as if it were his own flesh and blood.

The mother shifts on the hay, and we all take an involuntary step back as she rises to her feet and circles around to her calf. Jesse eases back and the pure joy on his face as the cow starts to lick and care for her calf touches me deeply.

Jesse drags his eyes away from the mother and baby, and when his gaze meets mine, he winks at me. It's like time freezes as the

ends of my lips lift. Jesse just delivered a baby, and I'm the one
he's choosing to include in his moment.

"All right," Mrs. Bergen says, "if you want extra credit, you
need to ask me questions."

As Monday evenings go in my house, it's pretty typical. Mom is
washing up after dinner, Isabelle is at the kitchen table finishing
her homework and Dad has retreated to his office to do whatever
it is CEOs do.

I was so caught up in my own head that Jesse helped birth a
cow, I forgot to pick up the mail when Camila dropped me off at
home. Now, as I reach the mailbox, the evening is warm and the
sky a beautiful dark blue as the sun sets.

I stop and look at the old Lachlin home. The house is one of
those 1800s farmhouses that must have been beautiful in its day.
I can imagine that during its prime the wood on the outside was
pristine and painted white, the windowpanes full of glass and clear
of any grime, each tile on the roof neatly on point, and the porch
must have been filled with chairs for an afternoon of cookies and
lemonade.

The years have been tough on the aging house. Along with the
roof, the exterior is rotting, the steps of the porch gone and most
of the windows are cracked and covered in dirt. Dad hates that
the house still stands even though it has been condemned. He calls
the decaying structure and Jesse's trailer eyesores, but I've always
loved the old farmhouse. When I was younger, I used to dream of
bringing the old place back to life.

I tilt my head; something is off . . . The door is open. A flash
of light swirls through the inside of the house, and Jesse walks
past one of the windows. Adrenaline surges through me at the
thought of talking to him, of seeing him again, but I'm hesitant.
Because of my dad and because I'm not sure if I can truly trust
Jesse yet. But I watched as Jesse helped bring life into the world so
that must mean that I can trust him, at least for today.

With one look at my house to confirm light shines from Dad's office, I sprint across the road and jump up onto the old porch. It creaks with my weight, and the beam of light that had been moving away from the door does an abrupt about-face in my direction.

Jesse's hulking figure appears in the door, and he lowers the flashlight. His face softens the moment he sees me. "Hey, Tink. What are you doing here?"

"You have a cow." Brilliant declaration, I know.

Jesse grins at me like he's the happiest guy in the world and my heart flips. "I have two cows. The mom belonged to Gran and now the calf belongs to me."

I nervously glance over my shoulder, and as if sensing my unease that I might be seen across the road, Jesse moves so that I can seek refuge in the old house.

"How long you got?" he asks.

"Maybe five minutes."

He frowns. "Do you think you can sneak out later?"

So he can show me the special place. "I don't know." Because while I'm drawn to Jesse, I'm still wary. But when disappointment flashes in his eyes, I pathetically backtrack in a sad attempt to soften my rejection. "It's a school night."

I look away as I hate the twisting inside that comes from letting someone down.

"It's okay," Jesse says in his deep, smooth voice. "Everything that happens between us is at your pace. I'm the one on probation, and I'm fine with that."

I risk a glance to see if he's serious, and I can tell by the kind set of his mouth he is. I try to wrap my head around the concept of "my pace." Everything is always on Dad's pace, not my own.

Needing to change the subject, I scan the room then touch the intricate border on the corner of the wall. "I bet this place was beautiful once."

"Gran said there used to be stained glass in the living room, and when the sun shined through it was like streams of gold."

Jesse has a wistful expression that makes me wish I could climb into his head and see what he sees. He's cleaned up since the farm. His hair is fresh-out-of-the-shower wet, and he smells of soap and shampoo. He's also in a new pair of jeans and T-shirt. All of the signs that he had helped a cow give birth earlier are gone.

"I didn't know you had cows," I say.

"Gran sold the last of our herd about five years ago to Mr. Bergen, but he allowed Gran to keep ownership of one cow and he told her that he'd care for it as long as we let him have first option on renting our land."

"So why is Mr. Bergen giving you the calf?"

"It's a good-faith gesture now that Gran's gone. He depends upon me letting his cattle graze on my land so he can use his land for crops."

"Does he know you want to use your land?"

"Yeah. He knows it's going to take a few years to get everything I want up and running so I think the calf is a peace offering to not start my plans with the pasture he uses."

"How come your grandmother sold the herd?" I ask.

"She couldn't financially and physically handle their upkeep. I tried to help however I could, but I wasn't old enough or strong enough. By the time I could manage more things on the farm, Gran's health started to decline. I've wanted to do so many things with this farm for years, but Gran needed me. So I did what I could to keep the farm going, then spent the rest of my time taking her to doctor's appointments, making sure she was taking her meds, and doing her exercises with her. Between school, working for money, taking care of the trailer, making sure she ate and watching over her to make sure she was okay there wasn't much time to do much else."

I never had any idea how much Jesse did for his gran. "I'm sorry."

"I'm not. I loved her. I'd do anything to have her back."

Before I can respond, Jesse places his hand on the rickety stair railing and pins me with a gaze that dares. "I want to show you something."

A part of me wants to continue to talk about Suzanne as there was something very intimate in how he shared so easily with me, but I think of how Jesse gives me space and realize if he's switching conversations so fast, he must need space from his overwhelming emotions, too. "Is it the thing you think will help make me feel better?"

"This might help, but it's not what I want to show you. That's farther on my land."

"What is it?"

"Follow me and find out." Jesse climbs the stairs, and curious, I trail behind. When I hit the top step, he turns off the flashlight, walks down the hallway and enters a room.

When I step in, I pause as the air is stolen from my lungs. Inside the ancient empty bedroom is a floor-to-ceiling arched vaulted window. In the very center of the window is a stone.

The window perfectly frames the sunset. The horizon is painted in strips of reds, purples, blues and oranges, and all those glorious colors fade into the rolling green hills of Jesse's farm. It's like the most beautiful, imaginative painting brought to life.

Jesse stands before the window with a sense of awe—as if he is standing in the presence of God.

"It's gorgeous," I say.

"It's not my favorite place, but it's one of them. It must have been heaven to sleep in this bedroom every night."

I edge up next to Jesse and the world around us is peaceful and quiet, and it's in such stark contrast to the constant screaming inside me. Sometimes when I stand next to Jesse, I swear he's magic. There's something about him that calms me, something that makes me feel as if I'm the one who is cursed and he is the only one with the cure.

"What do you see when you look out this window?" he asks.

"Beauty." Tranquility. Serenity. All the things that I'm without.

"I see possibility," he says.

"What's possible?"

Jesse places his palm against the glass as if he's touching an old friend. "I see corn in the east field. Soybeans in the north. I would love to plant some grapevines near the house. In the west field, I see cows. Lots of them. Dairy and beef. I see new barns, I see new outbuildings and equipment. I see dogs and barn cats. I see sunshine and gentle summer rains. Some days I stand here and feel as if I touch the glass that somehow my dreams will become reality."

Excitement courses through me because somehow as he talks, I see brief glimpses of his dream. The glimpses are so real, so vivid, it's as if he has entered my mind and placed them there. "Do you think you'll be able to do it?"

Jesse's emerald-green eyes bore into mine, and I'm hypnotized. "Yes."

Confusion worries my brow. "How can you be so sure?" How can he be so certain of his future when I'm terrified of everything?

"Let me show you." Jesse offers me his hand, palm up, and I nibble on my bottom lip. We've touched, several times, but each time we do, I feel as if I'm slowly being led into a fire I'm not sure I want to leave. That's a problem with fires—they have the ability to consume.

My curiosity is stronger than my fear, and I steel my courage to place my hand in his. The moment our palms meet, every cell in my body springs to life with a shot of electricity. He closes his eyes as if he feels it, too, but instead of holding on to me, he raises our combined hands and presses my palm against the stone set in the window.

"Do you feel it?" he asks.

I feel every inch of him against every inch of me even though the only part of us touching is the skin of our hands. I shiver in pleasure because it's as if somehow his touch has spread and left the ghost of a delicious kiss on my neck.

"Do you feel the heat of the sun?"

I close my eyes, focus on my palm, and nod as the late day's warmth still absorbed in the stone heats my skin. How is that possible? "Yes."

"This stone came from the heart of my land. Gran told me that just because I can't see the sun doesn't mean it isn't there. That block was put there to remind people of that. After the sun sets, I can't see the sun, but I can still feel its warmth. There isn't corn or soybeans in my ground, and the cows grazing in my field aren't mine, but they will be. Just like the sun will shine again."

Jesse's cell pings, and I jump. I lower my hand, and my palm still burns with the heat of the stone and his touch.

"I need to go," I whisper, and before he can respond, I run down the stairs and back across the street.

JESSE

A *ping* rouses me from that state where I'm dreaming but on the verge of being awake. For the past month I've waited for Scarlett to flash her lights, but each night, nothing. Last night, after waiting for her until one, I stayed up until three working on the plumbing in the bathroom.

My muscles heavy, I roll over in bed and grab my cell. I consider throwing it across the room when I spot Glory's name: *I'm here for you, remember that. We aren't a conventional family, but we're a family, and whether you believe it or not, you are loved.*

Evidently Glory's taken to recreational drug use. I scroll through my cell to find a few nonsense messages from V and Leo. They tag me and Nazareth to piss us off because we hate being spammed. Then there's one from Marshall: *I'll be by at eleven. I need to discuss something with you.*

Another meeting with Marshall is the last thing I want, but it's necessary. I have a half hour to shower and make this place look halfway decent. I push off the bed and get to work.

I barely have the last dish dried when there's a knock on the front door. The sick feeling in my gut makes me walk slowly to where Marshall's waiting. I open the door, and he's decked out in a pair of jeans and a University of Kentucky polo shirt. He's an alum, and the fact that he's a UK basketball fan is one of the few things we have in common.

Mumbling, "Hey," I wave him in, and he does a good scan of the living room and kitchen. His surprise is noticeable. I'm betting he was expecting to find a graveyard of pizza boxes, a pyramid of empty beer cans and a few naked, passed-out girls.

Preferring not to have a repeat of our last conversation, I head to the kitchen and lean back against the counter as I wait for him to give me whatever new speech he's concocted. He follows me into the kitchen and asks me a few questions about school. I answer them with short sentences. To be nice, I ask about his family. His answers are fake and to the point.

"I meant what I said after your grandmother died," Marshall says. "I'm here for you."

I don't buy it, but I do want my land. "Why are you here?"

Marshall glances away, and a pit forms in my stomach. He's not the type to dodge things. In fact, he's the type that races through a wall at a hundred miles per hour. Direct and fast. Makes him a good lawyer and a pain in my ass. So this pause means bad things for me.

"I was contacted by the Parole Victims Services Office. Your father's up for parole."

Parole. Flashes of memory. My father. My mother. The yelling. The screaming. The crying. The searing pain down my back. Her blood and mine. Anger rushes through me so quickly I begin to shake. "How the hell is that possible?"

Marshall opens his mouth then mashes his lips together. After a few more beats, he tries again. "There's not a good enough reason to give you other than it's happening."

I scrub my hands over my face, then over my head. Scratching along the way because the pain has to wake me up from this nightmare. Three years. It's only been three years. "You told me he would serve twenty."

"This wasn't my understanding of the plea deal, and I have friends who specialize in criminal law looking into it for me. I know nothing I'm saying makes it okay."

"Okay?" I shout. "He killed my mother! He should die in jail!"

"I agree. Keep in mind it's a parole hearing. It doesn't mean he'll be released. In fact, I think we have a good chance of keeping him in. I think this is a mistake, and if I can't have all this reversed before his hearing, I've secured a victim hearing with the parole board. I'll be speaking there. You can come with me and speak or you can complete a Victim Impact Statement, which I can read to them. It's whatever you're comfortable with."

My head's a mess. Too many thoughts, too many emotions collide. Unable to stand anymore, I sink to the floor and rest my head in my hands. The hits keep coming.

"Will he be there?" I ask, my voice hoarse. "Because I don't want to see him."

My mom. God, I miss my mom.

The linoleum floor creaks as Marshall crouches in front of me. "No, he won't. You don't have to go. Instead, you can write a statement of what you want the parole board to know."

"If I do that, you'll say I'm not strong enough."

"You saw your father murder your mother. I don't get the right to think one way or another on how you handle this. I only have the right to respect you for still breathing."

The words sound good, but I don't put weight into them. After Mom died, he told Gran to send me away. I can't deal with this, not now. I'll make a decision. Later. Though my knees are weak, I force myself to stand. "Thanks for letting me know."

Marshall stretches to his full height. "We should talk about your mom—"

"I can't," I cut him off, and when he starts to argue, I shut him down. "I can't."

Marshall raises his hands in submission, and the silence between us grows uncomfortable by the second. If Glory is psychic, she could have warned me that my life was about to implode.

"I need my land," I say. "If you take it from me, you take my only shot at being happy."

"You think this is the best time to discuss this?"

"No, but I don't think there's a good time."

He tilts his head in agreement. "What if I told you one of the reasons I'm pushing you so hard is because you think this farm is all you have? There's more to life than this land."

"The guidance counselor already gave me a speech on college this week."

"Did you listen?"

I snort as an answer, and Marshall is good enough to chuckle with me. Then he sobers up and so do I. My gut twists because I don't know how to make him understand. "I need this land."

"You're more capable than what you think, and you'll never figure that out because you limit yourself at every turn. Some days . . ." He pauses. "Some days I'm scared there *is* a curse. Some days I'd prefer you unsupervised in the world rather than you staying on this farm."

That catches my attention. "You believe?"

"No, but I have to admit believing in a curse would make more sense than believing that doomed coincidence happens to this family over and over again. Julia dying so young, taking our unborn child with her, your mom being murdered, your gran losing everyone she loved."

"She had me," I say, and I don't know why.

"She did," he agrees. "But think of how you came to her and how hard it was for you to trust. That wasn't your fault. I just wish something had been easy for your grandmother."

Yeah, me, too. "You think sending me away from this land will break the curse?" The exact opposite of what my mother believed.

Marshall stares out the back window. "What do you think? When so many in your family have failed at happiness, what do you think is going to break the cycle?"

"I don't know. It seems like every time I get a taste of happy, something else nails me in the head. But if I want to leave, then it's up to me to leave, and it should be my choice if the land is here waiting for me when I return."

Marshall studies me, and for one of the first times, it's not in contempt. "This is the first real conversation we've had since you moved in with your gran."

"Does that mean you're going to vote for me?" I ask. Marshall slightly grins and my lips slightly turn up as well, but then his face falls.

"It means you aren't your mom and you aren't your dad, and you aren't a product of their choices. I hope someday you'll see that. Believe it or not, I want you happy, and I believe you'll be happier without the land and the doomed legacy that follows it. I loved your aunt Julia. More than you can imagine. We had the opportunity to stay out of this town, and I let Julia talk me into coming back. If I had disagreed, she'd still be alive."

A muscle ticks in my jaw. "That sounds like you have no intention of voting for me."

He doesn't say anything. Just stands there, hands on his hips, and I know without a doubt I'm screwed. I have Scarlett's vote, but if I don't convince the pastor to vote for me, I'll lose my land.

"You think your vision is clear, but it's not," Marshall says. "You have to trust me on this. I can see the happiness you need even when you can't."

"I think you were right. I don't think it's time for us to talk about this."

Marshall rubs his eyes then heads for the door. "You'll need to decide what you want to do about the hearing. Take your time, think on it and get back to me." Then he leaves.

SCARLETT

Isabelle sits on the landing of the stairway in the foyer with her arms crossed over her chest. Her cheeks are red, there's moisture rimming the bottom of her eyes, but it's not sadness that's radiating from her, it's anger. I have the urge to give her a high-five.

My sister is in time-out. She didn't remove every item off her dresser and dust every inch. She only dusted the areas in front of her porcelain dolls and that didn't follow my father's explicit instructions. Therefore, she's being punished.

In the living room, Dad sits with his computer on his lap, and he types. Occasionally he glances over the top of the screen to confirm my sister's doing what she's told. Control. My father thrives off of it.

"Did you take out the garbage, Scarlett?" Dad must not like me lingering.

I don't answer him, but I do leave the couch and head to the kitchen. Funny, as I leave, Mom passes me and takes my seat on the couch. She can talk forgiveness, but she doesn't seem to trust Dad alone with Isabelle either. Mom takes up her knitting like that was her plan, but once in the kitchen I see the pan caked in lasagna in the sink.

I yank the bag out of the can and twist it up. I'd love to take the overflowing garbage and dump it over his head. Instead, I yank open the back door and walk the bag to the trash cans that are lined up neatly against the garage.

The autumn evening is clear and brisk. Across the street the lights are on in Jesse's trailer, and I can spot smoke and smell the burning embers from a bonfire in one of the fields. Since my freshman year, I've sat envious at my bedroom window and watched as Jesse has led his friends from the driveway to his back field. I hated them for being so happy together. I hated them more that I wasn't invited.

If I wanted to be invited tonight, I could be. But something has been holding me back. A hesitation. A distrust. It's almost nine. I could be across the road and part of the action in three hours, but I don't know if I should or if he wants me there.

A shadow in the night, and I squint to make out the movement. My heart picks up speed when I hear footsteps—fear that it's Jesse, fear that it's not, fear of my father poking his head out and finding me with anyone.

Not wanting to take the risk of being caught, I head for the house but stop at the sound of my name being called by a female voice: "Scarlett."

Veronica walks into the light from the overhead lamp hanging from the garage. I sneak a quick peek at the house. "What are you doing here?"

Veronica's eyes are ice-cold blue, and when she tilts her head, her short blond curls bounce along her shoulder. "I don't know you and you don't know me, and I imagine you're like the rest of your friends and think I'm garbage."

I flinch as if she had hit me in the stomach because it doesn't feel good for anyone to admit they aren't liked. "I don't think that."

She ignores me. "But Jesse, Nazareth, Leo and I—we're friends. Real friends. We will do anything to help each other."

"Okay," I say slowly.

She crosses her arms over her chest and purses her lips like I'm releasing the smell equivalent to a skunk. "Jesse's upset and for some stupid reason he wants you."

"He sent you here?"

"No. He said you couldn't come, but Jesse never says he wants anything, but then he had to go and say that he wished you were there. You better figure out how to see him tonight or I swear to God I will take you out on Monday."

I double blink; she pivots on her toes and leaves.

"Why is Jesse upset?" I call out.

Veronica doesn't answer as she keeps walking.

I drop to the ground and inhale deeply to steady my shaking hands. Climbing down the tree was easy. It was that first leap from my window to the limb that was death defying. I can't grasp the level of stupidity and courage I must have had when I was younger. I don't remember ever thinking before I leapt out that window to Jesse when I was a kid.

I wipe my clammy hands against my jeans as I walk across the street. It's eleven-thirty. My mom had a headache, and my father sent us to bed early, around nine. Jesse said he'd meet me at midnight, but I couldn't wait thirty more minutes, though it may have been less intimidating to have Jesse waiting for me at the bottom of the tree instead of me strolling up to his yard.

I pass the trailer, and four figures circle a bonfire in Jesse's back field. At least it's not a long walk from his trailer, yet it's still far enough away that my parents couldn't make me out from their bedroom window. Jesse and his friends are loud and full of cheer, guitar chords are being plucked and occasionally there's laughter.

Nerves threaten to swallow me whole yet I walk into the firelight. The conversation halts. Shock covers Nazareth's and Leo's faces, Veronica offers a satisfied smirk, and when I lay my gaze on Jesse I have to prevent myself from laughing with how wide his eyes have become. "Tink?"

"Tink?" Veronica repeats as she turns her head toward him. "Is that what you said?"

Jesse ignores her and scrambles to his feet. He sways, just a tad, and his smile is a bit goofy. This is new, at least for me. Jesse's some level of inebriated.

"Are you drunk?" I ask.

He chuckles and flips the baseball cap on his head backward. "Not yet, but I'm working on it. Won't lie, I do have a good buzz going on." Jesse yanks his cell out of his pocket. "I'm sorry I messed up, Tink. I had my alarm set for eleven-fifty. I don't know what happened."

"Seriously, did anyone else hear that?" Veronica asks. "Or am I experiencing delusions? I mean, I knew it was going to happen at some point, but I didn't think it would happen tonight. Do I look crazy to you?"

She looks over at Nazareth, and he nods in agreement. Veronica bobs her head as if the answer was a gimme, and then drinks from a can of beer.

"I don't know what happened." Jesse checks the time on his cell, and his mood lightens as he looks at me with the most adorable expression. Sort of like a cuddly puppy. "You're early."

"Yeah." Poetic, I know, but with so many eyes on me, I'll admit to being self-conscious.

Leo opens a cooler, reaches in and tosses a can of beer to Nazareth, who plants it in the dirt next to another unopened can. Leo then tosses one to Jesse, who catches it with one hand.

"Want one, Scarlett?" Leo asks with a friendly grin.

I twine and untwine my fingers. I'm not a drinker. It's not like I've had much of an opportunity to decide if it's for me, but now is a bizarre time to experiment. "No, thank you."

"Who's polite at a bonfire?" Veronica asks everyone and no one.

"The better question is, who's polite around us?" Leo pops open his can of beer.

"Maybe we should try manners," Veronica says, and then her face brightens as if she has the best idea ever. "We should talk in English accents. Doesn't that mean we have manners?"

"Have you had your rabies shots, V?" Leo asks. "Because I'm worried about your brain. Connecting those two thoughts together is weird. Even for you."

She sticks her tongue out at him and then the two of them lapse into a fit of giggles. They then push on each other as if they're five-year-old siblings. This entire situation is strange.

Nazareth strums chords on the guitar, and Veronica announces, "Sing-along!"

Leo groans as he dramatically flops to the ground like a fish.

"What d'you think?" Jesse tilts his head toward his friends. "Want to sit?"

"Okay."

Jesse surprises me when he takes my hand, loosely linking his fingers with mine, and guides me over to where he was sitting. The grass is cool, the weather cooler, and I'm grateful when Jesse sits close to me because the sweater I have on isn't enough to keep out the chill. There's a bit of a letdown when he releases my hand, but I take comfort in how his shoulder brushes against mine.

Above us are a million stars, and beyond the scent of the smoldering wood and smoke, I taste the night air. Hundreds of memories of my childhood flood my mind—of laughter, of being free with Jesse.

Nazareth starts a new song, and this time Jesse sings along. Not to all the parts, just certain lyrics, and I can't help but smile that he gets half of those wrong. They harass him for it, he harasses them back, but the teasing is good-natured and fun.

Jesse has a smooth voice, can hit some notes, but not others. But he doesn't care that he's not perfect. Doesn't care he's not precisely right. He sings, loudly when the song is fun, a bit softer when the lyrics are serious. I envy him because while I'll tap my foot along to the beat, while I'll laugh along with them, I don't sing, which is a shame.

I want to. If it counts, I sing in my head, but there's a lost connection between my heart and my mouth.

At a faster song, Leo pulls Veronica up to dance, and he has an easy way of moving his body around hers. He teases her through most of the dance, cracking jokes, and Veronica laughs, so much that I smile just from the pure joy of watching someone else being happy. The song changes, he draws her close, she rests her head on his shoulder, and for a moment, there's a pang of jealousy. I want to feel as peaceful in that brief second as she does.

Leo places his hand on her back, but she jerks then pushes him away. She laughs, but it's forced. She sits, so does he, neither of them acknowledging that brief moment, and that makes me sad.

The songs become mellow, the joining in less frequent. Finally, Nazareth plays a song that is slow, that is sorrowful, and he's the only one who sings. He has a melodic voice, a deep voice. Somehow the beauty is found in the pain of the words. I stare at him, enamored. How is it that every word, every note describes me so well when he's a stranger to me and I'm a stranger to him?

Jesse watches the fire and finishes his beer. The twinkle in his eye has been replaced with a bleary-eyed look that causes me to place my hand over his. Jesse threads our fingers together, and my body aches with his gentle squeeze. I don't know what's broken him tonight or maybe Jesse is like me, hurting all the time, and puts on a show for the world.

"You're cold," Jesse says.

I am. The fire's dying, and the temperature has dropped as the stars have moved. We've been out here for an hour, maybe two, but I'm not ready to go home. "I'm okay."

"Come on." Jesse stands and pulls me up with him. "I'll get you a hoodie."

He keeps my hand as we walk past his friends. Both Leo and Nazareth reach up and offer Jesse their fists for a bump as he passes. They tell him that they'll take care of the fire. Jesse tells them we'll be coming back.

When we leave the circle of light created by the fire, Jesse slips an arm around my shoulder. He draws me into the shelter of his body, and I greedily inhale his rich, dark scent. His touch is warm, it's strong and makes me feel as if I belong.

The sliding back door isn't locked and we go in. Jesse releases me and flicks on the kitchen light. I freeze in the middle of the room, lost in a snow globe of a memory. It's been years since I've been here, years since Jesse's grandmother gave me hot oatmeal cookies with a glass of milk, and the sadness of her passing causes my heart to sink.

What's it like for Jesse to walk in here every day knowing she's gone? "I'm sorry."

Jesse's eyes are red and heavy. "For what?"

"Anything. Everything."

He takes off his cap, tosses it onto the kitchen table and runs his fingers through his red hair, causing it to stick up in multiple directions. "I know I promised you that I'd take you some place special, but I swear I'll take you on another night. I'm afraid I'll pass out between here and there, and that would suck for us both."

"Because you're buzzed?" I tease.

He releases a glorious smile. "Because I'm drunk."

At least he's honest. "So this is you drunk?"

His smile fades. "I guess so. It's been a weird day, and that's left me messed up in the head, sort of like I've been hit by the right hook of a heavyweight belt winner."

"Are you okay?" I ask.

Jesse closes his eyes then rubs his hand over his face. The answer is no, and I'm mad at myself because I don't know how to make him better. I turn away, hoping doing so will give me a revelation of what to do, and I'm surprised to find on the fridge a picture of Jesse and me.

"Gran never forgave me for when I stopped being your friend," Jesse says. "I think that's why she picked you for the vote. Her way of forcing me to stop being a jackass."

My lips lift up briefly, but then fall. "I miss her."

He releases a long breath. "I do, too. Can I show you something?"

"Sure."

He goes down the hall, I follow and when he reaches Suzanne's room, he pauses. One of his hands is on the knob, and the other is on the closed door. I reach out and touch his arm. "Are you sure you're okay?"

"No," he says, but opens the door anyway. He walks in, and several beats pass before he turns on the light. Suzanne's room is like I remember, down to the crocheted blanket on the bed.

"I haven't been in here since she died." Jesse's voice isn't quite his own. Before I can say anything, he moves through the room, opens the drawer of her bedside table and takes out a book. He tosses it to me and then moves to the record player in the corner. "That's yours."

The old, worn book is heavy in my hand and the title steals my breath: *Peter and Wendy*. "Jesse, I can't. You said Suzanne used to read this to you."

"She did." Jesse slips a record out of an album sleeve, places it on the record player then delicately drops the needle onto the vinyl. There's a crackling sound coming from the speakers and then there's a guitar being strummed. The song is rough yet has a smooth country twang, and it's a sad song about blue eyes crying and rain.

Jesse turns up the speakers and walks out of the room, ignoring me as I try to return the book to him.

"She read me that book because of you. I know she'd want you to have it, and if that's not enough for you, then *I* want you to have it. You're southern-mannered enough to not turn your nose up at a gift."

He's right, I am, and I press the book to my chest, wishing it were Suzanne I was hugging.

Another click of a light and Jesse walks into the room he and his mother used to share. I lean my shoulder against the door-frame. Jesse stands in the middle of the room, seemingly un-aware I'm there, and he strips off his shirt. He's gorgeous. A pure waterfall of muscle, and his jeans ride low enough that I'm inca-pable of coherent thought. My mouth immediately dries out, and I'm flustered. I should move. I should stay. I should definitely stop staring.

Jesse looks up, spots me, and his lips move into a pirate smile. "That's a beautiful blush spreading across your face."

I overly roll my eyes. "You're half naked, and I thought you were getting me a hoodie."

"True, but I had meant to change my shirt earlier then got dis-tracted. V has a way of plowing in and taking over." He roots through a drawer, not finding what he's searching for.

I survey the room, and it's exactly how I remember except the bed his mother used to sleep in is missing. We didn't hang much in here, only when it was raining so hard Suzanne refused to let us out for fear of flash flooding. Otherwise, the outdoors was too appealing.

The walls are still covered with a wallpaper of maps. State maps, county maps, national maps. Maps of foreign countries, maps of highway systems, maps of mountain ranges. I step into the room and brush my fingers along my name in second-grade print alongside Jesse's on the map of California. Putting our toes in the Pacific Ocean—that was our dream.

"I can't believe you still have these," I say.

Jesse looks over at our names on the wall then at the other maps overlapping each other. "When Mom was crashing here, she used to sit with me in the dark and point a flashlight at each map and tell me the places she wanted to visit. She knew every town, every route and every sight to be seen along the way."

"She visited them?" It's odd. I know only a little about his mom, and even less about her death.

"Not a one. Mom left the state once, and doing that killed her. It nearly killed me, too."

Jesse turns his back, and I suck in an audible breath. There's a scar running along Jesse's right shoulder blade. It's not long, and if I weren't this close, I probably wouldn't have seen it, but the scar is thick, it's rigid and it causes a chill along my spine. "What happened to you?"

"Don't guess you've seen that before, huh?"

"No." My voice is a combination of a whisper and a croak.

"That happened a few weeks before I cut you out." Looking dead on his feet, Jesse drops onto his bed. He appears so emotionally and physically drained, like he could sleep for years.

"Do you want me to go?" I ask.

"No, but I understand if you do."

I don't want to go so that means I need to do something. Steeling myself against the nerves tickling my stomach, I weigh the pros and cons of standing in front of Jesse or sitting on his bed. I choose his bed because my own fatigue is catching up. I don't sit as if I own the place. Instead, I'm perched on the edge of the bed, a few inches away from him, and my heart beats so hard I can scarcely breathe.

"How did you get the scar?" I ask.

"My dad hit me with a chair."

My stomach surges to my throat. "Your dad hit you? I . . ." My forehead wrinkles. "I didn't even know you saw your dad."

"I didn't, not much. I'd see him for a weekend here and there. Maybe once a year. It turns out Mom had been seeing him on and off between the guys she was dating. Part of their sleeping arrangement was for her to leave the kid with Gran. Not sure if you know, but I'm a downer."

He tries to smile at his joke, but he fails, and I reach out and place my hand over his. He laces his fingers with mine and nudges me closer. I give in to the gravitational pull and rest my head on his shoulder. "I'm sorry."

"Don't be," he says. "It's not your fault."

"I know, but it sucks all the same."

Jesse's mom was an in-and-out type of parent. She'd leave a guy, show up here at Suzanne's with Jesse in tow, find a new guy, leave Jesse with Suzanne, then come and get Jesse to live with her. Jesse would never be gone longer than two weeks. As a child, I never thought to ask what was going on. I was happy my best friend was home.

"Your dad hit you?" I whisper-ask, and I hate how I hurt for him, yet at the same time I have this strange hope that there's someone else who could possibly understand my life.

"Once."

I lift my head. "Once?"

He raises one eyebrow. "Isn't once enough?"

Blood drains from my body, leaving me dizzy, and Jesse's eyes flicker over my face. "What's wrong?"

I shudder from the ice overtaking me. "I'm just tired."

Jesse lifts his hand and tucks my hair behind my ear. His hot fingers graze my cheek and my skin tingles with his touch. "Someday, you're going to trust me enough to let me in."

I'm terrified to trust, yet I'm terrified not to. I'm terrified Jesse's going to touch me again in the same way, that causes every cell to spark to life, and I'm even more terrified I'm never going to feel his hands on my body again.

"Do you want me to walk you home?" he asks.

"Do you want me to go home?"

"Scarlett, there are two times that I can breathe in deeply without wincing in pain, and being with you is one of them. If I could, I'd keep you here forever."

Jesse stares at my lips, and his attention there causes me to lick them. His eyes darken and butterfly wings flap wildly in my chest.

"You're saying things that don't make sense."

The rebellious spark to him returns. "You know you're beautiful, right?"

Heat floods my cheeks, and Jesse brushes his fingers along my face again. They linger along the skin of my neck, causing pleasing goose bumps to form.

"You're definitely drunk," I whisper.

He lightly chuckles and tugs on my hand, which he still holds. Jesse slips up his bed, tempting me to go along with him. "Lay with me, Scarlett."

Just when my cheeks couldn't get much hotter, they do.

"I swear on my land that laying with you is all I want." His green eyes soften, and I melt. "For a few minutes, I want to feel okay, and when I touch you, it's the closest I am to being whole. If you don't feel the same, I promise I'll back off."

Warmth at the idea of lying next to him, of touching him and of him touching me. "If I lay with you, then what does that make us? I don't think friends do this."

"Do you want to lay with me?" he asks.

I nod, not trusting myself to speak.

"Do you need us to stay only friends?"

I glance down because . . . "I don't know."

"How about you lay with me tonight, and then we'll go back to friends tomorrow."

"Okay." That I can do. At least, it's what I think I can do. I scoot up the bed, and as Jesse rests his head on his pillow, I allow myself to place my head on his chest. My arm goes across his stomach as he wraps me tight to him.

Every nerve ending is on fire, so aware of his hands on my body, so aware of his legs brushing against mine. Jesse nuzzles his nose into my hair, and when his breath caresses my neck, my skin becomes insanely sensitive.

A part of me wants so badly to lift my head and allow him the opportunity to kiss me, to allow myself the opportunity to kiss him in return, but I can't. I'm too afraid.

Jesse rubs his hand along my back, slowly, methodically, and I hold on tighter to him, wishing I never had to let go.

JESSE

J esse." The voice sounds far away, in a tunnel, but it's urgent. My sleep was heavy, deep, and every inhale was of honeysuckle—of Scarlett. I don't want to wake up, but there's a warning siren screaming at me to wake up.

"Jesse." The voice again. "It's four in the morning. Scarlett should go."

My eyes snap open, and I glance at the beauty sound asleep in my arms. Scarlett's completely out, peaceful, and I hate that I had fallen asleep and missed seeing her like this.

I rub my eyes and look over at the form standing in my doorway. It's V, giving us space by not walking in, but she wouldn't be waking me if she wasn't concerned.

"There are lights on in her house. I may not have a normal family, but I watch enough TV to know that lights on in a fancy house and a girl who snuck out a few hours ago is bad."

Crap. "Give me a sec."

V leaves, and I shift so I can touch Scarlett's face. "Scarlett."

She stirs, but she doesn't wake. I run my hand through her hair and try again. "Tink."

Her eyelids flutter open, and the edges of her lips tug up. "I was dreaming of you."

Best words I've ever heard, but . . . "You need to go home."

Realization strikes her like a lightning bolt, and she jumps out of bed. "What time is it?"

"Four. V came in because she said there are lights on in your house."

"Four?" She starts to shake. "Oh my God. What if they know? What am I going to do?"

"Don't panic. The lights on could be unrelated." I swing my legs off the bed and stand, ignoring how the room sways. I guess there's still some alcohol in my system. "I'll walk you home."

"N . . . no, please don't," Scarlett blurts out, and the fear on her face causes a rumble of concern. "I can get myself home."

"I've walked you home before."

"Yes, but what if Dad is up and he's waiting for me and he sees me with you and . . ." She trails off as I watch her, wishing I could somehow crawl into her brain and understand what's going on in her world.

If her dad is watching, he'll see her leaving here. Me being with her won't change that trouble is trouble, but I respect her and her decisions. I gently take Scarlett's hand because this is not how I want her to leave after laying with me in my bed. "It's okay. Someone probably forgot to turn off a light before going to bed. The light on doesn't mean anything."

"You promised we'd stay friends." Scarlett searches my eyes, and I hate how she's pulling away.

There's a sinking in my gut because I want more than friends, but I'll take her in any capacity I can get her. "Whatever you need."

"Then we're friends." And with that, she grabs the book and leaves.

SCARLETT

I'm hot, I'm cold and my brain can't process thought. My father is awake, and I'm not home. This is a real-life nightmare.

Leo is passed out on the couch in the living room, and Nazareth is in the recliner watching TV. It's weird how calm they are. How is that possible when my father is awake? Nazareth looks at me as I pass, nodding his head at me as if we're friends. I nod back like a robot and randomly wonder if somehow tonight made us friends.

I walk out the door, and Veronica follows.

Confused, I stop at the bottom of the trailer steps. "What are you doing?"

"Walking with you." She offers me an adorable and disarming grin, yet I'm still full of anxiety.

"Thank you," I say slowly because it's a sweet offer, but I really don't want the company. "But I can do this on my own."

"I'm sure you can, but me and you need to talk." And the kitten-grin is gone.

The light is on in my father's study. The room right by the tree. I shiver so hard my teeth chatter.

"Are you going to be able to sneak back in?" Veronica asks. It's nice how she sounds sympathetic to my plight.

"Yes." I don't have much of a choice. I start walking and she joins me.

"Did you find out what was wrong with Jesse?" she probes, and that catches my attention. And here I thought she and Jesse were the best of friends. I don't answer, and she continues, "Unlike all the rumors, he doesn't drink very often, and if he does drink, he doesn't do it to get drunk. I brought you here, the least you could do is tell me what's going on."

Jesse didn't open up to me either—at least not with why he is in pain. "Jesse's private."

"Yes, he is. If I asked you to stay away from him, would you?"

I glance over at her to see if she's serious. Unfortunately, she is. "No."

"If I threatened you?" It's strangely intimidating how she appears super cute as she flutters her eyelashes in a menacing way.

Being threatened by Veronica doesn't sound like anything fun I'd choose to partake in, but she fails in comparison to my father's wrath so I have a hard time fearing her. "No."

She glowers at the ground.

"Why don't you like me?" I ask.

"I never said I don't like you."

"You just asked me to stay away from Jesse."

"Yes, I did. That has nothing to do with like. Anyway, you don't like me."

I straighten my shirt. "I never said I don't like you."

"I forgot. We're best friends. You're the girl who sits in the cafeteria at lunch, and I'm the girl who doesn't. We have so much in common."

"You can sit with me at lunch if you want," I say.

That brings her up short, but then she brushes her hair away from her face and shrugs. "I don't think your friends would be okay with that."

My heart sinks because she's probably right.

"Don't take any of this personally," Veronica says. "Life is what it is, right?"

Unfortunately, yes.

"I think you should stay away from Jesse because he's going through a lot, and he doesn't need anyone else making him hurt. You're a wild card, and he doesn't need surprises."

I stop at the road and look her in the eye. "Why do you think I'll hurt Jesse?"

"You don't know, do you?"

"Know what?"

"He calls you Tink and that book you're holding is *Peter Pan*."

I have no idea what that has to do with anything.

"Then to put it in those terms, if you're Tink, and he's Peter Pan, then Nazareth, Leo and I are the Lost Boys. What do those characters have in common?"

Not a clue. "What?"

"They felt abandoned at home, not wanted, that is until Peter Pan took them in and gave them a place to belong. Jesse is the ultimate Island of Misfit Toys. As in 'all who enter here have been damaged.' Even though you live in that big fancy house, I don't believe you're immune to broken. If you found your way here, then something or someone along the way has shattered you and that scares me.

"All of us are cracked, but Jesse takes *damaged* to another level. He doesn't need whatever is wrong with you destroying whatever parts of him are still intact. You won't mean to hurt him, but you might and I'm not okay with that. Jesse is my family, and it's clear you're more than a friend to him. Those types of feelings are dangerous. Especially when you're both broken."

"I'm not broken," I say, the defiance clear in my voice. I'm empty. I hurt. There's a difference, and someday, once I leave, I'm going to be okay.

"It's all right," she says, and holds out her hands, palms up. "My broken can't be fixed either so you're not alone in this. Broken doesn't mean death. Well . . . at least for you."

I've been reading the books Glory gave me, and the lines on her palm are hard to ignore. From the faint porch light from Jesse's trailer, her health line is visible—very visible. Very deep. Healthy people aren't supposed to have health lines, at least not one like hers. My stomach sinks in sympathy. But the psychic stuff isn't real, right? "Are you sick?"

The answer is plain on her face—*yes.* "Haven't you heard? I have the Black Death."

Ha. Very funny.

"You made Jesse happy today so thanks for that. And for the record, it's not that I don't like you, it's just that I like Jesse more. Anyway, I hope you don't get caught."

Caught. The word vibrates through my body. She steps back, an indication our conversation is done, and I walk toward my house, toward the light in my father's office. At the tree, I tuck *Peter and Wendy* into my jeans, at the small of my back, for safe keeping. The climb up the tree is long; each slight sound I make causes my heart to stutter.

I hold my breath as I slip through the window into my dark room. My pulse beats in my ears as my eyes adjust, and I quickly glance about to make sure Dad's not in my room. Some shadow of a monster waiting in the dark to jump out at me in anger.

I peel off my clothes that smell of Jesse, put on my PJs and lie in bed. I should feel relief that I'm safe, but instead I'm confused and I'm empty. Does that mean Veronica is right and I'm broken? If I am broken, am I so broken that I can't be repaired?

There's footsteps on the stairs, down the hall, and they stop outside my room. Fear paralyzes me as the knob turns, and the hinges squeak. Dad opens my door, and I force myself to look at him. If he's going to come in screaming then I want to see him coming.

"I'm sorry," he says. "I didn't mean to wake you. I thought I heard something and wanted to check in on you."

"I heard something, too, outside, but it went away," I say. "Why are you awake?"

"I couldn't sleep so I decided to get some work done. Squirrels are probably getting into the attic. That tree is close to the house and gives them access. I should probably cut it down."

"I like the tree."

"Your mom does, too. Go back to sleep, and I'll see you in the morning."

"Okay," I say, grateful that I wasn't busted. "Good night."

Dad doesn't leave like I expect. Instead he stands there like a statue. "I know you don't believe me, but I promise you, I'm trying to change."

I'm not sure what the proper response to this should be so I go for safe. "Okay."

"Do you know that's that longest conversation we've had without an argument in weeks?"

"Yeah."

"Okay then, just . . . have a good sleep." And he shuts the door, but I don't hear footsteps. He hasn't left, and I don't close my eyes.

JESSE

Lying in bed, I wish the room would stop spinning. The constant rotation makes it tough to pay attention to the sound of the front door. I heard V leave with Scarlett. I don't know if that's good or bad, and I want to talk to her before crashing again.

V should be back by now. I become edgy, muscles locking. Maybe there were problems. Maybe V already returned and I didn't hear. Maybe V left. Maybe V's standing on the front steps because she can't come in since no one gave her permission.

I take a deep breath, preparing to force myself to my feet, and the front door shuts. Footsteps down the hallway and I open my eyes to catch V entering my room. She plops at the end of my bed, pushing my feet out of the way so she can lean her back against the wall.

"How'd you get in?" I ask.

"Nazareth gave me permission to enter."

"Why do you do that?"

"Why do you have maps on your walls?"

I'm silent because I'm not going to answer.

"I refuse to walk into a house without permission. You have a hundred maps on your wall. You have your weird and I have mine. Though I'll give you that I have a lot more weird than you."

Touché. "Scarlett okay?"

"She's home, and the light in her bedroom never came on. I'm assuming that's good."

Only way to know for sure is when I see her again. "Thanks, V."

"How's the start of that hangover?"

"Fantastic." My head is already starting to pound like a bass drum.

"It's not like you can actually hold your alcohol." She fingers one of her bouncy, blond curls. "What happened today? And please don't say *nothing*. You don't drink to get drunk and that was your goal tonight."

I wish she'd back off. "I thought we were going to ignore my problems."

"I only said that because other people's grief makes me uncomfortable. Anyhow, maybe I'm evolving as a person and I'm trying to be more attuned to my feelings. That's what adults do, right?"

"That's the theory."

"Does Scarlett know what's going on with your land?" V asks.

"Yes."

"Does she know what your maps mean?"

Because V is one of my best friends, I give her the truth. "Yes."

"Does she know what caused the scar on your back?"

"Yes."

"Does she know why you were upset tonight?"

"No." And because I'm not the only one who had drama going on tonight, I throw the ball back in her court. "Does Leo know you have feelings for him?"

She stares at her hands in her lap. "I don't have feelings for him."

"I saw the look on your face when you placed your head on his shoulder."

"I don't have feelings for him."

"V—"

"It doesn't matter because he doesn't see me."

My forehead furrows. "He sees you all the time."

"*Me.*" She slams her hands against the bed. "He sees V, not me—Veronica, and on bad days, he sees my illness, but he never sees me. I'm more than V, and I'm more than my illness. Leo only sees Leo, and he only sees what's fun and what's blocking his path to fun."

I stare at her, not blinking, wondering if that's how she feels about all of us. "I think you should give Leo more credit than that."

"I've decided I don't like you drunk. You talk too much. I've also decided that becoming attuned to feelings is overrated."

I open my mouth to argue, but she cuts me off. "It doesn't matter what you say because it's not going to change my mind. I'm dying, Jesse, so none of it matters."

I hate it when she talks that way. Hate it because she has more life in front of her than she thinks. I hate it more because she could be right. The thought causes sadness, and I have to rub my eyes to fight off the way they burn.

"Are you in love with her?" V asks in a quiet voice.

"I think I was born in love with her, but that doesn't mean she wants me to do anything about it. Doesn't mean that I should do anything either."

V falls silent and the two of us stare at the other. It's not uncomfortable. Just two old friends in the same spot we always are—no idea what tomorrow will bring.

"She's lucky to have someone like you in love with her," V says.

I close my eyes and settle into the pillow. "No, she's not. Anything I love is cursed."

SCARLETT

"You look tired." It's a Friday, and Jesse Lachlin lazily leans against the locker next to mine. I glance at him out of the corner of my eye. Doesn't he know it's too early to be social? The first bell hasn't even rung.

"Is that a nice way of saying I look like crap?" I ask.

He chuckles. "You always look good, Scarlett."

The compliment is nice but untrue. I should be wearing a paper bag over my head with cut-outs for my eyes. I haven't slept well this week. One, after three weeks of Mom and Dad getting along, this week has brought on very serious, unknown-to-me discussions between them at night. A few times their voices raised and that was enough to make me sick to my stomach. It's baffling because I've been on my best behavior, yet they still find a way to fight.

The second reason is because I'm freaking myself out at night. I've been reading Glory's books, and that is a tragic mistake. I see forms in the shadows now—my mind tricking me that there are ghosts from another realm in my room.

When I visited Glory a few days ago, I told her that her books were scaring me. She told me that it wasn't a trick, but me opening myself to the awareness of the spiritual world, that I was awakening my psychic senses.

I need my head examined.

"You haven't signaled for me yet," Jesse says, as if he's asking if

I did my math homework. "I still need to show you that special place on my land."

I continue moving the dial on my lock one way then another and with a click, it opens. It's been three weeks since I snuck out to see Jesse and laid with him in his bed. It's not that I haven't wanted to take Jesse up on his offer, it's just . . . "Things are busy."

Between schoolwork, my mom staring at me twenty-four/seven because she's *so* disappointed that I lied about the job, trying to sneak in working for Glory at night so my parents don't find out I'm lying to them again and sleep, there's not a lot of time.

"Is that the only reason?" he asks.

I stop rummaging through my locker and study him. He's not watching me, but instead observing the people coming and going along the narrow hallway. Most girls turn their heads in his direction, and I understand why. He's in faded blue jeans that fit him perfectly, his solid-blue T-shirt is stretched taut across the muscles of his chest and the red stubble on his face makes him look more like a rugged man on a magazine cover than a high school boy.

Jesse Lachlin has this sexy presence that's impossible to ignore, and the more time I spend with him, I find myself thinking way too much of our unspoken night in his bed. Of how our bodies were twined tight, the tickle of his hot breath on my neck and how I'd like him to touch me again.

"Are you testing me?" Jesse looks over at me, and while he keeps the lazy, relaxed posture, there's a flash of hurt in his green eyes that causes me to ache. Because I have never liked seeing Jesse in pain and because I *am* testing him.

Testing him sucks, but I'm scared. I don't know why I'm scared and that makes me angry . . . and then that ticks me off more. Aggravated with myself, I shove two of my books into my backpack harder than needed, causing three of my folders to fall to the ground. I sigh heavily, and Jesse crouches and picks up my scattered papers before I have a chance to dip for them myself.

His eyes flicker along the page. "You're right. You've been busy."

On the sheet is math—not Calculus or Trig or even Algebra

Two. It's real-life math. It's estimates of how much I'll make working for Glory if I continue at my current rate, and comparing that to estimates for renting an apartment versus living in a dorm at the University of Kentucky. It's me trying to figure out my path to freedom.

"Where are these apartments that you're looking at?" he asks.

"Somewhere close to UK." Close, but not super-near. More important, they're cheaper than the dorms.

"Are you familiar with the areas these apartments are at?" he asks.

"No, but you should see the pictures. The places look great."

Jesse hands the papers to me. When I take them from him, his finger slips against mine. My heart pounds against my chest, and I lose the ability to make eye contact. I pathetically mumble some sort of thank-you and then my heart stutters again when he offers me a half-devilish grin in response.

I wish I weren't such an awkward mess. I wish his touch would have lasted longer. I really wish the blush on my cheeks would disappear.

I shove the folders back in, shut my locker and head to class before anything else embarrassing has a chance to happen. Jesse is there beside me, loping along as if he doesn't have a care in the world. Since the night in his bed, he does this now—finds me at my locker in the morning then walks me to class. Sometimes we talk. Sometimes we don't. I find his presence strangely exhilarating, as if I were willingly holding on to a live wire.

Besides the morning routine, he hangs with his friends, I hang with my friends and the world returns to its normal social axis of him on one side and me on the other. Except I catch him watching me, openly, and he doesn't turn away when caught. I notice this because I'm watching him, too.

"What if I told you those apartments probably aren't what you think they are?"

I roll my eyes. "What makes you say that?"

"Living on your own is tough. It can get financially hairy quick."

"Do you know everything?" I ask. "Or are there some elements on the periodic table you haven't memorized yet?"

"Barium is BA and its atomic number is fifty-six. All I'm saying is that you might need to lower your expectations of what you're getting into by living on your own. Have you thought about applying for financial aid?"

"Have *you* thought about applying for financial aid?"

"Nope, and you never answered before," he says. "About if you're testing me."

Because I don't want to answer. "What does that question have to do with barium or apartments? And why do you think I'm testing you?"

"When will you answer a direct question?"

"I answer plenty of questions."

"You evade or you answer a question with a question. Neither are real answers."

I scowl, and he smirks. Why must smug look so adorable on him?

With a deep breath, I force out a better and truer response. "I'm sorry." *For the test.* "I don't mean to be so messed up." And I think of what Veronica said about being broken.

"I don't think any of us mean to be messed up, but messed up happens regardless."

Neither of us speaks for a span of a section of lockers because that is so real and raw.

"Will the test be much longer?" he asks.

I give him my most honest answer. "I hope not."

"Me, too."

At the water fountain, Jesse's friends watch as we go by. Leo waggles his eyebrows at us while grinning, Nazareth watches with impassive interest and Veronica barely looks up from behind a piece of paper she's cutting into a snowflake.

It's fall, the leaves are a beautiful array of colors and there are dozens of snowflakes on her locker. She's dressed in a red plaid, pleated skirt, an off-the-shoulder low-cut blue shirt, and a scarf and matching toboggan hat when today will be a high of eighty. Last week, she celebrated Thanksgiving and it's only September. Veronica is definitely different.

"I can't tell if your friends like me," I say.

"You're an unknown to them," he replies. "Give them time and V will be putting snowflakes on your locker, too. If you aren't careful, you'll be her friend in time to celebrate Easter, which will probably be next week. As a warning, she doesn't hard-boil her eggs and she likes us to throw them."

"Awesome." I think.

"On the other hand, your friends hate me."

This is a very true story. The Jesse Lachlin bashing has reached near-epidemic status at our lunch table, and Camila is the one leading the charge.

"Does it bother you," I ask. "That my friends don't like you?"

"No."

Crystal clear and simple. I wish I were more like that, instead of muddy and complex.

"Does it bother you about my friends?" he asks.

"Everything bothers me." I pause at the corner, where we go our separate ways for the day, and he raises an eyebrow. I typically keep walking, and because I'm impaired, I also typically don't say goodbye.

Jesse waits for whatever it is that I have to offer him, and the words are stuck. I need to go to Glory's this weekend for work, and I don't want to go by myself as odds are I'll get lost once night falls. Glory told me she'd give me a bonus if I can pass her "test" on palm reading, but in order to pass, I need to read someone's palm, and considering my friends are in the dark about my extracurricular activities, Jesse is the best choice.

I need his help, but I don't know how to ask him and I don't know how to explain that I hate asking anyone for help. Asking makes me weak, makes me think of Dad pushing me to depend on him, and my mouth turns down because I don't want to be me for at least five seconds.

"Do . . . do you ever wish you were somebody else?" My words come out in a rushed cluster, and I'm not sure they make sense.

His green eyes soften as he looks at me as if I'm the only person in the world. As if there aren't hundreds of people pushing past in their quest for the next destination. As if there aren't loud voices demanding that we pay attention to them and not to what's going on between us. He takes a step toward me, so close that the heat of his body wraps me in an embrace. My breath catches as my blood tingles.

"I used to feel that way," he says. "About wanting to be somebody else."

I inhale his sweet, dark scent and I become a bit light-headed from his presence. "How did you make it stop?" Because I so desperately need answers to fill the hole in my soul.

"I spend time with you, and because you let me, I held you in my bed. Why would I want to be anyone else when I get to be the guy who holds you?"

The warning bell rings and my pulse beats erratically. Then, as if he didn't blow my mind, Jesse walks away.

I jump at the stack of books slammed onto the circulation desk. Camila's glare is red-hot. I finish scanning in the book that was in my hand before I was so rudely interrupted, place it on the cart of books that need to be shelved, then offer Camila my full attention.

"What are you doing?" Camila asks.

"I'm scanning books."

Evangeline nervously watches us from the other side of the library. I inwardly roll my eyes because I should have seen this coming. The two of them have been whispering to each other nonstop since the first time Jesse stopped by my locker. Not that them being in each other's ears is unusual, but typically they wouldn't be staring at me so much while conversing.

"What are you doing with Jesse Lachlin?" she rephrases.

"Nothing."

"He has been at your locker every day for the past month and walks with you in the hallway. And you two *talk*."

I have to fight the urge to laugh because the utter disbelief and shock that I would *talk* to Jesse Lachlin is a bit hilarious. "Would it be better if I didn't talk to him?"

"Yes."

My brief bit of levity fades, and I sit on the stool beside me. "That would be rude."

"That would be lifesaving."

"That is overdramatic." I pick up the scanner to start my work again.

"No, it's not."

My response is the *beep* of the book being swept back into the system.

Camila reaches over and snatches the scanner from me. This time, she isn't red-hot, but full of concern. Camila is overdramatic, but she rarely gets this emotional. "He hurt you, and if you become friends with him again, or worse, if you date him, he's going to hurt you again."

A fast debate in my head of how to answer any of this without tipping my hand. If I say the wrong thing, it could open a floodgate of questions I can't answer.

I rest the book in my hand on the counter and look Camila straight in the eye. "The night of the readings, Glory couldn't take me home so Jesse did. We talked, and he's simply been stopping by my locker to talk some more. That's it." It's a lie, but the truth will set her off.

She squishes her face in disagreement. "But talking is a gateway drug. Talking leads to more talking, and more talking leads to hanging out, and the next thing I know you'll be smoking pot with Veronica, tattooed like Nazareth, and having a baby with Jesse Lachlin and living in his trailer. Soon after that you'll die because of the Lachlin curse. Is that what you want, Scarlett? To be dead by twenty leaving Jesse behind to raise your infant triplets in his broken-down trailer?"

"Now that is definitely overdramatic."

"Is it?" She's dead serious. "Besides the fact the curse is real, you are who you hang out with. I know I'm not the friend I could be, but my way of being a friend doesn't include destroying you. He's going to hurt you again. I'm the one who held your hand when no one else would. Don't be stupid and make the same mistake again. You can't trust him."

Bluntly honest. That's Camila. She's speaking her mind, and it's not her fault there is menacing truth to her words.

"I know I'm not easy to be friends with," Camila says in a low voice, a soft voice, one full of regret and sadness. One I've never heard from Camila before, "but you stick by me when not many people do. I care for you, and I don't want to see him hurt you again."

"This isn't a big deal," I say. "We're just talk—"

"You have a date tomorrow with Stewart Mitchell." Camila drops the gauntlet.

"What?"

"The only thing we can come up with as to why you're talking with Jesse is that you're finally considering going on a date so instead of giving the opportunity to some guy who won't appreciate you, we found someone who will."

"What do you mean by *we*? And what do you mean by *date*? And Stewart Mitchell?"

Camila laughs like I told a joke and that must be the sign Evangeline was waiting for, as she joins us at the counter. "Isn't it exciting?"

Um . . . no. But I don't say that. My head tilts because I have no idea what just happened.

Camila rounds the desk. "The whole lunch table is in on this. First dinner, then a movie, then dessert. Fifteen of us will be going. It is going to be the most epic first date on the planet."

"It's not a pity date," Evangeline adds, as if that was a worry. "Stewart has been working up the nerve to ask you out all summer, but none of us thought you were ready so we told him to enter at his own risk, but now that you've been talking to Jesse, we know you're ready."

How any of that makes sense, I have no idea. "I don't want to date Jesse," I say slowly, but a small part of my brain dissents. "I'm just talking to him."

"*Just talking* is code for flirting." Camila playfully pats my hand. "Please, the only reason any girl at this school talks to Jesse is in the hopes of dating him."

"Or kissing him," Evangeline adds. "I'll be honest, I'd kiss him."

Camila takes my hand. "But we aren't going to waste Scarlett's first date, or first kiss, on some boy who is going to be voted most likely to end up in jail."

Mental whiplash. First date? And did she say . . . "First kiss?"

"You don't have to," Camila says, then frowns. "I'm not sure if Stewart will get the opportunity. Your parents are letting you go on a group date. But we can work out a system. Like blink three times and everyone will turn their back."

My head spins, and I grab the desk for support. "My parents are letting me go?"

Camila releases a blazing smile. "My mom called your mom. I know how protective your parents are, and I thought if my mom brought up the group date they would be on board."

I swear with the way my tongue is twisted, I'm having a seizure. "They said yes?"

"It took until last night for your parents to get back to my mom. They took forever to agree to it, and there are like a gazillion rules, but you can go! Aren't you excited?"

"I'm not okay with this," I say.

"Give it a few minutes," Camila waves off my concern, "then you'll be fine. Besides, it's all set so you have no choice but to go, which is the brilliant part of my plan because I know you better than you think. You'd be fine holing up in your room for the rest of your life pushing everyone away as long as people let you. So what that Jesse Lachlin hurt you years ago? The rest of the world isn't out to hurt you. He's cursed, and you're not. It's time to live, Scarlett."

My mouth pops open, but nothing comes out. Camila twirls her hair as she examines me. "I think she's in shock."

"It is shocking," Evangeline says. "You didn't work up to the date. You blurted it out."

"How does one work up to a surprise first date?"

"I don't know. Maybe you could have said that Stewart thinks Scarlett is pretty, then you work your way up to the surprise first date."

"That's boring, and time-consuming. My way worked fine. She has to know she has no choice." The bell rings, Camila loops her arm around mine, Evangeline gathers my things and I'm swooped off to lunch.

JESSE

I swing the ax and the wood splits. The chunks are small enough to stack, but I'm pissed so I swing the ax again, making the hunks of wood smaller. Besides a bonfire, there's no reason I need to cut wood. I don't have a fireplace, and I could have rented a wood shredder to get rid of this old tree that was downed by last night's storm. But since this afternoon I've been Godzilla tearing through Tokyo. I thought chopping the wood would help erase my anger or that I'd tire myself out. I've been home an hour from school and neither has transpired. Guess I am cursed.

"That looks like hard work," an unfamiliar voice calls out.

I pause mid-swing and glance over at the man intruding upon my land. A silent swear under my breath as I'm not in the mood for company, especially not someone I need to impress. I turn toward the thick trunk lying on the ground and whack the ax into it. I then pick my shirt off the ground and wipe my brow as I turn to welcome Pastor Hughes.

"It's not so bad," I say.

"You looked like a machine as I pulled up. I had a great-uncle who had a farm when I was younger. I remember chopping wood like you just did when I was angry at the world."

Not the world. Just a girl named Scarlett who's giving me heartburn. What sucks about school is even when you don't talk, you hear things, and I heard more about her and some other guy than I wanted. She's testing me, yet she'll go out with him. My fingers twitch with the need to pick up the ax again.

"The storm was rough last night," he says.

"Several trees are down, and I need to cut them up." The storm wasn't bad enough for so many of the trees to have toppled, which means the ones that fell were probably diseased. I have no idea what that means for the rest of my trees or if this could affect future crops. So far a Google search has been more of a labyrinth than helpful. This is one of those rare moments when I wish I had a mentor or some help.

"What brings you out?" I ask.

"You." His eyes flicker over me, and I have no doubt he noticed the scar on my back. "I promised your grandmother I'd check in on you from time to time."

Thanks, Gran. "Consider me checked-in on."

Pastor Hughes doesn't remind me much of a man of God in his jeans and red short-sleeved shirt. More like a guy who's about to hit up fast food with his family on a Friday night. Guess I've watched too much TV to think these guys only wear black.

He offers me his hand, I accept, and the man has a firm grip and a friendly smile. The trailer's in sight, but he had a decent walk. Because Gran raised me to do southern hospitality with guests, I say, "Do you want to go back to the trailer? I can get you something to drink."

"Nah, it's a nice day, and I'll admit that I'd like to stay outside. I'm inside too much for my liking. But why don't you go ahead and get a drink. Looks like you could use it."

Fair enough. I grab a bottle of cold water from the cooler, down it fast, then set it on the ground. Near the weeping willow, Pastor Hughes scans the land as if in appreciation, and that makes me like him enough that I'm disarmed. At least enough to not tell him to leave.

"You have a beautiful piece of property," he says. "I can see why your grandmother liked it. I don't think I've ever seen anything so rich in my life."

"*Loved*," I correct him. "Gran loved this land." Like I do.

He nods his agreement and starts in on questions about my

well-being: Am I getting along okay alone in the house, how has school gone, what have I been working on with the property? They're questions meant to be deep, but allow me enough space to give surface answers. The type of answers, I'm sure, a busy man like him wants to hear.

Then he throws a curveball. "Have you considered applying for college?"

I pause for too long. "I'm not interested in college."

"Why?"

If I tell him the real reason, because I want to work the land full-time, it could backfire and he could vote against me keeping the land. He, and every other adult, seems to have this quest for higher education. "Not my thing."

"It could be."

I shrug.

"There's a big world out there." Pastor Hughes looks off to the horizon. "Aren't you curious what's out there? Your grandmother told me you really haven't left the state."

Memories of Mom come rushing back and the hurt mixing with my previous anger becomes a toxic mix. "Let's cut the crap. I know you're part of the tribunal."

I like that he has to pause to take in my words. "Did your uncle tell you?"

"No, and I know Scarlett Copeland is the other person. I told her the truth."

"Is your uncle aware of your knowledge on any of this?"

"That I know the full truth? No."

"Why are you telling me?"

"Because I'm getting played in a game I never wanted to participate in. Seems fair to swing the game back in my direction."

He's not mad like I expected with the bombshell. Instead, he relaxes and that doesn't sit well with me. Pastor Hughes places his thumbs in his back pockets. "How does telling me this swing the game, as you call it, in your direction?"

"Scarlett's already agreed to vote for me. As for telling you, I figured it would be better if you and I shot straight. I'd bet the western part of this land you know I've left the state twice in my life, and I'm betting you know why and what happened on both occasions."

He probably also knows how those occasions broke me in ways that makes fixing me impossible. If he does, he knows secrets I wish Gran would have allowed to live only with me.

"Your grandmother was hurting," he says. "She wasn't trying to betray you by talking to me. She was trying to find a way to let go of her grief before she passed."

I'm tempted to ask him if it worked, but don't. He'll lie the same way Glory does to the people who pay for her time. "I don't want to go to college, and I don't want to analyze the *why* with you. But I do want this land. Whatever it is you need me to do to win your vote, I'll do it. Losing this land isn't an option. I hope that's something you can understand."

Pastor Hughes nods like he hears everything I'm saying and not saying. Maybe some things I'm not even hearing myself. "There are many ways you could have tried to manipulate this situation, but you took the most direct method and that, I respect."

"Does that mean you're going to vote for me?" I ask.

"It means you have my ear."

It's not a vote, but it's a start.

"I'll tell you what," Pastor Hughes says. "I have an important decision to make regarding your future, and I take that responsibility seriously. So I have two requests for you."

"You mean rules?"

He chuckles. "I mean more of an agreement. You agree to meet with me every month or so, when it's convenient for you. We'll talk, have dinner if you'd like."

I can do that. "Sure."

"The second part is for you to have dinner with your uncle. At least a couple of times a month. It'll go a long way in earning my vote if you can fix your relationship with him."

"It takes two people to fix things." The words come out fast and bitter. "And he's not the saint you think he is."

"No one is above reproach. Not you, not me and not your uncle. You two share a complicated relationship. True colors will win out on this—for good or possibly bad."

The idea causes me to want to grind my teeth, but I stay still, as my reaction will be judged. I'm tired of being tested, but this is what my life is going to be for the next year—me constantly being held over the fire. "Fine."

Pastor Hughes holds out his hand to me again, I shake it and he says those nice things people do, "goodbye" and "see you later." He's four steps away when he glances back at me. "I didn't know you and Scarlett Copeland were friends."

Not liking the question, I yank the ax out of the trunk and use my foot to roll another, larger log to where I'm splitting the wood. "What makes you assume we are?"

"You mentioning that you have spoken to her."

"We know each other."

"Do you talk much to her father?" The question is casual but causes warning alarms.

I swing the ax and split the log in half with the first try. "Can't say that I do. Do you?"

"Not much. I'll leave my card in your mailbox. Call me when you want to meet up."

"Sounds good." I continue to split wood until his car disappears down the dirt road. Once he's long gone, I wedge the ax back into the log, and I sit beside it wondering what level of hell I've unleashed by talking to him about Scarlett.

My cell vibrates, and if it's Glory, I swear I'll take an ax to my phone. I switch gears quick when I spot Nazareth's name. The kid's not the type to text. *V's in bad pain. Migraine from hell, and she can barely move. My parents laced their stash and it's too strong. I'm scared of what she'll be taking in if she smokes it. Can you help?*

A war takes place in my brain. I need to stay straight and narrow in order to keep my land, but I have to help my friend. Me: *Might take me a few hours.*

Nazareth: *Leo is on the way. He doesn't want you to do it alone. I'll bring V by later.*

I sigh heavily, and my cell becomes a hundred-pound weight in my hands. Last time I did this to help V, I ended up in handcuffs. I was stupid, though. Didn't watch my back. Probably why Leo is going along for the ride. Nazareth's parents grow their own pot and if he's asking for me to buy, it means that any supply they have isn't stuff he's comfortable with V smoking.

Thanks or unthanks to Mom, I know people who deal and those people won't sell to strangers, only to people they know, which means I'm on the hook for the buy. I push buttons and send the text that's going to help V and hopefully not damn me.

SCARLETT

Help, my life has been hijacked! It's what I'd like to send in an emergency text, but the problem is that anyone I'd send the SOS to is involved in ruining my life. I'm in a fog in my mother's bathroom as she fusses over my hair and makeup. She's been talking nonstop since I arrived home from school. Meanwhile, I'm unable to speak, and no one seems to notice.

"You should be proud of your father." Mom uses the hot iron on a lock of my hair then uses her fingers to draw out the curl.

I try to avoid looking at her palm. Since reading Glory's books, I can't help but see things I don't want to know. Like how almost all the lines on Mom's hand are weak, broken and fragmented. None of which is a good sign.

"Your father didn't say no automatically like I thought he would. He listened to what I had to say, spoke with Camila's parents then Evangeline's parents, and even spoke to Stewart's parents. He's been calm and thoughtful. He wants you to have a good time, and to be happy."

Mom's gushing, and I'm sick to my stomach. "Why were you two arguing this week?"

"Your first date," Mom ignores me. "I can't believe my baby is going on her first date."

With a boy I didn't choose, on a date I never said yes to and that was orchestrated by my father. This is what every girl dreams of.

Mom tilts her head as she takes in my expression. "What's wrong? Are you scared? You don't have to be. You'll have plenty of friends with you to keep everything comfortable."

My eyes burn, and I blink rapidly to keep the tears away. "I don't want to go."

"That's absurd. Of course you want to go. It's normal to be nervous."

"It's not nerves. I should have chosen who my first date is with."

"You're being ungrateful. Besides, you have to go. You'd embarrass the poor boy if you don't. Is that what you'd want? To make him sad?"

No, it's not. Nor do I want to disappoint Camila and Evangeline. I don't want to disappoint anyone. But it's like I'm standing in the middle of a crowded cafeteria and I'm screaming and not a single person is listening. Why is no one asking me what *I* want? Why is no one concerned about *me* being sad?

A knock, and Dad stands in the doorway. He smiles at me like he loves me, and my throat swells as I turn away. God, I want to be loved. So badly that it's causing me pain.

"Our living room is full of teenagers, and one very nervous boy waiting for you," he says.

Mom beams at Dad. "She's ready."

No, I'm not, but Mom takes my hand and pulls me from the safety of my seat. As I pass Dad, he places an arm around me and kisses my temple.

"Scarlett," he says in such a sad tone that my stomach drops. I look up at him, and meet his anguished eyes. "Can't you see I'm trying? I love you, and I miss how we used to be."

Is he changing? Am I the monster by keeping away forgiveness?

Dad lets go of me when I step into the hallway. I glance down into the foyer, and my heart shatters into a thousand pieces. Standing at the base of the stairs is a boy who looks up at me with a radiant smile and hope.

I descend, and a cloud of doom hovers over me as I share hugs from friends who have an expectation of me I'll never be able to meet. Stewart and I exchange an awkward greeting. A side hug, and staged pictures, thanks to Mom.

The cloud becomes a thunderstorm when I walk out the front door. Jesse Lachlin exits his trailer and looks over at me. I should glance away, but I can't. I need him to understand. This isn't me. This isn't my choice.

He turns away as if I've slapped him, and my stomach sinks as if I had. Regret becomes a weight on my chest, and I suddenly wish that I hadn't been so stupid. I wish I had snuck out night after night to meet with Jesse. Even though he promised to be watching out for me at midnight for the rest of my life, I know I just lost my chance.

I claw at the neckline of my top. I can't breathe. I haven't been able to breathe all evening, but there was nothing I could do other than fake a front. But I'm home now, I'm behind the closed door of my bedroom, and I yank the blouse over my head and kick out of my skirt.

"Scarlett," Mom says. Another knock on my door, and I wipe at the moisture filling my eyes. "I was hoping we could talk. I've dreamed of this moment your whole life. I'll make cookies and tea. I want to hear every detail. He seemed like such a wonderful boy."

But I don't want to talk about how this guy was super-nice, did everything textbook perfect, and when he looked at me as if I was making his night, I felt awful because when I looked at him I felt nothing. I don't want to talk about how my friends had this expectation that I would like this boy. That I would want to hold his hand, and that I would have taken advantage of the moment they all moved from one side of the movie lobby to another to give us time alone.

I don't want to talk about how he went from talking nonstop to going silent, and I knew if I didn't start talking, if I didn't move an inch away, he would have leaned in and kissed me.

I don't want to talk about how he was understanding. That he didn't ignore what I did, but instead said he respected my boundaries and that he'd kiss me when I was ready. I don't want to talk about how I hate myself because I don't want to upset my friends and I don't want to hurt him. I hate myself because I wish I could feel. I wish I were normal. I wish I wasn't me.

Mom knocks on my door again. "Scarlett? Is everything okay?"

No. I open my closet and throw on a tank top and an old pair of jeans my dad told me to throw out. He didn't like they were so worn and had rips, but I didn't throw them away. An act of defiance I didn't understand at the time, but I do now.

"Scarlett," Mom says again.

I inhale, but that doesn't help the strain in my voice. "I'm okay, Mom. I want to go to bed. We'll talk in the morning."

Silence. It stretches for so long that my skin shrinks too tight for my bones.

"I love you," she finally says, and I cover my face with my hands because I don't want to cry. I'm so sick and tired of crying. "Good night, baby."

I drop my hands and catch sight of myself in the mirror. My hair is curled and pinned up into perfection. My makeup covers every flaw, and creates an image of a girl I don't recognize. I can't keep living like this. I can't keep being who everyone wants me to be or I'm going to die.

Headlights flash against the wall of my room, and Jesse pulls into his drive. It's ten-thirty. I could wait until midnight, flash my light three times and pray Jesse comes to me, but he's not a dog to be summoned and I can't stomach what would happen inside me if he didn't show.

Not caring if my parents come to check on me, I open the window and crawl out. I make a point of not looking down as I stealthily maneuver along the branches. Two car doors slam shut, which means Jesse has company, but I don't care. I need to see him. I need to figure out who I am.

JESSE

Standing outside my trailer, Leo checks the text on his phone. "Nazareth and V are down by the creek and have started a fire down there." That's on the other side of the farm, but closer to the road Nazareth uses to bring him and V home.

"He says she's hurting bad, but she keeps saying she's fine. He said she keeps holding her head and is close to doubled over. It sounds like this migraine is taking her down. I don't know why she thinks she has to front with us."

Probably for the same reason we all keep parts of ourselves private—even within our group that we trust. Self-protection can be a tough wall to break down, but it's there for a reason. I should know.

"Do you ever wonder how sick she really is?" Leo says. "I mean, we know it's bad, but if it's worse than bad?"

"Yeah." But then I think of how V says that the sickness is all Leo sees of her—that and the crazy side she has to make up for it.

Leo's head jerks up, and I follow his line of sight. A shadow sprints across the road, and a combination of hope and dread knots my gut. It's Scarlett, and I turn away from her and toward the direction of the creek.

If Leo and I move fast enough, maybe she'll take the hint and leave. I don't have it in me to contain my anger. Anger I don't have a right to. Anger I don't understand. Scarlett doesn't trust me to be friends, real friends, but she trusts that idiot from school to go on a date. The word *date* tastes so bad in my mouth I want to spit. I walk faster, and Leo scrambles to keep up.

"Let me get this straight." It takes everything I have not to punch Leo's wide smile off his face. "The girl you've been following around like a sad puppy is finally chasing after you and you won't stop to chat? That feels rude, and I think we should all pause for a moment to discuss your poor choices."

"I'm not in the mood for drama," I say.

"Funny, I find drama amusing, so we should stay."

"You're supposed to be my friend," I bite out and Leo's laughter grinds my bones.

"I've never seen you so worked up. This is going to be more fun than I could have imagined."

"Jesse!" Scarlett calls out. "Please, Jesse, wait!"

I drop my head and wonder why the hell everything has to be so hard. Scarlett goes from a run to a fast walk. As she approaches, I can hear her hurried breath.

"What do you want, Scarlett?" I demand, and my voice is as sharp as the razor blade that went through me when she walked out of her house on the arm of that moron from school.

She stops short of Leo and me, and thanks to the faint light of the moon, I can make out her wide, wild eyes. Curls fall from the elaborate bun on her head, and it hurts that she's so beautiful. Scarlett's always pretty, but there's something that catches in my chest when she looks so . . . untamed.

Scarlett swallows as if talking through her breaths is a chore. "I need to talk to you."

"Then talk."

Her eyes dart to Leo then back to me. "Can we talk alone?"

"But where would the fun in that be for me?" Leo asks.

None. I scowl at my, in theory, friend. "V needs us."

"She does." Leo's smile fades. V being in physical pain is no joke to either of us. He holds out his hand to make it clear he intends to go alone. "But I got it from here."

I toss the baggie in my grasp to Leo, and he catches it. Scarlett's eyes somehow open wider. "What's that?"

I could lie, but it's not worth it. Her going out with that six-foot beanpole means she's already made up her mind about me. "Pot."

"What did you say?"

"Pot. Marijuana. It's a drug people smoke."

"Some eat it," Leo adds. "I'm partial to brownies."

I shoot him a death glare because I don't need his help. He grins again.

"Why do you have it?" she fires off.

"Why do you think?" Pot helps numb V's pain. The goal tonight is for her to not cry herself to sleep. I cross my arms because no matter what I say, Scarlett's going to judge me, and like everyone else, judge me wrong. "Still want to talk or am I no longer worthy of your presence?"

She purses her lips as if she's the one who has the right to be pissed off, and the expression works under my skin. This girl drives me insane.

I should walk, but Scarlett and I need to have this out. "Go on, Leo."

"Seriously, that's how you're going to leave me?" Leo turns his back to me and heads into the trees. "Cliffhangers suck."

I can't look at Scarlett as I wait for his footsteps to fade into the night. My muscles lock up in anger, and I berate myself. *Keep it civil, keep it simple.* I was right years ago—we can't be friends. Scarlett and I are on two different wavelengths.

"What do you need?" I say, and gather my courage to look her in the eye. What I wasn't prepared for was the hurt in them.

She drops her gaze to the ground. "I didn't want to go out with him. My friends set it up and told me about it today. I didn't know how to back out of it without upsetting anyone."

She's okay testing me, but won't say no to anyone else? Why do I get the short end of this stick? "You don't owe me an explanation. I'm not your boyfriend."

"But you're my friend," she rushes out.

"I don't know what we are anymore."

"You said we were friends," she says softly. "Are we not anymore?"

"You should go home. My *friends* need me." And she doesn't.

Her eyes fill with tears, and pain shoots through me. Each day has been torture as I've waited for her to trust me, and it's clear she has no intention of trusting me again. Not wanting to see the agony in her eyes, not wanting the guilt for being the one putting that ache there, I turn away and start for the forest.

"Jesse!" Scarlett calls with a tremble in her voice. "Please, stop!"

I round so quickly that my heart picks up speed. "Why should I? I've asked you for weeks to trust me, to give me a chance, and you put me off."

Nothing but stunned silence from her.

"If I met your friends' approval, your family's approval, you would have instantly been out your window. So your friends made you go on the date, but I gave you a choice and you didn't take it. I know you're messed up, but I'm messed up, too. If you want me to stay, you're going to have to give me a damned good reason and it has to be better than you're broken because I already own that excuse."

I wait for her to say something, to say anything to salvage us, but I'm met with her stoic silence. Forget this. Forget her. I don't need her or the pain she brings. I turn to go again, but her fragile voice stops me.

"He . . . he hits my mom," she says, then gasps as if she's fighting for air.

My vision tunnels and my brain goes fuzzy as I hear the memory of the slap as my mom was struck. My childhood screams reverberate in my mind.

"My . . . my d-dad hits my mom," she continues, and I look over my shoulder. Scarlett claws at her throat even though there's nothing there to strangle her. She begins to quake, or maybe I'm the one who can't stop shaking.

"I don't know what to do, and I'm scared and I'm angry. I'm sorry I never came to see you when you asked, and I'm sorry I've hurt you. I know I made a mistake, but I need a friend, and you said you were it. So are you? You made a mistake when you hurt me, and I know I've been making mistakes now, so we need to figure it out. Are we meant to be friends or are we one, big tragic mistake?"

SCARLETT

I struggle to breathe, and terror causes me to flinch. Oh my God, what did I do? I told him. I told Jesse he hits her.

My stomach lurches, a cold sweat breaks out along my body and dizziness hits my head so quickly I stumble. Oh God, I told someone. I told him and then he'll tell someone else and that someone will tell two more people and people will continue to talk until it reaches Dad.

Heat blasts through my body, and I convulse with a dry heave. My head becomes light as my body becomes heavy, and as I drop to my knees, strong arms wind around me and help lower me to the ground. Jesse's chest presses against my back. He holds me up as I dry heave again, and I don't have the energy to keep from planting face-first into the ground.

Tears stream down my cheeks, the entire world shudders and I hear whispering in my ear. Soft words with lips close to my skin. "It's okay. I promise it's okay."

My head shakes violently back and forth. So violently that I lose my ability to suck in air. It won't be okay. Nothing will be okay ever again.

"Shhhh." Jesse holds me closer and soothingly rocks us as he gently gathers my hair and raises it off the back of my neck. Cooler air hits my heated skin and it's welcome. "Deep breaths. Take deep breaths, Scarlett."

I try, but a strange sound leaves my mouth and it frightens me. I can't breathe. Something is strangling me. I can't breathe!

"Do it with me," Jesse says in such a calm tone, a commanding tone, and I will myself to listen. "Come on, do it with me. Breathe in." And he does, his chest moving in. "Then out." His long breath glides along my cheek, and I'm able to release a short breath.

He continues in the same reassuring voice, holds me with the same courageous strength, and slowly my inhales and exhales become longer, become more solid. The heat leaves my body, a strange calmness settles into my soul, and all the loud and angry voices in my head go silent. A wind blows through the trees, and I shiver as I'm left a clammy mess.

Jesse shifts slowly as if giving me room to bolt, but I don't. I move with him as he sits on the ground and gathers me onto his lap. He encourages me as I rest my head in the crook of his neck, and he rubs my arms to help ease my prickling skin.

I close my eyes and focus on the steady movement of his chest. In and then out. Slow and strong. I need this, I need him, and I'm terrified he'll let go.

"I'm sorry I went out with him," I whisper.

Jesse sighs heavily. "Don't be. I'm sorry I was angry. I didn't have the right."

"You were right. I was testing you. I—"

"Stop it. I was being a stupid, jealous ass and that's not a reason to be angry, nor should I have taken it out on you."

Stunned, I blink at his words. "Why were you jealous?"

His shoulders move up then down. "I can't say I understand much going on between us, but I'll ask you this—how would you feel if I went on a date with another girl?"

I stiffen, and he lightly chuckles, no doubt sensing my change. "Don't worry. I don't understand it either."

I cuddle closer to him and breathe in his familiar scent. I don't want to think about him with other girls or me with other boys or even try to wonder why the idea bothers either of us. We can hardly handle being friends. What happens if we wander into the category of *more*?

Our silence stretches, but it's not awkward or weird, but comforting. My thoughts are lazy, jumping from one place to another, and then I think of the night he promised that if I did venture out that he would show me something special. Something that could . . .

"Can you make me better?" I whisper. "You said there was something you could show me that makes you better when things are hard."

Jesse lightly traces his fingers along the skin of my arm, and I tremble again. Not from cold, but from the alien and desirable sensations his touch creates. He presses his cheek against the top of my head, and I wish I had kept my mouth shut, as I love this bubble we've created.

"I can't make anyone better," he says. "But I can show you what helps me."

I lift my head and look into his eyes. He's serious. Very serious. His red hair covers his forehead, and I sweep it away. But before letting my hand drop, I take a risk by allowing my fingertips to touch his face. His eyes darken and my heartbeat quickens. "Will you take me?"

He nods and offers me a hand to help as I push off of the ground.

JESSE

I hold Scarlett's hand as we hike. What I like is that she holds my hand back. Cool, silky-soft skin laced with my hot, callused fingers. Her grip is relaxed, as if touching me is as easy as breathing. For me, her touch settles portions of my constant internal chaos.

As we walk, sometimes her bicep slips against mine, and she's close enough that I can smell her sweet perfume. The scent reminds me of the honeysuckle we used to eat down by the creek. It also makes me want to gather her in my arms, and never let go.

We're quiet on the walk and the silence gives me needed time to process and recapture my own demons that had slipped through the cracks due to her admission. A growling in my head, and I hold her hand tighter.

So many questions and things I want to ask, but she doesn't need me demanding answers. I know what it's like to be hurt like she has. As if you're a shadow on the wall attached to the horror. Your pain is the ghost of the smack you witnessed, but it's still pain. Just a different type of pain. Your body may not be cut or bruised, but your soul is ripped apart all the same.

Part of me expects her to slow up when we start for the towering sugar maple in the middle of the field, but she doesn't. She keeps pace as if she's also called to this old tree like I have been since the day I learned to walk. This tree marks the center of the property, it's the heart, and when I hurt, this is where I come to relearn how to breathe.

The grass barely reaches our calves and bends easily under our feet. With each step we take toward the maple, the heartbeat of this land trembles within my veins. It's a familiar sensation. One I can't imagine living without.

Walking under the maple's protective leaves, Scarlett stops and her gaze roams to the same branch that has haunted my dreams since the summer before our freshman year. The moon casts a soft glow, giving everything a hazy grayish coloring.

"Do you remember the last time we were here?" she asks in a hushed tone. She releases my hand as she hugs herself. The memory probably scaring her like it still haunts me.

"Yeah." I remember every second as if it were yesterday. I remember racing through the field, how she outran me, how she scaled this tree with such ease that I was jealous, how she climbed higher and higher, and how I egged her to continue to the very top.

Then I remember the crack of the branch, the horrible tightness in my chest, her terrified expression as her head jerked down to look at me for help. Her wide eyes desperate for confirmation that the worst wasn't about to happen. Then she fell.

Fell.

My mouth still goes dry with fear.

She fell hard, she fell fast, crashing through limbs and leaves. She screamed, I yelled and I remember that the first few seconds of my jumping from my branch to capture her felt like flying.

Flying.

After I jumped, I wrapped my arms around her and wished that we were flying, that I could save her, save us. That flying sensation ended when I hit the ground.

I took the brunt of the fall. Me on my back, her in my arms, blood gushing from my chin. To this day, I don't know what I hit to cause that gash.

"How did we survive that fall?" she says in a whisper. "I was too high. Higher than I had ever been. I should have stopped climbing, but I loved the rush and didn't want it to end, and then I heard the crack."

She chokes up and my windpipe thickens.

"I would have died if you hadn't caught me. You risked your life to save mine."

I will always risk everything to save her. She didn't know it then. She doesn't know it now. Scarlett once said she was empty. I've never been empty. I've been loved, and I've loved in return, but I don't do it with many. She was one of the few. Still is. Always will be.

I reach out and touch the bark of the tree. "My mom once told me that as long as I love this land, the land will take care of me."

She raises a skeptical eyebrow. "Are you saying the land saved us that day?"

Yes. I don't believe in a lot, but I do believe that, and I don't think Scarlett will so I avoid her question. "Whenever life gets to be too much, I come here. My land makes me better, and I think it can help you, too."

She frowns. "Of course it helps you. This is your land."

"It's your land, too," I say, and this causes her to laugh.

"No, it's not."

"You were born on it." That doesn't make her cursed because she's not a Lachlin, and it doesn't make it safe for her to be with me, but being born on this land created a connection between her and it. She's always had a way of seeing this farm in ways others can't. This property has embraced her, and I'm convinced it saved her that day all those years ago.

She narrows her eyes, probably ruing the day she told me how her mom waited at home for her father to take her to the hospital. She thought the labor with her first child would be long, but it was short. So short Scarlett was born in their front yard. "I was born at home."

"Yeah, but the land your house sits on used to belong to the Lachlins."

"So?"

"This land . . ." I stop and try to find the right words to make her understand. Hell, I can't make myself understand. The best way would be to show her.

I hold out my hands to her, and she gives me a skeptical tilt of her head. "Jesse, this land is just land. It's land you love, but I don't see how it'll make me better."

"Trust me on this," I say.

"Fine." She places her hands in mine, and standing there in defiance is the force of nature who used to rule my land by my side. Strong, confident and full of trust.

I move us a safe distance away from the tree. "Spin with me."

"Spin?" Fire lights up her expression. "Like we're five?"

"Yeah, like we're five."

"You're crazy."

"Might be, but that doesn't change a thing."

Her smile grows. My God, she's gorgeous. With a flutter of her eyelashes, like she's the one about to pull massive mischief, she tugs on my hands, and we spin.

SCARLETT

As if we're carefree children again, we hold on to each other's hands and go faster and faster in a circle. Wind whips my cheeks, the world swirls around me, becoming one big blur, and all thoughts fall out of my head in a rush of dizziness.

Centrifugal force causes my head to fall back, my arms to strain, for me to have to fight to keep Jesse's hands in my own. The harder it becomes, the tighter Jesse holds on and I gasp for air as my lungs pump violently in my chest.

As the spinning enters another level, when my feet can no longer keep up, Jesse releases me, and I continue to rotate, but with no control. As if I'm the moon that has fallen off its axis. My feet try to concrete themselves into the ground, but my head is too heavy. I stumble and continue to turn, but then I remember the game. The goal is to fall.

So I do. My head is pillowed against the soft grass, my back supported by the land, my arms and legs stretched out, taking up as much space as I can. A *plop* beside me, and one of Jesse's fingers touches mine. "Close your eyes, Tink."

I do, and it's as if my soul leaves my body as I strangely move and float though the solid ground is beneath me.

"Do you feel it?" Jesse asks. "Do you feel the earth turning?"

"Yes." My entire body moves east, sliding along with the rhythm of the universe. I love this sensation. I've felt it before as a child. My soul slips away into the warm ground, my muscles lose their tension and the sweet memory of youth gathers me close in a hug.

I take in the welcome scent of cut grass, turned-over soil and the blooming wildflowers near the creek. A happy and contented sigh leaves my lips. Jesse was right. This was what I needed.

The glorious state of the earth moving fades, and Jesse caresses my wrist. "Stay there. Keep your eyes closed."

His fingers trail up and down my arm and the sensation tickles, causing pleasing goose bumps along my skin. There's a safety that radiates from his touch. A safety I wish I could take with me wherever I go.

"Now focus," he says. "Do you feel it?"

"The world turning?" I say. "Not so much anymore."

"No. Beyond that. The earth is breathing."

I settle into the ground as if the grass beneath me were a soft mattress and the stars above a homemade quilt. I reach out with my mind and try to discover Jesse's beyond. Discover if this "breathing" is an aftershock of spinning.

Concentrating so hard on anything beyond myself, I discover that the entire world surrounding us is alive. The crickets singing, the bats chirping and the owl calling out into the night. I strain to listen further and hear the quiet trickle of the creek lapping over the smooth rocks and the gentle breeze stirring through the leaves. The grass beneath my arms tickles my skin, the wind kisses my face and the taste of honeysuckle is sweet on my tongue.

"If you focus, you can sense the earth trying to suck us in with an inhale and then the gentle push of the exhale," he says in this deep, melodic tone. "This land, Tink, it's alive. The root systems, the veins; this very place that we lay, the heart. It has a heartbeat, a rhythm, and you and me, we're a part of it. It's alive, it's breathing and it loves. Every time life spirals out of control, I come here, I lay down and I feel the land breathe with me."

I suck in a deep breath and the rush of clean air fills my lungs. I hold it, longer than needed, and then there's a surprised jolt. A pulse nudges me from the ground below. A gentle tug, then a tender push. My eyes shoot open when the sensation happens again. It's a breath.

The land breathed.

Jesse's fingers drift to my wrist, the pads of his fingers delicately press upon my pulse, and I mirror his touch. My fingers sink into his hot skin and a shiver runs through me as I discover his heartbeat. It's strong, bold and exhilarating. Just like Jesse, my Peter Pan.

My heart beats, his heart beats and beneath us the land breathes in, it breathes out, and a rush fills my blood. I close my eyes again as a sensation like no other makes me feel as if I'm flying. As if my body is a permanent part of the land and my soul is free.

Free. No longer weighed down by my problems or the world. No longer trapped by my life and by my skin. Free. Flying and free.

I soar, and happiness sweeps through me like the wind through my hair. Tears of joy prick my eyes, and I grasp Jesse, terrified if he lets go, if I let go, that I'll never experience happiness again. I want this happiness. I want to forever soar.

"Jesse," I whisper, and there's a catch in my voice, emotion overwhelming me. "It's . . ." I can't find the words to describe this rare and beautiful buoyant sensation.

A shifting beside me and a caress across my cheek. "Don't cry, Tink."

I swallow as I open my eyes and find Jesse's concerned gaze. He's propped up on an elbow, his body grazes mine and I'm hypnotized by his closeness. "I'm not crying."

He inclines his head as wet tears slip down my cheek, but I smile, giggle even. As he starts to pull his hand away, I place my fingers over his, pressing to keep his hand against my cheek. "I'm not sad. It's . . . this place is so . . . beautiful."

Jesse's thumb slides against my skin, and I become pure liquid. "You're beautiful."

My skin heats from his words and shyness makes it tough to keep my gaze locked with his, but I do. "Thank you for sharing this with me."

"I can't think of anyone else I'd share this with."

"Surely you've shown someone else. One of your friends . . ." I trail off, but the serious set of his green eyes tells me the truth. I'm the only one.

Another slow swipe of his thumb across my cheek and then Jesse tucks a stray hair behind my ear. His fingers linger along my neck and the touch is so pleasing that liquid heat spreads to the tip of my toes.

"There's no one who has ever gotten me the way you do. No one who understands this land like you either. I've messed up in the past, but I promise, I won't mess up again. I'm here, and I promise I'm never going away."

His words are like soothing herbs on an old wound. We were friends, we fell apart, but we're friends again. As his fingers continue their leisurely, seductive dance along my arm, I peer deeper within myself. There's something more than friendship between us. A trust and love that had taken root when we were children, something that has grown, something that once took a wrong turn and had to be pruned. Something that has been allowed to reflourish and is on the verge of going wild.

"I've missed you," I whisper as I reach up to touch his face. The stubble of his chin tickles against the pads of my fingers, and a sensation of power and pleasure runs through me as he tilts his head into my touch.

Jesse edges nearer and my hand combs through his hair. His lips come close. So close.

"I missed you, too," he says against my mouth.

I lick my suddenly dry lips. "I've never kissed anyone before."

"You're the only girl that I've ever cared for, the only girl I've wanted to kiss."

If my heart fluttered any faster it would spread wings and fly.

"Can I kiss you?" he murmurs, and his lips are so near that the warmth of his breath caresses my lips.

Happiness explodes through me, and I nod, causing my lips to brush against his. He cradles my head in his hand, leans down and kisses me.

Kisses.

I can scarcely breathe. Kissing is warm, kissing is soft, kissing Jesse Lachlin is the closest I have ever felt to being alive, the closest I have ever felt to being comfortable in my own skin, the closest I have ever been to heaven.

My entire body becomes liquid, pliant, as I memorize each way his lips press against mine. I burn, head to toe, and the rush through my veins becomes so strong that it's like clinging to a flame. A flame that I love, a flame that frightens me because it's new, a flame I want to cuddle and hold for as long as I can.

Jesse takes my lower lip into his, a thrill races through me, and I pull back, excited and happy. I open my eyes as Jesse opens his. His face shines as bright as the millions of stars that rest in the night sky.

He takes my hand as he rolls to his back and guides me to rest my head on his chest. Jesse wraps his arms around me, I wrap my arms around him, and I close my eyes and listen to his heartbeat. I lose myself in the steady sound that shares the same rhythm as his land.

"We're going to be okay, aren't we?" I whisper, and it's not a question, but a statement, a fact. A declaration of this sense of peace and purpose in my soul.

"Yes." Jesse kisses the top of my head. "This was meant to be, Tink. We are meant to be."

JESSE

The surprised expression on Glory's face is enough to have made my day. Every ounce of me wants to gloat that I got one up on the "psychic," but I don't. I need her help, and in my experience, people only help if they feel like they're getting something out of the deal.

"Marshall's on his way," I say, then lift the bag in my hand. "I brought doughnuts."

In Hello Kitty PJs, Glory runs a hand through her long mane of unruly bed-head hair, pausing to scratch near her ear. It's near nine on Saturday morning. For as long as I've known Glory, she's a late-night, sleep-in psychic. I'm betting her tricks work better in the dark. Daylight has a way of ferreting out lies.

She yawns as she holds the door open for me, and I step into her cottage. It's the same combination of neat, clean, yet cluttered with books, rocks and crystals.

I head for the kitchen, but Glory doesn't follow. Instead she goes into the bedroom and closes the door. There's shifting and dresser drawers opening and closing. Minutes later, she's in the bathroom. Water runs from the sink, a toilet flushes, more water from the sink, and I'm impressed when she returns to the kitchen that she's in full Glory mode: a shimmering skirt, and an off-the-shoulder white blouse. There's only a hint of drowsiness from my early morning wake-up call.

Glory fills her teakettle with water, sets it on the back burner of the stove, then lays out three china cups with saucers on the counter. "It's about time you kissed Scarlett. You've been wanting to do that forever. But it's better you waited. It's not like a boy knows how to give a girl the proper toe-curling first kiss she deserves before he grows facial hair."

She sits in the chair across from me at the table and gives me a smug smirk. "Don't try to deny it, Jesse. The proof is all over your face."

I lean back in my seat and cross my arms. "Are you stalking me? Her? Or both of us?"

"I don't have to stalk you. I have angels who like to do it for me. But don't worry, no one was there for your first kiss. My spirits caught the giddiness of young love radiating off the both of you last night. If it makes you feel better, Scarlett couldn't go to sleep for a few hours either because she was thinking of you, too."

I have to look away because hearing that does worm its way into my heart, and I don't want Glory there. Letting Scarlett in is hard enough, but I can't keep her out. Fighting it was futile. I tried protecting her from me before, and that backfired. Now, I have to change tactics to protect us both. "I have to keep this land."

The land will protect me and it will protect Scarlett. Since we're together now and I'm not giving her up again, retaining ownership of the land is the only way to keep her safe from the Lachlin curse. Is it real? Is it not real? I don't know, but I'm not taking chances. Not with Scarlett.

"So you're going to build a relationship with Marshall to win his vote."

"The pastor won't give me his vote unless I make nice with Marshall. This vote will be all or nothing." Sucks, but it's how it is.

"Why bring Marshall here?" Glory asks. "He doesn't like me."

"Being alone with him doesn't sound like a good option. Going to his home turf with his family is unfair on my side. I'm relying on you to switch subjects or to kick me under the table if I go rogue."

"I'm to play referee?"

"Yeah, and I'm betting he doesn't like you more than he doesn't like me."

Glory laughs. Long, loud and hard. Enough that it feels good when I chuckle along with her. Steam shoots out of the teapot, and she returns to the stove. She pours the hot water into two cups then slips a basket of tea bags to the middle of the table. Dropping the bag she chose into her tea, she returns to her seat and draws her feet onto the chair. "You're going to need to be careful with Scarlett. Her life is complicated."

"I know." Scarlett and I talked last night. She explained her home life and her fears, and I told her that I didn't need to be the boy holding her hand in the hallway. I'm not a dog that needs to piss on a fire hydrant to mark that she's mine. If being with me— someone not on her father's approved list—creates problems, then we don't go public. "Thanks for helping her."

"I need you to come by with her sometime this week. She needs to practice reading palms. I'd prefer for her to use someone else, as reading you is like assigning advanced calculus to a kindergartener, but considering she's keeping so secret on things, you'll have to do."

"You're teaching her how to be a con? I didn't know there was a mentoring program."

"I like giving back. Good karma and all. And not that you'd know, but Scarlett has great potential. I've seen it in her since she was a child. She has a special connection with the land, and she has gifts that can't be taught. She has closed off her abilities because that is what society has told her to do. The benefit of being friends with you is that her little acts of rebellion are opening up her senses. She has the makings of being a great psychic should she choose."

I don't say anything because I'm not going to complain if Glory teaches Scarlett how to make a few extra bucks by conning until she can settle down with a real job. Money is money, especially when you're hungry.

"You don't believe she has talent, do you?" Glory raises her cup to her mouth.

"I believe she has plenty of talents."

"You perplex me. Always have. How you can believe you are cursed yet not believe in anything else baffles me." She sets her teacup on the saucer and meets my eyes in defiance.

A muscle ticks in my jaw at what she's inferred. "I don't be-lieve in the Lachlin curse." At least not the curse she believes in. I'm not going to lose what I love. I'll break this curse by keeping the land and staying.

"You can call it a water chicken all you want, but when it wad-dles like a duck and quacks like a duck, it's still a duck. A curse is a curse—you give it a different name."

"You're a lunatic."

"Listen to me good, Jesse. There's a curse, and it's real. Some-day, you're going to have to make a choice as to whether or not you're strong enough to defeat it."

Anger leaks into my blood, and I point at her. "If it's real, if I believe, if you believe, then stop talking in circles and help me. If you're all-knowing, if you're psychic and talk to spirits beyond the dead, then you tell me how to defeat the curse. Scarlett's in my life now, and I need to know how to keep her safe!"

"I *am* helping you." Glory looks at me as if she's amused, and it makes me want to smash my fist through the windowpane.

Rocks crackle outside along with the sound of a motor purr-ing. Marshall's here and Glory stands. She keeps her faded blue eyes on me as she walks past. I hate her faraway expression. The one that's supposed to make me think she's seeing more than she should.

"I'm helping you by creating the best weapon—to be honest, your only weapon. This family has been cursed for hundreds of years. It took all that time for someone to be born who could break the curse, but it finally happened. This means you have a chance to do what no Lachlin has ever done before. If you have courage, you have a chance to be free."

"What are you talking about?"

Her mouth edges up in a daring smile. "Scarlett felt the land breathe, didn't she?"

Blood drains from my face. There's no way anyone knows about that beyond me and Scarlett.

"There are only two other people alive who have felt this land breathe, and we're both in this kitchen. Scarlett was born on the land, she has a connection with you, with me, and when she laid down on the earth, it came alive for her when it breathes for nobody else.

"Even if you don't want to admit it, you two have always been connected. After what happened to your mom that bond scared you, and I don't blame you for that. You pushed Scarlett away in what you believed was an attempt to protect her, but you can't stop fate. Pushing her away only hurts you and devastates her. Your bond, even when you tried, can't be severed."

"She was born on the land, but she's not cursed," I say with finality.

"No," Glory says, "she's not. But you are and so am I. Whether I want it or not, our destinies are intertwined. I've searched my future and yours. If you lose all that you love, then so do I. I don't know the exact role Scarlett plays in all this, but I do know that if she becomes strong enough and you become strong enough then you can break the curse."

A knock on the front door and neither of us moves to let my uncle in. My brain swims. This isn't real. None of this is real.

"At Scarlett's earliest convenience, please bring her by. She has a lot to learn and not much time to do it." Glory heads for the door, but I stop her.

"The vote isn't until May," I say. "We have time."

Glory glances at me over her shoulder, and the sadness washing over her punches me hard in the gut. "Both of you will be tested before May. I don't know when, but it will be soon. I need to make sure that you will be strong enough because that's what the two of you will need—strength, not for yourselves, but strength to give the other. You will both be drained by what's ahead. You will be left empty, and you will need to trust the other enough in order to survive. Nothing about this will be easy."

Another knock on the front door, and I slump in my seat. "None of what you say is real."

"Not all of it," she says. "Just the true and important parts."

SCARLETT

Last thing I want to do is leave my room. If I stay in bed I can continue to close my eyes and relive my night with Jesse. His hands on my body, his lips on mine, the perfection of his land that breathes. The memory causes my pulse to quicken, my skin to flush, and I'm torn between lying still and sprinting across the road to lose myself in Jesse's arms again.

Freedom. It's several months away. It felt impossible weeks ago, but now I can practically taste it. I shift onto my back and stare at my ceiling fan. My lips squish to the side as anxiety sets in. I'm assuming Jesse will want to kiss me again. Jesse and I have always been confusing. What if last night was a last night thing? He said he cares, but does that mean we were a couple last night and today we're friends again?

Ugh. I place a pillow over my face and scream into it. For a brief few seconds, I consider smothering myself with it. Overanalyzing is, unfortunately, one of my best talents.

My cell vibrates, and I groan. It's been vibrating all morning. Mostly my friends who want to know what I thought of my date with Stewart. A few from Stewart asking if I want to go out again, and I am not looking forward to turning him down.

Mom: *I made something special for you. You can find it in the kitchen. Yes, you're allowed to have it for breakfast.* ☺ *I'm running errands this morning, but will be home for lunch. Your dad and sister are playing in the backyard. They'd LOVE for you to join them.*

Huh. Dad let Mom go someplace on her own on the weekend. That's impressive. As much as I hated the date, it's also impressive that Dad gave the date his blessing. Maybe he is changing.

I contemplate this as I roll out of bed, change clothes, run a quick brush through my hair, do all the essentials in the bathroom and make my way down the stairs. I enter the kitchen, and happiness causes me to smile.

On the counter is hot peanut butter cookies and a notecard with my name written on it propped up next to the platter in my mother's cursive penmanship. At my place at the table my sister has left me drawings of me and her holding hands against the backdrop of a rainbow and unicorns.

That is definitely love.

I nibble on my lower lip as I notice the menu from my favorite pizza place and a note scribbled from my father that tonight's my night to choose the toppings. That tonight's my night to choose the movie. A note that hints he'll give me those rights this night, tomorrow night, whatever night, if I'll participate in family movie night with him again.

The real question is, should I believe him?

A squeal from the backyard and through the windows I watch a memory in real time. Except the little girl with long black hair isn't me, but my sister.

Isabelle wears this brilliant smile as she races around my father's car with the hose in her little hands. Shockingly, my father allows her to spray him even though the morning is full of crisp autumn air. He fights past the mist of water to scoop her up and hug her as if she's the most precious person in the world.

Seeing them together, seeing them happy, causes heavy sorrow. She's happy and she believes my father loves her, but being her age once, having experienced that pure joy with my father, I can say it's easier to believe him when you have no other basis of comparison.

My father releases Isabelle, and she scurries away in a fit of giggles to behind the garage, no doubt planning her next phase of attack. Laughing to himself, Dad turns for the house and looks

up faster than I can turn away. Our eyes meet, and I hate how his
smile fades.

Part of me wants to retreat, sprint back to the safety of my
room, but I don't. I slink to the fridge and pretend to study it as Dad
enters the kitchen. He's slow as he walks toward me, and when he
stops by the island, he shoves his hands in his pants pockets.

He smells wet, as if he's been caught in a summer storm, and
I'm surprised to see him relaxed in clothes that are so drenched
that they stick to his body. Maybe he has changed because while
Dad did play with me like that as a child, he wouldn't have stayed
such a mess for long.

"How was your date?" Dad asks.

I grab a bottle of water from the fridge then hold the bottle
with both hands. I squeeze it tightly, as if it were a bomb and if I
let go it would explode. "Okay."

"Isabelle and I are washing the cars. Do you want to join us?"
He offers a hesitant grin full of desperate hope.

"I need to finish some schoolwork," I lie to him and myself. I
would love to believe he's changed and be as carefree as Isabelle,
but I'm terrified of letting my guard down because what if this is
just an act. What if he hasn't changed?

His grin flickers, but he forces it back as if my rejection didn't
sting. "We might be at this for a while if you change your mind.
Isabelle thinks it's fun to spray me more than the car."

I used to do that, too.

"Stewart seemed like a nice kid. Do you think there'll be a
second date?"

I shake my head no, and Dad deflates. "Your mom told me you
didn't want to go, and I'm sorry. When your friends came up with
the idea, I assumed they picked some guy you liked. I'm sorry I
pushed this on you."

The left portion of my brain tingles as if I'm having a stroke
because I don't think I heard any of that right. Did Dad apologize?

"Your mom and I feel bad," he says. "It was suggested in counseling that I give you some space to show that I trust you, and
hopefully you'll come to trust me. Your mom and Isabelle are
coming with me on a few weekend business trips. You're more

than welcome to come. In fact, I'd love for you to come, but I understand that you may need some space. So if you want to stay here, by yourself, then I'll allow it."

My eyebrows raise because beyond a few hours here and there, I've never been allowed alone, and the idea sounds like heaven. This means unlimited time away from him. Unlimited time to work and make money. Unlimited time to search for scholarships. Unlimited time with Jesse. Warmth spreads along my cheeks at the idea of being alone with him, and I drink my water to hide my reaction.

"Your mom and I would appreciate it if you tried talking with Pastor Hughes again, but I'm not going to push you. Isabelle has missed you hanging out with us so maybe if you participated in family movie night as a favor to her—"

"Okay," I say, and Dad's eyes snap to mine as if he is shocked to hear my voice.

"Okay on what part?"

I shrug as if I don't know or don't care. "To the movie tonight."

Dad beams, and he claps his hands together. "Pick the movie and pick the pizza."

I wish he wouldn't make this a big deal. Dad seems to read my mind and says a few other random things before he walks out. The moment the door shuts, my sister blasts him with the hose, and I'm surprised by the faint but real smile on my lips when he yelps in surprise.

Off balance, I touch my face. Is it possible my father has changed?

JESSE

It's two in the afternoon, and I'm starving. I've spent most of the morning and into the afternoon fixing the rail fence on the western side of the property. A guy pays me to put his horses out to pasture there. Sounded like a good deal until the horses started rubbing up against my fence and pushing it down. What I make in profit, I'll end up spending on fence upkeep.

My stomach's been growling for the past half hour, and I'm breaking for food. The doughnut I had earlier with Marshall and Glory wasn't enough to get me through the day.

We met for a half hour. None of us saying anything worth listening to. Me talking about school, Marshall asking more questions about school, Glory wondering aloud if me and Marshall would be more cordial if she scrubbed our auras clean. At least we shared one moment on the same page as we sat staring at Glory like she needed medication.

We left with the agreement that we would meet again at Glory's. Marshall seemed pleased I was trying.

As I approach the house, I squint at the figure on the swings. Probably V. No doubt she's pissed I cut out on hanging with her last night, and no doubt Leo told her that he had left me with Scarlett. But as I get closer, it's not short blond curls but long black hair. It's Scarlett.

She sways on the swing, her toes dragging along the ground.

A soft smile lights her up when she spots me, but there's a question there. The hesitancy I had chased away last night.

It makes sense. Last night, her walls were torn down; she let me in and now she needs to know nothing has changed in the morning light. I don't mind offering her proof. In fact, I'll offer her proof every second of every day. I even dreamed about offering her proof last night.

In two large strides, I reach Scarlett, and her eyes widen as I encircle my arms around her waist, lift her off the swing and pull her close. The breath rushes out of her body and before she has a chance to utter a word, I lean down and kiss her.

Her tense muscles quickly melt, and within a second, Scarlett's kissing me back. Her lips soft, her hands cautiously roaming, a test to herself and me if she's allowed to touch. She's allowed. She's more than allowed. Her touch alone is causing me to go up in flames, but Scarlett and I are in new territory and that requires patience.

Ignoring the urge to kiss her deeper, to lose myself in her for as long as humanly possible, I pull back. She gasps for air, a blush touches her cheeks and she falls into me, hugging me tight. I enjoy her embrace, inhale her sweet scent and kiss her head.

"What was that?" she asks.

"I figured that would be the easiest way to answer any questions. Plus I like kissing you."

She draws back and that shy lift of her lips makes me want to kiss her again. Scarlett eases to the swing and fidgets with the rusting metal chain. "I like kissing you, too."

"I can live with that." I wink at her and wonder if her parents would notice if I kept her here. "You're daring, Tink, but sneaking out during the day? That's hard-core."

"Dad took Mom and Isabelle into Lexington to go shopping."

Interesting. Her parents don't leave her alone much. "And you rebelled?"

"No, Dad said he's going to give me space. It's his attempt to show me he's changed."

"Space?"

"Space." She worries her lower lip. "He also apologized for forcing my date with Stewart. Do you think people can change?"

She's asking if her dad can change, and I'm not the right person to ask, but there's a growling inside me. A warning that I've heard these words before and the fallout caused a scar on my back and blood in my nightmares.

It's the middle of the day, blue sky, sun shining, but a darkness creeps into my peripheral vision. The ghosts who haunt me, they whisper in my ear and threaten my sanity. *People can't change. No one can change.* But I see the hope in her eyes, and I don't want to be the one to snuff it out. "I don't know."

Scarlett's lips flatten, and she looks to the ground. I don't want the demons of her dad to haunt her. Not now and not with me. "What do you want to do with your few hours of freedom? We can head inside if you'd like."

Scarlett glances at my trailer, and I have to hide my smile at how her face turns crimson. Don't have to be Glory to know she's contemplating me and her alone in a bed.

"Or we can head to Glory's," I suggest. "She wants you to practice palm reading on me."

"You're going to let me practice on you?"

Because that's how much I like her. "Yeah."

She laughs and the sound soothes my battered soul. "Then let's go."

SCARLETT

Jesse and I had to wait twenty minutes outside of Glory's while she finished a reading. We climbed trees and raced each other to the top. I laughed until it hurt to smile, and Jesse reached out to touch me when he felt like I was going too fast or too high. A gentle caress along my calf, my ankle, and each and every touch sent licks of fire along my veins.

There's a push and a pull within me. A need to let him touch me, to let him caress and kiss. Then there's a part that's terrified if I let him, I'll literally explode from excitement.

Sitting on a thick branch, I lean against the trunk of the tree and listen as Jesse talks about his frustration that another family farm in the county has been sold to a corporate farm. He sits beside me, his hand on my knee, and I wonder if he can feel how my heart beats erratically under his touch.

"People don't understand why it's a problem. By cutting out the family farm, you're cutting out competition. If there's no competition then the big companies can drive up food prices. When corporate farms take over an area then you'll see a lot of local economies collapse. It's like a food chain. You take one part of the chain out, and the rest can collapse."

Jesse is very passionate as he talks, and I can hear the ache in his voice.

"Is that who Marshall wants to sell the land to?" I ask. "A corporate farm?"

"I don't know. I've had at least two guys knocking on my trailer door representing the companies telling me that when I want to sell, they'll buy. It's not right, Tink. Not right at all."

"Then you gain ownership of this land, and you farm it."

Jesse picks a leaf and shreds it into small pieces. "I want to, but it's going to be tough to compete against the big companies. They have the resources to purchase the heavy equipment, and I don't."

"There must be some way for you to do this," I say.

"I need to figure it out fast. May is going to be here before we know it."

"Have you contacted the county extension office? I overheard Dad say once that they work with the University of Kentucky agriculture department on things concerning local farms. Maybe they know someone who can give you some advice."

A car engine starts and that's our cue. Jesse and I slip to the ground and head over to the cottage.

"You were flying today, Tink," Jesse says as we climb the steps of Glory's house. His green eyes flare with the recklessness that belongs only to him.

"Isn't that what Tink is supposed to do?" I ask. "Fly?"

"Feels good, doesn't it?"

It feels wonderful. "I thought Peter Pan was supposed to dare her to keep going." I playfully poke his arm. "You're going soft. We could have gone higher in the last tree."

Jesse's response is a wink as he opens the door and waves for me to head in. Even though I work for Glory, it's weird to enter without knocking. Jesse lops in behind me and passes me for the kitchen. I follow and discover Glory at the table in a ray of sunlight. She's looking out the window, and I'd willingly give an arm to experience the peace she currently wears.

"Hello." Glory turns away from the light. "Would you like some tea?"

We both decline. I'll admit I'm tired of tea, yet Glory makes some anyway, explaining that she's giving me lavender tea because lavender resonates with the third eye, the center of my clairvoyance.

Glory turns to the stove, and I glance over at Jesse, who is leaning against the wall. He's all relaxed and so sexy it hurts. I mouth,
Help me. He merely offers me a crooked grin along with a half
shrug.

She pours a cup for herself, a cup for me, and Jesse declines
with a flat, "No." Obviously, no third-eye cleansing for him today.
Just me, Glory and the room full of angels I, in theory, can't see,
but, once again in theory, will be able to "sense" soon.

We finish our tea, and Glory announces that I'll be reading
Jesse's palm at her table in the living room. "Jesse is a tough read,
and we need as many things as possible that will eat negative energy since he'll be uncooperative, even for you."

As we leave the sunshine of the kitchen, everything seems
darker in the living room, even with the lit candles, shimmering
crystals and glowing salt rocks that Glory says she purchased to
help with Jesse's negative extended presence in her home since
I've been working for her.

He snorts, and I have to try hard to not smile.

"Sit in my chair," Glory says to me. I do and have an internal
image of being a five-year-old sitting in the teacher's seat. It's not
that the chair is too tall or too big, as much as this is a position of
authority, and I feel as powerful as an ant looking down the mean
end of a shoe.

"Sit, Jesse," Glory says in reprimand and with a glare. He sits
and waggles his eyebrows at me. Not an ounce of him takes this
seriously, and that makes me intimidated.

"Why are you having me do this?" I ask.

Standing beside me, Glory grins. "Because I'm paying you."

Good point. I have a nice stash of cash in a shoebox under my
bed, thanks to this job. If she wants to pay me to learn reading
palms, I'll take the job.

"You have the gift to sense the spiritual realms," Glory says.
"I've seen it in your aura since you were a child, but negativity in
your life has blocked your chakras. You've wound yourself tight,
protecting yourself like the layers of an onion. What I'm doing is
slowly peeling each thin layer away so you can connect again with
your true self."

"Glory gave me a twenty-dollar cash card for my last birthday," Jesse says. "My gift is better than yours."

Ignoring him, Glory says, "Give her both of your hands, but she needs to start with your dominant hand. Palm up."

Jesse frowns, but he does what she's demanded.

Glory takes a seat next to me. "There is an art to reading a palm. You need knowledge, but if you're going to make money at it—"

"You mean be a con," Jesse interrupts.

"Be a businesswoman," Glory corrects. "There is an artistry, a performance aspect. You must lean on your knowledge of palm reading and your link to the spiritual world while making sure that your client understands what is happening in your head. Palm reading takes great concentration, but the longer you're silent and searching for the truth, the more impatient people become and believe they aren't getting what they paid for. We will take things slow, but I will need you to try to communicate with Jesse as you connect with the spiritual realm. Now take his hand."

I have officially left the freeway of sane and taken an off-ramp to weird. Yet I take Jesse's hand in mine and try to ignore the way my heart beats faster when he brushes his fingers seductively along my own.

"First, you meditate," Glory says in a soft voice. "The more you do this, the faster you'll be able to establish your link with the spiritual realm. Don't worry about fast now. Close your eyes, and focus on your breaths in and your breaths out. Become aware of your skin, how it stretches around your bones, how it fits, and then I want you to move inward. Become aware of your muscles relaxing, warming, like stepping into a hot bath. . . ."

I breathe in, I breathe out and my entire body grows heavy, like in a sleep state. My frame gives a slight tremble, like a radio frequency of a buzz, one I've never noticed before, and with another breath in, I realize it's my soul, the center of my being.

"Now let go." Glory's voice is airy, as if she's speaking more in my mind than in my ear. I do what she asks and breathe out, letting go of my body, and I become so light that I float.

"Without opening your eyes, feel Jesse's hand, and without breaking your link, your concentration, tell me what you discover."

It's weird to move my fingers after being so still.

"You have to talk, Ms. Copeland. You need to focus and speak at the same time."

"His hand is warm," I say. "Firm, like a rock."

"What does that mean?" Glory asks.

"He has energy and strength. Endurance."

"What else does it mean?"

My eyes snap open and Jesse's watching me with curious green eyes. I swallow because I don't want to say what it also means.

Glory rubs her hands together for longer than seems necessary and then places one on the skin of my arm. Her touch strangely burns and sends a jolt through me. The connection to the floating sensation I had started to lose returns.

"I also picked Jesse for you to read because he's not easily offended, are you, Jesse?"

"I'd have to believe for it to offend me. Give me your worst, Tink. I can take it."

"Good, now tell me what else having a hard hand means," Glory says.

I find courage and push forward. "It means he doesn't adapt to new situations easily, and he's not a fan of new ideas."

"Are you saying I'm stubborn?"

I can't stop the smile that spreads across my face, and I have to inhale to stay centered. "But his skin is soft." It's not that there aren't calluses on his hand from hard work or that he isn't strong, but the texture of his skin has a smooth quality.

"Which means?" Glory pushes.

"That he's sympathetic."

"So what does that mean for his character strengths and weaknesses?"

"Soft skin brings out the best."

"Tell me what his dominant mounts are," Glory says.

There are seven mounts on the hand, the mounts being the rising and falling of the flesh on the palm. The mounts that are raised higher than others are considered strong. I brush my fingers along the mounts of his hands, paying more attention to his right hand than his left, as Jesse favors his right hand. "Mars. Jesse is a warrior."

"That sounds promising," Jesse says.

I like good news, and I relax. "Because of the fine skin, it means you're brave, honest, direct, resilient, loyal and—" My cheeks burn red.

"It also means you're sexual," Glory adds, and I want to crawl under the table. "Ms. Copeland obviously read that part of you loud and clear."

Though his face is somber, I can tell he's laughing at me and I playfully kick his shin.

"Now take a look at the lines of both his hands."

I take my time studying Jesse's left hand. I then study his right. The chair beneath me jerks.

"Whatever it is, say it aloud," Glory says.

I don't know how. "What if you see something you think will upset them?"

"Then you find a way to focus on the positive until you discover a way to nicely tell them the negative. Depending upon the situation, you have to decide if you're going to keep information to yourself. That's when I really need my angels to guide me. Not everyone is ready to hear the truth that's in front of them. But you don't need to worry about that right now, because as I told you, Jesse can handle whatever it is you have to say."

"It's okay," Jesse says, but his hands become tense in mine. "It doesn't bother me that you know that I have detention next week."

That oddly captures my attention. "Why do you have detention?"

"Because Leo and I were making noises in Calculus."

"Noises?" And in Calculus, of all places. With a teacher who has two hearing aids and hates anyone under the age of twenty-one.

"I made a weird sound by mistake, and Leo wanted to see if we could replicate it."

"Why?" I ask.

Glory squeezes my arm. "Don't ask him why, reconnect with the universe and have the angels tell you the answer."

Doing what I'm told, I close my eyes and think of Jesse in the back of class with Leo by his side. I think of Jesse making some sort of noise. I see them both laughing and my lips twitch with their joy—joy in amusing themselves in a boring class. Their joy of sharing a tight friendship. The joy of something so simple making them laugh, and then other emotions appear in my mind. Emotions so strong that they almost create visual pictures of sadness and loneliness.

I open my eyes. "You continued to make noises because you think Leo is sad."

A shadow crosses over Jesse's face, and I have to strengthen my grip when he moves.

"Now tell him what you saw that upset you," Glory says.

I don't want to, but regardless, I take the plunge. "Your left hand, your weaker hand, is supposed to be who you were born to be. The life you were meant to live. And your right hand, your dominate hand, is what you've actually done with your life, the events that have shaped you and where you are heading because of your choices."

Jesse pulls back, and I have to hold on to him again. He wants this to end, I want this to end, yet I'm drawn to continue. I'm curious and consumed with seeing the things in front of me I have never noticed before. As if for the first time in my life, I've been introduced to the color red.

But, to be honest, I don't fully understand what I'm looking at. I don't quite understand how to decipher the lines. I do notice the difference in the palms, though, a huge difference. "This says who you are now is completely different from who you were born to be."

I glance to his right hand and fear drowns out the pulse that was in my ears. Jesse has islands on his right palm. Several islands at the start of the lines. More islands than I do. His lines—there are too many and they are so deep and too well defined and—

Glory reaches over, curls Jesse's fingers into a ball and pushes him away from me. "That's enough for today. We'll learn more about lines with somebody else."

But this has nothing to do with lines. This has to do with the shadow of fear in Jesse's eyes. "What happened to you?"

Jesse places his hands to where I can no longer see them. "Your showmanship is spot-on. If you decide to forgo college, you'd make a great con."

"I don't want to be a con," I say.

"Then you'll be great at whatever you decide to do." Jesse stands and goes for the boxes of necklaces and bags of tea Glory wants me to price before her next street fair. He lifts two as if they weigh nothing. "I'm going to take these out. Take your time wrapping up with Glory."

Jesse heads out and the screen door slams shut behind him. I watch through the window as he places the boxes in the truck then leans his back against the tailgate. His shoulders slump as if he's carrying a heavy unseen load.

I fall back into the chair. "What just happened?"

One by one, Glory blows out the burning candles. "You allowed yourself to be in tune with your psychic abilities. I told you that you were gifted."

None of that I believe. Yes, the reading was bizarre, but what I meant was . . . "Why is Jesse afraid? It's Jesse. He fears nothing."

Glory slips into the seat Jesse abandoned. "He fears the curse."

She says it so bluntly that I'm unnerved. "Jesse doesn't believe in the Lachlin curse."

"What is a curse?"

"A mark placed on you that something bad will happen."

"Mediate on that. In the meantime, keep reading, and I'll teach you more about the lines the next time you come by. You should be very proud of yourself today. I know I am."

I slowly comb my fingers through my hair and knot them in the ends. The compliment causes a sense of pride, but it also confuses me. "Can you expand upon what to do when you see something bad in someone's palm?"

Glory is pensive, quiet for so long that I wonder if she heard my question. "Do you know what a self-fulfilling prophecy is?"

"When someone tells you something is going to happen in your future, you believe it and it happens because you make choices in that direction."

She leans forward. "Give me your palms."

I do, and she holds them in both of her hands, stroking her thumbs over the lines. "As you know, the weaker hand shows what God intended us to become. The right hand shows what has happened and where we are going based on our current choices. Did you know the lines on your palm change?"

"No."

"They do. That's because our choices change. Whatever lines I see, whatever my guides tell me, that's a possible future based on the person's current choices. If I tell someone something horrible, like an impending heart attack and death, I can create a self-fulfilling prophecy, so instead I tell them that they need to watch what they eat, to exercise and to see a doctor. What I do for a living is considered good fun for people, but it's a terrible burden on me."

"Are you a real psychic?"

"Not all the time," she says. "There are times when I'm performing a reading and the angel guiding me finishes everything my client needs to know before their half hour is up. Sometimes my clients have questions my guides don't think are important to answer, so that's when I watch body language. I have to figure out what is really bothering my clients. Once I get to the root of the real problems, my guides will typically help me."

"So you *are* psychic."

"I believe I am. I see my job as one where people come for insight in their lives, insight that they need. My clients are so wrapped up in their problems that they can't see a true path. I show people a way to go, and sometimes that's all we need in life—a push in the right direction."

I glance out the window, and my stomach twists with how broken Jesse looks as he stares out onto the woods. "Does Jesse need a push?"

"Yes."

"In what direction?"

"That's the million-dollar question right there, and that's what I need you to figure out. So stay focused on your studies."

"Besides voting to help Jesse keep his land, there's nothing else I can do to help him."

"As long as you continue to limit yourself, then that's all you'll be able to do, but I believe you're capable of more," she says. "You ask if I'm psychic. I know that I am. That's the thing about life, Ms. Copeland. You're going to have plenty of people telling you what they believe you to be. I'm confident enough to know who I am, and I know that I'm strong enough to change the lines on my right hand if I so choose. Since you asked a question, I'll ask a question, too: Are you strong enough to change the lines on your hand?"

JESSE

Space and *time* have become two of my favorite words. *Space* means Scarlett's family has left, and I get to spend more time with her. *Time* means talking, whispering, holding hands, lazily lying together and kissing. I could kiss Scarlett for the rest of my life.

Scarlett's family went to the movies and dinner this evening, meaning we have had a few precious hours to ourselves. We're in the recliner leaned back, and she's cuddled close to me. We're half watching the movie and more absorbed in enjoying each other. There's a hunger to our kisses, yet a shyness. Scarlett explores, then will retreat, then will explore again and I allow her the space she needs. As I said, *space* is a beautiful word.

"We should stop," Scarlett whispers against my neck, but she kisses me there again. An open-mouth kiss that is driving me insane. "We should fill out college applications."

She needs to fill out college applications. I, on the other hand, have no intention of going, but she's insistent that I at least apply. "I'm staying on my land."

"Yes, but you can take online courses," she says softly in my ear, and she could possibly convince me of anything if she continues to speak to me in that slow way. Her hot breath caresses my skin and I have the urge to roll her underneath me and kiss her until we both forget who we are. "And you should really apply for financial aid."

I could have started applying for financial aid on October first, but I didn't because I have no intentions of going to college. Scarlett has been at me nonstop because the aid is awarded until the money is depleted. A lot of her pestering has been due to her own sorrow. Her father refuses to fill out the financial aid forms so that limits her ability to receive any help. Then she found out that because she's a dependent of her father, she can't apply on her own.

And people in power wonder why the powerless think the system is broken.

"If we're going to do anything," I run my hand along her back, and liking the caress, she further curls into me, "we should take a look at those apartments near UK."

She pulls back, not a lot, but enough that her lips are no longer on my neck, which is a damn shame. "They're cheaper than living in the dorms."

I think there's a reason for that. Scarlett's smart, and while she hasn't had it easy at home, she hasn't had to pay a bill. I gently hug her as I rest my forehead against hers. "You don't need your dad's permission to apply for scholarships so you need to focus on that. The money you're making with Glory is going to help, but it's not enough to pay for tuition and living expenses."

She frowns. "I know, but those apartments are a lot cheaper than the dorms, and if I live in the dorms I think I might have to have the meal plan and that's a ton of money and . . ."

If she's going to make it after graduation without her father's help, she's going to need solid answers. "Maybe we should visit."

Her surprise and joy are hesitant. "Visit what?"

"The apartments and UK. If you're going to do this on your own, you need to know exactly how much it costs so you can be prepared to pay for it."

"Really?"

To get her to smile like that regularly, we'll visit every weekend. "Sure. If you want, that's what we can do when your family goes away for the weekend."

My cell buzzes, and I gently kiss Scarlett's lips before reaching over to the end table to find a text from V: *On our way. You better be there when we get there or else. You owe me dinner.*

I groan. So much for time and space. "My friends are coming over."

Her lips squish to the side, and I understand why. We're still mainly a secret. Her friends watch us, no doubt sensing the changes between us. Even though we aren't flaunting our relationship in the hallways, they've been slowly shutting Scarlett out. She doesn't say much about it, but I can tell it bothers her. I hate how I'm slowly cursing her.

A part of me screams I should let her go, but I can't. I've fallen too far down this hole to be saved now. Glory has some big idea that through Scarlett I can somehow break the curse, but unless Glory can give me step-by-step instructions, I'm sticking with my original plan. The blueprint Mom laid out for me years ago: keep and stay on the land.

She stretches, and places space between us. "I'll head home."

I draw her closer. "Stay."

"I don't know."

"I promise they won't say anything to anyone about us, and if you stay, then I'll fill out a college application."

Scarlett tilts her head as if my proposal surprises her. "Two college applications."

"Don't go getting crazy, now."

"Two." She stands firm, and the way her lower lip protrudes entices me to kiss her again.

As if I could say no to her. "Fine."

SCARLETT

Staying true to his word, my father has allowed me space. Not a ton, several hours here and there on the weekends, but that time is mine. Soon, I'll be alone for an entire weekend, and I'm so excited. The only requirement Dad has for me being left alone for the weekend is to meet with Pastor Hughes. I could think of worst hoops of fire to dive through, so I agreed. He and I meet tomorrow.

Since Dad has given me space, I decided to dip my toe into being a part of the family again. My Friday nights are full of pizza, movie watching and then later, after my parents go to bed, spending time with Jesse.

Last Friday night, we watched the last movie in our *Harry Potter* marathon. Tonight is the start of the *Star Wars* marathon. Before starting the movie, Dad and I shared a long discussion as to whether we should start with *Episode I* or *Episode IV*. The entire time we debated, I knew we'd start with *Episode IV* because that's how the story should be told, but I found it oddly fun to tease Dad with the idea that *Episode I* should be the first.

To be honest, it was a test to see if he would lose his temper if I disagreed. He didn't. Instead he laughed, and that returned my lost sense of safety in my home.

The credits on the movie roll, and my sister is sound asleep beside me in the recliner. She's that sticky-skinned hot that happens when two people have been under the same covers for too long. My arm is numb, my leg aches, but I hate the idea of waking her up.

Mom giggles, and I glance over at her and Dad. They're on the couch, cuddled together like they are two teenagers on a date. Mom is settled on Dad's lap, and they have this expression of pure love as they look in each other's eyes.

The sight is a hug and a pinch. This is what I want for my family, and I'm scared to have faith in what I see. Can it be like this forever?

This looks good and it feels slightly good, but Dad still wants me to stay in town for college. He still doesn't want me to have a job. He still checks my cell every night. He's changing, but how far does change go? Will it ever be enough?

Mom glances over at me, and she wears her real smile. My lips lift in return and that causes her to beam.

"Isabelle fell asleep," I say in a soft tone so as not to awaken Sleeping Beauty. "I'm afraid if I stand with her, I'll fall over."

"I'll put her to bed." Dad kisses Mom's lips, and I don't look away like most teens would. Instead, seeing this is like rain on parched land.

Mom slips off Dad's lap, he stands and he's so gentle as he lifts Isabelle off of me. My sister rests her head on Dad's shoulder as if that's the place she is meant to be.

"You're a good sister, Scarlett." Dad readjusts Isabelle's floppy arm.

"She makes it easy," I say. Dad's response is a smile of agreement, and I feel a softening toward him. He crosses the carpet of the finished basement then goes up the stairs.

"Tonight was fun," Mom says.

"Yeah." It was, and I hate the conflicted feelings that creates. I draw my knees up to my chest and wrap my arms around them. How is it possible to equal parts resent and love Dad? Will life ever be less confusing?

"I'm so happy you're forgiving him, Scarlett. We're becoming a normal family again."

Mom uses the remote to find the next *Star Wars* movie so she misses how I flinch. I haven't forgiven him. I'm still angry and sad and does that make me a horrible person because I'm not ready? I want to ask Mom, but I don't. She's happy, and I'm tired of being the person who brings this entire family down.

So far the conversation between me and the good pastor has been harmless. We discovered that we both love Netflix binging, and that's led to a serious plot discussion.

"How are things with your dad?" Pastor Hughes asks.

I find myself taking a deep breath to answer, but then pause. "That was impressive."

"What?" His feigned innocence act is awful.

"You got me talking, and then I almost answered a question I don't want to answer."

He chuckles then leans back in his chair. "I try. So let me ask a different question. Why don't you want to answer the question?"

I pick lint from my blue sweater. "Can I ask you something instead?"

"Sure."

"When people talk to you about what's happening in their home, and bad stuff has happened, do you call the police?"

There's an understanding that flashes over Pastor Hughes's face that is sad yet comforting. As if he comprehends what's going on in my mind, even if I don't. "I'm what's called a mandatory reporter. If there is abuse with a minor, I'm obligated to report it. Period. For an adult, I'm obligated to report it if the abuse is currently happening or if there is a credible threat of impending violence. Other than that, it's confidential."

Dad is no longer hitting Mom, and he's not a current threat. I chip away at the pink paint my sister put on my pinkie yesterday. It's odd and welcoming how Pastor Hughes allows me this silence to process this new information.

I have so many questions about my dad, and I do need someone to talk to—an adult who maybe has answers, but what if Dad is changing and then I go and say something that screws things up for us? What if Dad isn't changing and Dad finds out I told? Either way, it seems better to talk in circles. "Can we talk about the hypothetical family like we did last time?"

"Sure. Hypothetically," Pastor Hughes says, "what's the dynamics of this family like?"

I shrug one shoulder. "I don't know. I guess there's a daughter and her dad can get angry."

"In this family, does the dad hit the daughter?"

"No."

"Does he hit the mom?"

I don't answer and after a few beats he continues, "How does the daughter feel about the father?"

"She doesn't want to talk about him."

"Why?"

"Because while he's changing, she's not ready to forgive. Then you're going to tell me that she should forgive him and that's going to make me angry. I'm not in the mood for angry so why have the conversation?"

Pastor Hughes links his hands over his stomach. "Who do you think forgiveness is for?"

"The person who wants to be forgiven. They feel bad and they want to stop feeling bad so you forgive them to make them feel better. If I don't forgive, then everyone else is mad at me for not forgiving because then I'm dragging out the issues. Then they blame me that no one can pretend the problem didn't happen and they can't move on in their pretend little lives."

He subtly nods as if he somehow can commiserate with me, but I seriously don't think that's true. If he could understand, we wouldn't be talking forgiveness.

"What if I told you forgiveness can be beneficial to the other person, but forgiveness exists to benefit you?"

"I'd ask if you've recently experienced a hard hit to the head or if you've taken part in recreational drug use in the past twenty-four hours. Not sure if they covered this in pastor school, but you should say no to meth."

He chuckles and my lips twitch along with him.

"Let me tell you a story," he says. "There was this young man named Jacob and he stole something very important from his brother, Esau. Esau was very angry and Jacob feared for his life so he ran away. He was gone for several years. Long enough that he had married and started a family, but one day God told Jacob to return home. Jacob was hesitant. He thought for sure if he returned that his brother would kill him.

"Listening to God, Jacob took his entire family and all his livestock and started on the long journey for his hometown. Jacob was fearful, though. He sent ahead messengers with lavish gifts to inform Esau of his homecoming.

"Finally, Jacob met Esau face-to-face. Jacob thought Esau meant to harm him, but instead Esau embraced his brother and welcomed Jacob and his family to live with him. God put it on both of their hearts to forgive, but God told Jacob to not live with his brother, but instead to live on the other side of town from him."

"No offense," I say, "but I'm not understanding the moral to the story."

"Jacob spent years in fear of his brother. Could you imagine how that fear ate at him? I'm sure Esau spent many years in anger toward his brother, and I'm sure that anger ate at him, too. But when the two finally met, they were able to forgive each other for the terrible things that they had done to each other and were able to start new, fresh lives without that fear and anger."

"Once again, all I'm hearing is you saying I have to forgive so everyone can live happily ever after, and I'm not feeling happily-ever-after-ish at the moment."

"True, but you're missing the important part. God didn't force them to have a relationship. He didn't force two puzzle pieces that don't fit together. He allowed space and time between the brothers before the forgiveness happened, and once they did forgive, He didn't say they had to be friends again. In fact, He put much-needed space between the two brothers."

Pastor Hughes gives me an opportunity to speak, but I'm a prisoner of the town of Mute.

He leans forward on his desk. "If abuse happens in your home, I'm not telling you to accept the abuse. I'm telling you the opposite. Abuse of any type is wrong. If your father or your mother hit each other or if they were to hit you or your sister, you call the police. If you don't feel like you can, then put it on me, and I will."

"We're talking hypotheticals," I whisper.

"And I'm not. This is advice everyone, regardless of who they are, should know."

I grab the arms of my chair as anger rushes through me. "But the mom will lie to the police."

"Let her. That's her choice, but it will put the family on the authorities' radar. God does not want anyone in any situation that causes harm."

"Then why this push to forgive?"

"Because you shouldn't be consumed with anger and sadness, and a father's sins shouldn't destroy a child. Anger and sadness make it difficult to let love and joy into your life.

"Scarlett, hypothetical family or not, you're sitting here today because your relationship with your father is complicated. Anyone could pick up on the tension between the two of you when you were sitting in my office together. I want to help you and I need you to listen to me.

"What I want you to take away from Jacob's story is that forgiveness is possible, but forgiveness does not mean that you have to let that person back in your life. Forgiveness does not mean you condone or accept abuse. Forgiveness means that you're going to be turning eighteen soon, graduating from high school, making choices for your own life. When you start fresh with a brand-new life, do you want to start that life full of anger, or do you want to focus on joy?"

What type of question is that? "Of course I want joy."

"Then find a way to look at your father as someone who is broken and needs counseling and prayer. Forgiveness removes yourself from inside the situation and gives you the ability to look upon it with different eyes. God gave us free will. He does not like it when we choose to harm others, but that's still a choice we can make. God teaches us forgiveness to help us realize that you aren't responsible for someone else's bad choices. That your father's mistakes are his fault, not yours. That the anger only keeps you tied to the harm, not setting you free from it.

"I don't want you to forgive your father to make his life easier, I want you to find forgiveness so you can move on with your life without your father's demons becoming yours."

I shift in my seat as my nerves demand for me to run, but as much as I want to run, I need to stay. I need answers. I need to know what to do. I'm nervous, I'm sick, I'm dizzy, but more important, I'm desperate. "Mom . . . Mom says Dad is changing. Dad says he's changing, too. Is he? Is change possible?"

"I can't answer the question as to whether or not he's changing as I don't counsel him. Even if I did, I couldn't betray my trust with him, but I will say that I do believe that change is possible. Over the years I've seen many broken people who never thought they'd find joy be happy again. The question I have for you is, do you think your dad is changing?"

"I don't know," I answer honestly. "He's not angry anymore."

"I need you to hear me on this," Pastor Hughes says. "Letting go of your anger and sadness does not give your father permission to hurt you or your family. I pray daily he is changing, and that you find peace. But you finding peace does not mean that you or your family are punching bags. There are no more second chances when it comes to abuse. Let me say it again: if your father hurts your mother or hurts you or your sister, you call the police. Do you understand?"

I slowly nod as I attempt to comprehend all he's said. Letting the anger go doesn't mean Dad has permission to hurt me again. It's such a strange concept that my brain disconnects.

"A part of my job is to discuss what is called a *safety plan* with people who are in complicated relationships. It's a plan of how to stay safe if you find yourself in a dangerous situation and a plan in case you need to leave home."

I'm so overwhelmed that I can do nothing more than listen. Pastor Hughes continues to talk about the plan and then he talks about websites he wants me to visit, websites to show me that help is available, but suggests doing so at school or at a friend's house.

I listen, yet I don't because I'm still lost in the last part of our conversation. It is possible? Can I let the anger go? Can I let go of my sadness? I honestly don't know.

There are several suitcases in the foyer and not a single one of them is mine. I sit on the steps, and I'm so stinking excited that my knee bounces. Dad is taking Mom and Isabelle to Atlanta for the weekend, and I'm staying here by myself, which is the most fascinating and exhilarating experience of my life. I'm not staying home either. I'm heading into Lexington with Jesse to go apartment hunting and to tour the University of Kentucky. Life is absolutely amazing.

In a suit, Dad walks out of his study and places his laptop bag near the pile. He takes in the baggage then looks at me. I don't glower in return—that's a major improvement for me. The anger I've been holding on to is becoming harder to muster, and I don't know how I feel about that.

"Can I bring you anything back from Atlanta?"

"An ice cream sundae?" I ask.

Dad grins. "Not sure that's going to travel well in my suitcase."

I snap my fingers in a fake *dang it*.

"Seriously, though, do you want anything?"

"I don't need anything, but thank you."

Mom and Isabelle walk down the stairs, and Mom's verbalizing a nonstop list of who I should call if there's an emergency, and whatever random thing pops into her head.

Isabelle gives me a wet kiss on the cheek, and my mom gives me a long, warm hug. Dad, on the other hand, gives me space. He has kept his word. He's going to counseling, he seems to be listening to me, seems to be listening to Mom and he seems to be . . . changing. Like Pastor Hughes, I do believe change is possible, but I have to decide if change is possible for my dad.

"Be safe if you go out with your friends or if they come over," Dad says. "Either way, let your mom know of your plans. Otherwise, call us if you need anything."

His hands shake, and I think of what it must have been like

for him to wait for a phone call from his sister that would never come. Just the idea hurts. I can't imagine having lived it.

I walk across the foyer and hug my father. It takes a moment before he hugs me back. I close my eyes and revel. As a child this hug was the favorite part of my day. I've missed this. I've missed him. I've missed having a real home.

I pull back, and my chest tightens at the sight of Dad's eyes filled with tears. "Thank you."

The emotion in me is so powerful that I only say, "Thank you for giving me space."

"You're welcome."

Yes, I do believe change is possible. For me and for him.

"When you get back," my palms sweat and my skin is clammy, "I'd like to talk to you."

"What do you want to talk about?"

About my job, about Jesse, about how I don't want to lie anymore and how I'd like him to, maybe not approve, but deal with my choices. "Things like how I'd like to get my driver's license and a few other things. Maybe we could talk about them with Pastor Hughes."

Happiness spreads over my dad's face. "I'd love to."

"You're okay with letting me get my driver's permit?" I'm testing him because if he's not okay with me driving, then he won't be okay with Jesse, my job or UK.

"It's time, but we'll discuss this more in counseling, okay?"

I'm absolutely blown away because it's happening—he's changing. "Sure."

Dad says a few other things, reminding me of important numbers and where they will be, and then he finally leaves. Standing alone in my house, I'm filled with a sense of hope that maybe, just maybe, we can be a family again.

I wrap my arms around myself because while that hope is uplifting, it is possibly the most terrifying emotion I have ever felt.

JESSE

Pen in my hand, I stare at the piece of paper. None of the sentences do justice to what it was like to lose my mother. I don't know how to describe how Mom's cries are a constant background noise, that at times the wound on my back still aches, or how to describe the ever-present hole that can never be filled.

Mom died, Dad lived and it doesn't make sense. It's not fair. It's not right. And some person in power thinks it's okay to let him go.

To do what? Hurt someone else? Three years. He was supposed to serve a minimum of twenty. When will life be okay?

The clock is ticking down. I either write this letter, show up in person to explain why Dad should stay in jail, or I do nothing. I've started the letter countless times, but I can't get through the first paragraph. The blank parts of the paper make me a failure.

A knock on the door, and I crumple the paper and toss it in the trash. I'll deal with it later. Right now, I'd rather deal with what's good in my world.

I open the door, and Scarlett's smile is bright enough to drive my demons away. She's been a piece of heaven in hell. She walks in, no purse in hand as she's convinced her father is still tracking her cell. Scarlett raises on her toes for a kiss, and I'm more than happy to oblige. My fingers thread into her hair and I press my lips to hers. I could do this every day for the rest of my life, and it still wouldn't be enough.

"You ready?" I ask.

I expect a quick confirmation, but instead she steps back. "I think so."

My eyebrows draw together. "Think so?"

"I think Dad is changing. He's willing to consider letting me get my driver's permit."

Changing. The word tries to settle in my stomach, but it doesn't. It hangs there as a foreign object that needs to be surgically removed. Maybe this change she speaks of is real, but just in case . . . "Looking at apartments and taking a tour at the University of Kentucky doesn't mean you're taking out a thirty-year mortgage. He can change and yet you can still look."

"I know." She fiddles with the ends of her sweater, an indication a ton is going on in her brain. "How would you feel if I told my father about us?"

My gut reaction is that what Scarlett and I have going on now is fine, but if I tell her to keep us quiet, she might see that as me having a problem with us going public. Which I don't have a problem with, but I am concerned with her safety. "I want what is best for you."

"I think he's changed," she says. "I think he might listen."

There's an awful lot at stake with words like *think* and *might*, but saying so isn't going to help, but hurt. "Are we leaving or staying?"

"Leaving." A daring fire glows in her eyes, and my Tink has returned. "If anything, this will be an adventure, right?"

SCARLETT

Panic attack. That's what I'm on the verge of. The world's not okay, and my dreams are being swept away. I don't know what apartment this is, but it's not the one pictured on the internet. I try to inhale deeply, but my lungs won't take in air.

This is the last apartment on the list and each one has been worse than the one before. Evidently, for me to afford a decent place to live, I must sell either my liver or my soul.

Jesse stands next to the large open window looking down at the squalor below. On the corner, someone is selling heroin. When we were on the sidewalk, there were two people shooting up. Jesse tugged on my hand, mumbling how we didn't need to see the inside, but I did. I needed this place to be an oasis in the proverbial desert.

Jesse jumps, catches the bottom of the open window, performs a pull-up, and soon his feet are no longer touching the floor. He drops, and I blink. "Why isn't it shutting?"

"It's painted open. I'm guessing management keeps it this way so they don't have to replace the glass for when the place is broken into. Easy access and all." Jesse grins like a lunatic at the woman showing us the apartment. "Am I right?"

The realtor, who is in a pencil suit, stares blankly at Jesse, but she then glances at me with a smile. "Have you seen the bathroom? It has a claw-foot tub!"

"Did you hear that, Tink? Claw-foot. Practically sells the

place." He walks into the bathroom, I hear the sound of water in a sink and then he calls out, "Cool, brown water."

The realtor's cell rings, and she excuses herself to answer it in the hallway.

The printout of the gorgeous apartment in my price range crackles in my hand, and I spin as I try to find something redeemable. Anything. A tickling near my ankle; I glance down and my heart bursts past my rib cage. I scream and sprint across the room.

Jesse comes running out, and when he looks at the corner I'm pointing at while shouting something even I can't understand, he places his hands in his pockets. "Look, it comes with pets."

"It's a rat!" I shout.

Jessie looks at me like I stated the obvious, because I just did.

"I hear rats are all the rage now. It's the new dog. They're supposed to be super-smart. Like how they know how to tie you down to the bed first before they gnaw your eyes out."

Not helping. "I can't live with rats!"

"They do get a bad rap. Bubonic plague can do that. Do you think they can domesticate the stray ones or do you think that's a genetic thing they breed into them?"

A new level of panic sets in, and I start to shake. "What am I going to do? I can't live like this. I can't live in any of these places and I had hoped and I had dreamed and . . ." I hold out the piece of paper that had contained my dreams. "They lied. All these places lied."

"Yes," he states plainly, and for a few seconds, I consider throwing the rat at him.

I spin, praying for an answer. "I'll get a roommate. That will help. They can pay half, I can pay half." We can move into an apartment where I won't die of tetanus.

"Where are you going to find a roommate? Are any of your friends planning on moving out from their parents' financial umbrella upon graduation as well?"

My friends are heading to college, maybe some to UK, but they'll move into the dorms because they have parents who will help them. "I can find someone on the internet?"

"Great thinking," Jesse says. "In your internet ad, are you going to be specific about the way you want them to kill you? I'd go with fast, but what do I know?"

I swing around and the glare I give Jesse causes him to step back two feet. "I'm teasing."

"This isn't funny!" I roar.

"I know, but if you don't learn to laugh during the bad moments, life—a life that is already rough—will be rougher."

My shoulders collapse, and Jesse crosses the room to me. He weaves an arm around my waist, and I press my head into his shoulder. His embrace is strong, it's safe and I'm completely and utterly lost. "What am I going to do?"

"Take it one step at a time. You're going to work for Glory as much as you can, you're going to save every penny and you will think of better ways to get a roommate other than the internet. If you can't afford to move into the dorms, I would find a better realtor, one who isn't obsessed with claw-foot tubs, for help finding suitable studios in other parts of the city."

I lift my head, and I'm grateful he still holds me close. "You knew this is what would happen, didn't you?"

He nods, and I appreciate he doesn't gloat. "If I told you, I don't think you would have believed me. Reality is sometimes something people have to experience to believe."

Sad part is, he's right.

"You have six months until graduation. That's a long time, but it's going to go by fast. I know you want college, but college, working a job and paying your own bills is a lot of work. It's doable, but work. You need to buckle down, apply for a ton of scholarships and get that meeting with the financial aid counselor at the university like our tour guide suggested. If you remember, she said that they still might be able to help you financially even though your father is refusing to help."

I sigh heavily. There's a lot I haven't considered, and there's a lot I need to learn. Dreams don't happen because I wish them into being. If I want freedom, I'll have to work and work hard.

"I don't know about you, but I've had enough of real-world problems for the day," he says. "Want to get out of here?"

"Definitely."

JESSE

After grabbing a quick bite to eat for dinner, we're headed home. Nice part of having an old truck is that Scarlett's able to ride next to me on the bench seat. My heater's not the best, the fall evening is cool and Scarlett wants to be warm. Fine by me. My arm's around her, her head is on my shoulder and every inch of her is squeezed tight to every inch of me. There's a flame that's been lit inside me, creating a smoldering fire.

At first, she had placed her hand on my thigh. Just laid flat. That alone got my mind buzzing. So then I fantasized about kissing her and how I'd love to have more time alone with her, and my fingers began brushing along her arm. Sometime later, can't remember when because the blood had drained from my brain, she made slow and tempting circles on my leg.

Alone. I need to get to this girl alone. It's become my single-most obsession. Scarlett in my bed, in my field, hell, the bed of this truck would work.

"Pull over!" Scarlett shouts, and I jump after the long, comfortable silence.

I hit the brakes and glance in my rearview mirror. Thankfully there isn't anyone behind me, and I take the turn into the deserted parking area next to the low rock wall that had to be built back in the 1800s. Scarlett undoes her seatbelt, leans forward and looks through the windshield. "My parents have driven past this place hundreds of times, and we have never once stopped. No matter how many times I've asked."

Funny, Gran stopped here almost every single time we drove by. Never occurred to me that anyone in our county hadn't parked here at one point or another. We're at the top of the highest hill of our county and below us are the twinkling lights of our hometown.

Our town has a county courthouse, a government building, a police station, a few two-story buildings, some fast food joints out on Massey Street and then the elementary, middle and high schools. Most people would turn their noses up at the sight, but for me it's home.

Scarlett's radiant as she looks upon the landscape. "It's beautiful, isn't it?"

"Yeah, it is."

She glances over at me and pushes my arm. "You weren't even looking."

"I like looking at what's inside my truck more than what's outside."

Her eyes soften to the deep blue of the sea. She relaxes back into the seat and cuddles closer to me. "Do you think I'm stupid for wanting to strike out on my own? Do you think I should suck it up and let Dad pay for everything for the next four years before cutting ties?"

"Do you want to go to a business college?"

"No."

"If he's hurting you, then you leave. It's that plain and simple."

"There is nothing simple about leaving."

"I wish my mom had left."

Her hair brushes my shoulder as she turns her head to look at me. "What do you mean?"

I push forward rapidly in an attempt to ignore the memory of the screams. "My mom had a habit of dating guys that hurt her until one day the guy didn't just hurt her, he killed her."

"Oh my God, Jesse, that's awful."

"You knew she died." Scarlett had left a note in my locker for me even though I had stopped talking to her by that point. I had continued to ignore Scarlett, but I had kept the note. It's still in my room, in a box at the bottom of my dresser.

"But I thought she died in an accident. I had no idea she was murdered."

Not many people do. "It happened out of state. Gran thought it would be easier for me if we didn't share the details." I can't say she made the wrong decision. I consider telling Scarlett the truth— that Mom didn't die that autumn, but had died that last summer while we were still friends, but that would bring on questions I don't think I can answer.

"I'm so sorry," she says.

"You do that a lot—apologize for things you don't need to apologize for."

She places her hand on my arm. "I hurt for you, and I don't know what else to say."

"I'm not telling you this so you'll pity me. I'm telling you this because I don't want you to make the same mistakes she did. I don't want you to put your hope in some guy who isn't worth an ounce of your love. I know your dad hasn't laid a hand on you, but he struck a blow to you every time he hit your mom. I can tell you want to forgive him. I can tell you're hoping he's changed, but I'm telling you that if you decide to strike out on your own after you graduate and he's pissed, then I say he's a bastard you need to leave behind. If he loves you, he'll support you.

"If any guy, including me, gets in the way of your happiness, if he stands in the way of you reaching your dreams, if he can't understand that harming someone is wrong, then walk away, Scarlett. It *is* that simple."

SCARLETT

For years, I've wondered what love was, and this is it. It's his words, it's his actions, and it's the way he's holding me as if he'd willingly walk through fire to love me. I caress Jesse's face, and the stubble along his jaw tickles my skin. He leans into my touch then kisses the palm of my hand. The sensitive brush of his lips sends tingles through my blood.

Over the past couple of weeks, we've kissed. We kiss a lot. We kiss often, but that's all we've done, all I've been comfortable with, and Jesse has been patient. So incredibly patient. Never pushing or asking for more. Stopping with my lightest change of body language. Allowing me room, allowing me to be in charge, allowing me to take the lead.

Now, though, I want more. I want him to kiss me, I want to get lost in him and I want to lose myself. I lean forward and touch my lips to his. It's a soft brush at first, so light, but it doesn't take long for our embrace to deepen. Our lips part, our tongues dance. Gentle tugs and nips. Hands roaming along backs, in hair, and there's this pulse, this energy, this need.

I want closer. I need closer. I desire closer, and unsure how to ask Jesse for more, I boldly kiss my way down his neck. Jesse sucks in a breath and his hold on me tightens.

"That feels good," he whispers, and his admission gives me courage. Courage to kiss, courage to explore, courage to sneak my hand up his shirt and touch the hot skin of his stomach. Jesse moans. My eyes snap open, so do his and we pant for breath.

"You sure?" he asks. "I don't want you doing anything you don't want to do."

"I want to," I say, but give him the truth, "but I'll want to stop."

Jesse unleashes his pirate grin, and that in itself is like a kiss I can feel down to my toes. "Scarlett, I am at your mercy. You're in control so lead the way."

"I like the sound of that." I love the sound of that. Before I over-think the situation, I yank my shirt over my head and have to bite my lower lip to stop the fit of giggles begging to be released at Jesse's adorable expression.

"Have I told you you're beautiful?" he says.

"Several times."

I grab the hem of his shirt, and Jesse is helpful and compliant as I free him of his shirt and toss it onto the floorboard. I circle my arms around his neck, nudge him in my direction, and Jesse is like a domino, falling onto me exactly how I want.

My head on the seat, his body covering mine, our legs tangled, and there's a rush of sensation as we continue to move and kiss and touch and explore. He whispers things to me, beautiful things, wonderful things, and I hold him tighter when he tells me he never wants to live life without me. I'm so full of joy, so full of happiness that I whisper, "I love you."

Banging on the window, my heart jumps, and as we sit up Jesse gathers me close.

"Hands on the dashboard. Driver, roll down your window. Do as we say and do it now!"

"Jesse?" I whisper into his neck.

He kisses the side of my head. "Get your shirt on then do what they say. It's the police."

JESSE

Scarlett reaches for her shirt and the police officer bangs on the window again. "Put your hands on the dashboard now!"

She turns ghost white, and that causes my blood to boil. Two teenagers making out in a truck doesn't equate to his pissed-off reaction. He's scaring Scarlett, and that doesn't sit well with me.

"Roll down the window or I'll break it."

He does and I'll have Marshall sue his ass. Scarlett looks over at me and her entire body quakes. "You should open the window."

"Put your shirt on first," I say in as even a tone as I can. "I'm not going to have some jerk cop checking you out."

In a rush, Scarlett slips on her shirt as the cop bangs at the window. I place my hands on the steering wheel and when Scarlett has her hands on the dashboard, I look over at the cop. The windows are fogged, but I can see him glaring at me. He gestures to my window, where there stands another cop.

"Window down," I shout, "or door open?"

"Unlock the door, window open."

I do what he asks and the cool fall air races in and bites at my skin. "What can I do for you, Officer?" Not a bit of that sounds sincere.

"License and registration. License first."

I slowly go for my wallet, hand him my license and as I do, the cop says, "Give me your license, ma'am."

"I don't have one," Scarlett says. "Or any ID."

The cop's eyes flicker over my license. "You're a Lachlin?"

Super. My family's name proceeds me. "Yes."

"What's your name, miss?" the cop asks.

"Scarlett Copeland."

The cop's head snaps up and he flicks his chin toward Scarlett in some sort of nonverbal to the other police officer. "What did you say your name is?"

"Scarlett Copeland."

The situation changes, quick, too quick. The police officer reaches for his sidearm. "Sir, we're going to need you to step out of the car."

"What for?" I ask.

"Do what you're told."

The passenger side door opens, and the other police officer grabs Scarlett's arm. Pure fear overwhelms her expression and I'm consumed with adrenaline. "Let her go!"

"Step out of the car!" the police officer shouts at me, but I don't. Scarlett's being dragged out. She reaches for me, I snatch her hand, but her fingers slip from my grip.

"Jesse!" Scarlett screams.

I'm being yanked then, and I go with it because I need to get to Scarlett. I need to protect her. The police officer hauls Scarlett toward his car, and a million scenarios run through my mind. Are they some sort of sick perverts? Are they even cops? "What's going on?"

"Put your hands on the car!" the cop yells in my ear.

"What the hell are you doing with Scarlett?"

"Jesse!" she shouts again, and as I go to step in her direction, the cop shoves me against the car, my head hitting the door. Hurts like hell, but I don't care. I round to go for Scarlett again, but as I turn the cop snatches my arm. He attempts to twist it behind my back, and when I hear her shout again, I push him away and he stumbles.

Curses from the man, shouts from other places as headlights flash over us. I'm rammed into the car again, but as I struggle I realize there are multiple arms pinning me. My own arms are pulled back, one after another, and handcuffs are being placed on my wrists.

"What's going on?" I shout.

"You're under arrest for kidnapping Scarlett Copeland."

SCARLETT

The police officer eases into my driveway, and I shake as if I'm naked in the artic. Dad's going to kill me. "This . . . this . . ." My stuttering is back, and I'm having a hard time reigning it in. "This . . . This is a mistake. I . . . I wasn't kidnapped. I willingly went with Jesse Lachlin today."

Like he has the entire time, the police officer says nothing. He exits the car as the front door to my house opens and my parents come out, Mom nearly at a run, my father not too far behind. Dad pauses by the police officer at the front of the car, but Mom rushes to my door. She presses her hands against the glass as if I'm an animal in the zoo.

"Why is she in the back? Why won't you let her out?"

My father nods and the police officer opens my door. The moment I'm out, Mom has me wrapped tight in a hug. "We were so worried. So worried."

"I don't understand." I try to lean back, but it's impossible. "What are you doing here? Why are they saying I was kidnapped? What is going on?"

Mom smooths back my hair as if I need comfort. "Our flight was cancelled, and when we came home you weren't here. Your cell was here, your purse was here, but you weren't. We called your friends, we called so many people, and no one knew where you were." Her eyes fill with tears. "We came home and you were gone. You were gone."

"Where were you?" Dad's voice breaks in and the entire world goes silent.

"I . . . I was out . . . I—"

"We found her with the Lachlin boy," the cop says in a low tone, but we all hear it. "They were at the overlook . . . in his truck . . ."

Dad's eyes harden and nausea hits me so hard, so fast, I sway.

"Go inside," Dad says. "I want to finish talking with the officer alone."

"Jesse didn't kidnap me," I spit out. "They handcuffed him, they said they were charging him with kidnapping. They said—"

"Get in the house!" Dad roars, and I flinch. So does Mom. She takes my hand, and she whispers for me to move quickly and I follow her directions, as I realize that we just entered hell.

JESSE

Resisting arrest!" Marshall busts into the holding room I'm in, and I lower my head, half wishing that they would have left me in lockup. "And you wonder why I don't think you're responsible enough to own the land."

I had one phone call, and I called him. Wouldn't have mattered if I didn't call him, the police would have. Marshall is my guardian. "I thought I was being arrested for kidnapping."

The glare Marshall gives scares even me. "Is this a joke to you? Because let me assure you, there is nothing funny about this."

I couldn't agree more. "I'm being serious. Am I being arrested for kidnapping?"

"Should you be?"

I look my uncle straight in the eye. "No."

"Why did you think it was a good idea to hit a police officer? You're lucky you aren't being charged with assaulting an officer!"

"I didn't hit him. I shoved him, but he shoved me first. Two police officers come up to my truck, and tell me to open my window. I tell Scarlett to get her shirt on first, then I open my window. They find out I'm a Lachlin, and the next thing I know they open Scarlett's door and drag her out. *Drag.* She's terrified, screaming my name, and when I get out, I'm slammed against my truck."

"You should have complied!"

"They should have never touched Scarlett!" I shout. "What would you have done? Scarlett and I were making out in a car, we weren't knocking over a convenience store! I may not have been right, but I wasn't wrong."

Marshall kicks the legs of a chair and pivots away from me. "This is serious, Jesse. These aren't charges I can easily have dismissed."

"I shouldn't have pushed him. I know that, but everything happened fast. She was scared, and that scared me."

Marshall rolls his neck, returns to the table, and with a mumbled curse takes the chair across from me. "The kidnapping charges are expected to be dropped soon. Scarlett told the police officers she went willingly with you. As for the resisting arrest charge, I don't know how to handle that one yet, but give me some time and I'll figure it out."

"Thank you for helping." It's all I can say.

"This is the reason I want you to leave town. The Lachlin name carries a heavy load. Scarlett's parents come home to find her gone, they contact the police, and when they find her with you, everyone assumes you did the worst because of your family name. If you stay, you will forever be living under a storm cloud you'll never be able to outrun."

There's no doubt I lost his vote. There's a good possibility I lost the pastor's vote, too, but I'll handle that once I'm free. At least I still have Scarlett's vote. My gut twists as I think of her. "Is Scarlett okay?"

"She's home," he answers.

But that doesn't mean she's fine. I weigh the pros and cons of asking Marshall to check in on her, but don't know how to voice my concerns without breaking Scarlett's trust.

"Maybe I should have told you who's responsible for the vote," Marshall says. "If I had, then maybe you wouldn't be in this scenario."

I forget he's not aware I know the identities of the people in the tribunal. "How's that?"

"I could be wrong, but maybe you wouldn't have gotten into a relationship with the daughter of the man who is going to vote on your future."

My brain vibrates with the impact of his words. "What did you say?"

"Besides me and Pastor Hughes, Scarlett's father is the third member of the tribunal."

SCARLETT

My father left the house, and I'm in my room. Mom hasn't visited. Isabelle hasn't either. I've sat on my bed, knees drawn to my chest, and I look out the window, searching for some sign of life at Jesse's, but there's none. The place is dark, shut tight, and his truck is missing from the driveway.

It's late. So late. Hours have passed since I've been home. What's happened to Jesse? Will my choices cost him his land and me my freedom? What have I done?

Headlights down our dark road and I will those lights to turn into Jesse's drive, but they don't. They instead turn into my driveway. Nausea ravages my stomach. My father's home.

I strain to listen in the silence. From my bedroom, I can't hear the kitchen door open, but I do hear his footsteps in the foyer then pounding on the stairs. My heart picks up speed and my chest becomes tight. My mother. He's going to go after her, he's going to yell at her, he's going to hurt her.

The doorknob turns and there's a crash as my door flies open and bangs against the wall. My father shoots in, he flicks the light on and I'm temporarily blinded.

"How long have you been lying to me?"

I don't know how to answer. I don't know if I should answer.

"How long have you been lying to me!" he yells, and I flinch.

Dad turns to my dresser, opens the drawers and he goes

through them. Ransacking through folded clothes. I'm so shocked
I'm up and out of my bed. "What are you doing?"

"This is my house." He goes for another drawer and then another. "Everything in here belongs to me, not you. I'm the one who
works. I buy everything. It all belongs to me, and if I want to go
through it, I can go through it. If I want to burn it, I can."

"Bryant," Mom says in soft voice from the safety of my doorway. In a long, white nightgown, she clings to the doorframe as if
she needs the support.

Dad doesn't respond to her, he probably doesn't even hear her.
He's in my room, but in his head he's in a different universe. A
hostile universe. A place where madness reigns. He crosses the
room, rummages through my bedside table, tossing out my pens
and notebooks.

I scramble out of the way as he grabs my mattress and flips the
bed. The mattress lands on me as I try to get away. I push it off
and tears prick my eyes as he tosses the box spring and it hits the
floor with a *boom*.

Exposed is my closed shoebox full of cash, my laptop from
Glory and the boxes of necklaces that I priced. He leans down,
flicks off the top of my shoebox and I slap a hand over my mouth
in an effort to stay quiet.

Dad straightens, a stack of cash in his hands, and he shakes it
at me. "Are you selling drugs with Jesse Lachlin?"

My eyes widen and my heart stops beating. "No."

"I don't believe you."

I stumble forward to make him believe. "I work for Glory
Gardner. You can ask her. I track her purchases on the laptop.
Look at it and you can see. I price her jewelry. I do clerical work
for her and she pays me. That's it."

"Are you doing drugs with him?"

"No."

"So you're sleeping with him then? My daughter's a whore?"

The air rushes out of my body.

"The police told me how they found you. Naked in his truck
at the top of the hill. Do you know how humiliated I am? Do you
know how upset I was? How sick with worry? Do you know what

it was like to wonder if you were hurt or dead? If you needed me and I wasn't there? That I couldn't protect you? I called everyone. Your friends, your mother's friends, people I work with, and I told them that my daughter was missing and instead she's having sex?"

"We weren't having sex!" I yell.

Dad turns an unnatural shade of red, and he's a steamroller as he rushes at me. I stumble, fear weakening my knees, and my back smacks the wall.

"Don't you lie!" Spit flies from his mouth. "They found you with your shirt off!"

"Bryant," Mom says a little louder. "Please, stop."

"Admit what you did!" Dad yells. "Admit what everyone in this town is going to think by tomorrow morning! Admit that you're a whore!"

"I am not a whore!" I shout.

"You've made me an embarrassment! You're costing me my reputation so you could throw your life away with that trailer trash? You could have at least had the self-respect to sleep with someone reputable."

Anger sweeps through me. I push off the wall and shout in his face, "I'll take Jesse over anyone! Anyone else would have bowed down to you, but Jesse is helping me leave!"

"What did you say?" Dad's voice goes deadpan and a warning chill runs through me.

"Bryant." Mom touches Dad's arm, and Dad turns on her.

"I told you years ago to never let her play with that boy."

"They were only children," Mom whispers.

"This is what happens when you don't listen!" he shouts.

He raises his hand, she covers her face and he hits her. The smack of flesh against flesh is a knife through my windpipe. Mom's head flops back, her body transforms to that of a rag doll, and she falls to the floor. Mom's a lifeless lump, and I shout her name. She jerks, a quick glance up, and raises her arms as Dad lifts his hand again.

I scream, but I don't hear the sound, I don't hear anything but a high-pitched buzzing. I grab at my father, attempting to hold on to his arm, but he shoves me off.

He strikes her again, and she squeezes into a ball. He lifts his arm, and I run in between them, but he grabs me. His fingers dig into my skin, I screech with the blinding pain and he throws me. I hit the wall; my muscles spasm with the impact and I crumple to the floor.

Mom sobs, a gut-wrenching sound that cuts me deep, and I look up to see him strike her again and again. Blood gushes from her nose, her mouth. Dad kicks her and a strange sound leaves Mom's mouth, a croaking wheeze as if she can't get in enough air.

"You're killing her," I yell, and Dad staggers back.

He looks at me, he looks at Mom, then becomes frozen. A demented statue.

Mom's crying, her entire body shaking. She tries to push up, but her arm gives as if there is no bone. She hits the floor, wincing as if breathing causes her agony. Blood stains her face, her hair, her clothing, my floor.

"Leave!" I scream at my father.

He slowly turns his head toward me as if he doesn't comprehend my words.

"Leave!" I yell again, and he does. A slow, stiff walk that's not fast enough for me.

I crawl, wrap my body around her and start to sob as if I'm a child. "I'm sorry, Mom. I'm so sorry."

"Mommy?" Isabelle says from the doorway. She's in PJs and an American Girl doll dangles from her hand. She shakes from head to toe. We're broken, so broken, and no one in this family will ever be fixed again.

JESSE

It's nearly impossible to keep my eyes open in the passenger side of Marshall's car. I had to spend the night in lockup and made bail this morning. Marshall then took me to the ER to have the bump on my head examined. There, he talked to the doctor behind the curtain. I didn't pay much attention as my thoughts were swamped by Scarlett.

Now, he's taking me to his house. Not my first choice, but he's my guardian and doesn't think going home is in my best interest. But there's a nagging in my gut to confirm that Scarlett is safe. It's so strong that a part of me wants to open the car door, even though Marshall's speeding down the road, jump out, run toward home and hold Scarlett in my arms.

"Can we at least swing by my house? Maybe pick up some stuff?" Give me a few minutes to sneak across the road, climb up the tree and check on Scarlett?

"Scarlett's father was on the warpath last night," Marshall says as if he's reading my mind. Maybe he's now psychic. "I hate to admit it, but he has some major connections at the police department. The last thing you need is a confrontation with him, and being across the road is begging for one."

"Did you see Scarlett?" I ask. "Was she okay?"

Marshall shakes his head, and I'm so damn edgy I swear my skin is molting.

"I heard someone say that the police took her home. Scarlett's father came to the station to talk to the chief. A friend of mine said the meeting wasn't pretty. Mr. Copeland was mad it took so long to find her, and then he was angry with what happened when they did. He wasn't happy to hear his daughter was manhandled. I'm hoping the last part will work in our favor."

"Is there any way you can check on Scarlett?"

"Is there something you want to tell me? Maybe the big something I feel you've been leaving out?"

I'm silent as I don't know what to tell him. At least not without possibly upsetting Scarlett because I betrayed her secret.

"I'll see if anyone has seen her since the arrest."

"I'd appreciate that."

"That doesn't mean I'm forgetting the question. I'm just allowing you some time to get your thoughts together."

I check my cell again, and besides a few texts from V, Leo and Nazareth, there's nothing from Scarlett and nothing from Glory. Silence from Scarlett is disappointing yet expected. We've never reached out to each other via cell. The silence from Glory, though, hits me hard. It's sad to admit, but I had started to believe Glory had a gift and that she cared.

"I called in every favor I have," Marshall continues. "And even called in a few favors that aren't owed to me."

I can't explain how grateful I am for him. I'd hate to think what would happen to someone who didn't have an Uncle Marshall in their corner.

"Even if this goes in front of a judge," he continues, "we have a good chance of getting this thrown out. Your initial arrest for kidnapping was an unlawful arrest, which means you have a justification to resist within reasonable limits. If that doesn't work, we can use the case of self-defense. That nice bump on your forehead will be the proof we need."

That explains the photos he had the doctor take. "I didn't think you did criminal law."

"I don't, but I did stay up most of the night reading."

"Thank you." Probably the most sincere thing I've said to him.

"Regardless of what you think, I care, Jesse. I always have."

I believe him, but I'm too drained to deal with much. "I don't get it. Why is Scarlett's father one of the people voting?"

"A few years ago, he began checking up on your grandmother at least twice a week. He paid for some of the repairs on the trailer. Mrs. Copeland would come over, too, and visit with her. You were either at school or working the land. This isn't a slap in the face to you, but your grandmother was lonely."

Heavy with exhaustion, I'm slow looking over at him. "I never knew."

Marshall looks as exhausted as me. Black circles under his eyes, his white dress shirt wrinkled. He stops at a red light and rubs his eyes. "Suzanne didn't want you to know. She thought it would upset you that she had become close with Scarlett's parents after you and Scarlett had stopped being friends."

It doesn't make sense. Maybe it's because I'm tired. Maybe it's because there's no straight process to understand. "He's not a good man."

Marshall glances over at me with sharp eyes. "Do you want to elaborate on that?"

"You already granted me a delay on that subject."

Marshall swears under his breath. "How deep is this rabbit hole?

"Deep." But I switch the subject back to Gran. "I don't believe Mr. Copeland was checking on and helping Gran out of the kindness of his heart."

"He was a sweet talker to your gran, and I didn't see anything wrong with it as the whole community thinks the man is a god. Your grandmother was a force of nature, but she was old, and as I said, she could get lonely.

"The day before her death, I had heard through friends that Mr. Copeland was asking around how much the land would be worth and if he would have any competition on buying it. That didn't sit right with me so I had planned on going over the next day and convincing your gran to change the vote from him to Glory, but I was too late. If you want to be mad at me for that, I don't blame you, but don't be mad at your gran. Even the best of us can be conned."

"Does he know he's one of the votes on the tribunal?"

"Yes."

Glory lied to me the entire time. "I'm going to lose the land, aren't I?"

The light turns green, and Marshall presses on the gas. "I know this is tough on you, but I can't give you the land. Seeing how hard you've worked over the past few months has impressed me, but the maturity aspect is only a portion. If you stay here you'll be fighting a legacy you have nothing to do with. What happened last night should be proof. Everyone will always think the worst of you because of your last name."

"I can prove them wrong," I say.

"If you stay here, you'll become a self-fulfilling prophecy."

My head hits the back of the seat, and I close my eyes. It's a surreal moment of sinking. Forty-eight hours ago, I had it all— possibly two votes to keep my land and the girl I loved in my arms. For a brief moment, I was happy. My throat constricts as I realize my mom was wrong and the world was right. The original curse is real, the land didn't protect me and I've lost everything I love.

We pull into the driveway, Marshall turns off the car and there's a few moments of silence.

"I'm sorry, Jesse," he says. "But I promise you'll get good money for the land. I'll invest it well for you, and it will give you plenty of time to figure out what you'd like to do with your life. And I promise you, you'll build a good life, a great life, and you'll look back on all of this as a bad dream. But in order for you to have a decent future, you have to learn how to let this life and this town go."

He stares at me, waiting for a response, but what do you say when you've lost it all? What do you say when all that you've loved has died?

"Gena made up the spare bedroom for you, and she took the kids to her mom's so we could get a few hours of uninterrupted sleep. We'll tackle the rest later, okay?"

I'm grateful that his wife and children are gone. They're innocent, and I don't need to curse anyone else.

SCARLETT

Dad's locked himself in the basement. As far as I'm concerned, he can lock himself in hell. Isabelle is plastic-wrap tight to me as we lay together on Mom's bed. The TV is on. My eyes are on it, but I don't watch. I wonder if Isabelle is able to lose herself in the flashing, loud cartoon. I wonder if Isabelle will ever be okay again, because I'm not. I'm consumed with the darkness of violation, betrayal and shame.

He hit Mom, and he tossed me into the wall. My wrist throbs and so does my back. But my pain is nothing compared to Mom's. Was Dad hitting Mom the same as him shoving me? Is it abuse? Is that the same or is it different?

There's a numbness in my brain that won't let me connect his actions with my emotions. I'm like one of Isabelle's bandaged-by-toilet-paper dolls. Frozen, empty and emotionless.

Isabelle and I stayed in here with Mom last night. Most of it was spent consoling my sobbing mother and pressing ice to her wounds. We had the same mantra of a conversation.

Call the police, Mom.

I can't.

Call the police, Mom.

I can't. They won't help me. They can't help me. No one can.

I'm going to call the police. I'm going to tell them what happened.

Who will believe you? The cops just pulled you half-naked out of a car with Jesse Lachlin. They arrested him and pity you.

Mom went in to take a shower thirty minutes ago. The water ran for fifteen minutes, but since then there's been silence. I glance at the door and light peeks out from underneath. A slice of worry breaks through my emotional paralysis. Yes, her body was broken and bruised, but so was her spirit. Her state of mind is fragile, and a question dances around the crazy in my mind. Would she hurt herself to escape?

I kiss Isabelle on the top of the head and cuddle her closer for a second, whispering that I'll be right back. What I'm not prepared for is how she clings to me.

"Don't go." Isabelle's grip on my arm becomes painful.

I place my hand over hers and try to gently peel her fingers off of me. "I need to check on Mom. I'll be right back, okay?"

She slides off the bed, dragging the king-size comforter with her. Unfortunately, the biggest security blanket in the world can't help us. "I'll come with you."

Realizing I won't win this battle, I give up, and when I knock on the door of the bathroom, Isabelle fastens herself to my leg.

"Mom," I call out. "Are you okay?"

Some shifting and she says, "I'm fine."

No, she's not. "Will you please open the door?"

Mom doesn't open the door, but she does undo the lock. I bundle my sister like a burrito by the door, face her toward the TV and convince her to stay put, promising to keep the door ajar.

The hinges squeak as it opens, and it's weird to think that a few weeks ago I was in here preparing for a date with Stewart. Mom was happy, my father was happy, but I wasn't. I was sick, my soul was sick and I was dying. Now everyone is dying.

Mom's wrapped in a wet towel and sits up in ball on the tile floor near her sunken bathtub. Her hair is wet, uncombed, and she shivers. I grab a stack of towels and drape them over her. It's hard to look directly at her as the right side of her face is bruised and her lip is swollen.

I sit beside her and wonder what to say or what to do. I'm confused because she's the parent and she should take care of me. But maybe that's what she's been doing, protecting me the only way she knew how. "You came into my room and touched him on purpose, didn't you?"

She's silent, and there's a part of me that wants her to stay quiet, but she eventually says, "It's better that he hits me. I don't want you to be hurt. I have never wanted you to hurt."

"Throw him out."

"I can't."

So sick and tired of hearing *I can't*, I hit the floor with my fist. "Throw him out."

"I can't!" she shouts, and that causes me to look at her. Mom never loses her temper. That's Dad's job. "I've tried, Scarlett. For years. He won't go. Just because I tell him to leave doesn't mean he has to. This is his house, his home. The deed is in his name. So is every car and every bank account. Don't you understand? I own nothing. I have no legal right to a thing. I can't throw him out. He's the one who can throw me out, and then who's going to be here to protect you girls? No one, and I can't live with that. I have never been able to stomach the idea of leaving here to save myself and risk putting you girls in the path of his wrath."

"Then *we* leave," I say. "We pack our bags, we grab Isabelle and we leave."

"With what?" Mom demands. "Didn't you hear me? We don't have anything. You don't think I've thought of leaving hundreds of times over the years? If I leave here, I leave with the clothes on my back.

"I have no money to feed you, no money to house you, no money for a lawyer, and your father would have full custody of the two of you before I could turn the doorknob of the front door. Your father has money, he has influence. He has friends in the system, friends who have gone through ugly divorces, powerful friends who will side with him. I'll lose, and I cannot leave you here to defend yourselves. I can't. I won't."

"But he's hurting you. The law will protect us."

"Do you remember Nikki Harvey? Her husband was a police officer, and he hit her for years. The abuse became so bad that she ended up in surgery. While she was in surgery, he filed a protection order against her claiming that she had attacked him and what he did to her was self-defense. By the time she made it out of surgery, he already had emergency custody of the children and she didn't have a penny to her name. It took her years to rebuild her life. TV makes leaving look so easy, but it's not, Scarlett. The system can be manipulated. The system is broken."

My mind is a whirlwind as I try to grasp an answer. Any answer. And like a miracle, the answer is there. The plan. The one Pastor Hughes went over with me. The one he said could save my life. "Then we go to a women's shelter. We don't have to stay here. We don't need anything. We start from scratch, as a family. Just you, me and Isabelle."

"The nearest one is an hour away," she says quietly.

"Then we take his car and we go there."

"He'll follow. He'll say we stole his car."

"Then we give him the car back after we get there, and the shelter will find a way to help us." I visited one of the websites Pastor Hughes shared with me. Their message was clear—all we have to do is leave. "Pastor Hughes says we aren't alone. We can go to a shelter."

"We're staying." Mom sounds like Isabelle when she doesn't want to eat her vegetables.

"If you can't throw Dad out, then we need to leave. I hear what you're saying, and I'm not suggesting that this will be easy, but we have to give this a shot. We need to leave."

Mom clutches the towel I laid over her. "It's easier to stay. It's easier to make it work. He was doing well, and he was changing. If you think about it, you lied, and you continued to lie when we trusted you to tell us the truth.

"And think of how much pain you put your father through last night. We were so terrified something horrible had happened to you. After what your father went through with his sister, what you did last night with Jesse Lachlin was heartless."

A dangerous flip of a switch in my brain and my head tilts. "What are you saying?"

"I should have done a better job with you. I should have never let you be friends with Jesse when you were younger. Maybe I should have sent you to a private school. I should have done better to teach you to follow the rules. If we follow the rules then everything will be perfect. Your father would never be angry, and then we'd be happy."

Her words vibrate along my body, and my mind starts to split into tiny fractures. "Are you blaming me? Are you blaming yourself?"

Mom's eyes water, and she wipes the tears away. "Why couldn't you forgive your father? Why couldn't you have just learned to not be so upset? If we had just followed the rules, we would have been okay. He doesn't get angry when we follow the rules, but now we have to start all over again and he's going to be so hurt."

He's hurt? She's the one with bruises on her body. "Dad hurt you, Mom. He hurt me. This isn't my fault, and this isn't your fault. This is Dad's fault, and it's time for you to stop making excuses for him."

Mom stands. I'm shaking as I rise and follow her into her bedroom. She doesn't go for her closet, nor does she go for her dresser. Instead she slips on her robe and heads for the door.

"Where are you going?"

She glances over her shoulder, but she doesn't look me in the eye. "Think of how heartbroken your father has to be. He thought he lost you. I should have been more supportive. I should have done a better job helping him calm down last night."

My mind completely cracks, and I try to grasp how the conversation turned so wrong, so quickly. "This isn't your fault."

She shakes her head as if she doesn't agree and then leaves the room.

"It's not your fault," I yell, but it doesn't matter how loud I am. She's not listening. "It's none of our faults! It's his! He's to blame!"

"Scarlett?" Isabelle's child-like voice, the voice of fear and innocence, cuts me deep. "Are things better now?"

I tremble so violently that my teeth chatter. "We need to leave."

"What?"

We need to leave. But how? I have no car, and even if I did, I don't know how to drive. Dad took my money, and I'm broke. We have no place to go, no one who will believe us, no one who will take us in. I spin as the walls of the room start to close in. We're trapped, and there's nothing I can do. I sink to the floor as bile rises in my throat. What do I do? God, what do I do?

A touch on my arm, and Isabelle has moved in front of me. "Do you want to hold my hand? When I get scared at school, my teacher holds my hand."

She holds out both of her hands, palms up, and I blink as I see the little lines on her left hand—who she was born to be. Then lines on her right hand—who she is due to her choices and circumstances. On her right hand, her life line is broken and so is her heart line.

Glory asked me if I had the courage to change the lines on my hand. I don't know if I can change me, but I have to be strong enough to change the lines on my sister's. "If I ask you to be quiet, and do absolutely everything I tell you to do, will you leave me with me?"

"Where are we going?"

"Somewhere safe."

Isabelle nods her agreement.

"How do you feel about climbing a tree?"

Climbing down the tree with my sister was terrifying. She was a little too eager, going a little too fast, and I finally have an appreciation of how Jesse feels when he climbs with me.

Going out one of the doors would have been preferable, but opening the door would set off the alarm throughout the house, alerting my parents we were leaving, and I don't know the code to turn off the security system.

I feel like a fugitive, and it's a terrible sensation. I have this itch between my shoulder blades, a sensation that there's a bull's-eye painted on my back.

If the cycle holds true then Mom and Dad will spend hours drowning in each other's misery before they reemerge in their attempt to be parents again. When they do emerge and find us gone, Dad will search, and I don't want him to find me, not until I'm ready.

A cold, light rain mists over me, and it makes the hike through the field treacherous, especially with my sister riding piggyback. Her arms are knotted tight around my neck, choking me, but I don't reprimand her. She's scared enough, and I do my best to readjust.

It's Sunday, and the tiny white church comes into view. It seems like a lifetime since I was here for Suzanne's funeral. I guess it has been. I'm not the same person I was back then, and I'll never be that person again.

People who had been gathered together talking after service wave goodbye to each other, get in their cars and pull away. There's only one car left, and I'm praying it belongs to the one person I need. At the street, I stop, slip my sister to the ground and have a moment of déjà vu. I glance over my shoulder at the weeping willow and there's a flash of disappointment that Glory's not there. I didn't think I did real friendships, but I now consider her one.

I take Isabelle's hand in mine and we cross the street, walk up the steps and into the aging church. Pastor Hughes is near the front, busying himself at the altar, but he freezes when he spots me and my sister.

The circulating air in the church hits my wet skin, and goose bumps form. I can imagine how we look—bedraggled, drowned rats. Wet hair stuck to our scalps, and our jeans and sweaters are darkened from the rain. Beads of water drop from us onto the carpet.

"What happened?" Pastor Hughes asks.

What if I made the wrong choice? What if I tell him and he sends us back? What if he just tells me to give counseling another try?

"My daddy hit my mom," Isabelle says, and the admission in her soft voice rocks through me like rolling thunder.

Pastor Hughes slowly walks toward us as if we're wounded animals he's scared he'll frighten off. When he reaches us, he pulls his cell out of his pocket and offers it to me. "What did I tell you do to when your dad hit your mom?"

My throat swells as a million voices of doubt enter my head. "Can you call?"

"I can if that's what you want me to do, and I will if you don't.

But you need to take control of the situation. You need to do this, Scarlett. You need to take control of your life."

My lips pull down and it's hard to speak. "Mom will deny what he did."

"But that doesn't mean they won't believe you."

"They won't."

"I believe you."

"Because you already knew he hit her."

"I knew there was past abuse between your parents, but we were under the impression that the abuse had happened years ago."

My eyes snap shut as disappointment rolls through me. Mom lied to me. She lied to the counselors, but she wouldn't see it that way. She'd see it as telling most of the truth. Then again, I shouldn't be shocked.

"You need to understand this," Pastor Hughes says. "Even if I didn't know about the past abuse, I still would believe you."

I grip my sister's hand tighter. Is this real? Is he lying?

"I believe you," he repeats.

The sweet words hold me like a hug, and I pray to God I'm making the right choice. I accept the cell, and Pastor Hughes holds out his hand to my sister for her to take. "I'm Pastor Hughes. Something tells me you haven't had anything to eat yet today. Which one would you like? Breakfast or lunch?"

My sister looks up at me, waiting for my judgment if this man is friend or foe. If he is to be trusted or denied. I understand her need for confirmation. Our trust radars have been broken for years, but now that I know what love is, I'm getting a better sense of where to turn.

I give Isabelle a nod, and she places her hand in his. She doesn't answer his question, but I know my sister. "Breakfast. Her favorite is pancakes."

"Then pancakes you will get. Scarlett, you hold on to that cell until you make the call. Once you do, you can give it back to me. Until then, let's go to my office so we can call my wife and ask her to bring breakfast and some warm clothes for both of you."

With Isabelle holding both of our hands, the three of us walk toward his office.

JESSE

A knocking drags me out of a deep sleep, and I sit up in bed. Disorientation sets in when I do a scan and have no idea where I am. The doorbell rings, another knock, and little kids' voices squeal that someone's at the door.

I rub the sleep out of my head as I slowly realize I'm at Marshall's. I'm shirtless and in a pair of old sweats that belong to my uncle. Near the door on a wooden chair are my neatly folded clothes. I didn't do that. I barely remember stripping down, leaving my clothes as a mess on the floor and stumbling into bed.

I pick up the clothes and they're warm as if fresh out of the dryer and have the sweet scent of fabric softener. The niceness that someone would do my laundry disarms me. I take my time changing and try to figure out how I should act or what I should say when I leave this room. My relationship with Marshall is complicated enough, and I don't want to do anything to insult or upset his wife and children.

I'm saved from having to figure it out with another knock, this time on the door to my room. It opens right as I finish pulling the shirt over my head. Marshall pops his head in. "Hey, how are you?"

"Good." My voice is rougher than normal, deeper, and my head throbs. "How long was I asleep?"

"Not long. It's eleven."

"At night?"

"In the morning. I had hoped to let you sleep longer, but Mr. Copeland's here and he wants to talk to you."

I raise my eyebrows. "Is that a good idea?"

"I don't know, but he's here and he seems calm."

Yeah. The guy is all about appearances. I follow Marshall down the hallway and in the living room is Scarlett's father. He's in a pair of khakis, a collared shirt, and he turns away from the window when we walk in. His eyes narrow at the bump and bruise on my head, and he mashes his lips together. "I heard there was a scuffle when they found you and my daughter. I had no idea it was so bad."

I glance at Marshall, willing him to take the lead, and he doesn't disappoint. "Jesse's legal team is handling the altercation directly with the police."

I have a legal team? Sounds fancy.

"I'm here to offer my support," Mr. Copeland says. "I've talked to several people in the department, the chief of police is a friend of mine, and it sounds as if there was a severe overreaction. I have it on good authority that the resisting arrest charges will be dropped, but of course, it's up to Jesse and his legal team if you want to file a formal complaint against the officers. I have not ruled that out myself."

Spoken like a true manipulator, but I don't buy it. Not for a second.

"I can speak to the chief if you'd like, Jesse, and tell him that I believe that the officers were out of line with you and my daughter."

In exchange for what? My soul?

"Thank you for your offer," Marshall says. "We'll definitely keep that in mind. While we appreciate you coming by to check on Jesse, it's been a long night and we need some decent sleep before we discuss legalities. It's good to know that you're hoping for the same thing we are: a peaceful, quick and just resolution."

I'm assuming I'm not the lone one who picked up on the subtext that we aren't only talking about the arrest last night.

"I agree." Mr. Copeland waves his hand at the couches. "Please, why don't we sit?" As if this is his house to offer.

I'm proud of Marshall as he stands his ground. "I mean no dis-respect, but Jesse is recovering and my daughters just returned home. Unless there is something else that weighs heavily on you, we can set up a meeting to discuss anything else you'd like this coming week. My law practice is near your company, which will make it convenient for you."

No wonder Gran liked Marshall. It's nice being on his side in-stead of the one he's fighting.

"Of course," Mr. Copeland says. "I do have one question, and it's a private matter. Would it be possible for me to speak to Jesse alone?"

"No." Marshall has balls of steel.

Anger flashes over Mr. Copeland's face, but it's gone as quick as it was there. "I understand and respect that. Jesse," he hesi-tates, "my daughter is going through a lot in her life. She's very confused, and I apologize that you've been caught up in her erratic behavior."

"Erratic?" I spit out, but the warning glare Marshall sends me shuts me up.

"As a concerned father, I'm trying to figure a few things out. One of them being, do you have any knowledge of Scarlett using drugs?"

My muscles tighten and my fingers form a fist. Marshall moves his arm out in front of me as if the driver had hit the brakes too fast and I'm whiplashing forward. "Answer, Jesse, but yes or no only."

Yes or no only? I want to tell Scarlett's father where to shove his question, and then I want to smack him like he's been smack-ing his wife. It's hard as hell to stay in place and even harder to not run my mouth. "No."

"Has she been drinking?"

"No."

"Do you know where she currently is?"

My entire body recoils in fear. "Don't you?"

"Yes or no only," Marshall bites out.

"As I said, Scarlett has been having a rough time. She's con-fused, and not acting like herself. Her mother and I are very concerned, and we'd like to get her help. After the traumatic experience you and Scarlett went through, she was understandably very upset. She left home sometime this morning, and she took Isabelle with her. With how Scarlett has been behaving lately, we're concerned with her mental well-being. I'm begging you, Jesse, if you know where Scarlett is, please let us know. We're extremely worried."

"Do you know where Scarlett is?" Marshall asks.

"No." And that scares me.

"If you're concerned," Marshall says, "I would suggest involving the police."

It's obvious that's not a recommendation Mr. Copeland appreciates. "Her mother and I were hoping to avoid the dramatic scene from last night. We believe it traumatized her. If you hear from her, please let me know immediately."

Mr. Copeland offers Marshall his hand, they say short, obligatory goodbyes, then Mr. Copland shuts the front door behind him. Marshall pivots to stand directly in front of me. "There's more going on than two teenagers making out in a car, and it's going to be in your best interest to catch me up."

My brain swims—losing my land, and now Scarlett . . . The bump on my head throbs and I'd give anything to crawl back into bed, but that's not in the cards I've been dealt. Scarlett is missing and that means she's in danger. "Can I trust you?"

"Yes, but that's never been the problem. You have to decide to do the trusting."

Scarlett trusts me, but I love her. She needs help, more help than I can give, and Marshall might be the force of nature who can help her survive this storm. "Scarlett's father abuses her mother, and I've been helping Scarlett plan how to leave home after graduation. If she's gone, it means things are bad and she needs our help."

SCARLETT

It's weird. I've kissed Jesse, made out with Jesse, snuck out with Jesse, have fallen in love with Jesse, but I've never called him and have never sent him a text. I couldn't because of the fear of my father. So when Pastor Hughes asked me if there was anyone I wanted to contact, I wasn't able to reach out directly to Jesse as I don't have his number.

My father has stolen so much from me—the happiness of childhood, teenage normalcy, any concept of safety.

Pastor Hughes and his wife drove Isabelle and me from the small church to the main one in town where I did my counseling. In one of the church's children's playrooms, I sit in a chair in the back and flip Pastor Hughes's cell in my hand again and again. I haven't made the call. Not yet. Something's holding me back. Years of fear, years of being told not to, years of wondering what would happen if I did.

I watch as Isabelle plays with the Hughes children. They are adorable girls with bright smiles, and they are gracious and welcoming to my sister. No matter how friendly they are, Isabelle is shy and rarely talks. It's tough for her to engage, and that breaks my heart. My sister holds on to her doll as if her life depends on keeping her close.

"I can't believe I'm in a church, Tink. Two times in a year is a record for me, but I'll admit you're worth it."

My heart leaps at the sound of Jesse's voice, and I'm out of my seat. I ram into him and he doesn't rock with the impact. Instead, he weaves his arms around me and holds me close. I bury my head into his chest and for the first time since I was dragged out of his truck, I can breathe.

A light touch on my head and then another. He's kissing me and each one is like medicine on a wound. "Are you okay?"

"Yes," I say. "Are you?"

"I'm fine."

I draw back and his green eyes are so sad that I grab both of his hands for support. For me and for him. I just lied. I'm not fine. I'm anything but fine and I need to start being honest, beginning with being honest with myself. "It happened again last night."

"What?"

The words become lodged in my throat, but I'm done being silenced. "Dad hit Mom again."

"Did he hit you?"

Did he? The instinct is to say no, that it was just a push and a shove, but I think of how my back is sore and of the bruise forming on my wrist. I think of how Jesse told me that being hit once was enough. I think of the sadness and sense of betrayal.

I loved my father, and I had thought that he loved me. The ends of my mouth turn down as they quiver. "He shoved me." And because I can't think about it anymore, I place my hand in the air to stop the flood of anger that I know is poised on the tip of his tongue. "Pastor Hughes thinks I should call the police."

"He shoved you?" Jesse cups my face with the palm of his hand and the touch is so tender, I'm nearly undone. "Are you sure you're okay?"

"No, but I'm here and not there. That's good, right?"

"What do you think?" he asks. "Of calling the police?"

I think Jesse shouldn't have a large lump on his head. "Oh my God."

I reach up, barely brush the wound, and Jesse winces. "I'm okay."

"Did the police do that?"

"Marshall's handling everything so don't worry about me. We need to focus on you."

Not wanting to discuss this where Isabelle can overhear, I walk into the hallway and Jesse follows. I lean my back against a wall and Jesse props himself up on the opposite one.

"Talk to me, Tink," he says, and my heart melts over how much he cares.

"Mom said it was my fault Dad hit her. She also thinks it's her fault. What happened is everyone's fault but his."

"Do you believe that?"

The answer should be an immediate no. I'm aware of this, but there's this twisting in my stomach that keeps me from saying it. My foot taps the floor, and I hug myself. "He did hit her because of me. I made him mad. If I had kept my mouth shut, if I hadn't left the house, if I hadn't lied, if—"

"If you had never met me?" Jesse wears a sad smile.

My chest rips apart. "No. You're part of the small amount of good in my life."

"You aren't responsible for what your dad did. He's responsible for his choices."

"But if I hadn't caused problems it wouldn't have happened."

"So if you're perfect, there will be world peace? That's not how it works. Yeah, you lied, but for the rest of the world that means you're grounded from using your cell for a week, not watching your mom get beat. Your dad demanded his idea of perfection, and there is no one on this planet who can live up to that expectation. You aren't the one who messed up, he is."

My leg bounces as I fight the urge to cry. "What if I call the police and they blame me? I can't handle that."

"What if you call and they go over to your house and see the bruises on your mom? What if they believe you and tell you that you aren't to blame?"

I'm so nervous, I could peel off my own skin. "What's going to happen to me if I do call? What's going to happen to Isabelle? What if I make everything worse?"

Jesse drops his head, pinches the bridge of his nose, and when he lifts his head my heart cracks as his eyes hold tears. "What if you do nothing and the next time he kills her? Because that's what happened to me. My mom was hit by so many men, and I did nothing. I expected her to save me instead of me saving her, until one day my dad killed her. And that guilt that I carry? I'm dying every damn day. You once asked if I'm cursed, and the truth is I am. I'm doomed to hear her scream every day for the rest of my life and know that I did nothing. I knew she was being treated badly, and I never told anyone. Because of that *I'm* to blame."

I hold my breath, scared to breathe. Scared if I do then all the hurt, all the pain is going to come tumbling out and then I'll be broken. So broken. The unfixable kind, the devastating kind. But Jesse's head falls and his shoulders roll forward. He covers his face with his hands and his body shakes.

Jesse.

Carefree Jesse, strong Jesse, rebellious Jesse, Peter Pan in the flesh . . . is in pain.

I think of Jesse's pirate smile. The one he gave me as a child the first time he tapped on my window and offered me freedom. I think of the way he'd hold my hand as we crossed the field at night and I was still scared of the dark. I think of the way he'd offer his hand when jumping from branch to branch, the way he'd hold his breath when I would go a little too high. I think of long nights of laughter, of summer days of comforting silence. I think of Jesse. A bright soul, a candle in my ever-present darkness, and I see tears rolling down his cheeks.

For years he was my rock, and now I need to be his. I dash across the hall and pour myself into him, wrapping myself around Jesse in an effort to keep his pieces from falling to the ground and shattering. To keep me from going insane.

"We're going to be okay," I whisper to him. "I promise we're going to be okay."

Jesse holds on to me, his head buried into my shoulder, and I hold on to him. Both of us seeking comfort and holding the other up.

JESSE

I'm slumped in the chair outside of Pastor Hughes's office, and it's a lot like being in lockup: nerve-wracking and never-ending. Scarlett's in there with the police. Pastor Hughes is in there for support. My uncle Marshall is in there as legal counsel for Scarlett. It's hard to believe I used to hate that man with a passion reserved for Satan. Now, I have no idea how I'm going to repay him for all he's done to protect me and to protect the girl I love.

The door to the office opens, and I straighten as Pastor Hughes walks out then closes the door behind him. "They aren't done yet, but they're wrapping up."

"How's it going? Is Scarlett okay?"

He takes the seat next to me and folds his hands over his stomach. "It's going as well as these things can go. I can tell they believe her. It helps that your uncle is in there to help guide the questioning and the answering. He's a good man, and I wish everyone who is a victim had someone like him on their side when reporting a crime. It would make life incredibly easier for so many who are victimized again when telling their story."

"What will happen now?"

He releases a long breath that doesn't give me hope. "They'll investigate her claims and contact Child Protective Services. A caseworker will be assigned to the family. Odds are, since the children have never been abused before tonight, Isabelle will be returned to the family, but there will be state supervision."

Anger wells up inside me, and I bang the back of my head against the wall. "So nothing changes?"

Pastor Hughes stretches out his legs as if he's stiff and sore. "I can see how you'd think that, but that's not what I said."

"The government can't force Scarlett's dad to change."

"No, they can't. As a man of God, I have hope he will decide to change. And I'm hopeful that involving the police will be the wake-up call Scarlett's mother needs. She needs to come to terms with the reality of her situation, and she needs to start doing what is in the best interest of her daughters."

"And if she doesn't?"

"Then there are plenty of people in a position of authority watching."

"That sounds like a whole lot of nothing."

"The system isn't perfect, Jesse, but this family has a better shot with the truth being out in the open than it staying a secret."

"What's going to happen to Scarlett?" I ask.

"That depends on Scarlett. She'll be eighteen soon so her options are wider, but I'm going to let your uncle talk to her about that. To be honest, right now I'm more interested in what's going to happen to you."

Tension sets into my neck, and I roll it to help. "Marshall believes the charges will be dropped."

"That's good news, but that's not what I'm referring to. You can get mad at me for eavesdropping later, but I heard what you said to Scarlett in the hallway. I'm more curious of when you're going to take the advice you gave Scarlett and realize you aren't to blame for your mother's death or for anyone else's unhappiness. Because that's a terrible curse to carry, and it will taint every decision you make going forward."

I close my eyes because I don't want to face this—

"The better question I have for you is when will you allow yourself the room to figure out who you are out of the shadow of your mother's death? You've defined yourself by your guilt and have made that land your security blanket. Wouldn't it be freeing to rid yourself of that guilt and to throw off the security blanket and discover who you were meant to be?"

"That's not what the land is." My voice is rough and my throat tightens. "The land isn't a security blanket. It's more."

"I agree. The land could be more, but your family has made it a living shrine to your sins. Sins that don't even belong to you yet you take on the burden of blame. I've heard for years about the Lachlin curse, and if I had to guess, I'd say that's the curse—the belief that you're always to blame for other people's choices."

His words are like a hot sword through my stomach, and I'm saved from answering when the door to his office opens. Scarlett emerges. Her eyes are red and puffy, and she strangles a crumpled tissue in her hand. She takes one look at me, and I'm completely undone. I stand, gather her in my arms and hold the girl I love as she cries.

I'm going to owe Marshall a limb and/or an organ at the end of all this. After the police left, he had his wife pick up Isabelle, while Marshall and I took Scarlett to the hospital.

After the speech her father made at Marshall's house, my uncle wants to discredit any claim her father would have against her. Marshall had blood drawn to test for drugs and alcohol. He then had a nurse photograph the bruise on her wrist where her father grabbed her and the faint bruise on Scarlett's back from when she fell against the wall.

"What do people who have been abused do when they don't have lawyers?" Scarlett asked at one point, echoing my own earlier thoughts.

"Sometimes the system fails them," Marshall said. It wasn't the answer either Scarlett or I wanted to hear, but it was honest.

After the hospital, I retrieved my truck from the impound lot and said goodbye to Scarlett with a long kiss and hug. She's going to stay with Isabelle at Marshall's, and I thought that was a brilliant idea. If only she could stay there forever.

For myself, it's time to head home. Marshall told me to behave, which was a warning to avoid any conversation or confrontation with Scarlett's father. I promised to be on my best behavior. I'm not going to do a thing to ruin what my uncle has put in place to protect Scarlett.

As I pull onto the road that leads to my home, I pass three police cars. There's a grim sense of satisfaction that the bastard was placed in the hot seat for what he's done. Odds are Scarlett's father won't be punished how he should be, but at least he didn't win today.

Scarlett's house is lit up like airport runway lights. Every room in the house brightened even though there's only two people home.

I park in my driveway, turn off the engine and stare at my grandmother's trailer, at my home. The place looks dark, it looks empty, and the good pastor's words weave in and out of every thought and emotion. Mostly I keep tripping over the same thing: Have I let guilt guide my choices, and if so, who am I without the guilt? Better question, who am I without the land?

Movement toward the side of the trailer, like a flash of a moonbeam. I exit the truck and follow the light. I'm surprised when I spot Glory sitting on the swings in one of her shimmery, long skirts.

"How long were you watching me?" I ask.

Glory tilts her head in her patented faraway expression. "I have never stopped watching you. I've been doing it for so long I couldn't stop if I tried."

Not what I mean. "Do you have any idea what Scarlett and I have gone through? If you were really psychic, you would have warned us."

Glory leans back, raises her feet and swings. "Being psychic doesn't mean I know everything. It means I connect people with the universe for a brief few minutes so they can take a look at themselves and their choices."

"So you're saying you didn't know what was going to happen to us?"

She's quiet as she skims her toes on the ground to stop moving. "You and Scarlett have been hurtling toward the cliff that was last night for years. It had to happen."

A flash of anger. "Why? Scarlett's in pain." I'm in pain.

"Pain is what makes you grow, it's what makes you mature, it's what helps lead you to the path you are meant to be on. If everything is good all the time, there would never be change."

"What if I don't want change?"

"If it weren't for change, then you would have never fallen in love with Scarlett, and is that something you could say you didn't want?"

I wanted it, she knows this, and I drop onto the swing beside her. "Did you knowingly lie to me about Scarlett being one of the votes?"

"Yes."

Her honesty causes me to flinch. "Then you cost me my land."

"Did I? Because Scarlett's father paid me a visit today searching for her. He read me the riot act for giving his daughter a job. Once he blew himself out like a child's balloon, he let me know that if you convinced Scarlett to go home and to stop whatever it is that she's planning that he'd vote for you to keep your land."

"He's one vote. I need two."

"The pastor turned in his ballot in favor of you keeping the land the day he learned of the tribunal. He said the scenario was ridiculous, and that the decision shouldn't be up to him as to what happens to the land, but should be for you to decide."

"You're telling me the pastor lied, too? Because he made it sound like he hadn't made up his mind."

"Pastor Hughes wanted to bring peace to your soul and to the souls of Suzanne and Marshall. In his own way, he was trying to heal your family. Did he lie? I guess, but I don't think he's going to hell over it, do you?"

My head lowers as I think of the day he visited me on the farm. I had told him that Scarlett was the other person on the tribunal, and he probably knew I was wrong. Is that why he had brought up Scarlett and her father? Was it his way of warning me that I was wrong . . . or maybe that Scarlett was in danger?

I'm so mixed up right now my gut twists. "Why did you lie about Scarlett being on the tribunal?"

"Because of this exact moment. If you want your land, you can have it. You hold more influence over Scarlett than anyone else in this world. She's terrified, she's scared, she's confused and she could be easily swayed. If you told her to go home and give her father another chance, she might. If that didn't work, if you turned her away and shut her out like you did your freshman year, she might break and go running home."

"Scarlett won't budge. She's strong, she's solid and she can stand strong without me."

"You're right, but what I'm saying is, if you want your land you could possibly have it, but then you have to break Scarlett's heart."

I love my land, but . . . "I could never do that to Scarlett. I love her." It's true, but that doesn't stop the lashing pain. I'm losing my land. I'm losing a part of me. I literally feel as if I'm being torn in half. "I don't know who I am without this land."

Glory places her hand under my chin and forces me to look at her. "You're someone who is capable of love and letting someone truly love you in return, and that, Jesse, is what your grandmother wanted you to learn."

At the mention of my gran, my eyes burn. "Is love always going to hurt?"

"Sometimes, but it's also going to be as glorious as when you hold Scarlett in your arms, and you have to admit that feeling is worth walking through hell. I don't regret what I did to bring you and Scarlett together. You needed each other."

Glory is right. Scarlett is worth standing in an inferno for.

Sitting on this swing, I look over to the wooden picnic table that hasn't been used in years. Glory is the one who sees spirits, but I'm the one who sees ghosts—memories of my mom and Gran sitting with me at the table, eating dinner, and laughing with me.

I remember how my mom would make huge bubbles with me out of detergent. How she would smile when I would bring her frogs from the creek. I remember how she had the most beautiful singing voice, and how on dark nights, she would lie with me in bed and sing until I fell asleep.

"I miss my mom." My voice comes out rough. "I miss Gran, too."

Glory's mouth trembles as she tries to smile yet fails. "Me, too. If it helps, they miss us, as well. And your gran just told me to tell you to shut up and give me a hug."

"You're such a fake." Yet I have to wipe at the wetness in my eyes. She bumps my knee with hers. I bump it back to let her know we're good.

"Can I give you two more pieces of advice from the universe?" she asks.

"Sure."

"Be careful with Scarlett. The next few months to a year are going to be very trying for her, especially as she attempts to build her identity away from her father and mother."

"Away?" I'm hopeful this means Scarlett will find a better path than being forced home.

"The point I'm making is don't fall into a trap. There's a lot to be learned with what happened to your mother."

"What does that mean?"

"It means that whether you like it or not, this earth is the ultimate preschool. We're here to learn, not just one lesson, but multiple ones. Before you ask, I'm not going to tell you what the two of you will be facing because that would be cheating."

Fantastic. "What's your second piece of advice?"

"You know the connection you have with the land? How it breathes for you?"

And for Scarlett. "Yeah?"

"It's not the land that's special, that's you. You could go anywhere in the world, and the earth will breathe for you. You have to allow it the opportunity." With that, Glory stands, kisses my forehead the way mothers do and then she fades into the darkness.

SCARLETT

E *mancipation.*

It's a big word with an even bigger meaning. My mom stands in her kitchen and stares at me as if I had just taken the butcher knife and shoved it into my stomach. "What do you mean you want to be emancipated?"

It's a surreal feeling. On the counter is a plate of hot chocolate chip cookies, a bouquet of balloons and two letters of acceptance into colleges along with partial scholarship declarations. One from the college in town. The other from the University of Kentucky. My mother opened both of them before I arrived home from school.

I'm not angry Mom opened my mail. I didn't expect anything less. To be honest, I have such low expectations for my parents when it comes to respecting me that there isn't much that shocks me anymore.

"I'm filing in court for emancipation," I repeat. "My lawyer is handling it today."

It's the end of November, nearing the holiday break, and probably not the best timing, but I can't live like this anymore. Mom and Dad have made their choices, and I'm making mine.

A week after I reported what happened between my parents to the police, my mother was granted custody of me and Isabelle after she proved that my father had left the house and that he was renting an apartment in town. We also have a new, shiny social worker who confirms that our family attends therapy weekly and who reminds my father that she's watching him like a hawk on a field mouse.

I'll admit, I like our social worker. She's like a five-foot-four poodle who is half grizzly bear.

Dad has visitation rights, and I've gone along to keep an eye on my sister, but I don't talk to him. He tries to talk to me, but I'm not there to sweep up the ashes of the bridge we both lit on fire and burned. I'm there to make sure he respects my sister.

While Dad is "officially" out of the house, Mom hasn't truly thrown Dad out. He doesn't live here, but he's still in control of her life. The physical moving out is more for show for the court than a true reflection of our lives.

Last night, Mom crossed the huge, gaping moat I created that's filled with fire-breathing dragons and barbed wire when she invited Dad home for dinner. I'm not stupid. I know what that means. Dinner leads to staying to chat, to help with homework and to watch TV. That leads to a late night where he stays over, and that eventually leads to him returning home.

The merry-go-round my mom and dad is on goes round and round and it's broken because it never stops. Because it doesn't stop, I can be easily fooled to believe that I can't get off, but I refuse to be conned. I will exit this insane ride, and I'm leaving now, even though that means I have to jump. I have to prove to myself and show my sister that the two of us deserve better.

Like Pastor Hughes explained about Jacob, I don't have to let fear and anger rule my life, and that also means I don't have to settle here.

Mom drops onto a stool at the counter, looking utterly and completely destroyed. A part of me hurts for her, but she's made her choice and now I'm making mine.

"I don't want you to leave," Mom says.

"I don't want to leave either, but I can't watch Dad hurt you anymore. If I stay here, I'm condoning your behavior and his."

"He says he can change." My mother stares into space as if she's in shock. "He says he's going to really change this time."

"Good." I want him to change, and there's this small desperate hope in my heart that I don't think I'll ever get rid of that prays desperately for him to change. "But he needs to work on himself without us. Dad needs time, Dad needs space and he needs to figure out his problems before being involved with any of us again."

Mom slowly moves her head to look at me, as if she's stuck in sand. "If you do this, you'll be on your own. He'll cut you off financially. I won't be able to help you if you fail."

Even though I know this, my stomach roils. "I'd rather be on my own than live a life where I think it's my fault my father chooses to hit, and I'd rather live my own life than think it's okay for someone to abuse you and hurt me and my sister."

"You'll fail," she says. "You'll be broke, you'll be hungry, you'll be alone and you'll fail."

I swallow back tears because she could be right, but I'll hate myself if I never try.

JESSE

Scarlett turns on the bathroom light of the studio apartment and peeks her head in as if she's terrified a clown from a Stephen King novel might pop out. Obviously there's no psycho clown as she slowly makes her way in. The place is small, comes furnished with a fridge made for a dollhouse and a kitchen counter big enough for a low-wattage microwave. The living space has room for a twin bed and little else.

The tiny window by the front door will let in morning light, but this place will be midnight in the afternoon. It's not where I'd want to spend the rest of my life, but the rest of life isn't the plan. This place is a glorified waiting room. If Scarlett is granted emancipation, the idea is to live here until she can figure out her next step in life, which is graduation, only six to eight months away. After that will be college. Her hope is that if she is granted the emancipation that she'll be able to be awarded financial aid under her independent status.

Currently, Scarlett lives at home with her mom, but Scarlett is building her case for emancipation and that includes showing the judge that she has found a safe and affordable place to live away from her parents.

Scarlett walks out of the bathroom, the folder that contains leasing information pressed tight to her chest. The landlord is letting us tour the place on our own, and I appreciate that. Scarlett needs time to process.

"What do you think?" I ask. The apartment is within walking distance to the Save Mart, and it's on a bus route to school. I've already offered to pick her up and drop her off anytime she needs to go to Glory's for work. I'll also take her to anywhere else she needs.

"It's a definite improvement over the apartments in Lexington." She squeaks out a pathetic smile.

"What's wrong?" I ask.

She shakes her head and strands of her long black hair fall out of her makeshift bun. I push off the wall, cross the room and weave my arms around her. She falls into me, and like always, a sense of peace surrounds me with having her in my arms.

"What's wrong?" I ask again.

Scarlett draws back, and I let her go. Everything in her life is changing so quickly that I can't imagine how she's mentally keeping up. At the window, she undoes the lock, opens the window, closes it shut then relocks it. I smile—she's learning.

"I'm scared," she says as she looks out the window.

"Of what?"

She inhales deeply then slowly blows out air. "Of failing. Of being alone . . . Of failing. When I told Mom that I filed for emancipation, she said I'd fail. And some days I feel I already have. Camila won't talk to me. Evangeline says Camila feels like I betrayed her by not telling her everything going on between you and me. They don't even know what has fully happened between me and Dad yet, so I'm sure those friendships are beyond repair. And then I don't know if I'll be able to afford food and rent and a car and car insurance and—"

"Do you want to do this?" I interrupt her. "Do you want to be emancipated?"

"Do I want to be emancipated? No. I want Mom and Dad to take a very long break from each other while Dad works on his problems. But that's not going to happen. They've made their choices and now I need to make mine. But what if I fail?"

I walk over to the corner of the room, slide down to the floor and gesture for her to follow. "Come here."

Her face scrunches in confusion. "What are you doing?"

"You have to come here to find out." I waggle my eyebrows.

Sighing loudly to show her annoyance, she crosses the room to me. I widen my knees and wave both of my hands, welcoming her to sit. She settles between my legs, her back flush to my chest, and her legs brush against mine. I tuck her hair over her shoulder, wind my arms around her waist, then level my head so I can whisper in her ear, "Close your eyes."

"We're touring an apartment, Jesse. The manager will be in here soon."

"Just do it."

With another annoyed sigh, she does, and after a few deep breaths, she relaxes into me.

"Now open."

Her eyelashes flutter open.

"Do you see it?" I ask.

"What?"

"The tea bags on the counter. We should have known Glory was going to give you those and the teacups. She also gave you that large ugly rock on the folding table by the window. I know she says it brings good energy, but I think she's full of crap."

Scarlett giggles in my arms, and the friction feels good. I drag my mind away from kissing her and focus on helping. "Leo complains about the size of the TV on the wall, but you've figured out that the guy whines too much to begin with. Plus he's jealous we received such a good deal. Nazareth found it at a flea market. I know it stunk like smoke when you first got it, but that candle you keep burning covers the smell."

"Do I have a couch?" she asks.

"Not yet, but we're looking for one. But you got the financial aid you needed so you move into the dorms soon. You're debating whether it's worth it to have one. Plus V prefers to sit on the floor. She's recently developed a phobia to furniture, and after listening to her reasons as to why, you're starting to wonder how many bugs are in your bed."

Scarlett laughs, and I nibble on her ear in praise. She cuddles closer and I kiss her neck, wishing we were truly alone.

"And what are we sitting on now?" she whispers.

I turn my head and breathe into her ear, "Your bed. I gave you the one I had in storage."

She shivers and leans her neck closer to my mouth. I'd love to take her up on her invitation, but we do want her to take the apartment and not get kicked out. I press my lips lightly to her skin and then tell her the truth I've learned from my past couple of months alone.

"Scarlett. . . . you're going to fail. You're going to melt plastic mac-and-cheese cups in the microwave because you forgot to fill them with water. You're going to forget homework and get a zero on it because you were so busy working to make sure you can buy another mac-and-cheese cup. You're going to eat nothing but mac-and-cheese and ramen because you're more concerned about your grades at school than taking on more hours to afford more groceries."

"You make it sound so promising," she says.

"But," I emphasize, "what makes the difference is how you choose to look at it. You melted the mac-and-cheese cup, but you learned not to do that again, and you learned you're handy with a fire extinguisher. In fact, you feel like a warrior because your quick thinking stopped the entire complex from burning down.

"You get pissed off at yourself for forgetting your homework, but you figure out a system to remind yourself what's due and check it every night before you go to bed, and then you realize that the world isn't coming to an end because you messed up on one thing.

"And then when your friends are sick and tired of watching you eat ramen, they take you out for dollar tacos. Then when you get tired of watching your friends eat ramen, you take them for dollar tacos. While eating tacos, you laugh because Leo will only speak in Old English, complete with an accent, and then you'll watch him crash and burn as he tries to pick up the girl at the table next to us while speaking like Kermit the Frog."

She snorts because she's already seen this act in real life, and it's as horrifying as it sounds.

"The point I'm making is that you can choose to look at the tough moments as failures or you can choose to look at them as a bad few minutes in a good day. It's okay to feel sorry for yourself for a few seconds, but then you need to pick yourself up and brush yourself off. If you do that, you never fail."

Scarlett leans her head back onto my shoulder. "Is it possible? Can I succeed?"

"Yes, Tink." Calling her that makes me think of Gran and the hours she spent reading *Peter and Wendy* to me over and over again. "Do you want to know why Gran called you Tink?"

"I thought it was because I was loyal."

"It is, but there's more. It was said in the story that Tinker Bell was so small that she could only experience one emotion at a time. She was either all happy, all sad, all mad and so on. Gran said you were all or nothing. You were either all in or all out. All mad, sad or happy. Failure and success isn't an all-or-nothing. It's a little bit of both and everything in between."

She's silent for a while, taking in what I said, and I'm just as quiet, reminding myself that I have to play by the same rules.

Scarlett turns to look at me. "I want so badly to succeed and to do it on my own. I want to prove to myself, to my mom and to my sister, that this can be done. That I can support myself. That I don't need someone to take care of me."

I caress her face and spot the determination in her eyes. I wish my mom had been more like her, but she wasn't and that cost both me and her. "You're going to do it, Tink. I know you will."

The smile she gives me is the most blinding and brilliant I've ever seen, and I lean forward and kiss her sweet lips.

"What do you think of the apartment?" I ask her between kisses.

"I'm taking it."

SCARLETT

My pulse beats in my ears as the judge looks over his glasses at me then back at the paperwork in front of him. My social worker just finished testifying how I can afford the rent for the studio apartment, which Marshall has agreed to cosign for. She also detailed how, with the fact I am turning eighteen soon and won't be bound by the Graduated Driver Licensing program, I'm working toward earning my driver's license, and how I've lined up a very used car that probably shouldn't be driven longer than fifty miles. My lawyer also laid out that I seem to have a good understanding of the responsibilities of living on my own.

The underlying theme: yes, Scarlett is aware, for the foreseeable future, she'll be eating ramen noodles for every meal, will learn to wear layers and work by candlelight to save on energy costs, and will be shopping at Goodwill in the desperate scenario that she has to purchase something.

My lawyer, Susan Adachi, covers my hand with hers. She's a rock, she's a queen, and I love her even more because she's taken me on as a favor to Marshall and because she believes in me. This is family court, and in theory, the room is closed, but all the people who have spoken on my behalf are behind me: Marshall, Glory, Pastor Hughes, the police officer who handed me a tissue as I cried and told him what happened between my mom and dad, and then there's Jesse.

Strong Jesse. Beautiful Jesse. A lighthouse in the midst of my storm. I peek over my shoulder, and he sits as if he's the most care-free person in the world. He's not watching the judge like every-one else, but me. Our eyes meet and he winks. A flurry of butterflies in my chest, and I force myself to focus.

It's going to be okay. Everything is going to be fine.

My parents aren't here. They sent in signed statements with their lawyer, stating that they don't agree with my choices but that they will respect the decision of the court. I'm not sure how I feel about that—a bit empty, a bit relieved, a bit sad that they aren't here begging for me to give them another chance. Even if they did, it wouldn't change my mind. It's just that every child wants their parents to want them. There's this ache inside me that is begging for me to be loved—by them.

I still see Pastor Hughes once a week, by my choice, and I asked him during one of our sessions if that ache would ever go away. He didn't answer me directly, but I saw the honesty in his eyes—children always want their parents to love them and he told me that his Father, his God, offered the type of unconditional love that heals all wounds.

The judge takes a deep breath, nerves overtake my stomach, and with a few words of encouragement, the judge announces that I'm free.

"We also asked for visitation for her sister, Isabelle," Susan says.

"I'm also granting the visitation." And my entire world is right.

Dad is in the basement, Mom is in her room crying, Isabelle is watching cartoons and I'm wondering for the millionth time if I'm making the right choice. I'm leaving. Tonight. I'm terrified, and I want to puke. Across the street, Jesse and Marshall are sitting on the front steps of Jesse's trailer. They're there in case something goes wrong.

Jesse wanted to come in with me, but Marshall had worked it out with my parents for them to give me space to pack. Marshall believes that we should handle everything with as little emotion and confrontation as possible. Problem is, I don't know how to stop feeling.

Hot and clammy, I fold another shirt and place it on top of the others in the suitcase. I'm taking my clothes, some items like makeup and then some personal things like my favorite stuffed animal as a child and a photo of me and my sister. Marshall told me to only take things that I can prove were given to me as a gift—otherwise Dad could claim I'm stealing from him. Is he that bitter? I don't know, and I don't plan on finding out.

"You don't have to do this," my father says in his deep, sad tone.

My stomach sinks, and I briefly close my eyes before turning to look at him. He stands in the doorway with his hands in his pockets, looking so regretful. A slow throb starts in my head—and the merry-go-round starts up again.

"Yes, I do," I say.

"You can stay, and we can try again." Dad rubs the back of his neck, reminding me of the conversation we had in front of Glory's booth back in August. "I was wrong to get so angry that night, and I was wrong to hit your mother. It's just that when we came home and found you gone, it terrified me. I thought of how I lost my sister and—"

"Stop!" I hold out my hand, and I notice that it has a slight tremor. Standing up for myself is terrifying. In my back pocket is the prepaid cell I bought for myself last night, and it's my only security blanket in this horrendous situation. One call to Jesse or Marshall, and they'll be here in a heartbeat.

"You don't get to do this anymore," I say. "You don't get to excuse away your behavior. Something horrible happened to you, but that does not give you the excuse to do something horrible to Isabelle, Mom or me."

"I know," he starts, "and I'm truly working on this. I'm still in counseling. I'm attending several times a week now. I just need more time—"

"That's great, but you should be figuring this out away from here. You should be giving Mom space to figure out why she's okay with how you treat her, and you should be allowing me and Isabelle space to heal from our wounds. But you aren't. You're staying here so I have to leave. I'm no longer going to allow your problems to be my problems."

Dad's face and posture crumple, but while I hurt, while I feel sorry for him, I also feel sorry for me. He's broken, and I can't fix him. That's not my job anymore. It should have never been my job to begin with.

"I don't want to lose you," he says. "I love you."

I feel sick because I still love him, too, but I've decided to love me more. "I hope you stick with the counseling, and I hope you get better."

"Is that it?" Dad pushes. The tears in his eyes are real and the wetness in my eyes burn. "You're just going to leave? You walk out the door and you're no longer my daughter?"

I'm still his daughter. He's still my father. That's why this hurts. I wish I could wave a wand and be gifted my fairy tale. That Dad is magically healed of his issues and that we could be a happy family, but that's not how the real world works. "Please take care of yourself. Mom, Isabelle and I deserve better."

It's an empowering sensation as I zip up my suitcase, pick that one up and then the other, and walk past him and out the door.

JESSE

The sound of a chair scraping the floor causes me to open my eyes. At Glory's, Scarlett and I are curled up on Glory's bed and Scarlett is sound asleep. Scarlett's staying here tonight and tomorrow she's moving into her apartment. It was a tough evening. She left home, and I held her as she wept—my T-shirt soaked with her tears.

I couldn't find the right words to help her broken heart so I stayed silent and held on. I wish I were better with words, the right words, at least, but I'm not so I offered the only comfort I could give—being here. She's sad, she's scared, but I tried to tell her through my touch that she's not alone.

A glance at the clock on the wall. It's ten at night, and there are voices and footsteps as Glory wraps up her last client session of the evening. The front door opens, it shuts and then there is the sound of an engine and headlights flash into the room I'm in with Scarlett.

Light footsteps and the door doesn't squeak as Glory opens it. She leans her shoulder against the doorframe as she takes in the TV that plays a movie on low volume, Scarlett asleep and then me.

"Hey." My voice is cracked from sleep.

"She okay?" she asks.

No, but I hope she will be. "It was a rough day."

Glory tilts her head toward the living room, and I nod. I'm gentle as I sit up, and then place a blanket over Scarlett. In the moonlight, she appears young and at peace. I hope to God this all works out for her as she's gone through enough pain to last a lifetime.

I leave the door open an inch to let her know that Glory's done with clients in case she wakes. Glory's not in the kitchen pouring tea like I expect, but in the living room at her table and in her chair. In her hands is her deck of tarot cards.

As I sit, she hands them to me. I raise an eyebrow, yet I accept the cards.

"What do you want to know?" Glory asks.

The obvious. "Is Scarlett going to be okay?"

"That's up to her, but I have faith she'll make enough of the right choices that she'll overcome all of this."

"Enough of the right choices?"

"We're human, and we're built to make mistakes. Success isn't making the right choice every time. Success is trying again after you've failed. Now tell me what you'd like to know."

I shuffle the cards, think about all that's happened over the past few months. Truth is, after all this time I don't have the courage to ask her what I want to know—if I'm going to keep my land.

"I would have thought you would have asked me about your land," she says, somehow reading my mind for the millionth time since I've known her.

I keep shuffling. "Maybe I'm scared of the answer."

"Are you scared I'm going to tell you that you're keeping it or losing it?"

My stomach tightens as I don't know.

"After all we've been through, do you think I'm real now?" Glory asks.

I think she knows weird stuff that I can't explain, and I think she's family. Family I care about and family who cares about me. "I think you put too much oregano in your spaghetti sauce."

Glory laughs, and I work up the courage to ask her at least one of the questions that plague me. "Is the curse real?"

"My answer doesn't matter, Jesse. The curse is as real as your answer. Anything is as real as you make it, including everything I do. People highly underestimate the power of thought and faith."

Not the answer I had hoped for, but it's honest. "People pay you for this nonsense?"

"And they pay me well." She has the balls to wink as she takes the tarot cards from me and places them in the same intricate pattern that she did back in August.

"I didn't ask a question."

"You asked two. One you just asked aloud. The other you said in your mind."

The Chariot is laid out again on the table, but this time the card faces Glory.

"This card likes you and Scarlett," Glory says. "I'm happy to see it in the upright position this time. The Chariot shows movement. When it is in reverse, like it was in August, it can mean that you're moving in the wrong direction, stuck and/or experiencing a loss of control. When it's upright, like now, it means forward movement or progression."

"That sounds like a lot of vague nonsense."

"Does it? Because it sounds to me like after some false starts you're starting to take the right path." Glory lifts her head and stares straight through me with that faraway expression. "Play nice, Jesse, because he's here to play nice with you."

I cock an eyebrow and seconds later there's the humming of a smooth car engine. Marshall's car pulls up alongside Glory's Beetle, and I'm baffled. "How do you do that?"

Glory waggles her eyebrows. "Marshall texted me earlier and told me he was on his way."

"I knew you were a con," I tease.

"I'm only a con when I'm not psychic. Now go on outside. My last two client meetings were draining, and I need some time to refocus my energy."

That's called being dismissed. I put on my shoes and a jacket, and by the time I step into the cool December night, Marshall is already walking toward the porch. He's as casual as I've ever seen him in a gray Destin, Florida, sweatshirt and a pair of faded jeans.

I sit on the bottom step so I can be in contact with my land. Here lately, I've needed its strength. I've always needed its strength.

Marshall joins me, and he glances over his shoulder at the house. "Glory still meeting with a client?"

"She's refocusing her energy."

Marshall shakes his head like he doesn't get it, but that's the thing, he doesn't have to. I'm figuring out that I don't either. It's not up to me to judge what works for other people. Glory has her angels, and Pastor Hughes has his God. I should just be happy for them that they have faith in something that helps them along in a tough life.

My uncle and I look out onto the night, listen to the wind chimes lightly tinkle with the wind and to the peaceful sound of silence that only my land provides. It's a cool evening as so far December has been mild.

"I feel like I owe you a kidney. If yours ever goes out then you can have one of mine."

"If I ever need one, I'll take you up on that." Marshall rubs his hands together, reminiscent of the day of Gran's funeral. A slow throb in my head as I don't have it in me for more bad news. "Have you decided if you're going to write a letter for me to read at the hearing or if you're going to show and talk yourself?"

My plan was to write a letter, but that now seems like a weak choice when Scarlett has stood up to her father multiple times. She faced her demon, and maybe it's time I face mine. "I'll go myself and speak."

"You sure?"

"Yeah."

"I'll be there with you—every step of the way."

I'm depending on that. "Thank you."

We fall into silence again, but it's not peaceful. Our feet are literally resting on the elephant in our conversation: the land. Marshall and I spent so many years fighting with each other that it's tough for me to switch gears into being on the same side.

"I promise not to get angry if you bring it up," I say, "and I also promise to listen to what you have to say as long as you promise to listen to me."

"That sounds fair." Marshall rubs his hands together a second time then folds them. "I'm not going to claim that I have all the answers or that I've handled everything with the land right, but I want you to know that everything I've done, it's because I care. I wish that everything with the land would have gone down differently than what it has, but what's done is done. Now we have to figure out where to go from here."

"I have the pastor's vote."

"You do."

"I lost Mr. Copeland's vote," I say.

"I think that's a given."

The decision as to whether or not I keep my land is solely up to Marshall. It bothers me, but not nearly as much as I thought it would. "What do I have to do to keep the land?"

"Are you ready to have a mature conversation about that land? Not how you feel about it, but a financial one? If you want to keep the land, you can't keep thinking about the land in terms of dreams. You need to understand what's on paper."

I open my mouth to argue that I have been dealing with the financials, but then close it shut. One, I just told him I would listen. Two, I recently spent an entire day trying to show Scarlett the hardships and responsibilities of living on her own. From the money I make, I've been able to feed myself and keep the electricity running. Marshall's the one who has been handling the bills for the farm. "I'm listening."

"You're losing money on the land monthly between the taxes and upkeep. If you were to keep the land, you'd have to initially figure out how to make it self-sustaining and then figure out quick how to make it profitable. I wish I could help, but other than writing checks and subtracting from the land's account, I don't know a thing about how to help you manage the property."

Farming is a morning, noon and night position with no days off. I've taken off too many days recently and the to-do list only grows. It's not easy work. It's possibly the toughest, most grueling work there is.

"There are multiple people interested in the land, and they'll give you top dollar for it. Since your gran's death, several corporate

farms have inquired about the land. To be honest, we could probably have a very profitable auction on our hands. You can sell this
land, and if you manage the money correctly, you'd be set for the
rest of your life.

"You can leave town, never have anyone assume the worst
about who you are ever again due to your last name, nor will you
have to listen to nonsense about that curse. It'll be a fresh start."

"Will the money be mine or will it always be up to you as to
what happens?"

"Yes and no. How the will is set up, the money would go into
a trust. You'll receive three payments over ten years. The first payment will happen when the land is sold. What you do with the
payments when you receive them will be up to you, but if you'd
accept my help, I'll teach you how to manage the money to not
only make it last, but so the money will work for you."

This could be a fresh start for me and it could be a fresh start
for Scarlett. I could sell the land and make her dreams come true.
I could help her with college and living expenses. After all, one
of us needs a dream to work out. Besides loving Scarlett, I have no
idea what my dreams are anymore.

"Now is my turn to listen," Marshall says. "I'll admit to not listening to you when you first heard about the tribunal, when you
said you had ideas of how to make the land profitable. I'm listening now. Maybe between the two of us, we can figure out if we
can make your ideas work."

God, I've had so many ideas. Clearing out the fields and putting in corn and soybeans. Using other fields for dairy and beef
cattle. Keeping some of the property for hay and then using other
portions for other crops. But as I try to tell him my plans, my voice
box is as still as this night.

To do any of that, we need money and lots of it. Money that
the big corporate farms can invest in their properties and still
make a profit. They can hire people, and I can barely keep up with
the land on my own now and keep myself fed. Marshall's right: if
I mortgage the property for my dreams and I mess up and don't
make the monthly payments, I could lose everything. "I need to
think about this first. Once I do, we'll talk."

"Do you still want to keep the land?" he asks.

Truth is? I don't know what I want. I lower my head and clasp my hands together. I'm not sure if I'm praying, but this might be the closest I've ever gotten to it if it is.

It's time to be honest with myself. "The will said that the vote won't officially happen until May. Is there enough money in Gran's account to keep the land going until then?"

"I'll make the funds work. If things get bad, we can sell a few acres, but that's not something I'd advise we do often. You'll get more for the land with the acreage intact."

"I need time."

"Then that's what we'll do." Marshall pats my back as he stands. "Let me know if you or Scarlett need anything."

"I will."

Marshall leaves, and I sit for a while after his car goes down the long road. Whatever I decide, it's going to have a long-lasting effect on so many. For me, Scarlett and Glory.

This is Glory's home, and I can't ask her to leave it. That's something to consider if I do sell the land or mortgage the property in an attempt to make this a real working farm—making sure she stays.

I enter the cottage, and Glory's asleep on the tiny love seat in the corner of the room. She gave up her bedroom so Scarlett had a place to crash tonight. Marshall's niece and nephew are in from out of town taking up his guest room, and with it being Scarlett's first night away from home, I didn't think crashing with me, across the road from her family, would be helpful.

I lock the front door, grab a blanket out of the hall closet, toss it over Glory then turn off the lights. The TV is still on when I enter the bedroom. Using the remote, I power it off then take off my jacket, sit on the chair in the corner and take off my shoes. I relax back and wonder if I should sleep here instead of making the assumption Scarlett wants me in bed. Holding her is how she fell asleep, and while I ache to hold her again, I want to respect her and her space.

When I stretch out my legs, I glance over at her and Scarlett's groggy lids open. There's a moment there of fog, that misty place between sleep and consciousness, and then she blinks into awareness as her gaze lands on me. "Hi."

"Hi," I whisper. "How are you?"

"Better." Her blue eyes that were raging with a violent storm earlier tonight are calmer now and that settles some of the uneasiness inside me. "Are you okay?"

No, I'm not. "You should go back to sleep."

"I will, once you lay with me."

I don't have to be asked twice. She holds the blanket up for me and I slip in beside her. Scarlett's warm body melts into me, heating my cold skin and my broken heart.

"What's wrong?" she whispers against my chest.

"I'm fine." Scarlett's gone through hell tonight. She doesn't need to take on my burdens.

"Don't lie to me. That's not going to help either of us."

She's right. More than she knows. "Do you remember when I told you the reason why I stopped talking to you before our freshman year?"

She nods and her long, silky hair slides against the bare skin of my arm. For courage, I nuzzle my nose into her hair and inhale her sweet scent. She snuggles closer to me, almost as if she's aware how terrified I am.

"You didn't like how people treated me because of you," she says.

I run my fingers along her back, not to comfort her, but to comfort me. After all that I've done, she's still here lying with me. I need to be truthful with myself and with Scarlett. I've been lying to both of us for too long. "That's not the full reason why I cut you off."

Scarlett lifts her head and rests her chin on my chest. Her eyebrows pinch together as she looks at me. "What do you mean?

"I did overhear the conversation between you and your mom, but there was more." How do I tell her my darkest fear? How do I let the thing that's festered inside me like a spider laying eggs in a dark, deep hole come forth and be seen?

"Tell me," she encourages.

"My mom didn't die after we stopped talking like everyone in town thinks. She died during the summer. My father murdered her and I saw the whole thing."

I close my eyes to fight off the memories. "I grew up with my mom in my ear telling me that the curse was real, and I had Gran in the other telling me it wasn't. That summer, when I saw my mom in a pool of her own blood, when I laid down beside her and begged her to wake up and she didn't, I decided Mom was right— the curse was real. It had to be, because I had never hurt like I had before that day, and I made the decision to never hurt like that again."

A feathering touch on my cheek, but I ignore it. "Oh, Jesse."

"I cut myself off from you because I was terrified if I stayed friends with you then the curse would affect you. I loved you, which meant the curse would hurt you in order to hurt me. And I couldn't do that. I barely survived losing Mom, and I knew I couldn't survive losing you. I loved you too much for that."

There's silence, a stillness. That heavy, weighted second before the razor of the guillotine is released. My heart thrashes wildly in my chest as the emotion of losing Mom clogs up my throat. Then soft shifting as Scarlett drags her body up the bed. I open my eyes and stare straight at the ceiling, waiting for her to bolt.

"What did you say?" Scarlett whispers.

"That I believed in the curse. That it's my fault my mom died, and it would be my fault if anything happened to you."

"No, that I heard. What did you say about loving me?"

The world zones out as her question causes me to snap my head to look at her. There's hope on her face and that causes confusion in my chest. A sharp quickening and stalling of my heart. Is it possible that she loves me regardless of the curse?

My forehead furrows as maybe she didn't understand. "I'm cursed, Scarlett."

Scarlett cups my face with her hand and the soft feel of her skin against mine is too close to heaven. This can't be real.

"You love me?" she says.

"I've been in love with you for as long as I can remember. I don't remember not loving you." It's always been there—as easy and beautiful as the sun rising in the morning.

"You're not cursed."

"My mom died—"

"You're not cursed."

"And since being with me, your problems have intensified."

"Do you believe I love you?"

Even if I wanted to deny it, I couldn't. Love for me radiates from her in waves. "Yes."

"Then there is no curse, and if there was, it's not there anymore. Because if you were cursed, we wouldn't be having this moment right here, right now. My dad doesn't know how to love—that's a curse. My mom doesn't know how to love—that's a curse. There is absolutely nothing you can say to me to convince me that you're cursed when love actually exists. We love each other—that defeats everything else in our path."

I knot my fingers in her hair, and she kisses me. The type of kiss where your heart breaks and bleeds and then is sown back together. The type of kiss that is experienced once in a lifetime, and I'm not cursed because after she briefly pulls away to shift closer to me, we share the same kiss again.

Scarlett pulls back breathless, and I'm breathing hard myself. It would be easy to keep kissing her tonight—to go further than we have before, to press upon boundaries and get lost in each other. She's lost, I'm lost and we're both begging to be found, but I don't want to find each other that way. From the way she touches me with hunger, yet keeps her lips a small distance apart from mine, she's feeling the same way.

"I love you," I whisper.

Scarlett's mouth hesitantly lifts. "Do you know that besides tonight, you've never said that to me before?"

I frown. "Yes, I have."

She laughs and the sound brings me peace. "No, you haven't."

"Yes," I start, but she places a finger against my mouth, silencing me.

"You haven't. Trust me, I'd remember something like that."

I search back in my brain, thinking of all the times she's brought me joy, and while the memories are numerous, there's no declaration from me. I squeeze her gently in a hug for loving an idiot, then rest my forehead on hers. "I don't know what to do with the land."

She squints as if she doesn't understand. "What do you mean?"

"Most of the choices I've made in the past have been my attempt to avoid the curse. Some of them have worked out in my favor, but plenty haven't."

"What's that have to do with your land?"

"What if everybody is right and the only reason I've wanted the land is because I'm afraid what would happen if I left it? That I was afraid of the curse?"

She tilts her head in sympathy. "You love this land."

I do. "But what if I fear this land more than I love it, and I just have never given myself the opportunity to know the difference between love and fear?"

It's a tough question without an easy answer and because Scarlett is perfect in every way, she understands that I don't need words right now, but just her. She cuddles in close to me and holds me as I hold her.

JESSE

Icouldn't say 100 percent before, but I can now: suits aren't my thing. They smother me from the inside out.

Marshall and I wait outside a conference room for the parole board to call us in. I don't know what I was expecting. A courtroom, I guess, or maybe some grimy room within the prison itself where when I walked down the hallways I'd hear the yells from prisoners getting into fights.

I need to stop watching so much late-night TV.

My cell vibrates in my pocket, and along with good wishes from Nazareth, Leo and V, there's a text from Scarlett. A text from her own phone that she pays for herself. It's simple and strikes straight to the heart: *I love you.*

Three little words and her faith gives me the courage to move mountains, which is what I need. Me: *I love you, too. I'll text when I'm done.*

Scarlett: *Good luck. Just think how fantastically boring life will be when the hearing is over and we head back to school. New normal for the win.*

It's early January, and it's our last week of winter break. What no one else knows is that I'm not going back. On the last day of school before break, I went into the school board office and picked up my high school diploma. No fanfare, no cap and gown, just me knowing I have a lot of decisions to make and a few months left to make them.

I glance up to spot Marshall stalking my cell, and I raise an eyebrow. "Privacy?"

"You haven't told her."

No, I haven't. "I'm telling her tonight."

"Cutting it short, aren't you?"

The honest answer? "I'm afraid if I told her earlier I'd let her talk me out of it." I'm not as brave as Scarlett. If she were me, she would have already told me what's going on and have gone forward full throttle, and that's the reason why I'm doing what I'm doing. I need to become her equal. I need to be as brave as she is in how she lives life.

Marshall places a hand on my shoulder then squeezes. "You're making the right choice."

I think so, but the question is, will Scarlett? Will she understand that what I'm doing will hopefully help me figure out who I am? Or will she feel betrayed?

"Do you think she'll go with you?" Marshall asks.

The idea of being without Scarlett causes my chest to hollow out. I want her with me, every step of the way, but I don't think she'll follow me. She's stronger than that, and I need to become just as strong as she is. "No."

"Mr. Lachlin?" A woman with short brown hair sticks her head out the door. "We're ready for your statement."

I nod, and Marshall slides in front of me. "Remember, this isn't the parole hearing. It's an opportunity for you to tell them your emotions regarding your mother's death and your father's possible parole. Are you ready?"

As I'm going to be. "Let's go."

We walk in, take seats and some words are said. Marshall talks, the people at the other end of the conference table talk, and while it's important to listen, I can't. It's all buzzing in my head. Then there's a nudge on my arm, Marshall angling his head to the words I had written on the piece of paper to keep my thoughts in order. It's my turn to speak, my turn to announce my truth and no longer stay silent.

"First, I want to thank you for the opportunity to speak to you on behalf of my mother. To be honest, I wish I could say that if she had lived through what happened that night between her and my father that she would be in this chair talking to you and telling you not to offer him parole, but I can't say that because it would be a lie."

I glance up, and each of them watch me. Not one of them is on their phones or taking notes. I have their full, undivided attention.

"Throughout my childhood, my mother bounced from guy to guy. Many of them I met, probably many more I didn't. My mom needed someone in her life to feel secure, which is ironic because rarely was she safe in any of those situations.

"Mom and I were vagabonds drifting in the world. In between staying with guys she dated, I found a home base with my grandmother, Suzanne. She was my mother's mother. Sometimes my mom would stay with us, but there was a hole inside her that drove her away and into another man's arms.

"I lived my life fearing the day my mother would show up at my grandmother's and tell me she had found someone new. Someone who would love and take care of us. I never understood why she couldn't see the people who loved her in the safety of my grandmother's trailer, but she didn't, and I'll never know why.

"I've spent nights on cold floors, went hungry more times than I can count, and watched as my mother was physically and verbally abused again and again. There were a few times I found myself at the wrong end of one of her boyfriends' fists, and I have to admit that I found myself grateful that I was the one who was hit, not her, because somehow in my eight-year-old mind, I thought I could handle the pain better.

"It hasn't been until recent years that I learned that my mother had kept in contact with my father—a man she had met when she had turned eighteen. She had told me once that she had fallen madly in love. I don't know much about the love my parents shared, but I do know about the mad. Of all the people my mother had been with, it turns out he was the most abusive.

"What had driven them apart initially was me. My father didn't want me, my mother did, but she agreed to never bring me so they could be together. I tell you this to paint a picture of who my mother was. She made bad choices, but she also loved me. Her love might have been destructive, but it was mine, and as a child, I took any type of love I could get."

I think of how Mom would hug me tight when she'd walk in the door. I think of how we'd stay up for hours, and she'd talk to me about the maps. I think of how I'll never be able to show her another report card with an *A*. Of how I'll never be able to tell her about Scarlett and how I learned to love. I think of how someday, I'll never dance with my mom at my wedding, and I'll never place my child in her arms.

A million moments stolen from me. Moments I'll never be given back.

"The summer before my freshman year, my mother and father had entered what I presume would be called a honeymoon period. She thought they were fixed and would be together forever. One of her last mistakes was making this assumption and bringing me to stay with him. It was a day of many firsts for me. It was the first day I left the state of Kentucky, it was the first day I had a strawberry milkshake, it was the first time I had ever seen anyone so angry that my heart literally stopped beating.

"I'm not going to go into detail on what happened that night. There was a trial, and I'm sure you have the information and evidence that convicted my father. I understand that three years have passed, and that he possibly has had time to change, but I'm going to be selfish here and explain to you that three years has not been enough time for me to change.

"When my father killed my mother in front of me, I froze. I froze after my father smashed a chair over my back in anger. I froze when my father started beating my mother. I froze as I watched her die by his hand. I froze on the witness stand during the trial. I froze whenever my grandmother or my older cousin tried to touch me in comfort. I froze whenever I tried to tell my best friend what happened. I froze, and I've stayed that way for years."

My throat closes and the edges of my mouth turn down. I clear my throat once, twice, a third time and when I take a deep breath, I'm too close to a sob.

"It's okay, Mr. Lachlin," says a man with gray hair and a kind expression. "Take your time."

I take a drink and hate how the hand that holds the bottled water shakes. I clear my throat again. This time, I create enough of an air passage to continue.

"Over the past few months, through the love and dedication of some very important people in my life, I'm starting to change. The change has been hard. It's been a push and a pull, and there are times I have fought it every inch of the way.

"Even though there has been change, I'm going to admit, I don't know who I am, and I'd like a chance to figure that out. I've spent a good portion of my life believing I had to stay on my family's property, but I know now I can leave, and that has opened a whole realm of possibilities.

"It's overwhelming and frightening, but for the first time since my mother's death, I feel alive. It has taken me three years to get to this point, and I'm asking you to please allow me more time to explore myself, these changes and my new possibilities.

"What my father did froze me. He might have had time to change, but I haven't. I need this time, and if he's released, I'm scared it's going to return me to my previous state. He's the one who put me in this position, and it's up to me to change, but I need that time. I ask that you please take a long look at the crime, at how violent it was, at how he hurt me physically and emotionally, and then remember what I asked you here today. I ask that you please deny him parole and to keep him in prison. Thank you."

SCARLETT

I am the master of microwave spaghetti, and today I'm going fancy and I bought a loaf of Italian bread. Jesse had a long day meeting with the parole committee—exhausting, I'm sure, and I want to do something special for him. Dinner, TV and holding him tight.

I've been in the apartment for a few weeks, and so far, so good. Money is tight, the balancing act between school and work a bit tighter, but I've survived and for that I'm proud.

A knock on the door, and I cross the room. I smile at the Louisville Slugger Leo bought me as a housewarming gift that leans next to the door. He had a twinkle in his eye as he told me it was my home security system. Sort of freaked me out, but it was honest.

I check the peephole and my heart happily flips when I spot Jesse with a bouquet of flowers. Appears I wasn't the only one who planned on making tonight special. I undo the two security locks and the lock on the knob and then open the door. Jesse flashes his pirate smile as he walks in and offers me the bouquet of mixed wildflowers. I absolutely melt.

I raise onto my toes, and Jesse gives me one of his fantastic slow kisses. I heat up fast, and so does the kiss. Hands in hair, caresses along curves of backs, both of us pressing our bodies together in glorious ways.

We're alone, in a room, where there's a bed and not much else.

My blood pounds in my veins. If I don't break this off now, we'll never eat dinner. "I should put these into water."

My cheeks are hot from kissing, and there's shy embarrassment at how my voice comes out shaky. Vase-less, I decide upon a plastic cup I saved from a fast food restaurant, fill it with water and then stand at the counter as I arrange the bouquet.

Jesse cocks a hip against the counter and watches me as if I'm performing the most interesting act in the world. I'd like to offer him a place to sit, but other than the floor, there's the bed, and if we plan on eating dinner, we better not start there.

"How did today go?" I ask, and Jesse tells me. I listen as I finish with the flowers, finish making our dinner and then place it on the picnic blanket on the floor. Jesse continues to talk as he cuts up the loaf of bread and butters a few pieces.

Last night, he had read to me what he was going to say to the parole board and each word tore me apart. As he finishes telling me how he had the courage to read those words to strangers and still be standing tall, I hug him close.

"I'm proud of you," I say. "I bet your mom and Suzanne would be, too."

Jesse squeezes me, then draws back. "Marshall said he'd be shocked if my dad is granted parole. He said I did a good job, plus my father hasn't served long enough for the crime he committed."

"That's good." Because it is. It's what Jesse needs.

We sit on the floor, and Jesse switches up the subject by asking me about work, and I let him. Jesse and I aren't used to sharing the darkest and scariest places of ourselves with anyone. Sharing can be raw and consuming, and understanding that, we're very patient of any steps forward, then of the retreat.

Jesse and I gorge ourselves with bread and use it to sop up any remaining spaghetti sauce. We chat, we laugh, we enjoy each other and soon we're kissing. We're kissing long, we're kissing deep, and Jesse takes my breath away when he lays us down on the blanket and rolls me underneath him.

I love this feeling. The heavy weight of his body over mine. The safe, protective sensation as he caresses my cheek, the tingles of my skin as he feathers kisses down my neck and the warm, melting tickle in my blood at how we fit perfectly together.

There's nothing rushed. Each and every touch, brush of fingertips and kiss is memorized and fully explored. A reverence for each other as if this is a gift, as if we are a gift, as if each second is to be savored.

Soon my head starts to spin, a wonderful and beautiful thrill sprints through me, and then I break away, gasping for air, and Jesse, ever-so-patient Jesse, kisses the side of my neck and rolls onto his side facing me.

He slides a finger along my hot cheek and looks down at me with such love and devotion that my heart's a cup that's running over. "I have something for you."

"You already bought me flowers."

"Yeah, but this will last longer than flowers."

Jesse pushes himself off the floor, walks out into the cold evening and quickly returns, shutting out the darkness and the winter wind. He has a large rolled-up poster held in place by rubber bands. He slips the bands off, unrolls the paper and in front of me is a map of the United States with little stickered stars of varying colors across the map. "I brought you a map for your wall."

Seeing how bare my walls are, this is absolutely . . . "Perfect."

"Where do you want it?" he asks.

I do a slow spin of my studio apartment and then skip over to my bed. I plop down on it and touch the wall next to me. "Here."

It takes longer for me to dig the tape out of my Tupperware box of miscellaneous things than it does for Jesse to tape the map in place on my wall.

Once he's done, he tosses the tape back into my box then joins me on my bed, climbing behind me. I settle between his legs, he holds me close and I snuggle contently in his arms. Jesse rests his head against mine, and I get lost in his deep voice as he tells me the places he's marked and what he hopes to find there someday. He describes wonders that if they are even half as beautiful as he says, to experience them would be life-altering.

"I've thought long and hard about this, and I've decided to visit these places."

A wave of shock rumbles through me, and I sit up in order to look straight at him. "Does this mean you're selling your land?"

Jesse twirls a lock of my hair around his finger then lets it unwind. "I don't know. Marshall and I have talked a lot, and he's told me that he's going to leave the decision of what to do with my land up to me."

Happiness swirls though me as this is the news Jesse has been waiting for, but then I pause at the confusion in his eyes. "What's wrong?"

"I love my land," Jesse says. "But how do I know if I truly want my land until I experience what else is out there?"

My mouth tips up. "You're planning an adventure."

He nods, but he doesn't look as excited as I thought he would. "Marshall's going to sell a handful of acres in the southern property. It's too wooded for me to clear without heavy equipment. The money we'll get is going to be enough for me to purchase a truck that can withstand some miles, and if I'm smart, the money will also be enough to get me to each of those stars on your map."

"This sounds great, so why do you look unhappy?"

Jesse glances down and my stomach sinks when he looks back up at me. "I'm leaving next week."

I twitch as I grow cold. "You're what?"

"Leaving next week."

I open my mouth to speak, but it's difficult to make words come out. "You . . . you can't. We have school."

"You have school. Preparing for Gran's death, I completed most of my courses this past summer. I picked up the straggling few credits this fall. They gave me my diploma during the last week of school."

My forehead furrows as I try to force sanity into the situation. "So you're leaving?"

"I'm not leaving you." He goes to touch me, but I draw back. My heart hurts, my soul hurts, everything hurts and I'm done with hurt. Because of my dad, I've been ingrained with hurt. And things were starting to be good.

"I'm leaving for however long it takes me to figure myself out."

"So, what?" Tears burn my eyes. "I sit here and wait for you to return?"

"I don't expect you to sit and wait on anything. In fact, I expect you to keep being the force of nature that you are."

I suck in my lower lip as it begins to tremble. "It feels like you're leaving me."

"I'm not. I love you."

I have to take several deep breaths to fight off the rejection yet I lose the battle.

"Do you remember when you first started talking emancipation, and I asked you to move in with me?" Jesse asks.

A bit of anger joins the sadness because I have an idea where this is headed, and I don't like my words being used against me. "I remember."

I told him that I needed to prove to myself, to my mom and sister that I could leave and succeed on my own. What sucks is that when I rejected his offer, Jesse didn't bat an eyelash. Unlike me now, on the verge of becoming a crying mess.

"You told me that you need to live on your own, and I understand that," Jesse says. "My entire life, I've been scared of anything beyond my land. I need to prove to myself that I can leave and that I'm not my mom. I need to know that if I choose my land it isn't because I'm scared, but because my land is where I truly need to be. I understand that you need to do this on your own, and I hope you understand that I need to leave."

But he's leaving, and I hate that and I hate him because every word he's said makes complete sense. My eyesight becomes blurry. "Wait for this summer and let me go with you."

Jesse tries to tuck my hair behind my ear, and I reject his touch again. "Is that what you want, Scarlett? To give up what you're building on your own—your job with Glory, this apartment, your hope of college, your independence—to travel with me?"

Everything in my chest twists and knots. One month. That's how long my mother lasted without my father. That was her limit on being alone.

Alone.

My eyes close with the dull spasm in my heart, and when I

open them again I have to blink away the wetness. Jesse reaches out to cup my face again, and this time, I let him. I lean into his warm palm and a traitorous tear escapes from the corner of my eyes. His thumb is heartbreakingly gentle as he wipes it away.

"Truth is, I'll wait until this summer if that's what you want," Jesse says. "I don't want to be without you, but I've defined myself by the curse and this land my entire life. I don't know who I am without it, and I need to leave and figure that out. I don't want to be without you, and I don't want to leave you alone, but I need to decide by May if I'm keeping or selling this land. I'm losing money on the farm with how it's being managed now. I need to grow up and make big decisions, and I'd like to know who I am first before I make them."

"You'd wait and let me come if I pressed, wouldn't you?" I ask.

He sadly nods.

"But you need to go now and . . ." I trail off because the pain slashing through me causes me to wince, but I understand what he needs because I need it, too. "You need to be alone."

"Yes. I also hope you'll understand that I don't want to shut you out, but I do want to take some time before I call. I'm scared the moment I hear your voice, I'll run home. I also need to know that the choices I end up making are my choices and my choices alone."

Just like the emancipation and living alone in this apartment were my choice.

"For us to have forever," he continues, "I need to know who I am first. Staying here without that knowledge isn't fair to me or you."

"I'm scared." The truth is so raw, so exposing that I feel as if I'm standing stark naked in a snowstorm. I shiver, and he rubs his hands up and down my arms.

"Of what?" he asks.

My stomach clenches, but I need to be honest with Jesse and myself. "Of being alone."

I almost wish I could take back the words, but he doesn't want me to hide what I feel, and I no longer want to be the girl who buries her emotions.

"What's your worst fear?" he asks.

I close my eyes as my throat swells shut. I'm terrified if I'm alone I'll return home. That I'll believe that living in fear of my father is better than living alone with my own thoughts. "I'm terrified I'm not strong enough."

"You are the strongest person I know. If I thought for one second you couldn't do this, I wouldn't leave. You've made me realize that if I'm going to be worthy of you that I have to be just as brave as you are. You inspire me, and I hope to God you'll understand that I'm doing this for me and for you. I'm doing this for us."

For us. The words are so soothing yet create an enormous anguish. He loves me and he's leaving, and I love him and I need to let him go. "I understand."

Jesse releases a long breath and lowers his forehead to mine. "I love you, Scarlett. We've been connected for as long as I can remember, and I want more than a connection. I want us to make it to forever."

Me, too. I press my lips to his and the taste is salty from tears. "You're leaving next week?"

"Yes," he confirms.

Then I have a few more days with him that I'm going to live to the fullest.

Subject: You didn't say anything about email
From: Scarlett
To: Jesse

Jesse,

Yes, this is a loophole in the no communication agreement, but I figure the odds of you checking your email is zero. I mean, besides for schoolwork and business, who uses email anymore?

It's been three weeks, and overall, I've been doing okay, but tonight, I'm lonely. A snowstorm has blown in. School has been cancelled for two days, and the storm has shut down practically everything else. Two days. Two days of staring at the four walls of my apartment and only myself for company. I'll be honest, I'm starting to feel a little insane.

It's weird that you sold some of the land. I went by the other day, and they've taken down some of the trees. I understand why you sold it, and I'm glad you did so you can take this trip, but it's still bizarre to know that a small parcel of your land belongs to someone else.

I've been getting your postcards from the places you've been visiting. Won't lie, they have been the highlight of my life. Just to see your handwriting puts a smile on my face. I've started taping the postcards on my wall. It's my own personal countdown. The more I receive, the closer you'll be to returning to me.

I know I was a bit stubborn about taking your old truck, but I do appreciate it. The car insurance is going to be more than I expected. Glory agreed with your assessment that the truck isn't worth much, but it means the world to me and someday I will repay you. Glory and Marshall have been teaching me to drive. Only a few more months until I graduate to an actual license.

Leo, Nazareth and V still hang out with me. I thought they put up with me because of you. I need to start shifting my mind-set from negative to positive. After seventeen years of being like this, I wonder how long it will take to switch speeds.

I miss you so much it hurts, but don't you dare think of coming home. Keep going. When you come back, I want it to be forever, as well.

I love you,

Scarlett

Subject: Thank You!!

From: Scarlett

To: Jesse

Jesse,

I received the red roses, and I LOVE them! And YES! I will definitely check on your home and your land. I have a hard time believing checking in on the land is as much work as you say it is, but it'll give me a good excuse to walk your property.

Not that I want to discourage this, but sending me flowers because I sent you an email is setting up a dangerous precedent. ☺

I love you,

Tink

Subject: I noticed the Tink

From: Jesse

To: Scarlett

Seeing you sign your email with Tink made me smile. Weird to admit, but I laid in bed last night and stared at Tink for a while.

Texas is huge. I put my feet in the Gulf of Mexico today. It made me think of how when we were kids, we used to talk about playing in the Pacific Ocean. I miss you, too. Every second of every day.

I've attached a list of things that need to be looked after on the land. Marshall has enough on his plate and doesn't need to be heading out there every couple of days. If you can do this for me, I'll consider it payment for the truck. Let Marshall know if there is anything that needs to be taken care of.

You know how much this lands means to me, Tink, and there isn't anyone else I trust it with other than you.

I love you more,

Jesse

Subject: Rough Night
From: Jesse
To: Scarlett
Scarlett,
I know I'm breaking my own rules, but I've convinced myself that email doesn't count.

Tonight's been rough. I fell asleep, dreamed of Mom and how I couldn't save her and then my mom turned into you. I woke up in a cold sweat, terrified that it was some type of omen that something happened to you.

Please let me know you're okay.

I love you,

Jesse

Subject: I'm okay and you have kittens!!!
From: Scarlett
To: Jesse
One of the barn cats you saved years ago had kittens! They are so freaking adorable I can hardly stand it. Don't worry, I brought the mom and kittens to my apartment. This is totally to help them and not because I'm lonely. ☺ Don't judge.

Camila is talking to me again. She stopped by today and

we cried for a few hours. I told her everything that happened between me and Dad. We're friends again, and I hope it stays that way.

Wish me luck. I'm going to read palms at the next vendor fair. We'll be offering my services at half the price of Glory's, and she's going to sit in on them to make sure I don't screw up. I still don't believe I have an "ability," but it is weird how there are things you can learn about people by staring at their palm.

V let me read her palm, and we had a long talk. I know her secret now, how much physical pain she's in and what you've done to help her through the years. V misses you. So do Leo and Nazareth.

By the way, V's claimed a kitten.

The "Oklahoma is OK" shirt made me laugh.

Guess who received A's and B's on her report card while working a full-time job? This girl!!!!

The mean world who said I'd fail: 0

Scarlett, the girl determined to prove she can do it: 1

☺

Stay safe and I love you,
Scarlett

SCARLETT

I don't think I've ever been so giddy-nervous in my life. I can't sit still. I pace my tiny apartment while flipping my cell in my hands. It's April and beyond emails, it's been months since I've talked to Jesse. Last night he emailed he was going to call. Tonight. Eight P.M. Eastern Standard Time. So much happiness surges through me that I could fly, but then there's this nausea—nerves.

Two months ago, Jesse made it to Southern California. He was eating dinner at a diner and an older man who was also sitting alone started a conversation. The man owned a farm, said he needed help, and Jesse told him he'd like the job. Since then, Jesse's lived in one of those weekly rent motels, and he's emailed several times to tell me all he's learned. Stuff he didn't know about farming, tricks of the trade, and of the gentle patience of this man's teaching.

I've been equal parts happy for Jesse for the experience and fearful, wondering if he would choose to stay in California over coming home, but then my stomach drops. It's not like I'm going to be here much longer myself. I found out last week that I can move in early to the dorms, which means, after graduation, I'll be leaving town.

Jesse was happy for me, and I'm happy for me, too, but will our paths ever cross again?

Seven fifty-nine and my mouth dries out and my extremities tingle. What if he forgets? What if he doesn't call? What if my cell is on silent and he did call and I missed it? I check my cell, the volume's up, and as I breathe out in relief, my cell rings.

I place the phone to my ear. "Jesse?"

"What's going on, Tink?"

I smile as my eyes become wet. God, he sounds incredibly good. "How are you?"

"Good," he says. "For the first time in my life, I'm sitting on the beach at the Pacific Ocean, and this was a moment I had to spend with you."

I think of our names written in second-grade script on the map in his room. I walk over to my bed, stand on it and press my hand to California. "I miss you."

"I miss you, too." His voice goes deep and the sincerity in it is the equivalent of a hug.

"How has it been?" I ask. "How is the farm and the trip and did you end up figuring out what was wrong with the strawberries?"

Jesse chuckles and the sound is the best caress in the world. "Still figuring out the strawberries; the farm is fine and as for the trip, why don't you take a look for yourself?"

There's a *ping*, and I pull down my cell to find a text waiting. I open it, and see a picture of Jesse's palms. I switch Jesse to speaker then enlarge the photo. All the air rushes out of my lungs, and I place a hand to my chest. The lines on his right palm have changed. "You know your way."

"There were a lot of long, restless nights battling some demons. I lost a few rounds, but I won some, too. I know what I want now. I know who I am. I'm going to stay out here for another month or so to help with some things, but then I'm coming home, Tink. I'm coming home to you."

"What about your land?" I'm nervous asking. He loves his land, so do I, but Jesse needs to do what is best for him.

"I've learned a lot by working the farm out here and one of those things is how to work with the local extension office, government agencies and grant funding. There are people who want to keep family farms alive, and that's what I'll be as compared to the corporate ones. It'll be an uphill battle, but Marshall and I think this is one I can win. Be on the lookout for some action on the land, Tink. I've called in some favors, and the farmers I've helped out over the years are going to be doing the initial work. I'm putting in crops this year, and I'll be buying some cattle once I get home. I'm going to be a real farmer."

Joy and sadness at the same time. The curse is broken. He left his land, he's happy and he's coming home to what he loves. And he'll be coming home when I'm leaving.

I take a deep breath and focus on the positive. That's what Glory and Pastor Hughes have taught me to do. It's what has kept me together when times get tough. Jesse and I will be okay. An hour away from each other will be nothing as compared to a continent away. "I'm so happy for you."

"Me, too." He goes silent and then clears his throat. "I'm hoping you'll still want me."

"I will." Grateful, I close my eyes. "I will."

SCARLETT

The bad part of taking in the kittens is that I kept one for myself and now I have to give Eloise up. Not give up as much as
I have to allow Eloise to live with someone else until I have a
proper home. Unfortunately, no matter who I talked to at the university, no one would allow Eloise to live with me in the dorms.
People who work in college administration must be bitter, bitter
people. Who doesn't want a kitten?

I place Eloise in the cat carrier Nazareth had salvaged from his
family's basement then take a look around my empty apartment.
My few possessions are packed up and in the bed of the truck.
Jesse's map and postcards were placed lovingly into one of my few
Tupperware containers, and will be one of the first things I unpack
when I reach my dorm.

Yesterday, Leo helped me return the twin bed to Jesse's home,
and my chest ached when I saw my father watching me from my
childhood home. I was able to look back at him without anger,
just pity.

He lives there again, and has lived there for a while. I'm grateful my sister has a cell now. She has it with her at all times, and
she texts me the moment my parents start to fight. I call her, and
I won't hang up until I know she's safe.

If Mom and Dad won't protect her, then Isabelle's social worker
and I will.

With one last glance at the apartment, I'm hit with a sense of pride and a sense of sadness. I'm proud I survived these months on my own, and I'm sad to leave the place I learned to call home.

I force myself to lock the door behind me and leave. It's time for another adventure.

As I walk toward the old, rusty truck, I notice a piece of paper under the wiper. I scowl. Exactly what I need, a ticket I seriously can't afford. I just earned my license, and this is my reward? Even with the partial scholarship and financial aid, moving into dorms isn't cheap and a ticket sucks.

I open the passenger side door, place Eloise in and grab the paper.

Dear Mr. Lachlin,

I rarely write a personal email like this, but this is one of the few cases where I felt it needed to be done. When you first reached out to me about the blight spreading in the strawberry fields in a small Southern California farm, I didn't think much of it. But what did catch my attention was your persistence, how you showed how you were digging into research yourself in an attempt to find an answer and how you were hopeful that by working together we could help.

Once we were in contact and I learned of you and your story, I became emotionally invested in helping this small farm, but also in helping you. Not very often do I come across young men who are as mature as you or have had as much life experience.

You're smart to take a business course this following fall. You're right, farming is a business and you need to be educated on how to handle finances. Since you'll be in Lexington one day a week due to the class, if you are amenable, I would like to mentor you as you work toward making your family farm functional again. We can meet before or after your business class. You are taking on a huge project, and I'd like to be an advisor to you during this challenge.

You were made for great things, Mr. Lachlin, and I believe you will be one of the best and brightest of the next generation of farmers. Someday, I hope you'll study with the University of Kentucky's School of Agriculture. In the meantime, I do believe between your learned knowledge of farming over the years, taking advantage of your local extension office and hopefully accepting my help, you should be off to a good start . . .

Shock sets in, and I read the last paragraph again. The University of Kentucky. *The University of Kentucky.* The same University of Kentucky in Lexington where I'll be going to school.

Jesse.

My head pops up, and as I spin to find him he's there on the sidewalk. Red hair, a trimmed beard, a blue T-shirt taut against strong muscles and jeans riding lazily along his hips. He offers me a pirate smile and his green eyes twinkle with mischief.

"What do you think, Tink?" Jesse asks. "Are there trees worth climbing in Lexington?"

I don't answer. Instead I take two steps, and I spring into Jesse's arms. He holds me tight as I bury my head into the crook of his neck, inhaling deeply. It's him. Same deep, rich scent—turned over earth after a gentle rain, wildflowers in bloom and the slight scent of a bonfire at midnight.

Jesse kisses the side of my head, lifts me and squeezes as if he never wants to let go. When he does set me on the ground, I draw back so I can take in his beautiful face. "You're going to college?"

"One three-hour class, one day a week. I could take it online, but going into Lexington is one more day I get to spend with you."

A tingling in my blood. "You're keeping your land?"

"Yes. Not because I think this is what I have to do, but because deep down in my soul, this is what I'm meant to do. The real question is, are you ready for a new adventure?"

A smile stretches across my face as I'm filled with pure joy. "What type of adventure were you thinking?

"Second star to the right and straight on till morning."

Then Jesse Lachlin, my best friend, the man I love, leans down and kisses my lips.

PLAYLIST

THEME

"Rain on the Scarecrow" by John Mellencamp

"Amarillo Sky" by Jason Aldean

"Blue Eyes Crying in the Rain" by Willie Nelson

"Reckless Love" by Cory Asbury

"Something Just Like This" by The Chainsmokers & Coldplay

"Hard Love" by NEEDTOBREATHE (featuring Lauren Daigle)

"Parachute" by Chris Stapleton

JESSE

"Confession" by Florida Georgia Line

"Carry On Wayward Son" by Kansas

"These Days" by Rascal Flatts

"Record Year" by Eric Church

"Killer/Papa Was a Rollin' Stone" by George Michael

SCARLETT

"Million Reasons" by Lady Gaga

"Daughter" by Pearl Jam

"Better Man" by Pearl Jam

"Stay" by Rihanna (featuring Mikky Ekko)

SCARLETT AND JESSE'S FUTURE

"Perfect" by Ed Sheeran

"Oceans (Where Feet May Fail)" by Hillsong UNITED

ACKNOWLEDGMENTS

To God: Matthew 6:25–34 and Luke 5:1–11.
    —Thank you for your unconditional love, for taking my worry and anxiety and replacing it with hope and peace.

As always, for Dave.
    —I love you.

For A, N, and P.
    —For challenging me.

A huge thank-you to Suzie Townsend, Whitney Ross, Amy Stapp, and Tor Teen for loving Jesse and Scarlett as much as I do and for believing in my vision for *Only a Breath Apart*.

To my wonderful group of friends, family, critique partners, and beta readers who have helped and loved me along the way: Colette Ballard, Kelly Creagh, Bethany Griffin, Kurt Hampe, Bill Wolfe, Tiffany King, Wendy Higgins, Kristen Simmons, KP Simmons, and Angela Annalaro-Murphy.

Much love to my readers.
    —I am forever grateful for your support and love.